T0354061

Passion Crossing

Philip W. Kunz

iUniverse, Inc.
Bloomington

Passion Crossing

iUniverse books may be ordered through booksellers or by contacting:

iUniverse
1663 Liberty Drive
Bloomington, IN 47403
www.iuniverse.com
1-800-Authors (1-800-288-4677)

ISBN: 978-1-4697-9836-3 (sc)
ISBN: 978-1-4697-9837-0 (e)

Printed in the United States of America

iUniverse rev. date: 4/11/2012

Preface

I guess for a young bachelor, I was more than ready to end my hard college studies and enter the real world. My biological instincts led me to find a woman, a companion in life. I was certainly lonely and obviously overdue. I had accepted a good paying job in my chosen engineering vocation, which made me vulnerable to settling down; searching for a mate to share the spoils of my hard work with no play.

It was inevitable then, since my heart was ready. Although I was a novice at social skills, I went looking for that someone special. It didn't take long, though my sights were set very high…maybe too high.

Love at first sight…that's exactly what it was. Nevertheless, in my senior year of college, I somehow let that picture-perfect girl of my dreams slip away. I guess our meeting was too intense for my then weak-brained, panting, infatuated heartstrings. Our untimely togetherness, only passing moments, was priceless to me and my intentions were honorable.

Unbeknownst to me, she unexpectedly left college with no forwarding address. Therefore, not knowing her intimately, my thoughts of her left me searching frantically to find her, all in the last few hours before I departed UIC and Chicago.

Love sick when I could not find her, I feared I had lost that girl for eternity. She left me with only the faint-hearted memory of her beautiful face and that heavenly fragrance of hers. It is that same special perfume, which sometimes radiates her ghostly image before me in my mind.

Now and again, I see her face, especially whenever another attractive woman wearing that same fragrance passes nearby. That womanly scent still lingers there within my jasmine, igniting fond memories of her.

Absence makes a heart grow fonder, someone once said. I think that's just what had affected me more than anything all those years. My mental pictures of her were escalating in my brain. Thus, habitual to my heart her vision became, growing fonder and fonder, until after so very long I could barely remember her face clearly any longer.

Then some years later, it started all over again. Something completely unexpected and wonderful happened on a cross-country trip from Southern California to a friend's wedding in Chicago.

Chapter 1

Life for me began in Northfield, Illinois, a north side Chicago suburb. My family lived in a very nice home situated in an upper, middle-class neighborhood, where I was "the baby" in our family of four. Our family consisted of, Genevieve, my mother and our pillar, father Jonathon, the provider, sister Jillian the taker, and of course myself, Gregory Jonathon Wetmore. I do not know what part I actually portrayed in our family. I suppose I was just the baby boy. We went to church on Sunday mornings and out to eat together in the afternoon. We seemed to be having lots of togetherness and many fun family outings. There is much fondness for that part of my childhood. It was important to my mother and father that we supported one another with love…we did.

My adolescent years came quickly and continued to be full of those family outings. Sometimes we got in our car and Dad took us to Brookfield Zoo, the Chicago Museum, the Navy Pier, or shopping.

Sometimes we just strolled along together near the huge sailboat harbors, where sails of multi-colored fabrics strained in the wind by the hundreds, out upon Lake Michigan.

We often sat together in choice box seats behind the Cubs dugout at Wrigley Field. Nevertheless, from time to time, we enjoyed sitting in the blistering hot "bleacher bum" seats and tossed our opposing team's homerun balls back onto the field, unless, of course, they flew out of the park and over the fence onto Waveland Avenue.

In the fall we all bundled up and watched "Da Bears" play their games at Soldier Field. We seemed as if we were a more normal, happier family back then, until Dad became absorbed in his work. The family outings faded and eventually were non-existent, as Dad built his position into importance of corporate law and was making lots of money.

Of course, it was harder then on Mom for she searched in her own way to find relevance. I guess she went unappreciated by my sister and me, because we just expected great things from her always; as I mentioned, she was the pillar of our family. I suppose my sister and I did not show our true affections as often or as greatly then, as Mom needed.

She began a rather insignificant social life by entertaining other women in the neighborhood, who found comfort in their bridge club and small social get-togethers. We kids weren't invited, as if we would have liked being around those old forty year olds anyway.

The women often loudly divulged their personal lives rather vividly and sometimes too openly around the card tables. I could hear Mom ask to please keep it down, as her kids were still in the house upstairs. That lasted for only minutes and soon they'd be back at yakking again.

Sometimes I got an earful, when some of the other women said they found themselves left behind by their spouses, also, and even worse, sometimes because of another woman. That always brought negative responses and too much, "If I were you, I'd…," free advice.

Collectively, they hoped to find healing by sharing their misery, which helped them to ease their own concerns. I guess it was somewhat successful, as they seemed to laugh and agree a lot. Those social gatherings continued that way for years. Nevertheless, I personally recall those subsequent years as the loneliest for my sister and me.

I attended school at New Trier High, where my friends called me "Gregor the Terrible" in baseball, not because of my blazing fastball, but because I was just as likely to rip off a nasty curve ball, as to stick a wild fast ball in a batter's ear. Nevertheless, I got better each season, leading up to a 7-0 pitching record for my spring, varsity team, in my junior year. We finished fourth in state, class 3A that year. I was looking forward to my senior year in baseball for betterment.

I lettered in all the regular sports: basketball, baseball, and football, in season. My forte was pitching though, until I tore my ACL playing football against Township High School during my junior year for another sport championship.

Recovery was slow after the knee operation, and all future sports for me ended abruptly. Just as well, as I concentrated on academics, taking advanced college core courses when offered, all the while my ligaments slowly healed. I graduated near the top of my class of 800 and accepted a partial academic scholarship to the prestigious UIC's School of Engineering. The University of Illinois Chicago is the home of the Flames. I began, then took summer classes too, enough to finish early on a six-year program.

Chapter 2

I did not know her then though we lived just fifteen minutes apart most of our lives and we both visited the same beaches occasionally. If I had seen her then, I wonder sometimes now, if I would have loved her as much in her adolescent years. She was a Morgan and that name spelled money in Chi-town.

Her daddy was a fourth-generation Morgan, a Chicago-rich, business executive; his families' money made during the prohibition era. I do not know if their fortune was ill-gotten at that time, I just know they had an enormous bank account, because the Morgan family estate was extremely large.

Their individual pictures, often depicting them alongside an expensive Rolls Royce, Bentley or maybe their long, black Cadillac Coupe Deville, were eagerly posted in every social events' gathering of Illinois' governors, congressional figures, even sometimes U.S. presidents and occasionally foreign kings or queens. They held that kind of status in their lives.

Stanley Morgan often made or bankrupted someone's business on nothing more than a simple yes or no. His many lawyers oversaw his bidding. He helped build Chicago's greatest buildings and donated several parks and money to charity. The Morgan's partly owned many different factories, the mayor's office, and even a few of the cops, sometimes.

On the other hand, Stanley Morgan paid little attention in his wheeling and dealings, with his finest asset, Amanda. Stanley Morgan substituted his major cash account deposits into his daughter's, as payment for his unfulfilled roll of being a father. That is just how Amanda grew up…lonely, but herself, very self-sufficient and becoming rich before her time.

If you met Amanda though, because she never flaunted her daddy's wealth, you would not know that she herself was a multi-millionaire, but appeared as just any ordinary struggling college student.

Furthermore, Amanda's mother Olivia, who was almost twenty years younger than her father, led an agonizingly, troubled life, from about the time of Amanda's birth.

Olivia, a child model, who had grown quickly into a matured-looking woman very young, was a former Vogue model, from about age twelve. She was already extremely talented and very charming, beautiful, and very sexy when Stanley began pursuing her. He lavished young Olivia with expensive gifts.

Olivia married Stanley's money; Stanley married Olivia's body. When she was only seventeen and had become pregnant that gorgeous figure of hers was lost almost immediately to maternity. Olivia's feminine decline, seen only in Stanley's eyes, continued naturally around their home in childrearing their Amanda. However, when her body's chemistry began to return to normal, Olivia was as beautiful as ever. But that was too late for Stanley.

Olivia found out about Stanley's infidelity and they quarreled. She became miserable, and returned to the glamour she missed by sneaking away, all the while Stanley himself was out committing adultery.

When his own wife became a burden to Stanley's carousing; he threw her over for the next beautiful woman who was just as attracted to his money as Olivia had been. Except this time, he never married her. When Olivia confronted Stanley for the last time, he solved his family problem quickly through his lawyers.

He cut off Olivia's credit cards, removed her bank stocks, and closed her bank accounts, which dissolved her assets completely, leaving Olivia with nothing in the bank and no income.

The divorce was quick, but nasty, because Stanley had his lawyers. The judgment in favor of Stanley came on trumped-up charges that she had already hocked her expensive jewelry; sold her new $80,000 Jaguar for a $10,000 fix of heroin, and sold everything else she could get her shaking hands upon, just to hide her expensive drug addiction from Stanley, the divorce court records read.

When Olivia was about to be forced into permanent rehab by Stanley's attorney, she vanished before papers could be served. Stanley did not go looking for her, because he knew something no one but he could have. For him, Olivia's disappearance was a personal gratification. It was all lies.

Stanley's widowed mother, Marilyn, was summoned by her only son into his luxurious home to help raise Amanda; she did very well with her. Amanda regularly attended St. Mary's Catholic School for girls. She left for college at Vassar on grandmother's insistence, but returned after only two years. She did not quite fit in with the other girls who were tutored by their own socialite mothers on womanly ways.

Amanda changed her major to business and finance, minored in music. She decided she wanted to be nearer her father, after learning the reasons her mother vacated their lives, told to her by her dad.

Her understanding of her father's financial ways hardened Amanda to be stronger and forgiving to him, and maybe as she matured, her mother, also. Amanda and her father became closer in her absence at college, as Stanley suddenly realized he was alone and getting older.

Nevertheless, Amanda had often lain secretly awake nights, longing for the return of her mother. Amanda vowed to find out someday why her mother left them so suddenly and without warning. But time faded her vision.

Then, in time, Amanda asked her father if he would find Olivia for her. However, Amanda's wicked father told her he had just received word that Olivia was caught trying to smuggle dope into the United States near Tijuana, and was later sentenced to seven years in the California State Penal Institution for Women.

Amanda wrote to Olivia often, but Olivia never returned any of those letters, because her father never allowed them to be sent, therefore nor did Olivia come to see Amanda. Olivia wasn't really there in prison. After that, Olivia's whereabouts were unknown; she supposedly had just vanished.

I later learned first-hand why Olivia left, and remained reclusive, living her daunting life on the west coast.

After Amanda's grandmother, Marilyn, had passed away and Amanda left Vassar, she started over and enrolled at UIC ,where we conditionally met. The first time I glanced toward Amanda she instantly caught my eye. She was standing amidst a group of students looking stunningly, overly beautiful. Although she wore a scarf and wrapped-up in her herringbone-tweed overcoat, she looked great from the rear as well. But she had turned away from the howling, cold winter's wind.

The busy street was filled with an accumulation of snowdrifts, which displayed a mushy mixture of brown frozen sludge. Countless decaying sycamore leaves smelled putrid, assisted by a noxious, steamy cloud that was rising from the grill-covered curb sewer drain. The grayish, billowing blur became a dancing ghost-like figure, as it belched up in puffs, then danced merrily on its way down the street aboard a very biting, offshore wind. My ears were nearly frost bitten, my cheeks were red, and numbing, just like every forgetful hatless person I had seen that day.

I recall Amanda was standing in front of the university library waiting for one of the many shuttle buses to arrive. I knew even then that she could be the one by the way I felt just seeing her. She was the first ever who drew my biological attraction. I had to get to know her, but how, I was uncertain. I was hesitant, questioning myself that a girl, such as she, would not even cast an eye my way, at least without seeing my apprehension.

Now and then, I think of just how chic she looked...like a CEO businessperson-executive, yet, she held the innocence of a young woman in her face; the face that kept creeping into my thoughts with constant adoration.

Instantaneously, something inside of me awoke. My hormonal desires ignited as never before. I could not seem to help myself from staring and maybe lusting a bit, as I hurried to stand beside her, much too closely. She huddled amongst a small group of similarly winter-clothed, very chilled individuals, who had gathered around the bus stop. Carried closely to her bosom was a stack of books she held tightly, which helped her by blocking the gusting winds.

Obviously, looking at the folder's names: biochemistry, anthropology, and English lit, she was a student, also. I moved in closer. No one felt uneasy by my crowding in, as that is what everyone did in severe times such as this. Remarkably, the cold wind blowing in off Lake Michigan brought lots of strangers together.

I did not know her destination. Buses continually stopped there with sign placards of their destinations, going in all directions. You actually had to look at a time schedule and know your ride, or you would be left standing. I just knew I had to find out all about this woman as quickly as possible; therefore, I eased up beside her even closer, without her noticing me.

Her shiny, long, soft-looking, brown hair, underneath a cute beret, floated out on the wind and brushed my face as if an angel's kiss might. Her perfume's fragrance was sweet, warm, and sensual…it caused me to breathe deeply, as if I might inhale her all.

When the approaching bus's airbrakes swooshed loudly beside us, she turned around suddenly to avoid the exhaust fumes. Her books slammed against me causing them to tumble haphazardly onto the icy sidewalk.

"Oh, I'm sorry, I didn't see you standing there so closely," Amanda told me as we both hurriedly bent down to catch notebook papers blowing quickly under the bus.

Stupid me, for I could not even say back to her that I was sorry, also. Her speaking directly to me, face-to-face, up close and personal, embarrassed me. I was spellbound staring deeply into her lovely hazel eyes, which seemed to look right through me, while still searching past me for her runaway papers.

She hesitated though, as she looked curiously hard at me. For an instant, she maybe thought she knew me or made an effort to try to recognize me. On the other hand, maybe as we both stooped down to capture as many floating papers as possible, she noticed that look of awe on my face. Did she like it?

Then the bus driver yelled out for us to get on or he was leaving. He left with her as she quickly stepped onto the bus stairwell, while I had just stomped down on a maverick tumbling paper that I spotted. She was gone in a rush of diesel exhaust that hid the last smidgen of her feminine fragrance. I tried for a fleeting moment to halt the bus to no avail.

There I stood waving aimlessly, probably looking a fool to an uninterested woman who I had never seen before, and wasn't looking back for me. My only consolation then was that crumpled test paper that I retrieved under my pressed down foot.

I picked it up only to discover it was a handwritten exam paper. Upon one corner was her name and class. It read Amanda Morgan, Psychology 313, row 23, seat 8. Below her name was an A+ grade. Written in red were the class professor's words, "Good work!" This proved to be my primary plan to seeing her again.

As the shuttle bus abruptly turned a corner and disappeared, I chased down several more of Amanda's papers that I noticed had floated halfway down the block. I guess she thought she had them all, except the last two papers that I caught up with were her actual hand written class notes, due the next day at 8:00am, the note under a paper clip read. They were for her psych class. I had done those before and knew they were part of her grade. These were priceless and she would want them back. Things were looking up at that point.

It was noon; I was starving, so I headed back to my apartment along Greenwood Street. I don't really remember that particular walk that day, for I just somehow floated down the street with amorous thoughts of her, until suddenly I found the stairs to the entrance of my off-campus apartment before me; her lovely face still etched upon my mind. Was I in love? My heart thought so.

When I opened the door, I suddenly felt so all alone. Immediately, the phone rang out and broke my trance. It was my dear mother calling. Mom, in my eyes was almost regal, very noble, refined by Vassar standards herself, but always the confusing Genevieve Vandemere-Wetmore.

She told me that she and Dad were about to celebrate their twenty-fifth wedding anniversary. To celebrate they planned a weeklong honeymoon cruise to Nassau, Bahamas. They were flying down to Jacksonville, Florida in two weeks and then boarding a Norwegian ship from that port. She wanted to know if I would be okay. I laughed and assured her I was set, as I had big tests approaching and papers due. Finals week was then and I would not get home anyway.

Mom seemed worried about my social life, too. I told her since she knew the apartment owner that it really helped me financially. In addition, she and Dad had helped foot all my extra college bills that always popped up, therefore I was determined to give it my all to make them proud. My GPA was nearly an untainted 4.0, I assured her.

"Oh, you're such a wonderfully, appreciative and loving son. Why couldn't your sister be as excellent and do as well as you?" Mom sighed.

"Mom, Jill is a good person and is doing very well. Remember, it was both you and Dad who first spoiled her. She partied in high school and at college constantly on the money you gave her to be sociable. Anyway, that is what her close friends once told me. When you finally clamped down on her, it was too late for college. Taking away her checkbook and her Beemer right after she was put on scholastic probation and nearly failed all of her freshmen college courses embarrassed her so much she could not face her peers."

"I suppose Jill really thought she was hurting your father and me by joining up in the service, is my guess...her insensitive, spoiled-rotten revenge, I suppose. She naturally blamed us," Mom interjected, showing a bit of her disappointment.

"Nevertheless, I have hopes that being in the service will make a new man, ah new woman out of her. Jill seems to be excelling in her labors, Mom, and is a staff sergeant already. She is taking care of herself and supervising others, too. Jill has a great amount of responsibilities. As I said...it made a responsible adult out of her.

"It's only been two years. Have faith in my assessments, Mom. Someday she will meet the right guy and your worries will be over. She will be the wonderful woman and mother, just as you are...and I am sure of it. She will be twenty-five soon, remember? She's only eighteen months older than I am."

"I realize all that, except I had so many plans for Jill when she was growing up. I dreamed of her coming-out party and someday she'd graduate from Vassar, too," Mom reminisced.

"Mom, Vassar was out of the question and a coming-out party isn't what it was back in your day, believe me. It would never happen with Jill," I laughed.

"Oh! Oh! Ohhhh! The gay girl thing, huh?" was all Mom said when reality hit her.

Mom breathed deeply and then sighed. I could feel her disappointment. She was not as certain as I was, but I knew my sister. Jill was really just an immature rich kid's brat, who needed a quick, swift, kick in the pants.

I assured Mom, Jill was right where she could receive that swift kick in the butt, if she stepped out of line. However, apparently our Staff Sergeant Jill Wetmore was doing just fine.

Jill went to boot camp in San Diego after quickly enlisting to avoid Father's wrath for flunking out. It was roughly six weeks later, until Jill finally wrote to me. I right away noticed in her letter that there was a big difference in her attitude. She wrote that she really liked it there, though the hours were long and hard. She told me her baby fat was gone and she never felt so physically fit. Jill had lost twelve pounds in one month, she told me.

In addition, her efforts had caught the attention of a certain first lieutenant. They had their first date after boot. I knew the strict discipline was challenging her, shaping her mind set…she needed that, never having to answer to anyone before. However, maybe she also had met that person who tamed her wildness…who knew her intimately by close association.

Jill did boot with "Marine excellence" her certificate read. I guess they weren't looking for just a few good men.

Now stationed in Manila, Philippines for almost two years, Jill might be getting a furlough soon, maybe Easter, she wrote. I wished Mom happy anniversary and told her to tell Father the same, before she hung up.

Dad worked in the corporate world as a lawyer, but I never actually knew precisely what he did for his big company. I hated the lawyer jokes and Dad always being in demand to answer legal problems the company confronted. When Dad once tried to explain his work to me, I did not listen well enough. He became disgusted with my inattention and said I could never be a part of his team. I told him right back that I did not want to follow his example, since he was constantly away from us on those long business trips.

"Mom was always there for us alone, without you, most of the time," I told him.

Dad looked hard at me, then put his arms around me and hugged me.

"When you become a father, and I expect you will someday, you just do a better job than I have, okay? Nevertheless, remember how hard your mother and I worked to help you succeed. That, my son, will take up your time away from your family, but you will always think you are doing your best. Change that, if you can."

Then Dad released his tender hold, patted my shoulder affectionately, smiled, and then picked up his newspaper to go have his coffee in the study. I felt badly.

Mom was always worried about Dad when he left us, too, but she still spent much of her time with her bridge club parties and church affairs. She disappeared from us, too, sometimes, just like Pop, but not as often. Nevertheless, she always gave us extra cash, too, to spend at the movies when she felt guilty.

That is when I went to my piggy bank to make another deposit. Then, I'd begin a new Revelle plane to glue together. However, Jill was on her own schedule during this time of freedom. She hung out with her jet set friends from North Shore Drive who attended high school as the in-crowd. She disappeared more as soon as she got her driver's license and that expensive Beemer convertible. Jill often snuck in and out late at night without much worry someone would smell her breath.

I, on the other hand, hung out with my model airplanes, sniffing glue... not purposely, just putting together model Phantom F4J's, Harrier, and Stealth fighter jets, among many others including a U.S.S. Forestall aircraft carrier fully loaded.

I had each completed plane dangling from my ceiling fan by thread, so when I turned on the fan, the planes looked as though they were flying in a circular formation dogfight. I discarded them all as soon as I became a high school upper classman.

Now after all these years, Dad was soon to retire early with a healthy collection of company stocks. With his savings stockpiled, Dad promised Mom he was finally hers alone. Mom never had to work much after their marriage, not that it was beneath her. Before they met, she had been a men's clothing store manager. Mom eventually met Dad when he purchased several fancy suits for his employment, right after he was hired out of Harvard Law School.

Though their affections could be deemed love at first sight, they dated for almost three years, until Mom had to inform Dad that she was about to become a mother. Additionally, her notice read she was transferred out to Dallas on reassignment.

Ms. Genevieve Vandemere was the candidate-prospectus and new executive Neiman Markus manager in downtown Dallas. As soon as she told Dad, according to Mom's giggling tale, after we were older and knew the consequences of Jill's coming, Mom related to us how charming Dad performed that day.

Father took the news with a man's broad shoulders. Then the old man supposedly dropped down on one knee in front of shoppers, and romantically popped the question. He had had that ring in his pocket for some time, but never could get up the nerve or sever his ties to bachelorhood enough to ask her.

Of course, Mom said, "Yes!"

They were married that very afternoon in Mayor Daley's office, by a circuit judge, whom Dad knew. Their first planned honeymoon trip to the Bahamas had to be delayed, until two weeks later. Though Dad had to reschedule work around the trip, Mom's two-week notice of resignation also needed to be completed.

After their honeymoon, Mom immediately began seeing a gynecologist and found out she was in need of better nutrition because of her anemia. She went back to live with her parents when Dad was called away to Colorado on a multi-million dollar company lawsuit that required six weeks to conclude.

Dad became very motivated, successfully defended his company and his career then took off with new direction. Soon thereafter, he became a very highly respected corporate trial lawyer…Jill's unexpected forthcoming proved to be his catalyst.

Thus began Dad's career of frequent deployment nation-wide by his big law firm to oversee someone's legal representation or council on many different occasions. Dad was very good in his chosen field.

By birth certificate, Jill was born only seven months later. Mom always told Jill that she was a preemie baby, only 6 pounds. That sounded pretty regular to us. After we were older, Jill and I figured it all out and confronted Mom if she had been conceived out of wedlock. It really upset Jill's thinking. She thought she was a bastard and made me swear never to tell anyone. I promised and felt her grief.

I was compassionate to my older sister, because we actually were very close at times. She would always ask me if I had heard anything derogatory about the date she was about to go out with. I didn't know any of them, ever. I think she just wanted to show me she was attractive to men and brag a bit.

Jill's dates, mostly older guys, were sometimes Ivy League college students, too preppy and hoity-toity for my blood. Mom never really questioned Jill's selections and usually greeted them kindly in the study or foyer when Dad wasn't home. She assumed they were only very well dressed high school peers, children of the rich class; some were just that. Who could judge them unsuitable in her eyes?

It was about then that Jill became defiant and impossible, especially when Mom brought up the character of one chosen date from Winnetka. He was an uneducated service station mechanic who had tattoos and drove a big Harley. I cannot count the times I had heard Jill chastise Mom that she was not reckless as Mom was at her age.

Mom bowed out in embarrassment every single time and backed off. Maybe it was learning the truth that our parents were not as innocent as they demanded of her to be, or maybe Jill was at that age of rebellion all girls seem to excel in during those in-between years that made her become so difficult.

My parents' romance, however, has never diminished much after all these years. It seems absence did make the heart grow fonder in their lives. After Pop had been away for a week, Mom met his return with love and passion. Jill and I knew there was love in our family. Dad, too, related that he felt badly about leaving on long trips away from home.

To recompense, Dad readily provided us with individual bank accounts with no restrictions for anything we desired as long we kept expenses below the $1,000 balance. Now I know he felt guilty that he was often not there to provide those grown-up answers. He should not have. He was the best father any boy could have. He showed us love in many ways and the best he knew how was our security.

I remember how I saved my money, but Jill was older, shopped the malls regularly, and began a highly active social life. She was the knock-off of the original, "Little Miss Rich Bitch" and no one wanted to miss one of Jill's late-night, sometimes star-attending parties. I was not there, but I heard later that Oprah dropped by to say hi and gave her a hug. Jill just loved watching Oprah's show from here in Chicago and her appearance there would certainly have been a real social boost for Jill.

Downtown Chicago was not for me. The past events with the Sears Tower being a possible future Al-Qaeda target and many of the utilities' problems made me leery. Construction in Chicago could offer many job opportunities, but the hustle-bustle inside the Windy City was just too much for my tastes. I planned to finish my civil engineering degree, find some little company in a Midwest small town, and build condominiums and maybe interstate exit ramps and bridges.

My thoughts suddenly drifted to the present, as I began eating my evening meal when the UIC student directory caught my eye. Between bites, I searched the lists and found Amanda Morgan living off campus, also, and living only a few blocks away from my apartment. There I found her telephone number listed. Should I just walk over and give her the class notes, or call? I was pondering that phone call, but I would really like to see her face again, I thought.

An artist named Donald Stuart owned my apartment. He hired me to watch his studio, but only charged me $1400 which was half rent, because close-in housing was at a premium, at any price, especially furnished in such elaborate adornments as his.

His expensive paintings were hung upon every wall. He often toured Europe, mainly France and Italy, searching for sales' prospects at showings and other social involvements. I had never actually met the man, except over the telephone after I gave a reference. He knew Mother. Apparently, Stuart was an old college acquaintance, remembering her well, maybe too well it seemed, as he spoke very affectionately and asked me how she was. That was a bit uncomfortable for me, but not for him, as he related several brief encounters with Mother on campus in her day. Mom must have toned down her joie de vivre after becoming a wife and mother. He made her certainly sound like a completely different person than I knew, but related the guy she married swept her away.

Some of Stuart's art hung on rusty nails in a special room, where he used a humidifier to preserve the covered paintings. My job was to fill the small unit daily and keep the humidity adjusted, not bad for a $2800 monthly rent. I guess he wanted someone he could trust to watch his treasures.

Stuart sometimes had painted beautiful women, whom I believed were young college art students who needed money. However, once he must have found a gorgeous dark haired woman to pose in the nude on a couch. I became aware of the picture's rapture up close once, after receiving a call from Stuart to check the painting to see if it was properly storing and aging. I returned as often as necessary.

Stuart rarely came to Chicago in the cooler, fall-winter months, however, he hired a woman to clean once a month. She normally stayed two days. She cleaned all the rooms quietly, but sang softly the hymns of her church choir where she sang on Sundays. She slept in another part of the apartment for which only she had keys. Then she quietly left with all her buckets loaded with spray cans rattling loudly, mops sticking out in several directions and rags dangling about her waist. After about six months, I grew to know a lot about her.

Alberta Johnson was a middle-aged, woman, with the biggest bosom and warmest smile of anyone I had ever met. Her teeth were separated in the middle and offered her a way to intensify her spitting occasionally while cleaning up my apartment. She would spit between those teeth upon a real tough stain, to loosen up the crud. I'd just remember where I saw that spit land and sprayed there with Lysol.

Alberta was always jovial. While she was there, she constantly told me I needed a woman to do this work permanently for me. I would agree and then give her one of my cold lagers to enjoy. She would sit down with me and rest a while. Alberta beamed with pride telling me about her hard life growing up and making a go of life. She had eight kids, always spoke about the youngest three who were supposedly A+ students in college, two caught stealing and in prison and the others in the military.

"Henry and Jacob were unlike their half-brothers and sisters. They grew up when I was living with their father who was a drug-dealin', woman-chasin', good-for-nothin' gambler. Dat's why they done went bad," she sadly explained.

Then she would hop up with a sudden exclamation of, "Can't get done sitting here on my behind, now can I?"

When she finished cleaning up my apartment thoroughly, she went home, wherever that was. Alberta was always a very thorough cleaner. I liked her.

I finished my meal, searched for those notes, checked the address, and then headed for Amanda's apartment address with a quick step in that blustery wind. There it was only three blocks away on a corner with all the lights in the house on brightly. Her apartment looked like a knock-off of the one in which I resided. After I rang the buzzer listed to a Morgan, I glanced around and for the first time noticed all the old buildings looked alike. A government program must have built them many years ago; perhaps during the big depression, I thought to myself.

"Who is it?" the voice sounded perplexed over the outside intercom.

"Hi, I'm Greg Wetmore. I'm here to see Amanda Morgan, please."

"Go away. We don't need any, bye!" her voice sang out as if I just got a brush off.

I was about to turn around and let those papers just fly away, when I remembered the fragrance Amanda was wearing when I stood next to her. She was just too beautiful for me not to make an attempt to see her face again. Therefore, I pushed against her call button and held it down, just to get back at her rudeness.

"Didn't I just tell you, buster, we didn't want any?" she angrily yelled.

"Well then, missy, what the heck do you want me to do with all these pages of class notes of yours, which by the way I chased after all over the place in front of the library?" I retorted.

"Who is this?" she asked again.

"I'm the guy you accidentally bumped into in front of the library and who helped you gather up your class notes."

It got quiet then but I heard footsteps approaching the doorway. An eye peeked through the peephole, and then the door handle began to turn. When the door swung open, it was Amanda looking excited, but she had her hair in curlers and a facial cream on some zits. Still, she looked good to me…kind of domesticated this time, not so sophisticated.

"Step in, please…please excuse my reluctance, because I'm on a tight schedule tonight…who did you say you were?"

"Greg Wetmore…I'm a senior at UIC and know how important these papers must be, so I gathered them up, but you left on the shuttle before I could give them to you…here," I said, as I handed Amanda her papers and turned to go.

"Wait! You do not know how much I appreciate you doing this. Please, come in. Do you drink coffee? I just made a new pot to keep me going so that I could re-write these same darn notes after my leisure. I cannot believe they are all here and still in tact, not wet and ruined. Please?" she asked.

She extended her arm and actually took my arm in hers to show me the way up the staircase to her third floor apartment. We met other girls in various states of attire along the way. Some seemed headed out to night classes while others were in their robes and had just exited the community shower. They each acted nonchalant about my presence as if I wasn't even there. I guess guys came and went regularly.

Amanda stopped at her doorway and asked me not to notice her messy room. As I walked in all I saw in disorder were tons of books scattered about a small desk and papers strewn about. Otherwise, the place was very clean, warm and cozy, much smaller than mine, but enough for one person. She lived alone.

The smell of her fresh-brewed coffee in the cup eased the cold from my gloveless fingers as I rubbed them around the rim of the cup.

"Thanks…I needed this cup. That wind cuts right to the bone and I lost my gloves someplace…I think at Border's searching for a book."

Amanda placed the papers in order on her desk and smiled.

"They're all here…how can I ever thank you enough?" she begged.

"You already have, more than you'll ever know," I coyly told her, hoping she might suspect I was interested in knowing her better. "If I may ask, what was that perfume you wore today? I can't get that sweet fragrance out of my senses," I told her.

"Coffee!" she enlightened me.

"No, not the coffee, though it smells and tastes great…that perfume."

"As I said, it's called Coffee. It's something new I bought at Macy's. I'm glad you like it. I hope my date likes it as much."

She took my empty cup to her kitchen sink and then returned to open the door and offer another salutation.

"Well, again, thank you so much. I hope this wasn't too much trouble," she said with a slight push on my back to get me out of there more quickly.

My heart sank. I could tell my welcome was now over by my having drunk her coffee, so I turned to the door. Just then, a knock at the door sent Amanda around me to answer it. It was Carla Dionne. She was a girl I once dated a few times in my sophomore year, until Carla left on scholastic probation. I had not seen or heard of her since. She just stood there dumbfounded seeing me in Amanda's room.

"Greg…Greg Wetmore…I can't believe it's you!" as she rushed past Amanda smiling brightly to give me a rather long, warm, loving embrace.

"Good to see you again, Carla. I hadn't heard what had happened to you until later after summer break when you didn't return in the fall or write. I called but your phone was disconnected. How have you been?" I asked sincerely.

We chatted a moment, but Amanda interrupted us and told Carla I was just leaving and their dates were coming soon. Therefore, I hugged Carla once again. It was hello-good-bye, this time. Not to be out done by her friend, Amanda did the same. I was shocked, as she actually closed her eyes as she hugged me, just as if I were her closest friend. I did not want to leave her embrace, but she let go.

"Coffee, huh?" I sighed, inhaling that fragrance more deeply, once we had embraced farewell. It had the same affect of an aphrodisiac on me.

Amanda smiled, watched me get turned on, and then showed me the door. I left wanting more amidst the scurry of two women who apparently had dates and were probably late. I was out and the door closed behind me.

It was good to see Carla again, but my feelings were a bit perplexed after I learned my dream girl, Amanda, had a fella. Some young men seated in the vestibule looked hard at me coming from upstairs. Maybe they were not invited up there, as I had been. That thought was comforting. Maybe also, the boyfriend Amanda talked about was just a date and nothing more.

I had many dinner dates my first year, just trying to meet some nice girls, until I gave up looking for that special one. The very thought of Amanda raised my ambitions. I planned to bump into her again, but next time not so clumsily; with honorable intentions, because I then knew what I wanted. I had it bad.

I rushed back to my apartment. Again, it seemed very lonely there. I showered and lay in bed listening to soft music and reading my college book, "Better Avenues of Construction". All I could do was dream of Amanda. Did I mention, I already had it bad?

Chapter 3

The late winter snow continued to fall overnight and the sounds of silence were shattered by the zooming of mechanical snow blowers going down the street at a fast pace. The snow trucks were scraping the pavement with their plows and the swoosh of snow being forced up into the air by the huge blowers almost rattled the windows. Sometimes I recognized the sounds of cars being pelted by ice and snow, blown up high into the air then landing loudly with their squishy thuds.

I surmised all the cars on the street below would be half-buried by morning. I got up and then peeked through the curtain. Peering up through the dense falling snow was mesmerizing and amazingly beautiful, especially when it fell directly in front of a streetlight, illuminating every flake into becoming its own piece of sculpture. They said that no two snow crystals were alike; Amanda was made that way.

Looking across several blocks of rooftops of the many complexes, I could see a completely lit up apartment house. It was Amanda's building. I wondered if she was there or still out on that dinner date. Worse, was he there with her? That thought disgusted me and I had no right to think that, I told myself. She doesn't even know how you feel, stupid.

I went to the fridge and got a sip of water, then turned my radio on to late night Paul Harvey. Not only was his voice soothing and his programming very interesting, he had that certain ability to cause people like me to think. Therefore, I began to listen, then think and plan my next chance-rendezvous with Amanda.

Should I be nonchalant, aggressive, submissive or what? I decided she needed to be groomed into liking me. I would stroke her gently with little innuendos, flowers when appropriate, and love notes eventually, until she would know I really cared.

However, what if she doesn't care for me. I was already afraid of screwing up…after all, she was more than I deserved and much prettier and smarter than any woman I ever knew. All these questions and lack of my own certain attributes made it so hard for my limited Casanova abilities. I was very unsure of myself.

I had to hone my skills to win her heart. Eventually she would turn my way. It would take time, lots of time; I hoped it was sooner than later. I had to trust my heart.

I thought about her lovely face for many hours, as I listened to several Paul Harvey interludes with the current news. It was fourteen degrees with a gusty forty mile per hour wind, Paul let everyone know in Chicago. Nevertheless, it was the warmth from my thoughts of her that kept me warm inside.

My plan quickly became multi-faceted. First, I would be very nice to her after we met by accident; at a place of my choosing. Then, maybe invite her for an Espresso down at Starbucks' or just talk and hang out at Medici's on 57Th. We could take the rail there, since I had no car.

On the other hand, I could go for it and just ask her for a real date straight out. God, what if she laughs at me? No, I told myself, I must take it slow and move in little steps. I fell asleep and my alarm clock rang out immediately. Six o'clock and all is well went ringing in my brain. I managed to grab clean underwear out of my drawer and head off to the shower. My breakfast was cereal and toast.

There were always classes at UIC. Snow was just another obstacle that had to be addressed there on campus. The sidewalks hummed with more snow blowers and the flying snow from the blowers resembled tiny waterfalls, one by one, as I scurried off to my first class. My toes were frozen by the end of my trek. I should have bought those insulated Canadian snow boots I had promised myself in my freshman year.

Walking in snow wasn't really hazardous. It was that 10 degrees and forty miles per hour wind that did one in. I had to dress in layers and get to my class early to undress there or become overheated. I guess they named her "The Windy City" correctly; I thought to myself as I entered my classroom and felt the warmth of my seat. Boy was I tired. Then I felt light. I had forgotten my back pack… "Shit!" I shouted out in a sudden outburst of disgust.

"I beg your pardon!"

It was my professor, Max Davis.

"I apologize, sir. I came here without my backpack and my books were inside."

"Well, it looks as if this is your lucky day…what is your name, son?" he asked.

"Greg Wetmore, sir. I'm a fourth year student soon to graduate cum laude."

"Hum…that remains to be seen," he chuckled. "What are your plans after class today? I noticed on my grading list that Greg Wetmore is one of my best students. I did not even know you were he, before now. Wetmore…ah, Wetmore…yes, Ginny…I once dated a young, vibrant, strikingly beautiful girl named Genevieve Vandemere. She married a Wetmore, Jonathon, I think his name was…he stole her away…she was a real babe, as you kids say it…ahhh, Ginny, yes, Ginny…fond memories…ah um…anyway, I need a graduate cum laude this summer to assist me. I offer room and board…I have an excellent chef name Rosier who pays his board only by his service…he's that good… a gourmet chef extraordinaire downtown. I also offer a small stipend of fifty per week, grant money; not much but more than you'll need plus all the engineering knowledge I can put forward as recompense…interested?" he inquired very enthusiastically.

My mind suddenly knew that the professor, too, must have intimately known Mother. I was delirious that she was so well known around the suburbs, since she went to a New York college, not here in the Midwest. Maybe I didn't really know Mother.

"Well?" he then questioned when I did not immediately respond.

"Professor, may I please have time to think about this? I really enjoy your classes and this is my third with you. I would like to take your six hundred levels, advanced-engineering courses on material and fabric structure alternatives. I wish it were being taught at a lower level, because I could have used that info many times in our research. I discovered several structures in this city that are unsafe, and they are not even condemned. One building is at 26[Th] and Cal…the old police station."

"Oh, and how did you arrive at that conclusion, son? Were you incarcerated and tried to dig your way out?" he laugh-snorted through his nose as a geek might.

"Actually, sir, I have never been incarcerated, or even gotten a simple parking ticket. I read up on the old city building schematics on her, which included the nomenclature of the steel, stone, and mortar makeup. The city builder used regular sandstone to save money. It could easily crumble in an earthquake, sir," I tried to explain.

"I compliment you, Greg Wetmore. You must take my offer seriously. This summer would elevate you above my sixth level classes…you could be a great engineer or advanced architect one day, if you continued being observant that way with that burning desire to make the world a better place."

"Actually, I wasn't worried about the whole world, just mine. I need to find employment soon after graduation," I quipped too indifferently.

His stare was not without a hint of repugnance that he had even made me the offer and I recognized his ire, because it truly was an honor and a great privilege he offered to me.

"Please, sir, believe me, sir, this is quite the honor for me, sir. Could you give me a week to consider? I had plans to go south and this offer comes unexpectedly. I received an offer to be part of IDOT in Springfield. It doesn't pay as much as out in the private mainstream, but it's steady and the retirement is good."

"Take the time you need, Greg," he spoke with more sensitivity, "except one thing…call me, Max, please," he told me smiling. "This opportunity could lead to being my replacement in a few years. I would feel good about you eventually taking over here. We professors do get paid well, you know," he said grinning.

I was pleased that he wanted me to be a part of his department, but starting out in a steady job, building those bridges and highway on and off ramps seemed more appropriate for my finances. Sure, I had an almost free ride with Mom and Pop's generosity. Nevertheless, things would have to change in my world before I could.

Chapter 4

My following weeks involved no sleep, studying on library time and gallons of coffee. I kept very late hours reviewing my class notes and figures for finals. Advanced Metal Stress tests results were giving me problems. When I combined the angles and metal stress, they somehow got too weak to be safe; therefore, more products had to be included in the tally, thus costing a client more with higher cost overruns. Those same miscalculated costs someday would inevitably become the worst consequence one engineer could face… fired from a major project. That would possibly be the moratorium of one's career. I had to get it right before I went into the field.

As I hurriedly moved around campus from test to test, I searched for a glimpse of Amanda. I planned to ask her out. I missed her more than she knew, even more than I knew, but Amanda was nowhere to be found. I promised myself when my tests were over, I would go directly to her apartment and tell her how I felt about her and accept her answer, even if it were negative. I had to tell her how I felt. However, how could she even suspect this affection? Ours was a one-time, hit-miss confrontation where she was too busy to see me. Was all this love I had for her a one-way street and only a figment of my imagination?

For the moment, things looked hopeless without finding Amanda. Feeling lost, I shied away from intimate thoughts that drew me to remember embracing her. I hoped time would heal my heartsick infatuation though I really did not want that at all. Nevertheless, Amanda had vanished, just as Carla had once.

Two tough weeks passed and finals were over. I did well, so well, that my mom and dad surprised me with a new Ford pickup truck as a graduation present. They said it was something useful to go out to construction sites on my new job. I was thrilled and kissed them a fond farewell from our home doorstep. Both had tears in their eyes as we waved good-bye. No son could have loved or appreciated his parents more than I.

I drove my shiny new truck to campus to address the professor. He encouraged me again, about joining him as a graduate student. As fate would have it, I told him that I decided not to accept his offer. He stared at me long and then told me as he faced away that he too, had once told my mother he was leaving, just as I had then. He told me slowly, almost whispering in a moaning-like tone that he regretted leaving her ever since.

It was then I saw his anguish for not getting Mom as his life partner. Apparently, he had known her more intimately than I suspected. His sentiments somehow seemed linked to mine, for I was doing the same while leaving behind Amanda.

As I left the professor with a hardy handshake of farewell, he asked me to stop by now and again, whenever I ventured near campus. I drove to Amanda's apartment and rang her door buzzer, until I knew if she were there she could not stand the noise and would certainly respond, even cursing me angrily. I must have hit that button a hundred times. Then I held it down.

There was no response, except I overheard some woman's voice yell, "Get the hell off the door buzzer thingy." I suppose she thought I was leaning upon it. Amanda, sweet, Amanda…oh where had she gone I wondered? I drove back to my apartment.

I immediately began packing for Springfield, Illinois' capital city, as soon as Stuart returned that very afternoon to reclaim his Chicago condominium. He was pleased with my housesitting. Since his works had continued to sell so highly, he told me, he was refunding everything my parents and I had paid him. Then he emphatically asked about Mother. He wanted to know her happiness, her health and if she ever mentioned him to me. I assured him not. I guess he had a real thing for my mother once and this was his way of communicating that he was a success in life and she missed out. Dad was far more of everything good than he was, but the eye is in the beholder, as it is said.

Nevertheless, I was grateful to Stuart, as I really needed traveling money. At twenty-three, I was beginning my new life. This was my first step weaning away from my parents' financial teat.

I drove hastily down I-55 toward Springfield after I had received an encouraging telephone call from my future supervisor, Kurt Rakers, advising me to be there at the IDOT building in Springfield, Monday morning at six sharp.

My plans to see Amanda faded instantly into nothingness. If only I had known then that Amanda would have accepted a date after talking to Carla about me. It seems girls really only want what other girls find interesting. I left behind a dream I never expected to rediscover. The melancholy moments lived inside me as I turned into the old highway department's building in Springfield. It was a three-hour drive that I don't remember driving at all.

"Hello!" I bellowed through a locked door to a young woman pouring steaming coffee into several personalized cups from a huge coffee percolator. My first thought was how I'd appreciate some myself. The next thought was where was everyone else? When she looked up in surprise, she also took the time to look at her wristwatch, as she set the big pot down and advanced my way. She had the look of a secretary with several pencils stuck in her dark hair as she came to me.

"You the new guy?" she wanted to know before she opened the lock.

"Hi, I'm the new guy, all right. My name is Greg Wetmore…may I come in or is there a password?" I questioned.

"Hi, I'm Joyce…no password. The boss told me to expect you early. He always has the new people in early to meet me. Why? I have no idea, except he later asks me if I feel I can work with them. I only told him no once on a guy who was too aggressive and he shifted him off to the Carbondale office. Come in, I'm Joyce Dixon. Glad to meet you…ah, Greg," she said, while extending a handshake. "Want a cup? Take the red one off the wall, it's for guests, but you'll have to buy your own or use the Styrofoam cups from over there by the water cooler. I don't like the taste from those…here," she said, after she poured a steaming half-cup. "Tell me what you think."

I took a big sip, burned both lips, my tongue, and spewed her blouse with coffee as I was forced to spit it all out instantly.

"Man, was that too hot! I'm so sorry!" I shouted out to a very wide-eyed Joyce, who was stepping back, dripping wet and looking down upon the brown stains splattered upon her lovely new, ruffled, satin blouse.

She just stood there arms extended in shock before me, still looking ready to explode violent derogatory words at me when the door opened and Kurt walked in.

"Hey, Joy…I told you that darn pot got our coffee too hot," he said, as he hastily headed to the kitchenette area and the paper towel dispenser. He quickly returned with several sheets to help Joyce dab the stains.

It didn't work very well and she certainly didn't want help dabbing at the stains upon her bosom. She was fit to be tied but when she looked up and saw my concerned face, she let out a long sigh and said, "My fault, Greg… my fault."

"You must be my new man, Greg. Hi, call me Kurt, never boss," he said, turning away from Joy, then extending his handshake. "This cute little thing here's our wonderful secretary Joy, but I see you two have met, ha! Right now, I am giving her two hours leisure and you are giving her forty dollars or your credit card to go buy a new blouse. I know it cost forty, because she told me so, while hitting me up for a raise Friday night before quitting time."

"Now, I guess she could have waited, but I wanted her to look more professional when you arrived. She gets a bit lazy with her looks, wears those cowgirl duds, because usually she sits here in this fancy office and answers my calls, and types some, but nobody sees her beautiful face. Besides, you are filling a void in my team and I really need you out with me pronto. I saw your résumé, great grades…I talked to your teachers, and they each had great things to say about you. Sorry now I didn't meet you up there to warn you Joyce makes the best, but hottest damn coffee in Central Illinois.

"I really trust the people I've gotten out of UIC. They know their beans for sure," he continued. "Today, I want you to sit down with Joy after she gets back and get all of your personal paper work done…insurance, retirement, monthly schedule, and a place to live. I had Joy get the morning paper, so you can search together. Joy is our pillar here. You will learn to love her as we all have…here come the boys. Let's go meet them, get acquainted and look the shed over. There's two hundred sixty workers here who all directly depend on our speedy decisions to keeping them working safely," he told me, while leading me over to them to tell them to give me all the help I needed, and my name.

"Talking about speedy, I just have to be the first to ask you this important question…what is the slowest thing on Earth?" he asked smiling.

It was a local thing, I guess, but I suggested, "A snail?"

"Nope, an IDOT work truck driving down the road in front of you to the work shed, two hours before quittin' time!" he bellowed laughing.

"That's us!" I told him pretending to laugh.

I met most of my sleepy-eyed co-workers, both guys and gals who then lined up to greet me, I thought. They were very nice and seemed to have their routines down pat. As each walked past me they gave me a high-five. Then each one pulled out their respectively named punch cards from a vertical slotted card tray, which was conveniently situated next to me. They put their card into a clock's slot, and punched the time clock to get a timed arrival stamped upon it and put it in the opposite side card tray to check out. Now, the taxpayers were paying them.

Quickly they scurried to gulp the last of their coffee in a paper cup and pick up their lunchboxes, hardhats, and gloves. As they were walking away to the trucks, it was difficult discerning male from female, black, or white. They seemed to meld into a herd of beings.

Since they had a big interstate project ongoing for two months already, it had become routine and no meetings for assignments were needed today. Everyone knew his or her specific job and location. The groups broke into sixes and climbed into vans and trucks. Soon, Kurt put on his hardhat, grabbed up a few schematics and blueprints and squeezed into his small white supervisor's car he used to go to several job sites and drove away.

The dead silence of the shed being completely vacated was broken when I heard Joy yell, "Be back in a short short!" and then disappeared out the side door, got into her pick up, and sped away. I guess she was headed out to get that new blouse, although I hadn't given her my money yet. Maybe she didn't want my money or thought she could clean the blouse.

I looked around the empty, high-ceilinged shed, where sparrows flew around among the rafters and asked myself if I wanted this to be the rest of my life. Only time would tell me if I had made a proper life choice. I sat down at a rather old picnic table with knife carvings, which some of the workers used for their meals at break times.

I picked up a wrinkled, coffee-stained newspaper and sipped the rest of that cup of coffee, which Joy had served me earlier. I looked through the classifieds for rentals. There were many to choose from and I hoped Joy might give me insight.

It was now a quiet moment for me to reflect upon my decisions. I thought of my path getting to this wonderful, six-figures paying starting job. I knew how hard I worked in college to achieve great knowledge in civil engineering. I was thankful for the loving kindness and financial help Mom and Dad gave to me. I was very grateful. To show my appreciation, I would plan some sort of surprise gift to them; maybe a paid vacation.

Now, I was finally on my own and beginning to feel as one young man might feel while looking into his own future. I now had a good job, health, and dental insurance, an honorable position, which I was certain that it was going to be steady, with three weeks paid vacation. I had neither college loans, credit card debt nor personal loans outstanding. I was set, I surmised.

The only important missing element of my new life's puzzle was Amanda, I believed. Nevertheless, that apparently was over, for I assumed she was lost to me forever. I then suddenly accepted it, but sadly.

What I did learn from my short, infatuated, first-lost-love episode was that the next time, if there ever were a next time, I would be prepared to move more quickly, as a man would.

When she walked through the side door, I asked the casually dressed young woman if she needed help. I thought she was a visitor looking for something or someone. Her response caught me off guard when she asked, "Can you type?"

I stood up and realized it was Joy. In her tight-fitting jeans, a red plaid shirt just like one I personally owned, and her cowgirl boots, she hadn't that perfect secretary look anymore. Nevertheless, she was very attractive and even more appealing to me now, you might say.

"This is the real me," she told me. "So get used to it!" she quipped rather harshly.

"Here, let me pay for your ruined blouse. You left so unexpectedly, before I could give you the money…here, I insist," I said, as I yanked my wallet out of my back pocket and peeled off two twenties to hand her.

"Are you for real? It was my fault you burned your lips and I'm sorry, too.

No, keep your dough…I took it to the cleaners and they said since it was fresh they could get the stains out."

"Well, keep it for the cleaning then," I told her with my hand still extended holding the forty dollars.

She looked over the money, and then reached out and plucked one twenty.

"Okay, that's done…we're square…let's get started on the rest of your paperwork. Give me your DL and social. I have it down somewhere, but this will expedite matters."

She took them and typed my info into her desktop computer. A response immediately returned.

"Here's all of your pertinent info. It has your insurance, payroll schedule, rules, and regulations about calling in sick and taking a sick day, holidays, and vacation requests. You're on the bottom of the totem pole so don't expect every request to be granted. The workers, we workers, are union and you can't touch us, without first going through channels. Work place sexual harassment will be explained in a classroom during the next district meeting. Now, have you a permanent address?"

"No…thanks for all this," I told her as she neatly placed all the brochures and pamphlets in a folder and handed it to me. "I've been looking in the newspaper and there are lots of apartments listed," I explained.

"Yep, most of those classifieds are from our fellow tax-paying citizens' homes and apartments who lost their jobs. Rent is cheap, but now is the time to find a really good place."

"May I ask if you have any suggestions?"

"No, not really, but it sure is nice to roll out of bed and be close to the office, but then again, you have to contend with the locals and some are here to rob and steal…know what I mean? Therefore, I personally live out of town. It takes only a few extra minutes and our crews keep the roads open during the big snows."

"Ah, okay, is there an apartment or room available where you live?"

"You could live with me, but I have a nice roommate, Lila, she would get pissed. No, I suggest we go for a ride and find something. Then we'll head to the SOS."

"What's the SOS?"

"Secretary of State…you'll have to notify them that you have moved within ten days. You get caught and get a ticket, being a state employee they put a mark in your file…enough of them, and you are out-a-here, buster!" she explained, looking and sounding very arrogant.

If nothing else, I learned that Joy was very thorough and knowledgeable. She locked up the office and we left in my truck with Joy driving. She knew where we were going. The first place just out of the city was The Statehouse Apartments. It looked nice to me, but the sign read no-vacancies, so we searched a bit closer when I spotted a nice townhouse on College Street with a small sign in the window reading, "For lease soon". We got out.

"This is the high rent district," is all Joy mentioned.

I guess she meant it was too much for me. I noticed there was a nice heated pool, laundry, small gym, and security cameras at the gated entrance of the small complex, with few cars on the streets, as each had its own garage.

We met with the manager who showed us one available apartment.

It was perfect for me because it was close to work, newly painted, and carpeted throughout, with two completely furnished bedrooms, two baths, a gas fireplace, nice living room, dining and bedroom furniture, plus appliances with utilities paid. All these amenities were provided in the expensive lease, but you get what you pay for said Joe Petito, supervisor.

I agreed to a criminal background check and paid the $40 fee. Then I signed a one-year lease agreement to my new first floor townhouse apartment and gave $2,000 for first and last month's rent, plus another $1,000 damage deposit to the manager. I could move in pending their notification of a proper background check by the Sheriff's department in a few days, Joe the supervisor told me. I gave Joy's cell number as a way to contact me, since mine was probably out of my area of Chicago.

In less than an hour, we seated ourselves in the Secretary of State's office and I was completing my registration and driver's license transfers.

By eleven, Joy and I were back at the office.

"There's nothing for you to do here, right now. Maybe you could look over the place…like maybe get lost until three, maybe?" Joy hinted smiling.

Some of the workers were at her desk waiting with their personal requests, so she got right to work. Nevertheless, Joy opened her lunch bag and began eating a sandwich in front of the others, as she took their questions. I guess I should have offered to buy her lunch while we were out, but I thought she was in a hurry as it was our workday.

I looked around for hours, inside and out. While strolling around aimlessly, I passed many busy people who all seemed to be answering phones in their upstairs offices. I even checked out the intricate downstairs piped-in plumbing via the worker's elevator, when I punched the wrong button. It was only half-past two with more than an hour before quitting time. Therefore, I found soda and food vending machines in a lounge and bought a ham and Swiss sandwich, plus a 12-ounce Gatorade. I looked for a place to sit, eat, and hide as Joy suggested. I felt ignorant doing this. Was this the way of a state employee, I wondered?

When I had not begun eating yet, workers entered the lounge for their break, so I skedaddled. I mistakenly entered Kurt's office and saw a massive mess of paperwork thrown randomly upon his desk.

Therefore, as I munched, I worked on straightening things up, including dusting, cleaning the windows, and even aligning the pictures that hung cock-eyed upon the walls. I also sharpened all the loose, dull pencils off the floor. It was looking a bit more organized, so I opened the dusty curtain to let in more light from the clean windows. I found a mop in the bathroom and got it wet in the sink and then mopped the floor. It was streaked, but better. I was just about finished organizing everything when Joy suddenly walked in and stared hard at me.

"Oh, there you are...what do you think you're doing?" she said almost screaming. "I know you meant well, but the wrath that follows trying to get some sort of order to the boss's desk will bring you pain and suffering; I know. He has told me more than once he would fire me on the spot if I ever touched his papers again. He knows exactly where everything is, he says."

Then she looked at the full waste can and said I was in for it, just as Kurt strolled in, all six feet five of him, sweaty and dirty. He had had a hard day. He stopped, looked around his office, and said, "What happened?"

Joy appeared startled and quickly retreated backwards and pointed her finger directly at me.

"Well, it's about time someone cleaned up this office of ours. I called maintenance to find another desk and a drafting table for you. I'll need you in here with me. Looks like you've really made it look worthwhile working in...thanks!" he said, plopping his papers down in another careless disarrayed mess upon his desk.

If I hadn't witnessed it myself, I wouldn't have believed what was about to happen. Joy was really fuming because of Kurt's kind words to me. She had picked up a water jug, raised it up high and was about to douse Kurt over the head with the ice water left inside, as Kurt's back was turned. However, I quickly stepped between them and took it away before Kurt even knew what was about to happen to him.

Her wild blue eyes were flashing fire directly face-to-face into mine, as I grabbed onto the jug and then quietly whispered, "Will you have dinner with me tonight…please?"

It caught her off guard, unprepared even to think about what I had proposed. Very confused, her reaction was to frown at me, sigh loudly, and then release her death grip on the jug, while pushing it hard into my gut. Then she just turned and stomped away back to her desk.

Kurt had seen us face to face whispering, but did not say a word, until Joy was out of earshot. Then he whispered.

"Hey, that girl is acting strange…maybe she is on the rag or just maybe she already has the hots for you, huh? Did you two get acquainted and get all your paperwork done…a place to live?" he asked with a big sheepish smile.

"Yes, thanks to Joy. She sure is efficient!" I said loudly enough so Joy might hear my compliment.

I saw her eyes roll upward and another frown draw into a funny face with her tongue sticking out at me, as she gathered her things to end her workday.

"Well, Greg, tonight you have to come to my house for dinner. I called Martha, she's anxious to meet you. She's also expecting me to stop off at the market first to get some steaks. I hope you like to barbecue…I loathe it…so if I buy the meat…you get the honors tonight, okay? Bring Joy if you want. Is she pissed or something? She didn't say her usual, 'See ya tomorrow'," he suddenly added.

"I best explain that tomorrow, too. First, I have to catch her before she gets to her truck. What time?" I asked, headed out after Joy.

"Go home, clean up, and come on over as soon as you two can," he yelled out.

I nodded yes, waved okay to him, and hurriedly ran after Joy.

"Hey, wait up!" I summoned Joy.

"What do you want now?" Joy asked rather sarcastically, as I held onto her driver's door, so she couldn't close it. "Gee, I didn't want to make you angry. I know I'm a newbie, but I just wanted to ask you out for dinner so we could get to know each other better...Kurt wants me to bring you out to his house for barbecue."

"Not tonight...I've got things to do. I wouldn't be good company anyway after that."

"Please...let me be the judge. Besides, I don't know how to get to his house and I just remembered I don't even have a place to sleep tonight, since I have to wait for that criminal check to come back before I move in. Please?"

Joy stared at me hard, up and down, and then asked.

"Are you going to tell me about your girl back in Chicago, too?"

"No, I don't have a girl back in Chicago...anyway, I'm from Northfield."

"Oh, then tell me about your Northfield girlfriend...are you engaged?"

"Wait...I don't have anyone that I'm attached to in any kind of relationship. If I was, I'd tell you, if I thought it was important."

Joy sighed, then spouted rather reluctantly, "Okay, follow me, but I'll have to ask my roommate," she said, as if I had passed her test.

I think she was only trying to find out if I was available. She got on her cell; I think to call her roommate to tell her I was coming.

I hopped into my new truck, which had only seven hundred miles on the odometer and followed Joy south out of Springfield down I-55. In twenty minutes, we exited and drove into a nice little burg named Pawnee. Joy drove into an apartment complex parking lot with her cell phone still to her ear, so I stopped my truck and waited. I suppose she hadn't made contact with her roommate yet and was worried.

Joy pointed for me to park next to her and then told me to grab my bags and haul them inside as she got out of her truck. I guessed she had decided to allow me to stay with her, without Lila's okay. I understood from the get-go that my stay was just until my apartment was available in a few days.

I followed Joy inside. Lila was not home yet, so Joy scribbled out a note on the kitchen table and stuck it on their mutual message board explaining to Lila I was her guest and we both would be at Kurt's for dinner. Then she discovered a note from Lila and pulled it off the board. It read that Lila was headed up to Chicago overnight to visit her family and would return Wednesday. It read she took a sick day at her job for Tuesday.

I learned Lila was an office worker at the capital building and apparently took off whenever it was necessary. Joy then told me Lila had a seven-year-old boy who had been staying with her parents to attend school there and that she missed him terribly, but couldn't bring him here.

"Shucks! I thought Lila would surely have been here, at least by tonight. Do you promise to behave yourself, if I let you stay over?" she managed to ask.

"My word of honor as a gentleman," I swore, with my right hand held as if being sworn in by a judge.

"Take your stuff in the living room; you'll sleep on the couch. I'll give you some sheets later. Got it?" she quipped. "Better get going if we want to get to Kurt's in time and barbecue, too. You're driving, of course," she quickly added.

It only took Joy a minute to change into a dress and freshen up. I went as I was.

Martha was as sweet as my mother and quite the hostess, too. Kurt had our steaks seasoned, awaiting my touch. I quickly headed to the patio grill and in a bit more than thirty minutes, I had some good-looking grilled rib eyes still sizzling hot coming off the fire.

When we all had seated ourselves around the dining room table, Kurt was the first to bow his head to offer a blessing. Martha had a rich dinner wine already poured and we all raised our glasses to sip the nectar.

"To everyone's health and happiness," Martha toasted.

The evening was laid back, as the women scooped up the dishes and put them into the dishwasher, before joining us in the living room to watch the Cubs play. I suddenly felt exhausted. By nine, Joy and I thanked Kurt and Martha for the great meal and then we drove back to her apartment. In the morning, it would be a workday with both of us getting up early.

"Nice couple, huh?" I said to break the silence.

"Yep, they're two special people. Martha was my Sunday school teacher when I used to go to church as a kid," Joy related with a voice of recollection.

"You said, 'used to', why did you stop?" I asked.

"Oh, life got screwy and fell apart."

"Before, or after church-going?" I wanted to know.

"During," Joy related hesitantly. "I really don't want to discuss my life with a capuche," she told me bluntly, however looking over at me from the passenger side smiling.

I just wondered what a "capuche" was. It was not in my vocabulary nor was I certain it should be. Had she just politely criticized me?

Somehow, I felt she had big regrets about me staying over, especially without her roommate there. Therefore, I addressed her fears as best I could.

"Look, if you feel uncomfortable about me staying over, I'll gladly see if I can find a motel. It's late, but I saw that we just passed a big Ramada back there."

"I'm glad you said that. It does ease my worries. I offered you not knowing Lila would be out. But, since you have your job on the line, and I'm a black belt in karate, I guess I'm safe," she said, with a little judo chop on my arm to suggest she could defend herself, if necessary.

"Believe me you're safe…besides, you're not my type!" I laughed. It just came out.

"Well, I'll be hanged…you silly bum-turd…that wasn't nice!" she let out laughing with another chop, but this time it hurt.

I momentarily lost control of my truck, crossed the dividing line, and got loudly blasted by a cattle truck's air horn, which was racing up beside me speeding on the inside lane. The blast scared the hell out of both of us and Joy grabbed my arm again in fright.

"Whoa! That guy's really pissed!" Joy let out as we both laughed together.

"If the Good Lord let me live through that, I don't have to worry about you, huh?" she quipped. "Besides, you're definitely not my type either, so we'll get along, until you get into your apartment, hopefully soon."

Then Joy settled back in the seat. She looked out the window all the way to her apartment and did not speak another word. I had unintentionally hurt her feelings and I knew it. I pulled next to her truck in the parking slot that was meant for Lila's vehicle.

"Look, I'm thankful you trust me tonight, but I really didn't mean you weren't my type. You're a nice girl, but we haven't gotten to know each other that well."

"Sorry, too, but you really aren't my type, so forget it…apology accepted. Let's get you set on the couch and after I shower, you can have the bathroom."

"Oh, I always shave and shower in the mornings. Besides, I washed up at Kurt's after I barbecued. What time can I have the bathroom in the morning?"

"I'm up at six, you better be out by then, and don't stink up the place. Guys are filthy…don't be. Extra towels are in the cabinet, soap, too. See you in the morning," she said, as she handed me some linens from the hall closet and pointed me to the couch down the hall to the living room.

"Good night!" I offered with no return.

It is always strange to sleep in someone else's house at nighttime, and this was no exception. I heard everything happening in the complex, which was not limited to a lovers' quarrel, loud rap music, trashcans clanking outside at the dumpster, and a rather arousing sexual encounter going on in a bedroom somewhere at three in the morning. I guess some very religious person was enjoying life to its fullest. Nevertheless, the "Oh, God's" and the bed squeaking sounds were disturbing at that hour.

Eventually, I fell sound asleep and awoke to Joy flushing a toilet. Then the shower water turned on and I heard the shower door close.

It was six-fifteen. I could not use the bathroom now. However, I smelled the aroma of fresh-perked coffee and went into the kitchen to get a cup. Just then, the telephone rang, so with Joy in the shower I answered it.

"Hello!" I answered, and immediately heard a click of the receiver going down on the other end. It immediately rang again. "Hello!" I again answered.

"Is this 217-765-4151?" the voice questioned, as I looked for the number on the phone.

"Yes…Joy is in the shower, if that's who you are calling."

"Who in the hell are you is what I want to know?" the woman screamed rudely. "You're in my house!"

"Oh, sorry…I'm Greg Wetmore. I work with Joy…she allowed me to stay over until I get my new apartment. She is up, but taking a shower and I don't think she wants to come to this phone right now. Could this be Lila?" I asked.

"Oh, you know I'm her roommate…I guess everything's okay there. I thought there was an intruder. Tell Joy my son, Truman, is ill and I'm taking him to the doctor here. I might not return until Sunday, if I can take off that long…got that? And don't you dare sleep in my bedroom or steal anything or I'll cut your nuts out!" she bellowed.

I'm sure she couldn't see my wide eyes or the surprised look on my face, but the thought of castration made my voice come out squeaky as I told her, "Got that for sure!"

The phone went dead with no good-bye and I put the receiver back down. I heard Joy making noise so I searched for two cups and the toaster. I made two slices of toast and buttered both…one for Joy. Then she walked into the kitchen with a towel around her head and told me the shower was now mine.

"Well, warm toast…thanks. However, I have to eat sustenance. Want some bacon and eggs over easy?" she asked.

"No, thanks, just this toast, please…your roommate called while you were in the shower. She said to tell you Truman is sick and she's going to take him to the doctor. If she can get off she'll be there till Sunday, I think."

"You think? I guess you can sleep in her room now," Joy suggested.

"No, maam, it's definitely the couch for me," I told her remembering Lila's orders. My balls seemed to twitch.

I gulped the coffee, ate the toast, and then headed to the bathroom. I quickly shaved, then took my shower. By six forty, I was stepping into my jeans when Joy looked in from the kitchen and told me she was leaving to go to work. We were going separately as I would need my truck to go out to a work site. Then Kurt called Joy to let her know I was to meet him out on I-55 south bound at the Glenarm exit, just a few miles from Pawnee. The crew was working on an exit ramp improvement and that was to be my first assignment.

Chapter 5

From a mile away, I could see the flashing sign, which alerted all vehicles to caution, as there were State of Illinois IDOT personnel at work one mile ahead. I also noticed the speed limit was reducing to 45M.P.H. and the right lane to the Glenarm exit was stop and go, with a hardhat, florescent-yellow vested worker holding a red stop sign on a pole. Big trucks downshifted and motors strained as several bumper-to-bumper semi trucks slowed down entering the speed zone. The fine was an automatic $350, if a trooper nailed you on radar speeding in a construction zone.

However, there was very little, if any, exiting traffic to Glenarm this sunny morning when I eased up to the signal person, who stood facing away from traffic. Therefore, when I honked my horn to get his attention, I found out how darn angry a person can be, sleeping, while leaning on a sign pole.

"You dumb son-of-a-bitch! I'll have you arrested for reckless endangerment of a highway worker!" he began to rant, while pointing his finger at me. I eased up slowly and wary he might take a swat at my truck with his sign. His brown eyes were bloodshot red and my guess was he had a late night drinking session and maybe had a hair that bites the dog, also. I rolled my window down, but waited for him to simmer down.

"Sir, could you please tell me where Kurt Rakers is?"

His brown eyelids began to bat and squint as he bent down to lean upon my open window and asked, "Who wants to know?" very sarcastically.

"I do, sir. I'm sorry I scared you. I didn't mean to."

"Looky here, nobody scares Ol' Smoke. You just snuck up on me too fast! Who is you anyway…you from front office or the shed…or just a nosey person?" he asked, becoming suddenly leery.

"I guess I'm from the shed," I concurred.

The sour smell of an alcoholic beverage was present upon his breath. He stood there a moment breathing towards me and I realized he was very intoxicated. When I showed a grimaced face to him, because of the way he smelled, he suddenly spoke more politely.

"You ain't gonna report me, is you, sir?"

"What…for sleeping at your post and being drunk on the job? I don't have to report you…you work for me, remember?"

I had no communication with the shed, so I fumbled around in my wallet to get the office's telephone number. I could not just leave a drunken person in charge who might cause an accident to happen or be killed himself, therefore I called on my cell.

"State shed…Joyce speaking," her voice chirped quickly.

"Joy, this is Greg. I have a problem out on I-55 at the Glenarm exit. Can you contact Kurt and ask him to come here. I have a worker here who is too drunk to direct traffic and I can't allow him to continue."

"Really? Hum…yep, hang on…IDOT one from base…IDOT one…come in."

"This is IDOT one, go ahead, Joy."

"Greg Wetmore needs you to come to the south bound exit ramp. He says he has a drunken worker…I guess it's Smoke again."

"Tell him I'm a mile away headed south…be there in a minute…over."

"He'll be there in a short-short, boss number two…anything else?"

"Yes, thanks. I think I need a radio."

"Guess what?"

"What?" I returned.

"You got one. There's a new truck with your name on it outside. You were supposed to come in and pick it up. No one told me…it must have come in overnight. It has all your tools in it, plus communication. That means when you are lonely you can talk to me," she giggled then said, "Oops, I've got a customer."

Then she just quit talking.

I heard Kurt's truck slowing as the big white tandem slid next to us on the berm. It didn't take long as he jumped out quickly to confront Smoke.

"Smoke...I warned you before...get your check at the shed and don't come back...hear me? You cannot come out here being drunk, buster. No... wait...Greg, you'll have to run him back to the shed. I can't let him leave here driving drunk, now can I? Anyway, there's a new truck for you and you have to leave it at the shed every night before quittin' time, like I do mine. Smoke, you get in Mr. Wetmore's truck and don't you dare give him any trouble... understand me?" Kurt screamed.

Ol' Smoke laid down his stop sign gently and asked very politely if he could get inside my truck. I unlocked the passenger's side door and he eased inside looking very sad.

"Nice truck, Mr. Wetmore," he spoke looking about. "Smells new, too. You know I'm union, don't ya?"

I used the median turnaround to head back to Springfield and our work shed. I looked in my rear view mirror and saw Kurt holding that stop-and-go sign in one hand and talking on his hand-held radio in the other. He was calling someone to take his place. Smoke soon leaned back against the door, fell asleep, and began snoring. His breathing almost made me gag, so I left my window cracked open the entire way.

We both got out, but Smoke had to straighten himself up first, before he was able to negotiate the side door entrance. I saw two men wearing white shirts waiting for him, who apparently were the upstairs office bosses in the hiring-firing department. The union surely would not back a person caught drunk on the job, I assumed.

As the door closed behind him, a mournful Smoke tried to avoid their wrath; his head bowed down, while he brought his palms together as if to pray for mercy. I could only see their mouths moving, while reprimanding him, but he looked beaten.

I headed for the new white Dodge Ram truck parked outside with a vehicle equipment sticker still pasted upon the rear window. I felt a bit tormented that it was I who had reported him drunk. Maybe I should have gotten a replacement for him, first, I thought. However, it was not the first time for

Smoke to show up drunk. His drinking had been addressed before, as Kurt mentioned to him in my presence. Then, I realized it would have been me, also, who would have mourned my poor judgment, if Smoke had errored and some worker had been killed or injured.

The keys were in the truck with a note. It was from Joy…"Good luck, roomie! Check to see if everything is there and then sign out for your new equipment. Return it to me by quitting time, your slave."

I immediately laughed, and then looked around, but could not see Joy. I checked the gas gauge and the tank was full. After I adjusted the driver's seat position and rear view mirror, I surveyed the list of equipment for which I was held responsible and then signed the required equipment-received receipt. There was quite the list of expensive engineering paraphernalia.

We civil engineers are hired to fabricate projects such as bridges, highways and waterways, and rely on very precise tools and instrumentation to guide us in designing. Without technology and civil engineering state-of-the art tools, structures might not be as safe. From now on, I realized, it is my sole responsibility to place safety first.

I learned very early in UIC's engineering classes how to use and rely upon special tools to make jobs easier, more efficient, and safer. It was my job to utilize weather, geology, and hydrology.

I also was thoroughly familiar with those important geographical websites needed to track down information for structural projects. There, too, I found my new lap top computer all charged with another note with Joy's office email, plus the job's blue prints and schematics. I was set.

Nevertheless, as great of a college is UIC, I had not been offered instruction on how to deal with firing unsafe, intoxicated employees. I learned that myself today. Smoke was peering out that side window and I saw tears running down his face. I do not think he was really just mad at me alone, but himself, also, for being an alcoholic who could not help himself. That made me sick enough to puke though I never met him before now. I drove to the job site thinking, "What a hell of a way to start off!"

It was just the beginning, as Kurt approached me at a fast pace, then greeted me instantly like a man on a mission.

"The backhoe just suffered a seizure. I plain-bobbed the ramp's grade, now it's seven degrees too lean because it settled more than I figured, and the farmer who has given us permission to dig him a new five acre lake to get our fill dirt here has now asked for seventy thousand. Yesterday he was jumping with joy anticipating all the fish he could catch out of his free five-acre lake. I also promised him the state would stock it for him like the others. Today, after probably talking to some of the other farmers along the interstate, who we borrowed fill from, they must have told him he could also get cash. Would you like to go dicker with him, if you can, while I re-shoot the grade for the ramp? He's out there on his John Deere blocking the cat from any digging. We will over-run the set costs and the governor will have our asses, if we do.

"We've only got sixteen days to get this completed if the weather holds and I'm not in a very good mood this morning after Smoke. The son-of-a-biscuit has six kids to feed and guess now what…I just got a call from Joy…Smoke got saved by the union anyway and has to be given state rehab counseling before termination and maybe keep his job. I should be happy that he'll try to get straight, but if I did that I'd be long gone…of course, I wouldn't do that…but if these things keep going haywire around here I might," he yelled. "Please get going and settle this fill dirt thing first, okay… thanks," Kurt continued like a whirl wind, then started motioning for the grader-packer to follow the dozers.

At least he had a handle on everything, which could have come only by his twenty-five years of experience. This would be another first, as I wasn't told I would have to be a negotiator, too. It was ten and I hadn't even lifted my pencil or looked to those new tools. Suddenly, a thought came to me as I drove over to the farmer's pasture. I parked a few hundred feet away, then got out my new GPS and quickly calibrated it. Then, as if I was using a Geiger counter, I moved it back and forth until I got up near Mr. Danby. He was sitting on his old tractor with an "I got you by the balls" look. I ignored him, which brought him down from the tractor. Curiosity, they say, killed the cat.

"Hey, you…whatcha foolin' with?" he questioned.

"Ten feet deep…five acres…third of one acre is 16,780 cubic yards minus truck spill…amounts to square root times one tenth equals…eh… near 85,000," I continued randomly calculating absolutely nothing to arouse his ire.

Mr. Danby stood about as much as he could of my jumbled mumbling that I used to aggravate him. The patched bib overalls and weaved straw hat he wore, fit the look of most Midwest farmers on workday.

"Hey! I asked you a question!" he became louder and more intense.

"How do you do, sir…are you the owner of this fine pasture?" I asked.

"Yes, it's a real valuable flat piece of land…good dirt with drainage from the interstate, too," he let me know. "I best ask for more money like the others did."

"Oh, didn't you sign a paper you were happy allowing IDOT to remove about 85,000 cubic yards of soil to use as fill for that exit ramp? It would have been one heck of a nice fishing hole…too bad."

"Yes, but…" he said then hesitated with a sudden look of being worried.

"Hum…I wondered why they've changed their minds," I said reaching down to examine the dirt in my fist. "It seems to me your place is closer to the project than driving way down to that other farmer's place to dig him a free pond. I guess he wanted to have a place, too, for his family to barbecue and fish with his grandkids more than you did, huh?"

"What do you mean?"

"What I'm saying to you is that your neighbor could have offered us more dirt than you have since he's close…and it might be free, too. He might have told someone he'd cooperate without any problems, especially if he got those super-sized state fish stocked free, also," I replied, looking out toward the other farmer's pasture.

"You mean Bill Folcum offered his useless choke-weeded pasture free and now IDOT wants his instead of mine? Why he's the one who told me yesterday to ask for money in the first place. So, he thought he'd pull one over on me, huh? You boys just do what you promised on that contract and I'll cancel the money part. I'll show that double-crossin' jackass…I won't speak to him any time soon…see if I milk his cows again, just so he and June can go on vacation to Branson, Dolly Wood and The Grand Ole Opry, ha…even if he is a third cousin."

"I guess he'll be really jealous, also, if you have this big lake filled with big fish. He'll probably beg you to go fishing, think? You had best keep this our secret lest he persuades the bosses to go ahead and use his pasture. Are you sure you haven't changed your mind…ahhh…wouldn't that be something to have a rope dangling from that leaning, big oak so the kids could swing out over the water and drop in on a hot, humid day, like today? On the other hand, you could put a floating dock over there by the big willow with a diving board on it too. I could tell the cat driver to dig it just a bit deeper over there on that level side, maybe twelve feet deep, or so, how's that?"

"Wonderful! I never thought of that...Minnie and I can even come here skinny dippin' after dark...now that's really sompthin', Mr.!" he laughed with gusto. "Go tell that fella on the cat to start scoopin'...and then you go back and tell Bill Folcum to go to hell!" he said sarcastically, while leaping up onto the tow bar of his John Deere and then cranking over his Johnny pop and backing it away from the Caterpillar's path.

I reached up, shook Mr. Danby's hand to reassert our contract, and then headed over to the cat operator. The pop, pop, pop of Danby's John Deere tractor's exhaust eliminated anything heard after that.

I then motioned by hand to the dozer driver to scoop out a nicer, deeper hole for swimming. That operating engineer knew I had dickered with Danby for something. He was glad to perform my request and glad to get going. He cranked up that diesel and soon the dirt began to roll up onto his big cat's blade. Again, the dump trucks were straining under their dirt overloads to build that ramp. I returned and found Kurt in a much better mood.

"I have to go to the office because of Smoke. He says you abused him by scaring him, which caused him much pain. He is threatening to sue."

"I'll go," I told Kurt. "Yes, I tooted my horn at him, because he turned his back on traffic and was sound asleep," I further explained. "I can't believe what our world is coming to," I moaned, for I was getting pissed quickly.

"Okay, if you think you can handle it. They just asked for his supervisor and that fits both of us. Go get justice," Kurt added as he patted me on the back. "Oh, what about that Danby fella...was he stubborn?"

"He's convinced now that lake will bring him happiness and maybe a little nasty lark after dark with his wife, Minnie, skinny-dippin', he told me."

"You sure must have a gifted silver tongue. From now on, I delegate all our negotiating and union disputes to be handled solely by you...good luck!" Kurt said happy to get out of that.

I used my radio for the first time without instructions to call Joy, but instead, I got the state police troopers' radio system, and was sternly told I was broadcasting on the emergency channel and if it wasn't an emergency to use my channel one.

I felt ignorant, but thanked the radio communicator. I looked closer at the switches and saw small letters stamped into tapes for my work channels. After that, I just turned the radio off and drove to the shed without calling ahead. It was good to know I had that if ever an emergency arose and needed the police. I had direct communication.

"Why didn't you call in? I heard the state police tell you that you were on the wrong channel…sorry…I should have told you about how our radios operate. Did you figure it out?" Joy asked, after I sat down in the air conditioning.

"Yep, I turned it off."

"Too bad…then you could have heard me advise you to 10-22…that means disregard and you could have stayed out there. I tried Kurt, but he didn't respond either. Anyway, when Smoke sobered up and heard you were coming in, he fessed-up to the upstairs people and shut up about suing us. He's going to rehab. Now that makes six…three guys and three girls…what a gimmick, huh? What I'd really like to know is, where they get all that dope shit…oops, pardon my French," Joy said with a bit of embarrassment.

"I guess it's everywhere. I never use the stuff and hope I never will. If I do, it will be because of days like this on the job that will have driven me to drinking and probably I'll decide to blow my own brains out. Seems like Kurt handles everything smoothly," I suggested.

"Yep, he's a peach. Look, I heard from your apartment super and you can move in Saturday…want to eat out on the way home? That way I won't have to wash dishes. It was Lila's week anyway. There's a nice Country Kitchen on the way. I love their salad bar and you can't beat their steaks…what say?"

"I say, great, it'll be my treat all week, but when is quitting time? Do I punch in…out…no one ever said?"

"No, I told you that. You apparently didn't listen…you're salaried, like me. We just come and go anytime, if we can get away with it, ha!" Joy laughed. "Might as well stick here cause by the time you return it'll be past quitting time."

Just then Kurt radioed I should just stay at the shop and could leave at four. Joy got busy typing and handed me Smoke's statement, which he had signed, relinquishing me of any wrongdoing. I was pleased, but fortunate, as being a new guy they'd probably throw me under the bus and discard me with the wash water. I'm certain if a lawsuit arose out of it, I'd get the pink slip. I got a bit wiser that day.

By four, I was starved to death and realized I hadn't even brought a lunch…what was I thinking, or more like it, not thinking?

Kurt was pulling up outside, so I waited for him to come inside. He was dusty and thirsty. After Kurt washed up in our private office's lavatory, I asked him to join Joy and me at the Country Kitchen Restaurant. He decided to join us and called Martha to tell her to meet us there. He really loved that woman. I was happy to return the favor of a meal. However, Kurt also wanted to talk shop. I concurred.

When a loud buzzer sounded it was quitting time, people started coming from everywhere…a closet, the furnace room, the cafeteria, the men's and women's johns and from several trucks, which came into the shed quickly one after the other. Where had they been all day, I asked myself?

They all crowded around the time clock and began lining up in a straight line. When the time clock hit four o'clock, they each strolled by the clock and systematically punched out. Amazingly, by one minute after four, everyone had left the building.

Joy told me to follow her and she was behind Kurt. We all arrived at a very busy Country Kitchen about the same time as Martha, who drove up in her red, white-topped, 1964 ½ Ford Mustang convertible. It looked as if it were showroom new. She looked different somehow with the scarf wrapped neatly around her hairdo. Kurt greeted Martha with a kiss and we all headed to our table, behind a very charming waitress appropriately named, Sugar. She exuded sweetness and her kindness was more than just ample.

Joy and Martha headed for the salad bar, while Kurt and I ordered everyone's steaks. Then Sugar brought them over, after they were grilled to perfection. Once again, Kurt offered a short prayer. This time, I closed my eyes tightly and really thanked Him for getting me through my first day safely. I also thanked Him for giving me these people dining with me as friends… they were good people.

The whole meal was a "Joy" as our Joy took over the conversation concerning Smoke's departure, then his sudden reprieve. Maybe his prayer had worked for him, who knows?

Somehow, I saw Joy in a different light, not as a very efficient secretary this time, but a real live person, who had feelings, opinions, and a very tight figure, which somehow I had not really noticed until she scooted in next to me in a booth. It was a bit disturbing, also, as suddenly her fragrance seeped into my mind, and I had flashbacks of a girl I left behind.

"Coffee!" I suddenly spoke without hesitating.

"Sugar! May we have more coffee over this way, please?" Kurt quickly summoned our waitress.

"No, Kurt, I think Joy is wearing perfume called Coffee...it reminded me of someone. My cup is still full, sorry."

"Then you better gulp it down, because our very efficient waitress is lickity-split headed this way with a hot pot," Kurt advised and also gulped his drink.

I almost exploded my gulp of hot java when Sugar greeted us happily and poured more coffee.

"The way you folks like our coffee, mind if I set the pot down? The tables are full tonight and I'm going to get my daily exercise starting right now...I'll be back," Sugar mentioned quickly and set the pot on a warmer for us to use at our own pace.

Martha then spoke, "It's so nice when a guy notices your perfume, don't you think, Joy?" she said coyly.

"If I didn't know better, a girl might think she was getting a compliment, it's that 'it reminded me of someone' which takes all the pleasure out of it," Joy said guardedly, without glancing my way.

"I'm sorry. I like that fragrance...it's become my favorite. It's a personal thing which I can't explain here," I said praying this moment might end.

I kept eating my salad, but Joy seemed to stab at her steak a bit too vigorously for me. I was worried that I had put my big foot in my mouth again.

"Umm...ahhh," I added while breathing in her perfume's aroma again to rectify my first missed response. "I think it smells much better on you," I told Joy turning her way.

Nevertheless, Joy avoided any eye contact with me, stabbed that steak, and changed the subject quickly to the annual sidewalk sale going on in downtown Springfield. Joy and Martha consumed the rest of their meals, while each relating to their marvelous buys found at last year's downtown summer sale-a-thon. Kurt just remained quiet, however gave out a sudden chuckle at my dismal attempt. He hid his face in his napkin to avoid his laughter.

Soon, I picked up the tab and left a nice tip for Sugar. Then Kurt and Martha thanked me for their meal, as we each bid ado to one another. We agreed that we would all do it again soon.

I followed behind Joy headed to Pawnee. She pulled into the complex's parking lot and headed straight for the door of her apartment. She closed the door fast, so I knocked first, without barging right in after her. She did not answer, so I knocked again, only louder. I thought she was overly upset with me.

"Come on in!" was Joy's shout from the bathroom.

As I walked in I saw the bathroom light coming from beneath the door and Joy sounded very uncomfortable.

"Peeeuuut!" a big thunderous fart exploded loudly. "Sorry!" she called out to me sounding very embarrassed as she then quickly flushed the toilet to cover the sounds.

Apparently, Joy had to go there badly and could not wait any longer, so I turned on the TV and put the volume up a bit to drown out her little noises she was trying to keep me from hearing. It was that funny intimate moment between friends when you realize they are human, too.

"Well you look very relieved," I kidded, when Joy came out with an embarrassed look upon her face.

"I don't need your comments…when Lila is here we don't say anything about these kinds of situations…go to bed," she advised rudely.

I did…I just got comfortable on the couch when I heard fast footsteps headed to the john. It was Joy again, and apparently, she had a really upset stomach.

"Can I help?" I asked, thinking I could get medicine.

"What…you want to wipe my ass!" she yelled, obviously very distressed.

"Got any Keopectate…that works sometimes?" I advised loudly.

"What's that? I took Imodium, I'll be better soon, I hope. Thanks, but don't you worry about it…go to sleep!"

"I'm sorry. I feel bad when you feel sick. I get that way sometimes, too. Do you think it was the meal?" I asked, just as the toilet flushed again. I heard the faucet running as she washed her hands.

Joy walked out in her terry robe and then curled up in the lounge chair, which had a big, colorful, tufted pillow that she then hid herself behind, and answered.

"No, except, I ate way too much…but I'm okay now, I think. That steak was so darn good I almost started chewing the bone right in front of everyone," she joked.

She looked at me as if she wanted to say something, but could not, so I asked her what else was bothering her.

"It's you being here...not because you're here...well, heck...I don't know," she said very confused.

"I feel sort of funny, too. Our sudden relationship, which has pushed us together so closely, is confusing us both. Is that it?" I questioned.

"Yeah, sort of...I'm not sure I can figure us out, if there even is an 'us'. Sometimes I feel like I'd like us to be more than friends, because we seemed to enjoy each other right from the get-go and you are easy to talk to...but then I feel it's no good because I don't know if you feel as I do...I don't know much about you...I'm confused."

"Only time will tell, Joy. Nevertheless, be assured I like you...I think an awful lot about you, even this soon. I guess that's good, huh? But I'm not even settled in yet, haven't gotten my first check and we haven't even kissed," I said looking for an invitation.

"Forget about it...I'm too tired now. Let's just say I get your drift and that's that...good night!" she said seemingly annoyed, but then again, maybe she was unprepared for my sudden advances.

"You think our friendship can even survive, until we both get to know each other better? I think we'll know it when we both want to be more than friends. Gee, we have only been friends for about two days, nevertheless, I do feel like you say...we are closer...I'm very comfortable being around you, too. I'm not certain if it's platonic, or not, but I respect you now...that's important. I want us to at least be good friends, don't you?"

"Good night, boss, number two," she said grinning and quickly arising from the chair, headed straight to her room.

I learned immediately she was female, fickle, and very moody. I liked that about her.

I do not think I could have explained better, because I was not in love with Joy, right then...not the same way as I was with Amanda. Nevertheless, I would never want to hurt Joy's feelings and getting to know her better was leveling the playing field, bit by bit. I decided just to let things be as they may with us, and whatever happens, happens. I laid down and shut my eyes. Tomorrow, I hoped, would be a much better day.

Chapter 6

A series of job mishaps occurred at the job site. It was first thing Wednesday morning, after a good Tuesday's digging, that the cat hit an underground spring in Mr. Danby's pasture. The cat got stuck ten feet down in a gusher of sandy mud. The cat driver had been smart enough to roll over the spouting water and plug it quickly, but we couldn't get another cat down there to wench him out of the muck. Then, Mr. Danby raced home to get his big six-wheeled tractor he used to pull his eight-bottom plow. He came back with two, however, one other tractor being driven by Minnie, his wife.

Before we could say Rumpelstiltskin, Minnie Danby climbed aboard that big six-wheeler while Mr. Danby hooked up his log chains to the rear of the cat. This cat wasn't equipped like the others with heavy digging cleats or it would have come out on its own. Nevertheless, with the assist from Mrs. Danby the cat eased off the sludge and made it out of that hole.

"Good thing the cat got it down to twelve feet. We have enough, I think. That water will fill his lake in about a week it appears by the flow...won't he be happy! Go tell him you have to charge him extra for filling his lake up, and then tell him thanks. We are through here. I read the water table charts in this area and it's only supposed to be nine and a half feet. We got lucky," Kurt, told me.

Just then, an air horn blasted loudly and when we looked toward the sound, we saw workers scattering in all directions. A speeding semi locked up its brakes when a state trooper coming from the opposite direction hit him with moving radar. The driver locked up the trailer tandem brakes and the trailer skidded out of control sideways knocking down traffic cones and a barricade. Luckily, the truck missed the workers and slid off into a drainage ditch where it came to rest.

The truck was stuck and the workers were infuriated at the semi's driver. Of all things, it was a female driver and she locked the cab's doors so the workers could not get to her. They shook their fists and shouted cuss words.

The trooper pulled up and ordered every worker to go back to work except the signalman who told the trooper that he clearly had the slow down sign displayed and the flashing road sign was operating to inform traffic that workers were present and the speed reduced to 45 M.P.H. That driver could get a $350 fine plus the price of a tow truck. Some people never learn.

Kurt and I got over to the scene just as the trooper cuffed the female driver, took her truck ignition keys, and placed her in the back of his squad car. Her eyes were very red, but I don't think it was from any tears. I heard the trooper tell her that her logbook was way behind, maybe over twenty-four hours.

He asked her why she failed to fill it out correctly, but she remained silent. Then he asked if she had had any sleep during that time.

The driver simply stated, "Nope!"

"You could have killed someone," the trooper sternly warned, to which she sarcastically replied, "Tell that to my laid off husband and six kids I have to feed."

"Yeah, how would I explain to them that their mother was a murderer… think how they'd feel then if you did kill someone, or yourself…that's also the same thing I'd probably have to explain to some of these workers' big families. Then see who puts food on their table. Let's go see the judge," he told her.

Two large wreckers responded to the trooper's request to assist removing the big rig. It was fully loaded with five-gallon cans of asphalt paving for home use, which had remained upon their pallets. A hefty wrecker hoist pulled the rig backwards out onto the shoulder very slowly, as the trooper diverted traffic, with our people's help directing traffic to the inside lane, until it was driven away by one of the helpers.

Then right before they left the trooper asked his headquarters if a judge was available and advised that he was transporting a female. He gave his mileage to his headquarters' radio, before they zoomed off to Springfield. That woman was a pitiful sight. Her eyes closed and she was beginning to snore before they finally left.

"The road supervisors advised me no one was hurt, so I guess this is over... what next?" Kurt said chuckling. "You'll get used to this eventually. Just when things look good, shit always happens."

We looked over the progress of the ramp by truck and I was impressed how efficient and hard working, also dedicated, these employees were. The job was ahead of schedule.

"I have an errand for you to do for me, if you don't mind, Greg. Use your GPS and head out to Saline County Road 45 and Blue Ridge Road. They have appropriated money to replace a bridge and asked IDOT to give them a suggestion or two, which structure would best suit the creek crossing. They have a rickety old bridge built in the twenties out of railroad track timbers and rails, but now the road commissioner load-limited it to just two tons... so the farmers are complaining they can't get to their fields. It's a hurry-up job...just check to see if Phil Fuhrman, their surveyor, has everything right, okay? They don't have our GPS equipment and ask sometimes to borrow it. You will have to do the precise coordinates for them.

"Then stop for the day and head into the shop...see you tomorrow out here. And thanks again for getting Danby straight...see ya tomorrow," Kurt repeated with a pat on my shoulder. No one could ask for a nicer boss than Kurt.

My GPS led me way out into the boonies to a site along a creek bottom road, which seemed well below the normal flood plain. My visual survey of their situation revealed there was a much better location for the new bridge just a few hundred yards beyond. Nevertheless, my job was to ascertain if their calculations were accurate and that was all.

I could not help wondering about my alternative selection. It would really save them costs now and in the future. I was not a brilliant wizard as it was just common sense. I met with their crew and asked them why they picked this particular spot to build. Their explanation was, "It's always been here."

I asked them if they would consider my choice, because cost-wise it would eliminate over a mile of continual, annual, blacktop repair, which also cut through a farmer's field using up fertile ground. In addition, it was diverting the normal waterway, which I was certain was washed out occasionally, because of flooding. I surmised the plan had originated there because of the horse and buggy days where a horse could not negotiate the steepness of the hill. It was no problem now for motor vehicles, I suggested.

"Now why didn't we think of that?" one said looking to the others gathered.

"We don't get paid to think like he does," another spoke out.

"He probably makes a half million a year doin' stuff like this here," another broke in.

"Well, how about it, fellas? Let's go back to the commish and see if it will work. It might be the first time anyone has ever attempted to save money on a project," he said chuckling.

"Thank you, what did you say your name was?" a man questioned extending a handshake.

"I'm an engineer, Wetmore. Call me Greg, please. I'd be glad to draw up a pre-plan on my computer if you have a couple of minutes."

"Yeah, go ahead. We can use all the help we can get."

They were wide-eyed with the computer's wizardry when it showed the new structure in place as well as the cost and savings. Since I didn't have a printer handy, I sent a copy to theirs and ours in Joy's office to alert Kurt of my suggestion. I still needed his okay.

However, the men were ready to adopt my idea and drop their plan to rebuild there. I told them they could begin the project without closing this one, until the other was in place, which also met with their approval. I shook their hands and left them scratching their heads. I had done a good job today and I was pleased with my own work. College studies were beginning to shine through.

It was well after quitting time, so I headed to the shed. When I got there, I could not even get inside as the gates were closed. Someone had parked my truck outside the gates and someone was sitting in it, leaned back listening to my stereo. It was Joy.

"Hey…how's it going? What happened?"

"After five, the gates are locked up. I thought you might be confused, so I waited for you."

"How did you move my truck?" I asked her.

"I hotwired it, silly!" she said to provoke me. "Not really, you left the keys in the ignition."

I immediately felt for my keys in my pocket and they weren't there.

"Don't do that again or I'll use it to go shopping while you're gone," Joy said smiling and handing the keys to me. "Besides, aren't you taking me to dinner, as planned?"

"Yep, as planned," I agreed. "Thanks for thinking of me, or for me, or whatever I mean."

"Still confused, huh?" she said grinning.

"No, just…well, yes…you're a very good friend to do this for me. Where shall we eat tonight?" I asked trying to avoid her inquiry.

"Bonanza sound okay? It's just up town a bit. We're both properly dressed for the occasion."

"What occasion is that?" I questioned.

"Day three!" she advised. "Two more and you've got your own place to go home to."

When she said day three, I suspected it was day three of our relationship. I looked at her wondering what she was really thinking. It was probably that she was happy for me to go. I later learned I was wrong.

After our meal, I drove Joy back to the shop to get her truck. Then I followed her home.

"Here, this is the extra key. Keep it, so I won't have to worry you're locked out. I might have to go somewhere, so until Saturday, keep it."

I took the key and opened the door. Joy changed into her usual robe after a shower and then we watched a movie. She made us buttered popcorn and by ten we both said goodnight. I thought of how nice it might be to follow her into her room and lay down with her. The couch was getting lumpy and it was a bit short for my frame. Joy was moderately attractive and good-natured in many ways. She was growing on me minute by minute and I had a hard time getting asleep when she closed her bedroom door.

Again, I somehow awoke at six in the morning to the sounds of Joy taking a shower. The smell of fresh coffee filled my nostrils as I climbed off the couch. I stretched and noticed there was rain falling and wondered what that would do to our ramp's schedule. Then I heard thunder and a bolt of lightning knocked out the power source. I heard Joy yell out asking what happened, so I hollered back, "Power went out!"

I felt around in only the light of dawn for two coffee cups and burnt my fingers on the very hot percolator. I managed to make four pieces of toast in the gas oven like my mother used to do sometimes in those Chicago winters and decided to scramble some eggs and do them in the oven as best I could. By the time Joy came out, spooked by my presence, she let out an, "Eek!" when she spotted me sitting in the dark.

"Oh, there you are. You can have the shower now, if you can find it. Hey, breakfast made already? Now that's the kind of guy every girl wants to wake up to…do dishes, too?" she quipped.

"I'm just an old handyman around the house. I've batched-it since beginning college; never had a roommate before now. I thought you might burn yourself if I did not cook your breakfast for you. I burned my pinky anyway."

"Well, there's cereal instead. Nevertheless, I do appreciate this. I'll repay breakfast with…" she hesitated, and then said, "with doing our laundry. Sort your clothes out and I will put them in on timed cycle, so they are finished when we get home from work."

"Thanks…I'm headed to the shower. Want to ride with me this time and save gas?"

"No, thank you. I have some girly shopping to do and I need my truck during noon hour. That sale is on downtown starting today and I want to slip out and find a bargain. Besides, Martha is coming, too."

I offered, but she refused. I guess I thought it was my time to share, but her plans were different. I took my shower and when I came out Joy had left. I put my dirty clothes in two piles in the hallway next to the utility room, before I left for work.

It was pouring outside and the rain was coming down horizontally with the wind. I didn't have an umbrella or raincoat, as if either might have helped, so I made a mad dash out to my truck. I got soaked. In five minutes, just as I was entering the city, the storm suddenly let up and the sun broke upon clear skies to the west. However, when I got to the office, I figured that I looked like I peed my pants.

Joy wasn't there and the phone at her desk rang continuously. Therefore, I picked up the receiver to hear one of the workers calling in sick and took down his name and time. Then the phone continued to ring repeatedly. I had ten workers calling in as being sick and my note pad was full.

When my own cell chimed, I was surprised. It was Mom. She just wanted to know why I had not called. Everything was good there; unfortunately, I had to cut our conversation short by telling her I loved her and missed her, but had to go.

I again picked up the ringing office phone, turned around, and there was Joy standing right behind me. She looked soaking wet, and very pissed for some reason. Joy reluctantly gripped the phone from my paw and talked to another employee about being late to work, then hung up, and went over and punched the girl's time clock. When she came back, she was exceptionally cold.

"Hey…I took down eight or ten people calling in sick this morning. I didn't know what else to do since you weren't here and I…"

"Thanks!" Joy broke in, and then casually walked away to another part of the building with my notepad. She came back, still obviously perturbed.

"Hey…what's the matter? I tried to do you a favor and you treat me like this…what's up?"

"You! That's what. You just passed me by, while that cop gave me a ticket for me making an illegal left turn in front of him. I didn't see him because of the hard rain. I'm not even sure he had his lights on. You'd think you might have stopped and have seen if I was okay, or not."

"I didn't see any red lights flashing anywhere. As a matter of fact, I didn't see anyone in trouble. Where were you?"

"On Jefferson…I took the back way here to avoid traffic."

"Then how in the heck could I have seen you? I didn't know there was a short cut here. I stayed on I-55 all the way until exit 34. Man, you are hard to get along with suddenly," I told her.

Joy turned her back on me and appeared to be crying, so I put my arms on her shoulder to see. Just then, Kurt walked in the door with one of the upstairs bosses and both stared hard at us. Kurt came over and spouted, "What's wrong, a lovers' spat?" he jived.

"I don't know. She's acting very strange. I can't figure her out."

"She's a woman…give up…you'll never figure them out," Kurt lavished in laughter then took Joy's chin in his hand to look her in the eyes.

"Okay, tell poppa what's the matter," he softly spoke, as if he were her father.

"I think I need a vacation, that's all. I'm sick and tired of being here, on time, every single day, and listening to all those assholes call in to say they're sick, when they're not. I wish I could take off like that!"

"Then do it, why don't you?" Kurt advised her. "You have sick days just like the rest of us, assholes," he beamed back at her.

"Because, if I take a day, and whenever I return, my work will have stacked up higher, waiting just for me...I'll get more tired just trying to catch up, that's why!"

"Well, sweetie, I think it's time I got you some assistance. Hang on a minute, Judd!" he called out. "I think you can help my girl out here," he said to the man he walked in with.

Then Kurt left for five minutes and came back with the cutest little girl in the upstairs. She was fresh out of high school and her uncle was a congressional representative looking for a summer job for his niece before her college began. She was just what Joy needed most...female company.

"Joy, meet Sheena. Sheena has been assigned to you for the summer, just to relieve you for any time you feel like the walls are coming in on you. Teach her the ropes. I understand all that you have done for everyone here. Hell, woman, if it weren't for you, half of us oldies would be lost and have constipation, too!" he laughed, and then Joy laughed.

Kurt hugged her and Joy him. I wondered if I had anything to do with her sudden sadness.

The girls shook hands and walked away to get better acquainted at the water fountain. For some reason, girls drink lots of water, and then wonder why they have to pee all the time...go figure.

Kurt told me the Glenarm project was delayed for the first half-day, but wanted to know about the Saline County Project.

"Tell me first, how'd you make those people so happy? I got a call last night from the county commissioner and he's thrilled with your idea to build the bridge three hundred yards up stream. How did you arrive at that location and the resulting cost saving estimates? He said estimates by you will save enough money to pay for another smaller project, too."

"Computer...I did it all by my new computer. Don't you use one?"

"Look, I can use any computer, it's what to tell that fuckin' thing to get those facts you got that I'm not trained in," he said dejectedly. "I guess it's time for this old dog to go back into training, huh?" Kurt softly mused.

"Hey, it's brand new technology. I can show you in twenty minutes and you're not old…you just are the brightest thing since compact fluorescent bulbs, boss," I said assuring him I respected him that much.

"I hope you're right. Martha gets lonely when I have to go up to Chicago for re-schooling. Home for the weekend is not enough. I skipped out once or twice the last time to come home and got in trouble. They caught me up there coming in at five in the morning through a side window. Boy, they nearly shot me…the cops that is!" he laughed.

I explained all the mechanics on the new computer, which I had used to evaluate and construct the cost estimate versus their project and subtracted the annual costs of their present projected road repair. Kurt thought I was a genius, but that particular downloaded computer was a tool that any well-schooled engineer could learn to use.

Nearing noon, after we both had eaten soup from the auto-meal dispenser, we arrived at the ramp on I-55 to see if construction could restart. It was better than ever, as the rain left puddles, which showed us best where water might stand in lower areas. We could easily correct that problem with leveling machines and fill dirt.

"Tomorrow we can bring in the paving contractor and end this thing by next Tuesday, with the rollers on the shoulders. It's happening!" Kurt said happily. "I always like to see the end of a successful project that comes in on budget…you will feel that way, also," he assured me.

The workers came in their pickup trucks. They arrived just as all the supervisors were called into the trailer, which had been parked on location and used as our office. Each supervisor had something to add, but all agreed the final stages were set and some of their workers should shift over to the next project. I inadvertently looked to Danby's new lake. It was already full and I asked Kurt if the Department of Conservation was coming to stock his lake anytime soon. I told him I would personally enjoy seeing that happen.

"Hey, that's a good idea. You call DOC. Get their telephone number from Joy and see if they've got his stocking permit and when they'll be here. Then tell Danby again how lucky he is and how thankful we are. I like to leave bridges behind me in good standing."

Before I could call them, I saw a white, fish tank truck, backing up to Danby's new lake. I hurriedly drove over in my truck, and got there just as a woman and a man both dressed in green fatigues began opening valves, draining the truck's load of two hundred 6-inch bass, three hundred 2-inch mixed red ear and bluegills, and two hundred pounds of fathead minnows for food. Those rosy reds were like a shimmering wave seeping out into the lake.

The lake was a bit cloudy, I heard the man speak, but she answered that it was good to avoid sun shock, whatever that was. They told Mr. Danby to feed them pelleted catfish food, until the pond aged with algae growth, about one full season.

"Where's those catfish I was promised?" Danby suddenly asked.

"Sorry, I saw you ordered the channels, but if we stocked even a few channels now, the other fish that we just put in would be gone by winter. Those cats will eat anything that moves, especially this size. You might want to invest in an aerator if the water gets too hot in August or freezes in December. A nice big dock would give them some protection for now and if you have a tree limb or two, evergreens or a few bales of barley hay, or alfalfa, put one bale at each end, scatter the evergreens and those fish reproduce there in the spring. It's just wait and see, now.

"Then, when the population is booming in a year or two, put a few young channels in, if you insist, and keep count when you take them out for restocking purposes. They usually won't reproduce without moving water. I've found a variety of fish species do best as they feed off one another. Put in some crappie, or maybe a few walleye. You might have some fish you catch at the river, except no carp, bowfin, or gar. Some clams pitched in will help a lot, too.

"Otherwise, sign here that we delivered these and if you still want cats, they sell them cheap enough at the grain elevators every spring. Again, I'd wait until it seems there's too many fish and use the channels to control the population and have good eating, also."

The fish tank truck left and Danby looked out on his new lake and I could tell he was dreaming of catching a big one someday.

"You know what, Mr. Danby, those midnight skinny dips will really be fun," I said shaking his hand, while thanking him. Then, I said good-bye.

When I looked in my rear view mirror, Danby had sat himself down on the bank, pulled a foxtail weed's stem up, and started sucking on it, while still admiring his new lake. Kurt would be happy with this ending and I began to get that feeling also.

The rest of our team's workweek went smoothly like clockwork. The weather held, the ramp's final grading went perfectly and the asphalt company on the project performed wonderfully. They laid down the entire exit ramp in seven hours and had the gravel berm tamped down off the trailer at quitting time. Their job wasn't yet completed, but our Tuesday deadline for this project would be met.

Kurt was already meeting with the white-collar men upstairs for the beginning of the next project when I drove into the Springfield garage to park my truck for the weekend. I had to fill my gas tank and log my miles, before I delivered my equipment checklist and the keys to the truck. Joy took care of my signed checklist and the truck keys were placed on hooks upon a key board behind her desk with "Boss#2" on the tag. She would also redistribute the same, come Monday morning.

"Well, one more night to put up with me. Where may I take us to dine tonight? How about we go to your apartment, get dressed up and you show me Springfield's fun places," I said, assuming it was a good gesture to help repay her for the hospitality.

Just then, a new fellow who had apparently been hired for the road crew strolled in looking like Tom Cruise. He looked around, spotted Joy, and had a big smile all the way to her desk.

"Hey, Babe, pick you up at seven and we'll do the town tonight, okay?" he said, bypassing me standing in his way.

"Hi, I'm Clint Edwards. I saw you out at mile post thirty-four when that female trucker almost wiped us out," he mentioned, turning around back to me still smiling brightly.

"Oh, yeah, I'm Greg Wetmore. I bet we'll be seeing a lot of each other, huh?" I said realizing my offer to Joy was about to be trumped by Ol' Clint.

"You have my address, see you at seven…threads or casual?" Joy asked.

"Lady, what I'm going to do with you, you'd best not wear anything that you're afraid might get torn," he chuckled, while leaning over Joy's desk to give her a big wink. "It's been a tough week and I'm looking for a real good time, aren't you, babe?" he said, with his big smile that showed his pearly-white teeth from ear to ear.

They touched fingertips and Joy actually offered up a blown kiss as he moved away to leave.

"Until seven," Joy advised him, with a very alluring look to his midsection, as if she was expecting what he was dreaming.

Then Clint hustled to the time clock, punched out, and yelled, "Nice meetin' ya, George…see YOU at seven!" he said, pointing his finger directly at Joy, who now was sitting straight up and noticing his John Wayne walk. I could tell she was very stimulated.

"Well, that takes care of that, huh?" I said to Joy, who was not listening at all to me, but still absorbed by the body movements of the much tanned, muscled construction man, in his hardhat.

"Ahh, huh!" I coughed, to get Joy's undivided attention. "I have a key, if you're not headed home right away," I told her.

"No, I'm headed there now, but I can't eat out with you. I guess you'll be moving out in the morning anyway, so if I don't see you until Monday, have a great weekend," she said nonchalantly, as if she could care less.

"Okay…well thanks so much for letting me stay with you and giving all the help you gave to me. I really, really appreciate that. I can see why Kurt praises you so highly. Well, I'm going back to Country Kitchen and sample a rare rib-eye that will moo back at me when I stick it with my fork. If you want, I can get a room at the Ramada, so you and Mr. Right can have your privacy. Roomies do that, you know," I told her smiling.

"Hey, you're old fashioned…you can do those things in a back seat just as well and don't cost more money nor do you have to mess up the bed sheets or cook breakfast in the morning for a stranger…nope, not necessary, thanks."

"Okay, then see ya!" I said, feeling a bit let down, but also glad Joy had a life of her own. This new situation made it much easier for me, also, I told myself. Nevertheless, I felt a bit sick for some reason knowing she was going to be with him. I guess it was meant to be, I thought.

Sugar spotted me coming in alone at Country Kitchen and had a smallish frown upon her face as she approached me to guide me to a table near the bar.

"Awe, where's that sweet little Joy tonight?" she asked, as if we were an item.

"Joy's dancing on air…she's just found Tom Cruise in a hardhat and tonight she's headed out to paint the Springfield skyline red," I spoke with a subdued jovial voice. Was I jealous? Maybe…maybe not.

"Too bad for you, huh? My daughter would like a guy just like you. She's a good-lookin' girl…senior at SIUC and is home this weekend…want a date?" she asked unexpectedly, but obviously serious.

"Oh, no thanks, not this weekend. However, maybe sometime in the future, if she is just as pretty as you are. I'm moving into my new apartment early in the morning," I said, to avoid complete denial to her idea.

"I'll tell you when she comes home again. Denise is majoring in business administration and making straight A's," she advised.

"That's super…does she cook, too?"

"Like her mother!" Sugar exclaimed.

"Well how about her mother asking the cook here to throw on his biggest rib-eye on the grill, burn both sides rare, with some onion rings and French fries tossed in, please," I interjected to get my dinner going.

Sugar took my hint, and hustled to the back grill and delivered my order. Luckily, I had just beaten the evening crowd; therefore, Sugar was too busy to do any more talking about her beautiful daughter, Denise.

I was starved, but that steak Sugar brought was melt-in-your-mouth tender. I actually cut it with my fork. I was almost done when a family group came in and began hugging Sugar. I learned later that they were her husband Fred, son Coby, and her knockout, gorgeous daughter Denise.

Man, was Denise beautiful! I could not help staring at her, as other gents began to do so, also. Then I wished I had accepted Sugar's offer for a date with her. Maybe I was a bit too quick about being alone tonight, I thought. After all, I only had a few bags of clothing to move. I caught the attention of Sugar who brought my bill over to me, accompanied by her family.

Sugar introduced her family to me, including her lovely daughter, Denise. Denise told her mother that she was meeting her date here. Then she asked if they could have a seat near the salad bar. I knew then not to bother her and just winked at Sugar to let her know Denise was all Sugar said her daughter was. Then, Poppa Smurf, Fred, leaned over and asked if I had something going on with his wife, because I winked at her.

"No, sir, it's a little joke about your daughter."

"You mean Sugar's still trying to get a "Mr. Right" for my Denise?" he said lowly, but with a scowl.

I shook my head slowly, yes, and he said, "Denise is doing just fine… forget it, bub."

"I have," I assured him with a bit of reluctance, and then put down a big tip and headed to the cashier.

I looked back just in time to see Denise hug her date. He was a college

Joe and looked rather frail and prissy to me, maybe he was the rich kid type, with whom early in life I used to associate. Nevertheless, he definitely was neatly dressed. I laughed to myself and chalked up another lost chance at love experience in life.

I drove back to Joy's Pawnee apartment at seven fifteen hoping she would have gone out already, though her truck was there. The apartment was empty as I sat on my couch and became engrossed in a baseball game between the Cards and the Cubs, at St. Louis. There was a Cardinals' farm team in Springfield, so most people at work liked the Cards and loathed the Cubs for their unanswered prayers for a World Series Championship.

Somewhere in the late innings of the ballgame, I had fallen asleep and then I awakened to the door opening without a key. I had not locked the door. I anticipated it was Joy and I hoped her date wasn't good and she was coming home early. However, I saw an arm slide around the door's edge and then flip on the light switch that was definitely from a black person. I suspected a burglar was about to enter and me helpless in my underwear. All I could do was watch the entry from the couch.

Then an attractive black woman slipped inside clumsily with her arms full of clothes and a bag.

"Hey, who are you?" I questioned loudly.

"I'm your greatest nightmare, buster, if you're not Joy's newest sleep-over. Are you him?" she spoke, squinting with the meanest scowl I'd ever seen a woman give anyone, since Whoopee Goldberg. What she pulled from her purse made me stand up and take notice…it was a chrome, 1911, Colt 45, just like General Patton himself used with a pearl handle.

"Are you, Lila?" I said very weakly and wide-eyed, I'm certain.

She put the automatic back in her purse and said, "Yeah! Put your pants on…where's Joyce?"

"She's on a date. I thought you weren't coming back until Sunday. How's Truman?" I asked suddenly recalling his name, which put her at ease.

"Little shit's doing good. He just missed his momma and had a touch of flu. I had to get a flu shot, too, because I was around him. That H1N1 flu is goin' around and spreading up in Chi-town, you know. You had your shot?" she asked.

"Yes, last fall before school."

"Oh yeah, what school was that?"

"I just graduated from UIC as an engineer. I'm working with Joy."

"Oh, yeah...where you call home?"

"Northfield!"

"You shittin' me, Northfield...I bet you went to New Trier High, huh?"

"Yep, home of the Tigers!"

"What'd you say your name was, again?" she said, with a disturbed look on her face.

"Greg Wetmore."

"Aren't you the quarterback cat that beat Township five-six years ago at state?"

"I guess that's me...were you there?" I asked.

"Hell, yes, I was there. I cheered my guts out for Township, until you threw that last fuckin' TD right over my ex-husband's head...remember, Earl Cabell?"

"Do I? Earl Cabell ended my career in sports that day by tackling me on a sack."

"Served you right...we'da won dat game without you being so hot-shotty good...still hurtin'?"

"I finished the game limping around, but tore my ACL...the next day they operated. I'm okay now."

"Too damn bad...Earl didn't get his scholarship to Eastern because you made him look bad...he joined up in the army instead. He's still there, but we unhitched right after Truman was born...here, grab some stuff and help me...I can tell you ain't no gentleman," she said, guardedly, but smiling.

I helped Lila get her things into her room and for the first time saw the inside.

"Gosh, is that a picture on the desk of you in your cheerleader's outfit... now I remember you! You tripped me coming off the field and called me a freaky asshole...yeah...that was you, wasn't it?" I accused her.

"I plead the fifth, but you were just a clumsy, white bread, hotdog anyway," she said, glaring hard enough so that I knew to drop the subject quickly.

"When you leavin'?" Lila questioned, as if now wasn't soon enough.

"I'm on the couch tonight leaving in the morning, early," I said headed back to the couch.

"Hey, white bread...thanks!" Lila said with a warmer smile and softer tone of voice. "Why didn't you and Joyce hookup tonight?"

"We're just friends...good friends. I hope she is having a good time tonight."

"Hell, it's only ten. You wanna go out and get a beer and celebrate your leavin' in the mornin'?" she quipped.

"No, I'm not much of a drinker...thanks anyway," I returned.

"Come on...do you good. Besides, we may never meet again...and since I know Joyce is really a good girl, maybe not tonight, but she'll probably wish we weren't here when she comes home with her boyfriend guy. You get it?"

"Oh, I guess you're right. I don't know any places, but I guess you do, huh?"

"Sure shittin' I do, honey. Lila knows where to hang. I won't even take you to the fairy clubs downtown. We'll head out to the Harness Club in the suburbs and listen to those silly-fool yokels sing their karaoke, how's that? Their beer's coldest in town."

"Sounds okay...lead on then, dear lady!" I spoke.

"Listen, honey, I ain't no lady," she told me grinning.

Lila quickly dropped her things on her bed. Then she just stripped off her blouse to put on a red, shiny, silky thing off a closet hanger. She turned around to see my surprised look and asked, "What's wrong, sugar, you never seen a black girl's boobs before?"

"No, I guess I haven't, sorry."

"You gonna be a stiff dick or we gonna have fun?" she questioned, staring hard at me still standing there gaping at her huge jugs inside a tiny black bra.

"I hope we can just get along and survive this night," I chuckled, but I also was getting a bit aroused by her nasty manner.

"You drive, or I'll drive your car?" she asked.

"I'll drive...you tell me where to go, your royal highness!" I joked.

"Hey, I like that...a girl could get used to that kind of treatment."

I put on a clean shirt, some cologne to mask the day's perspiration, and then asked Lila if I needed a shave.

"Nah, I like my men in fros best, but if not, dark stubbly cheeks are good," she said leading me out the door with a swaying of her hips.

I hoped I wasn't getting into something I couldn't tell my mother about, but it seemed I was headed for new ground. Then it happened...that sweet fragrance caught my senses following behind her.

"Is that Coffee I smell?" I asked, breathing in her scent.

"Honey, maybe you ain't as naive as I thought you were...if you know the exact perfume I have on, I might enjoy this night," was what she told me as we headed out to my truck.

I then wondered, if she knew, what Joy would say if I was headed out on a date with her roommate. It was an interesting thought, which seemed a bit of payback to my way of thinking, for Joy's obvious delight in rejecting my friendly offer to take her out on the town. Maybe I would try to impress Lila enough to get back at Joy. Then I asked myself, why?

"This way, honey," Lila pointed to a side road, which led us to an out-of-town nightclub with a bright marquee flashing and a parking lot mostly full of pickups with just a few cars. I parked almost a block away, the closest I could get, and immediately heard music blaring and a voice really getting down... it sounded a bit like Aretha Franklin singing RESPECT.

Immediately, Lila felt the vibes in her soul and began gyrating right there in the parking lot, dancing and singing to the rhythm all the way to the entrance. She knew the person at the door and he just motioned us inside without paying the ten-dollar cover charge. We stood there for a moment, letting our eyes adjust to the twirling spotlights, until Lila took me by the hand and more or less dragged me out on the dance floor, where she really let it all hang out. That girl could get down.

I did my best to use my white bread moves, but became mesmerized by Lila's complete self-satisfying, out of control, seductive motions, as she turned everyone's head doing her thing...she really was good and I was proud to be with her. I am not sure it was mutual, for Lila kept giving me advice like "Loosen up, child...move those hips!"

A really well-dressed female in a shimmering mini was on stage singing karaoke and if I had closed my eyes, I could not tell if she was singing real, or if it was Memorex. The applause was loud when her song was over and another person, not so talented took the mike. She was obviously intoxicated, now brave, and could not hold a note for her rendition of "The Way We Were", an old 60's song. Lila cringed at her singing, took my hand, and again literally dragged me to an open table for two.

"I'm thirsty...how about you? I'd like a cool, crispy, mint leaved mojito, honey," she informed me, as she pointed to a sudden opening of humans moving away from a spot at the bar.

"What the holy hell is that?" I asked, using her profanity. "Will the bartender know?"

Lila assured me I was an old fuddy-duddy and needed to get out more, so I moved through the crowd searching for a way to get to the open part of the bar. It was bumper-to-bumper people enjoying themselves on a Friday night.

I asked for Lila's six-dollar mojito drink. He did not bat an eye, but asked someone for some fresh mint leaves from the cooler. I then ordered my two dollar Ski, a soda that was made famous by a country song called "Down at Dumas Walker's", but originated right there in southern Illinois.

Everyone whoever tried Ski just loved it, wanted to buy a case or two to take home, but could not, because it hadn't taken over the nation in sales or distribution. The small company that made it hadn't taken to advertising it much for more profit. It seemed they were doing just fine with their locally sold product.

At UIC, the college kids from southern Illinois, often profited by loading up cases of Ski in their trunks, and brought it back to sell to their fellow students. It was a big hit with college students and with Lila as she poured some of my Ski into her already well mixed drink when I sat down with her at our table.

"Well, when you going to get up on stage and embarrass me?" I jokingly asked Lila, who was then mouthing the words to "Gimmie, Gimmie True Lovin'", which a young girl was singing rather poorly.

Lila's hard look back at me was colder than the ice in my glass of Ski.

"You best know Lila can sing, honey…used to be a real debutant. What we need to find out now is if Greg…what's your last name again, can sing!" she said very loudly, which suddenly brought a "It's your turn" yell from the people seated nearest us. After a chant grew for us to sing, I wished I had died at birth.

I told Lila that I couldn't even sing in the shower, so why did she think I could sing up on stage. She leaned over and drank my Ski, too, by accident. I watched the desire of Lila rise with every drink I brought back and every rotten singer who got applause for trying. It was a congenial crowd.

I guess Lila was getting up her courage to sing by downing that hard liquor. An hour went by and I changed to beer, any beer on draught. After just three, I was really feeling loose, but not as loose as Lila was. She was shit-faced stoned. When the last singer was jerked off the stage for imitating Michael Jackson's infamous crotch holding, while singing his version of "Beat It…Beat It!" and then attempted unzipping his jeans to expose himself, the bouncers showed up pronto to escort him out the door. I don't think they hurt him, but he never returned.

That was Lila's time to get brave. She got up and again dragged me…this time up onto the stage and took the mike away from another drunk stuck on the third verse of "Mary Had a Little Lamb", who then fell off the stage into the arms of several inebriated folks who led her back to her table.

That was Lila's opportunity to get down…"Listen up brothers and sisters. Tonight, tonight, right here in Springfield, Illinois, we have with us one of the greatest soul singers in the history of the business. He has volunteered to help me sing this song and you know you'll like it, because I'm singing it," she told everyone, then some began hoopin' and hollering for her to shut up and just sing.

"You know Ike's part in Rollin' Down a River…Proud Mary, fool?" she suddenly asked me.

Now everyone has sung a bit to Tina Turner's version, so I said loudly I'd try.

Lila turned to the DJ who put on the "Proud Mary" and then she nudged me… "Listen up, you is Ike, be him now…go!"

Therefore, I started out when the music began in the lowest key I could muster… "Rollin, rollin' yeah, rollin' on the river!"

Then the music beat picked up fast and you would have thought Tina Turner herself was on stage, except I wasn't Ike. That didn't bother Lila, as she mimicked the gyrations of Tina and even shook her booty to the crowd. It was over in a few minutes, but the crowd wanted an encore, so, we did it all over again. This time, I looked through the bright lights and noticed Joy was in the crowd with her hardhat date. He was cheering us on, but Joy just stood there with her mouth wide open in disbelief.

Therefore, I really did my best, which brought Lila to say over the mike to the cheering crowd, "Boy, that brother can sing!" and then we both jumped off the stage to another round of applause. Someone thought we were good enough and bought us both drinks and sent them to our table. Lila was strutting back the entire way like a star and then turned on me and kissed me hard. I could taste the liquor and feel her powerful grip on my lips.

"That kiss was for doin' so well," Lila told me after her kiss. "I thought you were gonna make a fool out of me, but, brother, you have good pipes," Lila told me trying to kiss me more.

It was three o'clock and things were still going strong. I felt sober, but I was exhausted and wasn't a drinker. I wasn't going to get behind the steering wheel. Then Joy appeared out of nowhere.

"Looks like you guys have hit it off…how'd that happen so fast when my back was turned?" Joy spouted rudely sounding a bit drunk.

"Where's Clint?" I asked.

"Hell if I know…he disappeared…somewhere…and I can't find him… probably in the john whacking off," she continued in her drunken voice.

I told both girls it was time we headed home and offered Joy a ride. She gladly accepted, without even mentioning Clint again. I guess he had left with another girl or passed out somewhere. Anyway, I looked for him, but he was nowhere to be seen.

I took the chance and got the women inside my truck. All Joy kept saying to Lila was, "How could you?" She said it repeatedly to Lila's face all the way back to Pawnee.

I drove into the parking lot, but there wasn't a place for me to park, so I parked illegally on the street, right next to the "No parking" sign. There were other cars there, so I thought I might get by until morning, and then I'd move it as soon as I could find a space.

The girls seemed very distant, and did not talk to one another until they both got inside. When we got inside, Lila announced that I need not sleep on the couch. I could sleep with her. That really irked Joy.

While they argued very confused at each other, I brushed my teeth, took a long needed pee and slipped into my pajamas. Then I led Joy to her room and she told me to undress her, right before she fell across her bed out like a light. Lila, on the other hand, asked me if I was going to "do her" and said, "Well go ahead, she really needs it, the bitch!" Lila screamed.

I pulled Joy's shoes off and threw her cover over her, and turned off the light in her bedroom. I suspected Joy would be hurting in the morning. Then I took Lila by the arm and though she wanted to play, I let her kiss me, before she just curled up with her clothes on and passed out on her bed, too.

Now it was my turn, but I was wide-awake at four thirty. I hoped to be out of there before the two awoke. I lay on that couch, until dawn. Then I got dressed, and snuck out quietly. It was seven, about our usual time to be up and going to work. I felt good for being up all night. I drove over to my new apartment and waited in front of the supervisor's office. He came at ten to let me into my new furnished home.

My tiredness must have caught up with me, because I fell asleep on my new bed as soon as my head hit the pillow. It was three in the afternoon, when my cell vibrated on the nightstand and fell off onto the floor, which awoke me. It was Jill. I must have sounded a bit strange to her yawning constantly, but we talked for an hour. She was coming home soon, she said. What she did not tell me was that it was a furlough before being shipped overseas to Afghanistan.

Chapter 7

My new apartment was cool, I mean very cool. The air conditioning was pre set and turned down to about 65degrees. I felt stupid searching to find a sweater to put on walking around the house. I heard the doorbell ring. It was the mail carrier with a piece of paper, which I had to sign to verify I was Greg J. Wetmore. When I did, he said maybe next time I'd have mail that was forwarded, but today, I could take some shoppers' market advertising coupons off his hands and he handed me several pages. I thanked him and he looked at me a second time. This time, I think he was wondering about my wearing a sweater in summer.

I noticed the hot outside air was streaming in and warming up the apartment, so I left it open to kill the chill. Then a soft tapping started, until I turned around and saw there was a girl at my door.

"Who is it?" I asked.

"It's Pat, your neighbor. I came over from next door to meet you and make sure that you're not Jack the Ripper," she said giggling.

"Nope, that's not me; he's dead and was from London, England, or someplace. I'm Greg, Greg Wetmore. Come in, so I can see you better. You're standing in the shadows of the overhang and casting just a dark image on the screen door with the sun at your back. Maybe you're the shadow now, huh?" I chuckled.

I noticed quickly when she came through the door that this girl was young, shapely, and very pretty. She walked in, looked around, and asked if my apartment was furnished, or did I have this good taste. I took that as a compliment at first, but she was jesting. When we shook hands, I felt her soft hand in mine and asked her to sit. She announced herself as being Beverly Kohn, but went by the name Pat…go figure? I dare ask her how she arrived at that name, but she quickly told me it was her patting of her feet in a high school English class that her teacher named her that nickname when it was obvious she, Beverly, could not stop patting her nervous foot. It just stuck.

I noticed she wasn't patting her foot then and she said it was an embarrassing story she might tell me about someday.

"You take a year lease here?" she wanted to know.

"Yes, with an option for another at the same rent…how about you?"

"Well, really that was why I came over to you hoping you hadn't. My roommate skipped out on me and I'm looking for a roommate. Mine is a two bedroom, also, like yours, with separate bedrooms, of course, so it could be a boy. I'm broke trying to pull the rent alone. I work downtown at Murphy's and haven't been there long enough to get a raise."

"Well, I know a lady who seems to get things done. She's my real boss. Her name is Joy. Monday I'll ask her if she knows any good person."

"She's your boss? Where do you work, if I may ask," she wanted to know.

"Actually, Joy is my secretary and I work for IDOT as an engineer. I just graduated and this is my first job…started Monday."

"I didn't know the state had trains," she added.

"You're kidding, right?"

When she looked puzzled at me, I knew she was not.

"I'm a civil engineer. I build highways, bridges and most of the other projects handled by the State of Illinois," I then explained.

"You don't look old enough to be that," she surprisingly quipped.

"Well, I am. I'm an old twenty-three year guy who is looking to start his life as part of the proletariat."

"Is that like a professional ball player?" she asked.

She could not be that dense, I thought, but she was blond. Maybe there was something to that.

"Look, ahhh, miss…what's your last name again?"

"Just call me Pat, remember?" she spoke getting up and ready to leave.

"I haven't a thing in my fridge. Mind telling me where the closest IGA, Piggly Wiggly or what grocery is close?"

"There are none of those here. I do shopping, when I can afford to, at the Super Wal-Mart. It's just about a mile straight down College Street. You can't miss it."

"Say, I haven't had breakfast yet…would you care to join me at a fast food place…my treat?"

"Sure! I haven't eaten in two days and that was just a dollar cheeseburger at Burger King. I've been saving to pay the rent, remember?"

I could not believe I had moved in a building with an obviously destitute little girl in poverty. How could she have put down all the money I just had, a damage deposit, plus first and last months' rents? Surely, she must have some other income. Then I thought she might have turned to prostitution. I became leery.

Her growling stomach told me I better feed her a meal, so I drove out to the Country Kitchen to see Sugar. Sugar wasn't working, but another nice lady was there to greet us. She stared at Pat and thought she knew her.

"Are you Lilly White's daughter, Bev?" she asked her politely.

"I don't know any Lilly White, lady," Pat told her very nervously.

"You sure look like her and she's been missing for six weeks, humm."

I then knew my hunch was right and ordered two big breakfasts for the both of us to hold her here. Pat wanted extra toast, extra pads of butter, extra sugar, and a doggy bag. Now that was telling it all. I tried to excuse myself to go to the restroom but Pat asked where I was going. I told her I had to pee and if she had to go also, now was the time to take care of her needs. She seemed younger by the minute.

I caught up to the server and told her the strange-acting girl claimed to be called Pat, but her real name she had told me was Beverly Kohn.

"Beverly White, that's her real name…not Kohn. That is her step daddy's last name and I am certain now that is her. I'll call the state police…as a matter of fact, Mr., I don't have to, because here come two in off patrol for coffee right now."

She went straight to the troopers and told them what I had told her. They called me over, while Pat was in the restroom, but she must have seen them talking to me and split out through the kitchen. When they couldn't locate her inside, a cook told them she went running out the back door into the woods.

One smart trooper used his noggin. He drove his squad car to the rear of the restaurant and spoke over his loud speaker to Pat.

"Beverly, this is Trooper Franklin speaking to you. We know who you are and know you ran away because your stepfather called the police when you took his car. I know you are afraid of him. You won't have to go back, but please...we fear for your safety. If you're in those woods, please be advised to watch out for those pygmy rattlesnakes...they're everywhere. Watch your step. If they bite you there's nothing we can do for you and the coyotes will grab you after dark...please come back," he cleverly told her.

It wasn't a minute, until I heard leaves rustling from the woods and a frail figure appeared about a block away, running fast as she could toward the trooper's squad. He got out when he saw her, took his hat off, and took Beverly's quick lunge into his arms. He held his arms around her to assure her that she was then safe.

It was an amazing scheme he used and I had to snicker a bit. I walked over and told the trooper I had ordered her breakfast and she was starving. He looked at Beverly White and told her if she would not run away again, and eat the meal I had bought for her, he would take her to a family that would love her and take care of her. She said she would.

After Beverly ate breakfast with the troopers, they got up and she came to thank me for her meal. Then she and the Troopers all left together. I felt good about meeting Beverly. I hoped that she would grow up to be a beautiful woman one day and a good parent. I headed for Wal-Mart and shopping.

I reviewed my bill from Wal-Mart out loud to myself to see if I missed anything, "groceries, toiletries, dishwasher liquid soap...washing machine powder, a sponge, and kitchen towels," was above two hundred dollars, but I was set.

As I tried to carry all those six bags inside at once, it became obvious I needed a second trip or a helping hand. Then I heard the complex super, Joe Petito, ask if he could help me out as he peeked into my garage. Of course, I was thankful and when we had everything upon the kitchen bar, I asked Joe if he cared for a fresh cup of instant coffee.

"I'll take a beer instead," he suggested.

I did buy some Bud Lite so he was in luck, I told him. As I took one beer right out of the shopping bag, I thought it was very early to imbibe, but Joe pulled the tab and chugged a gulp or two.

"You know," said Joe, "there have been some strange things happening around here lately. Some tenants told me their garbage had been rummaged-through and two of them even said they came home from work last week, after forgetting to lock their patio doors like I always tell everyone to do, you remember me telling, you, don't you? Yeah, yeah, you do...well anyway they found food missing and dirty dishes on their tables. One swore it was me, because she thought I had the keys...I do, but I don't ever do that...unless someone's way behind on their rent.

"I told one to call the police and have the plates fingerprinted, but the cops were too busy, she said. They wanted her to bring the plates to them instead...that's Loony Laura in six B...anyway, she was afraid the cops would think she was a dirty person, so she put them in the dishwasher first before she left. They thought she really was loony then all right. She has to stay four days for evaluation at Alton Mental facility. I'm going over there now to check her apartment. Wanna go along?" he asked, as if that wasn't the first beer he had drunk this day.

"No, I've got things to do, but I did just run into a young runaway girl here in my apartment who just happened by here. She is with the state troopers now and headed back to her parents or someone. She probably was the culprit as she was starving and told me she was saving up for her rent money for next door...that couldn't be right, could it?" I questioned a dizzy-looking Joe.

"Humm...yes that's probably the thief... heck I saw her, too, why didn't I realize that myself...good work...say, I ought to offer my sister as a date for you as a reward for catching her and turning her in...you did, didn't you?"

"Yes, I notified authorities with the help of an alert waitress...poor little thing was a runaway out on the street for six weeks."

"My sister did that street-walkin' thing, too...ran away from home for three whole years...dropped out of high school and disappeared...we thought she'd been kidnapped, or killed, or something...until one night the cops brought her back home all bloody and bruised...she got herself hurt by a hit and run driver car, but refused attention...she lived.

"Some guys who later said they had met her out there on the streets and didn't know she was my sister, said she could suck a golf ball through a twenty-foot garden hose, but I told them I didn't believe that...I'd like to have seen that, wouldn't you, huh? Why would she wanna do that stunt anyway? I can't figure it out how she thought of it, or why…for extra money…got another beer, Mr. Wetmore?" he rambled on to himself, appearing more intoxicated each passing moment.

Was this ignorant dope really our complex liaison and protection, I wondered? Maybe he was all right when he was sober, but this was not his moment.

"Yeah, that feat is a 'Ripley's Believe It Or Not' trick for TV," I jested.

I turned around to my dwindling six-pack and pulled another beer out and popped the tab for him. When I turned back around, Joe had gone. I looked out the back door and he was talking to a girl by the pool. She was opening her cooler to fetch a cold drink for him, also. I worried for him, his sister, and Loony Laura in six B, then I drank the beer myself before it got warmer.

Surprisingly, Dad called and seemed as if he really missed me. He had not called me much while I was in college. I guess he just knew I was okay and safe there. He discussed my one day leaving the state payroll to earn that big money in the private sector, but also told me he thought beginning my career with IDOT meant I was a highly selective prospect. He assured me outside companies would eventually seek me out to steal my type of employee, because the pay scale was so much lower here. Dad always considered making the most money possible as his main purpose in life. I did not.

Dad and Mom had taken their cruise, but gained ten pounds, so they both began a diet program after they returned. Dad also mentioned he was considering retirement and thought both he and Mom would move to a warmer climate. He was just afraid his savings might not get them far enough, although he always was afraid of not having enough money. Dad always worked like a man on a mission and I'm certain he was not hurting financially. I was proud of his ambitions, though I might have traded some of that ambition for him being home more. Nevertheless, it worked out well, I guess. Then Mom wanted to talk.

Everything was fine and back to normal. Except, Mom told me she inherited big bucks from her mother's family side. She and her sister, my Aunt Margaret, were sole heirs to their uncle's huge Vandemere business estate when he passed. I didn't even know him because he was so reclusive.

Mom and Aunt Margaret were always Uncle Art's little girls he never had, she said. She and Aunt Margaret planned to sell their stocks and business interests to one of their Uncle Arthur's business associates, instead of running it themselves when the time came to go before the board of trustees. I didn't know what he did.

Additionally, Mom said both Grandpa and Grandma Vandemere fell ill and had moved into a senior nursing home in La Porte, Indiana. She and Aunt Margaret had driven out and seen to their care. Unfortunately, we seldom saw one another, except when we were younger on holidays.

Then Mom told me she and Dad would have no difficulty retiring, except they were rejuvenating their love life and spent much more time together now than ever. That was probably because of Jill and me being so important to them. Mom also mentioned suddenly that she left Jill and me something in her will, as had our father in his, she said, which made me think that one day, unexpectedly, they were leaving us.

I appreciated Mom more than I showed her...she meant so much to everyone. Her words made me sad. It was the beginning of my constant worry. I could not repay their kindness towards me all my life. I had to find something suitable to give them when my checks began. Once, while I was in college, I mentioned my plan to buy her an expensive gift to show my appreciation. Mom said several good, healthy, God-fearing grandkids would do just fine.

Our conversation lasted over an hour, the longest I had ever spoken to each of my parents at the same time. I hung up feeling melancholy, when remembering their happy, smiling faces at graduation. I remembered, also, how pleased they were and could not love them more.

My mesmerizing was shaken by my new telephone ringing. It came with the apartment, so I expected it was a bogus call.

"Hello," is all I answered.

"Sugar, you sure caused one hell of an uproar...someone just got nuts! Did we do it last night?"

It was Lila speaking. I recognized her voice without telling me who she was.

"Who is nuts and what do I have to do with anything? Hey...how did you get this number anyway, Lila, I don't even know it myself?" I asked her.

"I called Joe...I used to live there in those nice quiet, but very expensive apartments, until this crazy chick person put an ad in the Springfield Gazette for a roommate and I was dumb enough to take her up on her word we could get along. She's accusing me of luring you away from her and she just stormed out cussing me. You two got something going on?"

"I guess you mean Joy. Yes, we're friends like you and I…and no, we didn't do anything last night," I reminded her. "I just put you both to bed and left early, before you sobered up," I chuckled. "Where'd Joy go?"

"Hell if I know…probably took herself a ride. She does that when she has to clear the air."

"Oh, it's happened before, huh?"

"Sure, every time she has her period she gets down right mean. But I think she's really got this thing going on for you…did you know that?"

"No, I don't think that's it. She has to go to work Monday morning knowing her hardhat jockey who she works with dumped her last night. Got any clue as to where she really is?"

"As I said…probably still out driving around in her truck."

"Okay, maybe Springfield isn't as big as I think it is…I might go riding around myself."

"Want company?"

"Not right now, thanks. If she comes back would you text me at 312-977-4161?"

"Okay, but you ain't gonna find her just tooling around the streets."

"Just please text me, okay?"

"Too bad you're who you are…I'd tell you to go kiss it, but since it's you, I'll send the message if she shows her big ass up here," Lila told me explicitly.

I didn't know what she meant by who she thought I was, but I decided to just drive out to my job site and maybe the office just to familiarize the route.

I drove out onto I-55 and got lucky when I noticed someone had run down the traffic cones, which blocked off the new exit ramp at Glenarm. It really hadn't hurt anything, so I pulled over and reset the cones.

While replacing the cones, at the top of the ramp, I looked out at a long row of pickups lining both sides of the streets in town, and one that looked like Joy's truck. It was parked outside of an old tavern that seemed to disgrace the place of God. I then drove into Glenarm and circled the block…it was Joy's truck, so I parked next to hers, which was actually the only place to park.

I wondered what this place had going for it to have that many customers so early on a Saturday morning.

I got out, opened the door of the old tavern, and peered inside. A voice quickly hollered for me to come in, or "Shut the damn door", as I was letting out the fucking air conditioning. Therefore, I closed that 'fucking door' and stepped further inside of the darkened tavern. I stood there searching a moment, allowing my eyes to focus and adjust to the sudden darkness.

Soon I saw a bearded man behind the bar and several "good old boys" sitting at the end of the bar, drinking whiskey and playing euchre. Two others were shooting pool and had stopped to look my way. I was evidently a stranger there, but where in the heck were all his other clientele who drove all those parked trucks outside, I wondered. I asked if there was a girl in there somewhere.

The foul-mouthed bartender said, "This ain't no damn whorehouse, fella, I only serve drinks! If you want pussy you best head out of here!" he spoke loudly with a tough sounding, growling voice, and over the sudden laughter of the fellas seated on bar stools.

I was a bit confused when I heard church bells ringing loudly and it was on a Saturday. Where was that church? Was it an early morning wedding? Then I vaguely remembered some religious sects thought Saturday was their real holy day, not Sunday. I supposed, since it was so long ago, and so many people rewrote the Bible to fit their needs, anything was possible.

I then exited backwards telling him I wasn't looking for that kind of girl and the bartender hollered out, "We ain't got no queers in here neither!" which brought another round of laughter before I could close the door.

Boy was I uncomfortable and puzzled when I realized Joy might have gone to church. There was a little stone church sitting back on a big lawn about five hundred feet away. Joy had told me something had occurred to keep her away from church. What had drawn her back?

I went back to my truck and waited an hour, until the big church doors swung wide open and people started coming out shaking hands with their pastor. They were dressed in their Sunday best clothes here, unlike our Lutheran church in Northfield, which encouraged followers to come more casually, even in shorts in the summer. Here, all the men appeared to be wearing hats, dark suits and ties, even the boys. All the females had lovely bonnets and dresses of many colors. It was a joyous sight to my eyes, as each person filed out like a rainbow of colors to greet the pastor's handshake. It was a nice setting and I liked its friendliness.

I saw the good pastor holding one woman's hands, expressing happiness to greet her and she him, which made the girl openly smile. When that same girl noticed who had parked next to her truck, she stood frozen there staring at me.

I got out of my truck and stood in front of it awaiting Joy to pass.

"What you doing here?" is what Joy asked sarcastically in passing, then stopped.

"Oh, I wanted to see where a crazy girl goes when a crazy girl goes out the door cussing at her roommate, I suppose."

"Lila called you, huh?"

"She was worried and upset…so am I. We both care about you."

"Well, I don't believe that for one minute. The way you two treated me last night is unforgivable," she told me, as other worshipers stopped to hear us.

"You want to talk about it? Maybe at the Country Kitchen over breakfast… my treat," I suggested.

"Go ahead, Joy!" yelled someone from the gathering crowd who must have known her.

Those remarks made Joy shuffle quickly to her truck. She told me quietly that she would meet me there. Then she peeled out like an Indy 500 driver leaving black marks on the tired old blacktop city street.

"That's our Joy, all right!" someone yelled with an additional, "Yahoo, look at her go!"

I followed her as best I could, but she drove very fast, as if she had something on her mind and was getting it out of her system through her gas pedal. The back roads were no stranger to her, but I almost lost her. If it were not for all the dust that her truck was blowing up, I would have lost sight of her.

Suddenly, I was following the billowing clouds of dust onto a side dirt road through tall timbered woods. Eventually, I drove up to the rear of the Country Kitchen's back door, with Joy standing outside of her truck smiling. I guess it worked for her, but I had grit in my teeth from all the dust I ate, which she had provided me so freely, I told her.

"Serves you right! Next time you do that…well, there won't be a next time, that's all."

I was confused then, because it was her hardhat date who left her little behind, behind, not me. Was Joy so drunk last night that she thought I was her date? When we entered through the restaurant's kitchen door, the cooks just said, "Hi, Joy, how you doin'? Good to see you again, Joy!" they all greeted her.

I guess she did this frequently after church, when she went.

We found a booth, not a table and slid in just as Martha spoke, "Look who's here, Kurt!"

We had sat down near the Rakers just as they were getting up leaving. Kurt walked over.

"Hey, good morning, you two, didn't you get enough of each other during the workweek?" he chuckled.

Joy didn't say a word and I just smiled. Kurt could see he was interrupting, so he added, "Somebody knocked all the cones down at the project, I'm going up there and reset them," he told me.

"Don't bother…I did it an hour ago. I'll check again on my way back home to my new apartment," I told him.

"Now that's why I liked you so much. Your instructors up there in Chicago told me you went the extra mile in your work…thanks. Well, I'll leave you two lovebirds alone. Joy, meet us in church tomorrow?"

"Just went…sorry you weren't there," Joy said quietly, unable to look Kurt straight on.

"Wish Martha and I had known, Joy. Well see you both Monday," Kurt said, as he held Martha close to his side and seemed to whisper as they walked away.

"Okay, let's get our order in then talk," I suggested.

"I'm really only good for a salad and iced tea today. Last night was more than I normally do. But you enjoy your big meal as boys always do," she related.

Our order arrived and Joy still had not explained her sudden discontent. Therefore, I began.

"Okay, tell me what's wrong. I thought we were friends. After all, you went out with Clint and he seems like a great guy. What happened?"

"An old flame came by Clint and like a moth he just couldn't stop looking at her, so I pushed him away while we were dancing and went to the john to powder my nose. When I came back, he was long gone and there you and Lila were up there havin' fun…so I started drinkin'. It was all my stupid fault. I did it to make you jealous, but you don't feel at all that way about me, I know…I guess I jumped to conclusions, huh?"

"Well, you're partly right. I do like you, but we've only known each other for a short-short, as you say. Hey, it may take a while. Let time make it better or worse for us. I'm congenial and you are a sweet, intelligent, beautiful girl, with lots of class. As time heals all wounds, it covers them too."

"Oooh, that sounds just like a scab!" she squealed, then laughed.

"I guess, but as I think I told you I remember a girl and she's still got my heart…that's all. I doubt if I'll ever see her again…only time will tell, understand?" I tried to explain.

"Yep, old Joyce is barkin' up the wrong tree, huh?" she quipped.

"No, I didn't say that. I just said let's take our time to be real friends and from friends grow the best relationships…capuche person," I jested. "By the way, I looked that word up and it's not what you think it means…what do you think it means?"

"Forget it…my French is rotten and I guess it just sort of sounded like the right word…I guess I should have just said shithead, huh?" she injected with sarcasm. "Last time you bought, it's my treat for ruining your day. I'll go back to Lila and tell her she did me a big favor, bye!" Joy said, then threw down a two-dollar tip and went to the cashier on the run, before I could even reply.

I felt badly then, but I just let Joy be Joy. I did not understand her then and probably never would. We were worlds apart. I hoped our workplace would not suffer.

After a wonderful breakfast, I cruised past the Glenarm exit ramp. Everything was still in place. On my northerly bound trip home, I noticed historical marker information on New Salem, the home of our sixteenth president, President Lincoln. I decided to follow the signs.

I arrived there in forty minutes. It was a quaint little frontier settlement, which looked as if it might still be livable. Some people were dressed up in the clothes of the period and I enjoyed everything about it. I spent two hours and bought a souvenir for Jill before I left.

On one of the brochures I accepted, there was info on President Lincoln's tomb in Springfield proper. I followed those signs and parked in a car-filled parking lot there. Many families were strolling towards a tall statue, so I just followed. I walked down a tree-shaded sidewalk and felt a nice soft breeze in my face. Unexpectedly, I discovered the gigantic monumental resting place had doors. A cordial invitation to enter from an attendant made me feel humble, as I walked inside and around the granite tomb; it was Lincoln's one-hundred and fifty-some years place of rest. His state had taken impeccable care of his tomb. When I left, I felt honored.

A vendor selling foot-long hotdogs from his little stand caught my eye, so I bought my lunch and sat in the cool breeze on a bench reading my many brochures. One mentioned the state museum and the Capital Building. It was nearing four o'clock, so I decided not to do it all in one day.

I got in my truck, immediately made a wrong turn, and then got lost in the city. I traveled past the State of Illinois Fairgrounds twice, before I realized I was traveling in circles. I stopped at a stop sign and noticed the cross street was College Street, which was my apartment's street. I chuckled for my dumb luck, but had to chuckle again when I realized I had headed in the wrong direction.

Soon I discovered Springfield had a large airport and a freeway called Senator Dirkson Boulevard. I remembered the fine man as being an honest politician and his talented speeches given on Chicago's television when I was very young. I remembered, because my father admired him so and made me watch.

I eventually found the IDOT signs and continued on only a half mile past the IDOT building to my apartment complex. Before I fiddled with my new garage door opener to get it to open my garage, I saw lots of activity by the pool. It was a hot Midwestern day, so I went into my apartment to change into my swimming trunks.

The pool was excellent, especially the view. The bikinis were out in number and I just stayed in the deep end and watched all the activity pass me by. Then I grabbed a youngster flailing in the water nearby, apparently trying to talk and drink lots of pool water at the same time, but going unnoticed. I simply swam to her rescue, grabbed her from a few feet below, and pitched her up to a woman I assumed was her mother, who by then was frantically watching us after finally observing her child drowning.

The girl just stood up coughing hard, then puked back into the pool. Everyone vacated, except I was caught behind a murky cloud, which appeared to be a combination of mucus and Campbell's mushroom soup with chunks.

I dove down to the bottom, pushed off the wall and arose out of the putrid stink. I walked up the steps and grabbed my towel. Cold arms suddenly hugged me around the knees. It was the little girl I had just pulled out of the pool thanking me while being coerced by her mother to do so.

I was delighted she had recovered so quickly.

"Hey, sweetheart...you have to learn to keep that little mouth shut and not talk when you go in the water...see what happens?" I said, bending down and hugged her back.

"Hi, I'm her mother, Laura," she told me.

My memory flashed quickly to Loony Laura, but surely not her? She was a very nice woman and thankful for my efforts, which was certainly sufficient for doing so.

"It was God's plan for me to be there right then at that moment," I suggested to her.

"I'm so grateful and Kitty is going to use her life vest from now on," she told her daughter, but looking at me. "It's her weekend with Mommy, but Daddy mustn't know about this, right, Kitty?" she said, kneeling down beside me, but hugging Kitty.

She must have been Loony Laura, I surmised, so I quickly told them both I had to leave. However, the little girl clung to me and asked me to stay. She was afraid for some reason. I hoped it was not from any of her mother's actions.

Someone had called Joe and he came running and jumped in the pool. Then he surfaced and yelled out, "I can't see anybody. Where's the body?"

"This is the little lady," I told him reluctantly. "She's safe," I further advised Joe who began dog paddling in the clouded water.

"He saved my little girl, Joe...he's a hero!" Laura told him.

Joe looked up at Laura and just said, "Thanks!" to me. Then he swam to the side of the pool and leaped out. He walked over to us and faced up to Laura.

"Hey, who's kid is this anyhow? I know it's not yours...whose is it? I'm calling the police," Joe shouted.

The little girl began to cry that she wanted her daddy, and then got behind me.

Joe bent down and asked the little girl where she lived. It seems that Laura was just babysitting her for a single parent and had brought her to the pool. Joe called her father. He knew every number from his notebook that he kept on his person. He discussed with her father why he had left his child with Loony Laura.

Then, rather disgustedly, Joe slammed his cell shut and told Laura to go back to her own apartment and that he was taking over the babysitting job. He was angry, so she scampered away.

"Come with me, honey," Joe said smiling very brightly. "You're daddy is out of town on business, but wants you to stay with my family for now. I have a daughter named Sheri. She is five. How old are you?" he asked, kneeling down to take her hand. His kind demeanor was far more intelligent than I expected.

"I'm four and a half," she told him. "My name is Kitty Higgins."

Joe leaned into me and whispered his job did not pay enough. Then he led Kitty away hand in hand.

"What about the soiled pool?" I asked Joe.

"Could you please just reach inside that box and pull out the "out of order sign and stand it up at the entrance. I'll be back. The whole damn pool has to be drained, I bet."

"Your little lady got sick in it, so I guess you're right. Want me to back wash it empty?"

"You know about pools, too? God Damn, you're good, fella. I should give you a free rental. I'll be back after I show her to my wife," Joe said turning the corner.

I reached inside the big fiberglass box and withdrew a little sign, "Pool is closed" to close the pool. Then I looked over the schematics and found the pool held 60,000 gallons and the seven-horse pump filter worked five hundred gallons per minute. By head calculations, emptying the pool would take about two hours.

I pulled the backwash lever up and began emptying the soiled pool. It discharged directly into the sewer system, but it was cleaner than toilets and sinks. I saw fill valves, so I ran to my apartment and grabbed my cell and hurried back to watch the pool. Joe did not return quickly and when he did, I had dozed off in a lounge chair as the last of the pool water was gurgling out the bottom drain. Joe was very happy. So happy he yanked his joint out and commenced to piss into the pool right while it finished emptying and right in front of me. He definitely regressed.

"Ahh, I always wanted to do that. There's nothing hurt," he suggested stuffing it back in his shorts, and then let a big juicy beer fart.

Joe then rolled out a fifty-gallon plastic barrel of pool bromine, dumped it into the bottom of the empty pool, and turned the water fill valves on.

"Watch this," Joe advised. "It will only take half the time to fill it. I like to watch it fill up like a sinking ship. Look at those bubbles when it hits that bromine. It will stop on its own after I dial up 60,000, be crystal clear, and clean enough to drink. Want to play some dominoes?" he asked.

"Out here?"

"Sure, I'll go get the bug spray and the dominoes. You do know how to play, don't you?"

"I played sometimes in grade school during winter recesses."

"That's good enough. I'll be back," Joe told me as he left barefooted to his apartment.

When Joe came back, he held the box of dominoes, bug spray, two cold cans of beer, and a real Les Paul Gibson Custom guitar. The Gibson was something I always wished I owned, since I first noticed Paul McCartney playing his in an old-time Beatles' movie I watched with my pop.

"You play that thing?" I asked Joe.

"Well, no, I hoped you did. You see a tenant screwed me out of two months' rent money one time and I took this in trade, thinking he would be honest and make it right with the rent. However, the bastard took off leaving this here with me about five years ago now, so he ain't comin' back for it. Want to buy a cheap guitar?" he asked while handing the guitar for me to look over.

I knew I wanted it right away, when I strummed the strings and it still was in tune.

"How much do you need for it?" I asked, knowing guitars like this one sold for thousands or more with age.

"To you, my courageous hero, fifty dollars…it has a fancy case, too. It's dusty because it's just been sitting behind our closet door," he said with a grin.

"Sold…I'll go get the money."

"Nope, nope, you paid it off in full with all the good things you've done here for me. My wife even had time for sex today, just because I didn't have to spend all my time sneaking around, looking for the God damned burglar girl you caught and now this, ha, you earned it. If you need a waterbed, I traded for one of those once, too," Joe jested.

I thanked him and laid the guitar down gently with admiration. Joe and I played dominoes, until the pool was full and the automatic fill-check stopped the inflow of water. He turned off the pool lights and locked the gate at nine. I followed him to his apartment and met his Mexican wife and several of his children along with Kitty. She was in her pajamas ready for bedtime. Kitty was happy being with Sheri.

"Get that guitar case for Greg here," he told Angelina. "I traded him your piece of ass time for it," he joked, but I was embarrassed. She was, also.

I left them all with one of my childhood dreams fulfilled. I held that Gibson reverently and very cautious not to bang it into anything. I decided to learn how to play it in my spare time, just as soon as I bought lessons.

Sunday morning I decided to dress up and find a church. I looked in the telephone directory and discovered the Glenarm church was Mennonite faith-based and had Saturday and Sunday services. I guess that was to give grace to their farmers so they could come out of their fields and not disrupt their harvesting. That made good sense to me.

I remembered those friendly faces and decided if I went, they could only throw me out. Surely one religion was as valued as another was. I arrived just five minutes ahead of the scheduled hour. The bells were ringing and I could hear the organ music and people clapping. I eased inside while everyone was standing, I realized all the men were in black, and my white shirt stood out. I then saw steps leading to the balcony and made my way upstairs, where mostly kids were seated in long pews. They were suspicious of me and began whispering, but sat down as the pastor gave death notices.

I picked up a hymnal and looked at their songs. They were the same songs as I sang in the Lutheran church back home. When the pastor asked everyone to rise again for the Lord's Prayer, my white shirt caught his eyes as he raised them for prayer. He hesitated, but began his prayer with everyone speaking in unison. After its finish, he again looked to me and asked all visitors to rise and give their names. There were none below, so he looked up to me. I announced my name and thanked everyone for allowing me to share their church.

"Mr. Wetmore," the pastor kindly spoke out loudly, "you are always welcome here in God's house. Thank you for coming."

Then a loud "Amen," erupted from the group of two hundred and I felt the vibrations bouncing off the walls. It was titillating to say the least…like hearing a herd of buffalo come stampeding at you.

I sat back down and listened to his sermon. I think he had several sheep in his flock he meant to shear as he stared hard at an apparent adulterous woman and made her wiggle in her seat speaking hell and damnation. He scowled at a lazy good for nothing, by telling everyone, "It's not a sin to be poor, but it is to be lazy. Go forth and earn your own keep and don't place that burden on your brethren," he continued, as he stared down one of his brethren.

He finally gave up and began his real sermon on hope. It was appropriate and I felt good afterward. I placed my offering in the basket being passed around. Mine was the only twenty not in an envelope as the kids dropped in their nickels and dimes inside small envelopes.

After church, Brother Kefir greeted me. He took the time to invite me again and thanked me for my generous donation. I guess he watched me drop it in the plate. He was a very kind man and I told him I would be happy to return.

Sunday for me is always special. I returned home after stopping by a newsstand's auto-vendor near a corner for the Sunday paper. I also picked up some drive through Taco Bell burritos before I headed to my apartment.

It was a good day to read, relax, and think. I was always thinking, maybe too much my first week, so instead of just going to my bed, I pulled the blankets off the bed and haphazardly flung them on the couch in front of the TV. I watched Tiger golf and fell asleep when he buried the rest of the field late in the afternoon. Sometime later, I became very comfortable and slept soundly.

I did not awaken from my needed deep sleep, until my Monday morning's alarm clock sounding, just before six. I also heard the whole complex come to life. There was the usual water running, motors starting up, and car security alarms outside deactivated by the driver before getting inside to go to work. Reluctantly, I headed to the shower. By seven, I headed for IDOT.

The employees were gathered around the coffee vendor and sandwich machines in the lounge so I, too, received my share of the hot revelation and was surprised how good that coffee really was. Then a service man came to replenish most of the machines with his new supply. I asked him what brand of coffee he provided that was so good. He looked over to me then pitched a foiled wrapper of instant coffee used in the machine to me without skipping a beat.

"Keep it!" he told me.

Then others asked for samples, too, so he threw several packets onto a table, rolled his eyes up at me and grimaced unhappily for what he started. He didn't hear my thank you, but finished quickly and left. The women, faster than the men were, scurried away with what they absconded to their offices. I headed to mine.

Seated at her desk with a telephone tight to her ear and a pen in one hand scribbling down info, Joy looked fresh and vigorous, except for the dark glasses she was wearing. Why those glasses here inside, I asked myself. Our eyes seem to avoid each other purposely as I entered Kurt's office. Several notes were pinned to the message board, none for me. I sipped my coffee, until I heard Kurt's voice tell Joy he would be in meetings upstairs, until ten or so. When he walked in, he told me immediately that I had better skedaddle out to supervise the ramp project and see to its completion.

"I'm tied up in committee with deciding on which project we'll begin tomorrow. The state is limited on this year's budget and I have to give input on the most considered necessary and money-saving project, which I'm sure, as usual, will be some congressional representative's choice, which his constituents will be happy with, and then vote him back in office for…you know the story. See you tonight."

Kurt left without any suggestions or orders. It was then for the first time I felt he trusted my judgment and treated me almost as his equal. Without talking with Joy, I left by the side door and drove off in my work truck. Then I decided I was a bit over doing it, so I turned on the IDOT radio.

"Headquarters…this is number two. Do you have any messages…come in?"

I repeated my message knowing it would be Joy and waited for her response.

"Number two, you have no messages…over and out!" she spoke seemingly annoyed, as if I was disturbing her.

Maybe I was, so I just returned a soft, "Thank you."

The road crew supervisors were doing their part to finish on time. Every person was working, or it appeared so. Regardless, by noon, huge dump trucks were finished depositing rock along both edges of the asphalt pavement and narrow one-man rollers compacted the stone nearing completion. By three, two workers in a stake truck drove along the cones to pick them up, one by one, stacking them on the bed for the next job. Two freshly planted stop signs had been placed at the ramp's end.

A white hat construction supervisor came to me and told me his crew was finished and asked me to relieve his crew. I told him they had done a fine job and of course, he could let the men go home.

"See you next time," he said, as he jumped into a large van, one of four, all filled with his workers. They sped off towards the shed. They would not have to take their time, as it was regular quitting time for them.

I hadn't seen Clint on the job all day and my list of workers didn't include him. Apparently, he was assigned to another location, or maybe he quit or called in sick. Traffic began to flow up the exit ramp and I watched for any adjustments needed. I surmised a lower speed limit upon the approach in cross traffic would benefit the intersecting road and put that on my final report.

This ramp job was being signed off by me as completed satisfactorily, so I made certain everything was right. I had done mock-up reviews at UIC. I was also pleased that this first project of mine was successfully completed early. I was given the honor by Kurt, as being the project's closer and signed off as, "Gregory Wetmore, engineer".

"Number two, to base!" I sent out my call.

"Go ahead number two, this is base," answered Joy more politely.

"This is number two, base. I am leaving the Glenarm project and it is complete. Please advise number one, over."

"Stand by, number two. Number two, number one says bring it home, over and out."

The fresh, hot smell of that asphalt might have been putrid before today, but now, seeing a plan come together with its finished, gleaming newness, and leveled smoothly into a picture-perfect completed project, I felt a bit of pride knowing I had assisted in a small way. What project came next I was unsure.

When I returned to the shed almost everyone had gone home as I gassed up for the next workday. I had to park inside and leave my keys, because of the equipment aboard. Joy was gone, so I filled out the sheet with my mileage and gas receipt, and then placed the keys on the board.

When I heard the time clock was being punched, I turned around to see

Clint of all people. He was working at the northbound truck scales on I-55, he told me, but had to punch in and out back here. He must have stopped off because he smelled like a brewery.

"Say, if I'm not too nosey, what happened with you and Joy last Friday night?"

"It is none of anyone's business, but she just isn't my type. She's all frigid and stuff…cold as a witch's toe in Chicago…wouldn't even let me touch her. I hooked up with some girls from high school and, ha, I just forgot she was there," he laughed.

"Didn't you have the decency to even tell her? You brought her out there…you should have taken her home early and then came back," I told him disgustedly.

"Eh, she'll get over it, they always do," he smirked.

My look must have told it all.

"What? She turns you on, huh? Well ol' buddy…take her, she's all yours," he told me so arrogantly that I lost it.

There were two hits. I hit him hard and he hit the floor. I saw he wasn't really injured, just dazed. He now had a fat lip and his pride tarnished, so I flipped over a mop bucket on his head with enough water to make him come up swinging, so I decked him again. He skidded on his behind up against the Coke machine and decided not to get up again.

"You sucker-punched me, buster. You've got me now," he said, while checking his teeth, "but I'll get even with you if it's the last thing I do," Clint warned me.

"You'll get over it…they always do," I told him sarcastically and left him trying to get straight.

Little did I know our confrontation was being taped by hidden security cameras, which were meant to capture thieves, not a punching match. Elvis left the building. I did, too.

I drove home and my knuckles on my right hand began to feel sore. I flexed them but it did not help. As I drove into my garage, I caught a wave from Joe as he was out and about seeing everything was in place at the complex. I guess he worked hard enough; it's just his way of performing his duties seemed very strange. I then decided to take a cool dip before dinner.

When I began to change into my swim trunks, I felt that lonely feeling a man gets coming home to an empty house. I quickly changed, slipped on my thongs, and grabbed a towel. I did not hesitate to try out the diving board and found out I hadn't done that for several years. That belly flop splash brought all eyes looking my way. My stomach was red, but the soreness of my fist, was removed by the pain in my midsection.

I heard laughing and I knew it was Joe.

"Hey, you're no Johnny Weissmuller, Greg!" he shouted.

"Who's he?"

"He's the first Tarzan, dummy…before your time, I guess. Anyway, come on over and meet Doyle. He's my brother-in-law and owns this pig sty he calls a beautiful complex, only because I make it that way," he laughed, poking Doyle jokingly.

"How do you do, sir…very glad to meet you. I'm Greg Wetmore," I told Doyle, who looked the part of a Mafia boss with his white linen suit, tropical shirt, a big green stogy and dark sunglasses.

"Same here…Joe tells me you saved me a lawsuit or two. Thanks! Do you like my complex?"

"Yes, very much…it's pricey, but you get what you pay for," I told him.

"Joe is a great super, kind of squirrelly, but gets the job done as I want. I like that in my employees. Although, I have to follow him up and tell him everything to do. I hate owning these, but they make me richer…what do you do?" he inquired, while inhaling another big puff off his Cuban cigar that caused him to cough.

"I work for the state as a highway civil engineer. I just started and finished my first project today," I advised.

"Yeah, and what was that and what did it pay?" he spoke wryly.

"An exit ramp on I-55 at Glenarm…enough," I answered to his pay question.

"You know what I build?" he wanted to know.

"I guess housing complexes."

"Nah, I bought this as a tax write-off and a place for my sister to raise her kids with this yahoo!" he said, reaching back to pull the hairs on Joe's legs just to aggravate him for turning his back on us to watch a hot pink bikini.

"Ouch! You son-of-a-bitch…you do that again and I'll whip your ass!" Joe let everyone in the complex hear as he hopped around complaining.

After Doyle quit laughing, he asked me to sit down with him.

"Have a cigar?" he offered.

"No thanks…I quit long ago when the surgeon general said smoking caused cancer. My great uncle supposedly died of lung cancer. He smoked… must be something to that, think?" I said waving all his blown smoke out of my face, then moving up-wind to another chair at his umbrella table.

"Okay, fine…Joe, Jerk-off, get him a drink…want a martini?"

"No, nothing right now, thanks. What is it you wish to talk to me about? Ah, Doyle, was it?" I asked as I was starting to feel hunger pangs.

Then things got a bit more serious.

"Mr. Wetmore…I might have a job for you…maybe."

"I already have a job and it has a good pension. No, thanks…is that it?" I said a bit perturbed by his uppity arrogance and rose up to leave.

"Oh yeah, you won't even listen to my offer?" he mused.

"Okay…shoot!" I said sitting back down.

"I know you don't really mean that I should shoot you, do ya, ha…look, you must surely make about $400,000 tax free a year, and drive a Mercedes, live in a pent house, and work three, maybe four hours a month, right?"

"Hardly," I laughed.

"Then why not listen to my offer?" he said, looking deeply into my eyes for a sign of weakening.

"What could pay so well? Do I have to kill somebody?" I chuckled.

Doyle wasn't laughing, but smug-looking. I thought he was about to get very serious with me, as he motioned for Joe to get out of there. He began to talk more quietly as he scooted his chair closer to mine.

"I need a guy like you around to make me look good. You look straight and got brains. I really run the Diamond Casino in Vegas. It's the old Sand Dune worked over…interested yet? Anyway, you come in with me and be my brain. I can tell you are exactly the guy I need. You're a quick thinker. You'll keep me on the right path and together I'll make you rich…your brains, my collateral…interested yet?"

"There are lots of people out there who could fill your needs…no, I have a job that I'm satisfied with…but for Christ sakes, how'd you get so rich?" I asked trying to pull his strings.

"Here, ever see this kind of dough?" he said reaching into his pants and withdrawing a wad of rolled up bills that could choke a horse.

"Here…take it…it's now yours…buy yourself a Mercedes and follow me out to Vegas…really, it's yours. Besides, you probably saved me from a fuckin' ten million lawsuit, already. I just want to show you my appreciation," he said, then pitching the money roll into my lap.

It was like a hot potato and I suspected there was over a hundred thousand in hundreds in that roll. Now that was hard to resist, but I pretended it did not affect my decision one bit, but I was nervous. I didn't know how to reject his offer, so I told him I was under a freshly drawn contract for this fiscal year ending July 1st.

"Can't you break it?" he wanted to know.

"No, I'm bound for at least six more months, and can't get tenured for two years on the job. I still don't understand," I said weakening, seeing all that money thrown at me.

I was living check to check. It came once every two weeks, but the first came late after one month to get the deductions, and insurances correct at my expense.

"Look, kid," he called me seeing me begin to sweat.

"I'm no kid. Call me Greg, please," I asked more manly.

"Kid's got manners, huh? I like that...but now you can call me Mr. Valero," he demanded rather sarcastically. "Respect your elders," he added.

Regaining my composure, I slid the money back across the table at Doyle and got up. Doyle was not happy.

"Look, pencil-dick, desk jockey...I just offered you the best fucking job you'll ever have in your whole fucking life and it's tax free...get it? All you have to do now is be smart for me with your education. That's as simple as I can make it. I'll buy your brains for money. I'll be in town at the capital with some very important friends for a week or two doing business," he said, more settled down. "I like you, kid. I like you a lot for your brains and guts. You think about it...I know where to find you...adios!" he said, drawing deep on his cigar then blowing his smoke at me.

It seems I was looking at a desperate man who always got what he wanted and I was pissing him off royally. I suspected immediately that he was a drug smuggler or big crime boss. He certainly fit the part as far as his appearance and that roll of hundred dollar bills he threw at me so casually. I left feeling he may send someone to do me in, so I looked for Joe for some answers. He wasn't around, so I continued to my apartment, looking back once, and seeing Doyle was gone.

I broke an egg on the stove, burned my fingers trying to get it off the glass top burner, and stepped back knocking over the glass of milk on the table I had just poured. I couldn't concentrate after my encounter with Doyle, so I scrambled more eggs, threw two egg sandwiches together, and sat down.

My cell rang and it was Kurt calling. He wanted to tell me the committee had chosen a bridge project in Saline County, using my calculations. They actually believed I could finish what I started and Saline County would pay the state for my salary, so Kurt could start another, he began.

"Greg, I have good news, bad news, and worse news. Which you want first? Well, anyway, first, Joy quit today. She went to work as a secretary at the capital building, I think. I hoped to change her mind, but she was set on leaving. She just cleaned out her desk and took off. Did you kids have a falling out?"

"No, I think it was because she got dumped by one of our own hardhat workers. He took her out Friday night and left her hangin'," I explained. "It wasn't pretty."

"She seemed to say it was because of you. She finds it hard to be around you…I think she really has it bad for you and it's getting to her."

"All I ever said to Joy was I liked her, but we were just friends. I'm sorry if she feels that way. Maybe if I call her she'll reconsider. I know she's your right arm."

"Darn tootin' she is…I love that little girl as my own. Actually, she is mine and Martha's. You knew her parents died in a car crash when she was in her early teens, didn't ya? Joyce and her parents were good active members in our church then. Martha immediately wanted to help when she told me about Joyce's bad situation and becoming an orphan. Joyce moved in with us, but quit going to church after Darrel and Jewell were killed; that is until you showed up. Anyway, as soon as we got her out of high school, I got her this job. She's been my right arm, yes, sir," he spoke out sullenly.

"Nothing could be good after that. What's next?" I complained.

"The state is running out of highway funds. That's why you're lucky you got that job offer with the county building that bridge. It'll take eight months to a year and by then finances might change for the better."

"Now that was a lot better, but now I have to worry next year, huh?"

"More than you know. What happened with you and Clint in the shed after work? They got you two on camera fighting. The security cam showed you decked him…what happened?"

"If it weren't for bad luck, I'd have no luck at all, huh?" I said subdued. "The bastard was the one who dumped Joy Saturday night. I asked him why he left her behind and alone out at the Harness Club and he just laughed it off and said she'll get over it. I couldn't help it and I hit him."

"The security chief said he didn't touch you and you hit him a second time," Kurt said.

"Did he mention I dumped a mop bucket with soapy water over his head, too?"

"I was getting to that," Kurt grumbled.

"What do I do?"

"Nothing…Clint took it on the chin after I talked with him. He knows I love Joy and his job anywhere in the state was at risk if he filed a complaint… not saying I wouldn't have done the same thing as you, but I didn't expect that from you, Greg. That's the bad news. In the mean time hang loose. Go out to the county's bridge tomorrow and get it done at your pace. If you run into trouble, give me a holler. Greg, I'll do what I can, but if you can get Joy back I'll be beholdin' to ya."

"I'm beholding to you…and Martha, and Joy. I don't know what to say yet, but I'll try my best to make her understand…see you later."

I hung up really disturbed and decided to get a beer. I just got my position with lots of financial responsibilities and now I'm already facing a timetable to becoming unemployed. How could this be? They did not discuss what to do in cases such as mine at UIC. Only time would tell.

Then Joe knocked at my back door and wanted to talk.

"Hey, don't get hung up on my asshole brother-in-law. He thinks because he's so fuckin' rich he can dictate to everyone. What'd he say to you?" Joe was curious.

"He offered me a job."

"Mine?" with a bit of distress.

"No, no, a job with him as a thinker in Vegas, I guess."

"Take it! That silly bastard does stupid things all the time and can't figure anything out for himself. He's fucked away millions on bitches and bad investments. He even backed some senator from Nevada who wanted to raise taxes on his casino. He didn't even ask the jerk about his platform and just wanted to be seen with him in public to look important…he pays really good, too. He looks like a hood, but isn't smart enough to think for himself.

He just somehow falls into money without trying. Then, he falls out just as fast. He's better now than ten years ago. You might be the best fucking thing that happens to him. Do it!"

"Yeah, then he'd change his fuck-ing mind and I'd be looking for another fuck-ing job," I spoke, mimicking his foul vocabulary.

"Eh, I think he's always good on his word, but he can treat you like his slave sometimes…he likes that…but he always pays good…did I mention that?

"However, he's not so good if someone screws with him. He's not the guy who would hire you just to fire you. He didn't get filthy rich doing that. My wife says he first robbed a small bank south of the border, disappeared for three years, and returned very rich. I don't believe that, but I think he started out as a mule for shipments of cocaine across the border and mooched some. Then he sold his mooched stash after he cut it down and got out quick. Some New York buyers don't know good shit from bad shit."

"And I should go with him…get outta here…get real!" I said.

Then Joe left insulted. Anyway, he let the door slam. He was a character, but somehow I felt I could trust him. I hated to admit it, but we talked openly and I think honestly to each other, maybe insulting, too, but we still remained friends.

With so much revolving in my mind, I decided to call Joy. Either she had her phone turned off or disconnected, so I tried Lila.

"Lila, I need to talk to Joy. Is she there?"

"Nope, and I ain't getting stuck with her side of the rent money neither… the bitch packed up and left."

"Where'd she go?"

"Hell if I know and damned if I care…just so she pays her half on time… bitch!"

Lila was totally cranked, so I gave up talking sense to her.

"How's Truman?" I asked to settle her down.

"He's doin' good…I miss the little shit," Lila said, sounding lonely for him.

"Well, maybe now you can have him there with you."

"No, he's with my momma and it's best…Galesburg!"

"What Galesburg?" I asked to her sudden burst.

"Joyce went to Galesburg…I think to work there."

"Do you know for whom?"

"Nah, but it's some kind of finance company. I saw it circled on her newspaper in the classified ads. Wait, the paper is in the wastebasket, I just pitched it. I'll go get it, hang on."

I heard her footsteps and then she cussed out. I think I heard a chair move and it was her big toe that moved it. She had stubbed her toes and after a short tirade of foul words and hopping sounds, Lila picked up on me again.

"Shit, I think I broke my toe…damn…let me look," she told me, as if she could give a cat's ass about Joy, but was doing this for me.

"Got a pencil? Here's the ad…Capital G Finance, 13678 South Boulevard, Galesburg…that's where she took off to…it's circled. It's a secretarial job opening and I think they hired her right over the phone. Anyway, she's gone. Got it?"

"Thanks, Lila…I got it down. I'll get back to you."

"If you find that bitch tell her I ain't takin' no hit on the rent money…I'll sue her ass…tell her that!" Lila screamed at me, and then hung up.

I had no idea how to quickly find Joy, except go to that finance company. I had to do it now or never, because of my new project's beginning. I was in a bind. I locked up, got in my truck, and drove to a gas station to fill up. I went inside, bought an Illinois highway map, and located Galesburg. I had been there once playing football in high school, but I couldn't remember how to get there, especially from Springfield. My thoughts were how I was going to find her there anyway, as it was already past working hours. I had no leeway. I just had to find her. Galesburg was about seventy miles northwest, off I-74, so there was no problem. I took off headed that way.

In an hour, I exited into Galesburg's business district, but it took me stopping and asking a man on the sidewalk to find out where South Boulevard was. I was driving parallel to it and it was just a block, if I'd turn right at the next stoplight. He had no idea where Capital G Finance was, but I had its address anyway. I thanked him and followed his directions.

The office lights were off and only the marquee was lit at Capital G Finance. There was a telephone number on the plate glass, so I tried it with my cell. The voice gave the business hours, no human, so I pulled over into a parking lot to gather my thoughts. I was now lost without a clue, so when I spotted an IHOP, I decided to grab a hot cup and a sandwich or something before I headed back. That was a stroke of good luck.

As I met the waitress about to lead me to a table, I saw Joy seated at a booth reading a newspaper. She didn't look very happy and didn't look up when I stood next to her table.

"Mind if I sit here with you?" I asked.

Joy slowly looked up at me and stared.

"May I sit down?" I repeated.

Joy seemed shocked and did not say a word, until I sat down anyway.

"How'd you get here?"

"I followed the tears…Kurt and everyone else wants you to come back…I do too," I pleaded.

She couldn't say a word, but only stared hard at me, then spoke.

"I heard what you did to Clint…why'd you do it?"

"Because, he's an asshole."

"I already knew that…why did it bother you? For what he did to me?"

"It made you sad," I told her, trying hard not to go where she was leading me. I think she wanted to hear me say I loved her, but I just couldn't.

"What I saw in you I'll never know now. But, I thought a lot about us… well, me really. I decided you aren't meant for me and I jumped to conclusions. However, coming here changes things. You must care some after all to come all the way here to find me…by the way, how did you?"

"I do care for you…you're my friend, remember? Lila said you found a job with Capital G Finance. She said you had read a help wanted ad and circled it in the newspaper, so I followed that lead…it was just dumb luck that I wandered into here…unbelievable, isn't it? A city of thousands and here you are. What happened to your head?"

Joy grimaced, looked up to the small bandage stuck to her forehead, and then yanked it off. Then she reached in her purse and pulled out two traffic tickets with her name on them.

"What's this?"

"Read the damn things. The cop scribbled so badly I can hardly read them either. I hit a car."

"When? Was anyone hurt…oh, besides you?"

"Nah, just me…I forgot to put on my seatbelt and my head hit the steering wheel when I hit the old fart. He pulled up to a stop sign, took off fast, and then suddenly stopped. I didn't see any brake lights, but I knocked those out, so the cop couldn't tell if they were working or not. I smacked him good…broke my radiator, bent up the grill and hood. I'm hoofin' it till I find a rental in the morning," she informed me.

"Where's your vehicle now?"

"At a body shop, somewhere…I called the guy and he said he could fix it in two or three weeks, if I had insurance. Otherwise, he said it would cost me about four grand plus labor."

"What about your new job?"

"Ha, that lasted fifteen minutes. The boss was just too friendly. He leaned over me to see if I could type and began rubbing his pecker against me without any underwear on. I elbowed him hard there and while he was on his knees praying, or something, I got the hell out of there. That's why I hit the old fart…I was fleeing the job scene," Joy explained very sadly, while looking into my eyes.

"Let me grab a snack and I'll take you home."

"I ain't got no home, if you want to know."

"When did your English turn so hillbilly?" I jested.

"The real me is a showin' up now," she snickered. "I just get very refined on the job," she admitted.

"Okay, well tonight is payback. You are now my guest and roomie tonight. You get my couch. Besides, Kurt wants you back immediately. We can work everything out…please?" I begged.

"Looks like this lady better take you up on it or sleep here all night. I gave the cop all I had for my bond money."

"Why didn't you just give him your driver's license?"

"Cause I have to have some kind of ID while wandering around this big city as a vagrant," she laughed. The waitress then looked hard at us from behind the cash register.

Everything seemed better after we both had dark coffee and strawberry filled crepes. Then Joy accompanied me to my truck, where she laughed, and said if I were a gentleman, I'd open her door for her. I did, and she slid inside.

"Put that seat belt on!" I told her, but had to put it on her myself when she couldn't find one end. I think she did that on purpose, as we got very close.

"I guess Lila is really pissed, huh?"

"Well, she just wants you to pay your half of the rent. I think she actually misses you though."

"Yeah, I bet. Well, I'll find out. I learned the hard way not to let your emotions guide you. From now on, if I meet a good-lookin' guy, he'll have to beg first before I ever fall again."

Joy seemed to be talking to herself. I wasn't sure if it was me or Clint she was thinking about. Women!

"I hope you didn't get too upset about losing your new job," Joy began. "I know a few people who can use a guy with your credentials," Joy suddenly advised.

"I didn't lose my job," I enlightened her.

"Well, why not? When the letter came down they were cutting finances and every department was to lose one of their new employees without tenure... you're the only one in engineering without tenure. That upset me, too."

"I didn't know about that. When Kurt called me moaning your loss, he told me I had a new project with Saline County building a new bridge that I'd given estimates on earlier in the week."

"That Kurt...he's an angel. He saved your butt by getting them to sign off on you. I guess he threatened to leave instead and that really upset their carts. Nope, you were tagged to be let go, sorry."

The ride home became quiet, when Joy fell asleep, and a light rain caused me to turn on the windshield wipers. The continuous rhythm of the wiper blades does that. I had time to think then and I even contemplated Doyle's offer. I felt tired by the time I pushed the remote that opened my garage.

"We're home!" I told Joy, who now was zonked-out and breathing hard.

When she awoke she asked, "Where are we anyhow?"

"My garage, my house, remember? You're staying over tonight."

"Ohhh, aren't you the coy one?" she said laughing, as if I was about to seduce her. She then slid off the seat slowly and entered through my kitchen door in front of me. I noticed her firm rear and imagined what it would be like if we were actually more than just good friends.

I felt much happier being with her and not that alone feeling I always got coming inside my empty apartment. It was only temporary, but much nicer.

"Where's your john?" was the first thing she asked.

"Down the hall, first door on the right...if you want to shower, there are a few towels hanging on hooks to use. It's only me and I haven't bought extras. That blue one wasn't used...take that," I told her.

"Well, unfortunately my luggage was in my truck when it got towed.

I thought I could go get it all, but I had no way to haul it, so it's back in Galesburg. Why didn't you think of that?" Joy yelled out as she closed the bathroom door.

"I do have some PJ shorts that I seldom wear and a robe that my mom gave me that you can have," I yelled back, but only heard the toilet seat open rapidly.

Again, I turned on the TV to make some noise to drown out her obvious gastric distress. She was the fartiest woman I had ever known. Nevertheless, you have to accept the good with the bad and Joy was all-good. I learned once before that roommates never discuss loud farting. They just accepted it.

When I heard the shower begin, I hurriedly got out my pajama bottoms and a top for Joy to slip into. I gave her my New Trier High School's jersey, which had my name and old number twelve on the back.

When I lightly knocked on the bathroom door to give Joy a change of clothes, she hadn't gotten into the shower yet. When the door suddenly eased open unexpectedly with my knock, it exposed Joy standing there naked in front of me. She "eked" and grabbed a towel.

"Now that wasn't necessary, bub!" she told be bluntly, still hiding behind the towel.

"Sorry, I'm sorry…I just wanted to give you these," I said, with one hand over my eyes. I pitched the clothes towards the vanity and backed out quickly, very embarrassed.

There was no response from Joy, but I immediately suspected she thought I did that on purpose. I decided to give Kurt a quick call and ask him what I should tell Joy about her job. I knew he would be very happy, and he was.

"You tell her everything's as it was and I expect her back in the morning. It's pouring down hard out here, you guys getting this storm?" Kurt injected. "And thanks, Greg. You don't know how much she means to me. I'd be lost without her. Good luck on your project…I doubt it will start up tomorrow, since this gully washer came up…man, it's really coming down… oh, boy, now hail…better head for the basement, Martha!" Kurt called to her. "See you tomorrow, I hope!" he yelled.

Though I could not hear any terrible storming over the cell, it was coming. I began to hear rumbling noises, which seemed to sound like Indians on their drums at a far distance.

Then I peeked outside through the living room curtains to observe the weather. I was just in time to see the first bright flash of a lightning bolt striking nearby, which knocked out the power to our whole complex. Immediately, all the electronics sounded out their tones and everything went dead.

It became pitch-black dark, very creepy, inside and out. There was dead silence then, with only those intermittent flashes of lightning and the sound of the shower running.

I was allowing my eyes to readjust from the brilliant flash that had temporarily blinded me and had left a hazy-white spot in both eyes to focus upon. The wind began howling outside, and I feared a tornado was nearing. I called out to Joy to hurry out of the shower.

Still unable to focus, I made a ruckus when I stumbled over the ottoman in front of my favorite chair. I arose staggering a bit, rubbing my eyes, then walked right into a wet, half-nude Joy, who had come out of the shower in my robe, dripping wet, probably thinking the world had come to an end, and was lost in a strange house. Very frightened, Joy bumped into me hard and suddenly embraced me clumsily. She locked us both up, arm in arm, and began holding on to me tightly.

Our collision was unplanned, yet with very surprising results. When our lips inadvertently crossed paths in the dark from being drawn so closely together by Mother Nature's wrath, it seemed so natural for them to touch again.

Our noticeably innocent encounter for beginners was stimulating, as her wet bare breasts now felt yet soapy and very slippery when they bounced out of her robe against my chest. She was much too chesty to wear it tightly. It was then I realized how diminutive she was when she was not wearing heels.

The now more frequent white flashes of lightning revealed her face looking up to me, exposing her large bare breasts, which I had no idea were so huge out of their bra. The outside deafening clap of thunder from another near-by lightning strike scared her, and she quickly drew me even more tightly to her. I could not resist that intimate moment to kiss her repeatedly, as she, too, kissed me back.

Joy allowed the borrowed robe to slip off her body onto the floor and our caresses became very intense. She tugged at my shirt that was tucked tightly inside my pants and felt me in all places where I was touching her. Our untamed, burning desires grew stronger and stronger. We continued our embrace in a deep, long-lasting French kiss, until we both breathlessly wanted the other. It was madness.

I took her hand in mine and managed to lead her to the couch. I sat down and let her gently descend on top of me, as we held our bond. Our passion was then out of control, as Joy got up, unbuckled my belt, and unzipped me. I quickly told her I needed a condom, but she said it was too late for that. She slid to the couch and we made union as I managed to shake off my pants eventually with her help.

The lightning with thunder was not only outside, but also there in my apartment with my now best friend. Our bodies seemed to meld into one, clashing violently sometimes, time after time. I could always feel her loving me back with no reserve.

It was a first union I would never forget, yet it didn't end there on the couch, as we moved to the bedroom and continued our lovemaking there, until we were both too exhausted to continue several hours later.

We then rested a bit and talked about work, pillow-talk shop, and of all things God. Joy told me on days like today, when the weather showed no mercy, the workers held close to the shed, because their work out on the projects halted. Many state employees took these times to use up accrued sick days, holiday time, and vacation time to be with their families, because they were virtually useless at work.

"What do you do when you get sick…who takes your place?" I asked.

"Oh, that's simple. First of all, I hardly ever get sick, maybe the flu, but someone gave it to me at work, but I work right through that. Kurt really needs me.

"But when I really need help, any kind of guidance, something important to me, I just say, 'Jesus, I need your help, save me.' He never fails me, and I'm happy to tell you that if you'll just say that at anytime you're in need, He will help you, but only if you truly believe. Do you?"

"Sure, I'm a Christian," I told her. "But I never really felt like I ever got His Divine help, especially back in high school when I did pray to Him, right before they cut on my knee to make me well. I prayed hard, but it didn't work," I told Joy reluctantly.

"Then did you think because He didn't help you immediately He didn't care? He did. Let's see if I can figure it out for you…humm…you ended up as a very highly intelligent, very important civil engineer, not a cripple working in a car wash, like most big-time athletes find themselves doing by age twenty-five. Think I just answered your question about God, huh? Good night!"

Spent physically, we both fell sound asleep in each other's arms on my bed, as the storm outside continued to wail to a tune of destructive 60 mph winds.

I awoke several hours later when the electric suddenly popped on, and then back off, then on again. Joy still slept soundly, nevertheless, with her head on my chest. The naked beauty of her entirety was a remarkable sight for any man.

I eased from Joy and gently lay her head upon my pillow. I looked down upon her sleeping so peacefully and felt very blessed to be with her. I wanted to kiss her soft lips again, but I did not want to wake her. She had gone the distance with me, never complaining once that I was too rough or clumsy. Therefore, I tiptoed to the restroom to wash up and brush my teeth. I wanted to do that quickly in the light, just in case the power went off again.

In the bathroom, I looked at myself in the vanity mirror, while brushing my teeth. I asked myself then if I now was prepared to marry Joy. I was a man and if she became pregnant from this rendezvous, and there was every possibility she might, by me not using a condom, yes, I would, with no regrets.

I also just might marry Joy even if she did not become pregnant. The answer would lie, also, in if she felt I was worthy of her. I knew I pleased her and she me. I hated to admit it, but Joy was my first real sexual adventure and I knew I was her first. She had given it up to me freely. Our union was a spontaneous, mutually enjoyed burst of lovemaking, which each made wonderful.

I believed now that good friends made the best lovers. I wondered if that held true with matrimony. We had come so far together in such a short time. My true feelings for Joy hoped our road together was never-ending.

When Joy suddenly appeared behind me and told me she had to pee, and then squatted on the toilet and did, I felt we were as close friends as any two humans could be; confiding in one another, responsive to each other's needs, and eager to share everything in life. My desire for a bachelor's life diminished abruptly and I am certain Joy was also feeling different emotions.

We showered together, drying ourselves while sharing just the one unused towel I had left, and then began laughing together about it, as we dressed only in underwear and then sat eating toast and drinking coffee at the dawning.

It continued to storm horribly. Tornado warnings continuously displayed on red warning banners running across the bottom of the TV screen and local reports of a twister on the ground had damaged some farmer's barn.

Therefore, we looked to one another, embracing more, not wanting to leave the other. Joy had the solution. We resumed our play in the light of day, right after we both called in sick to Kurt. He was thrilled and told Joy it was about time.

Chapter 8

About noon, the storm suddenly moved off easterly and the sun cast its brightness through the bedroom's curtain. I awoke when I heard Joy zip up her jeans, slip on her boots, and sat gently down on my bed to search for her bra. It was under my pillow. Her face was a bit rosy from the rubbing of my growth of whiskers, but in the midday's light… it glowed just like an angel's.

"What's up?" I asked Joy.

"A girl can't spend all her time in bed. I have work to do. I bet Sheena has her hands full today. She'll likely do okay, but when she goes back and tells her uncle that she was in charge and had control of the whole Springfield office, there will be a congressional investigation about the real need to have permanent state employees," she joked.

"Don't go…we need to talk, don't you think?"

"About what? It's over, and if I'm knocked up it's my own fault. You don't have to worry," she arrogantly blabbered, though I knew immediately she was testing me to see if I still wanted her, now, after the fact.

I grabbed Joy's hand and pulled her down to me on the bed. Then I kissed her hard, right before I got the courage to say what was on my mind.

"Joy, I want to marry you. There, I said it."

"What for? You got the milk free, why buy the cow? I got what I wanted, too, so we're even," she said, trying to get up off my bed.

I yanked her back down under me and forced her to look into my eyes. When she turned away, I saw a tear forming in the corner of her eye, so I kissed it away and with my fingers softly upon her chin, I turned her face gently toward mine.

"I just asked you to marry me, dummy. I won't take no for an answer. I love you, Miss Joyce Dixon…I really do…not because of the wonderful sex you and I just shared, but my eyes have been awakened to your wonderful loving personality. And, yes, you do have a great hot bod, too…but that's not all I desire…I want this to never end, don't you? I'm willing to work at our bonding closer for the rest of our lives together…will you marry me?…I don't have a ring to offer, yet…but just say yes and we'll go shopping right now."

"You sure know how to try and sweep a girl off her feet, don't you? Seems like you've had lots of practice. How do I know tomorrow you won't change your mind?"

"You don't…especially if you doubt me. Just give your whole to me and I'll surrender mine," I said, so eloquently that I had to think about exactly what I had just told her…she wasn't so eloquent.

"Looks like I already gave you my hole," she laughed. "Why would I want yours?" she began to giggle more loudly.

I could tell my wanting her still the morning after, relieved her, as Joy began letting loose with her happiness inside. Then she took a deep sigh and kissed me so wonderfully, I knew I had made the right decision. Her kiss was all I'd ever need.

"I guess we can make a go of it…especially if we get rained out once or twice a month like this, after we are hitched up, of course," she said, holding me tightly. "Yes, I'll become Misses Gregory Jonathon Wetmore… Joyce Wetmore…humm…sounds a bit classy, doesn't it?"

We did more planning right there in my bedroom and within an hour, I drove Joy into downtown Springfield and found a jeweler to buy her that ring. It was a "Joy-ess" moment that I recall fondly.

"That's the one I want, really…that one!" Joy insisted, when she selected a rather small titanium engagement ring with an also rather insignificant looking stone from the jeweler's case. I had suggested a larger two-carat stone, which could be mounted in any setting, but she still insisted on her choice, which was much lower priced, but evidently not "cheaper".

"This ring will last me forever and it won't constantly be getting hung up on things like laundry, vacuum cleaners, dish cloths, computers, bed clothes and your underwear," she then giggled, smiling at me, and causing the jeweler to roll his eyes. "Besides, it's not the quantity; it's the quality that counts. It reads there it's a flawless, .51 carat. That's really good, isn't it?" Joy asked the retailer.

"Yes, flawless diamonds are the best. These diamonds are sold commercially at this price, only in everything less than one full carat. This is a perfectly flawless diamond, small, yet a valued cut stone. It's a nice choice, especially combined with the setting that you have chosen," he said, holding the diamond ring up closer to his monocle magnifier to look hard into the diamond's center.

"Notice, Greg, I do not wear any rings for a reason," Joy announced, as she held up her ring less hands. "As much typing as I have to do, even in one day, a fancy gold ring with a big diamond sticking up on it would hang up on everything. Therefore, it wouldn't last very long or I'd end up having to take it off. If I put this on, it's never coming off, I guarantee you that. So, that one is perfect for me...there is a man's matching band beside it and they look good together, don't you agree? If we get these together, I'll be very happy always. It's what this ring means to the wearer that is most important."

Maybe it was not kosher, maybe it was not appropriate at all, but I took the ring from its box and again asked Joy to please make me the happiest man in the world and marry me. I got down on one knee, right in the store.

She said, "Certainly, because you already asked me...get up, you look silly!" with a beaming grin, as I slid that little ring upon her finger. When it fit perfectly, she jumped into my arms and we kissed to seal the deal.

The retailer then quickly mentioned to me it was the first time he had ever witnessed an actual proposal request and acceptance.

"It has never before happened here in this store, especially before we even discussed the price and paid for it," he hinted.

Therefore, I asked him if he would take my Visa card. He took it and said he gladly accepted them all. Joy stood beside me holding my arm and looking up to me very happily, as we waited to finalize the purchase.

This woman wasn't thinking only of herself, as much as she was thinking of us. I learned this was her way always and I loved her dearly for many reasons.

We had purchased the rings, but together decided to wait a while to give notice to the many people we loved. I had Mom, Dad, and possibly Jill. Joy had only one uncle and aunt and her grandmother. We both had Kurt and Martha.

We had many things to work out, including Lila. When Joy and I showed up at their apartment, Lila was at her work place.

"Good, she's not here…I'll call her on her cell at work and break the ice. She can't get violent over the telephone, can she?" Joy said after we entered.

I wasn't so sure of that, having been the target of Lila's aggression once or twice myself. Nevertheless, Joy was right and I heard a squeal over the phone from Lila when Joy told her our news. Then she wished us happiness and told Joy she had the say so over her next roommate.

"I think I have the perfect new roommate for you, but I have to ask her first. She just told me her uncle was allowing her to get an apartment of her own."

"Sounds like a kid to me, having to ask her uncle."

"Her uncle is Congressman Byrd and she works with me. Her name is Sheena Johnson."

"George Byrd's little niece? Hell, I voted for him…he's a brother and it might be a good way to get a better job here. Send her over to me quick," Lila chuckled before she agreed and then hung up.

Joy's cell phone chimed and it was her insurance company. They told her that the damage on her truck exceeded its value. Therefore, after their agent adjusted the Blue Book's value slightly upward for low mileage, they were mailing her a check for the total value. She got $9,800 and was very satisfied.

"Damn! If I had known, I could get that much for that junker I would have crashed it sooner. That was my first accident…I hope they don't raise my rates, but they probably will," Joy complained, as she looked up to me with a frown.

"That's okay, I'll buy you a new one, and that's that, except for the tickets. Send your $175 for them both and get that done, also, right now while we're talking about that. I don't want a sheriff's deputy showing up at our doorstep dragging you off in handcuffs, just because you forgot to pay your tickets. You were at fault and haven't got a diddley-crap-chance disputing it, it appears to me, so just get an envelope and send your check.

"And, I better never hear about or see you not wearing your seatbelt, ever," I sternly told her, looking to touch her small abrasion, but she just shrugged me off not wanting my input or me touching her little ouchie.

"Says here, I can call in to the circuit clerk's office and pay by credit card. I don't need a new truck. I'll search for a family car…maybe a big four door Buick. That way our kids can be comfortable on the way to church," Joy informed me, reassuring, also, that she was in it for the long haul; thinking as a mother would. She must have already known something then.

Before I left Joy, to get our simple wedding plans started, I told her that I would be there early in the morning to transport her to work. However, Joy told me, "No," she was taking another sick day to get things done. She told me just to concentrate on doing my job, because the next day she would already have purchased a different car. Then she was driving to Galesburg to get back her suitcases.

As it turned out, Lila drove near the state shed daily and could drop Joy off. Consequently, Joy began riding with Lila to work. Apparently, Joy could not find that car she hoped to find at her right price. Nevertheless, Sheena met Lila one day at the shed and they both hit it off which set up their relationship.

Two weeks flew by quickly, as I began work on the bridge project with the county. Unfortunately, I wasn't really the sole boss. Their engineer took over and he only consulted me when he hit an obstacle. I kept doing calculations and costs. He must have never gone to college, as he was confused continually, but agreed with my every suggestion and importantly, I still got paid. His being there made it easy for me to appropriate materials, but it was not like building one's own project. Still, the project was flowing as well as could be expected with just our small crew.

One evening after work, I picked up Joy. We met with Kurt and Martha out at the Country Kitchen for dinner to tell them we were in love and getting married. Joy asked Martha to be her matron of honor, so I asked Kurt to be my best man. They were both delighted and hugged us.

"I knew it that first day!" Kurt laughed. "I saw you two whispering behind my back. You didn't fool me!"

I didn't dare tell Kurt I had just saved him from a water dousing or a bump on his head.

I decided to drive Joy to Northfield on the next Friday evening after work to meet my parents and give them the news. They were certainly surprised, maybe even overwhelmed, showing us their astonished looks. Learning their baby was suddenly becoming a married man, almost overnight, was understandable for their concern. Mom cried, but said it would take a while to arrange all the formal guest lists and secure a church and reception hall. Joy settled that quickly.

"Mother Wetmore," Joy began, "with all due respects, Greg and I are getting married in Glenarm; two weeks come Saturday, at one. That's what we both came here to tell you," Joy told her, then looking to me. "It will be a very small wedding, no reception afterwards, but you two are welcome there. It's probably going to be a bit strange for you both to be in that church, it's Mennonite, my faith, but my parents were lain to rest there and still lie there behind the church. I feel they are still anxiously waiting for me to return to that little church to get married there. Please understand."

Mom, who quietly listened, told Joy she and Dad couldn't miss it, and would be proud to have her as a daughter-in-law, but asked the painful question of how her parents died. I never knew more than what Kurt had told me and had never asked Joy. It seemed almost too much for her, but Joy sighed, and then spoke softly.

"It was a Saturday morning," Joy began…"Dad and Mom were going shopping for groceries at Noble's in Glenarm, riding in Mom's brand new little car, which she chose and was so pleased Dad had bought for her, as being a gas-saver. I think it was eventually going to be mine, because Dad always drove big four-wheel drive pickups and being so tall, he had a difficult time adjusting to get his big frame into the tiny car…anyway…somehow, authorities said, Dad just turned right in front of a big semi truck. I think he wasn't used to Mom's car.

"My mother, Jewell, was killed instantly and was pronounced dead at the scene. They had to use those Jaws of Life to extract her. I never saw her again as it was a closed casket funeral. I didn't even get to say good-bye that day, because I had stayed over at my friend Julie's house. Maybe it was good, Martha told me because I missed the awfulness of the moment. Martha came, told me everything, and stayed with me. I could not have gotten through it all without her, especially after I realized I was an orphan. That was a world-ending experience for me.

"My dad, Darrel, was trapped inside also, really crushed badly. They said it took firefighters and EMTs forty minutes to free him. They flew him by Med-Vac helicopter into Springfield…he was placed on life support in the intensive care unit, after they amputated both his legs at the knees. He was in a coma for two days. I never talked to him and only saw him once from a distance with Martha. When Dad awoke, he immediately asked for my mother. Someone inadvertently told him Mother had been killed in the crash. His heart failed right then and they couldn't revive him," Joy told us, as tears suddenly formed in her eyes.

Joy seemed to be giving much more information than Mom wanted, as she grimaced at the awful thought of amputation. Nevertheless, by telling us everything, it seemed to be therapeutic for Joy…I could see something in her eyes as she seemed to drift back to that time remembering. Maybe she needed to tell us that, especially me before our vows. Then she continued, this time, with some sort of subtle tranquility.

"That night, I stayed with Kurt and Martha Rakers. They accompanied me to our church funeral and held my hand all the way, until we left my parents' graves behind the church. I lived with them for almost four years, until I moved out to Pawnee after Kurt got me a job with him as his secretary. They have been my parents and actually were my godparents, before all that happened. I love them both dearly and I'll be very proud for you to meet them," Joy sighed, with tears beginning to run down her face as she spoke.

"Kurt is my boss at work, Mom and Dad. He's a great person and so is Martha," I added, then hugged Joy.

Mom took Joy into her loving arms and said, "You poor child," and then hugged and patted her back softly, as she had always done for me as a child when I was disturbed. Dad joined in, but suddenly Joy backed away.

"Hey now!" Joy told us wiping away her tears…"this isn't a pity party for Joyce. This is a happy time. I'm marrying a fine man, your son, and I thank you two for doing such a wonderful job. We really haven't known each other very long, but we knew right away. Greg is my best friend and this ring gets a brother come two weeks Saturday. It's late; we have a three-hour drive back, so thank you for understanding and we'll hope to see you then."

I helped Joy move the rest of her things into my apartment late that night, when Lila told us Sheena had called and was moving in as quickly as Joy could get out. It worked perfectly for the monthly lease payment.

I delivered Joy and picked her up after work each day. At day's end, we ate out and searched for that family car. Joy spotted a white Buick locally, dealer-owned, that she wanted, and almost like my dad's car. It was a one-year-old, trade-in, and in almost new condition. Joy negotiated her own terms and without a trade-in; she made one hell of a deal, and for the exact insurance-money check. In addition, she demanded a full tank of gas and new floor mats to boot. That was my little girl. Then she politely informed me it was time.

"It's almost been two weeks. Your job is going well; I let Sheena have my apartment, got my share of the security deposit back, I think we are set. Now it is the time for us to visit Pastor Kefir in the morning. He is expecting us early."

Joy had insisted upon celibacy, until our official wedding night, so she actually had me sleeping on the couch in my apartment. I think she, too, was very anxious to resume our lovemaking, this time as man and wife. We headed out to Glenarm to talk with Pastor Kefir, Friday after work.

"I've taken it upon myself to have our organist, Pearl, here at eleven," Joy told Pastor Kefir. "I ordered some flowers for the alter, and a wedding bouquet for me and flowers for Martha. I have boutonnières for Greg and Kurt. I also have a wedding cake from Betty Wolf in our choir and she will also sing "The Ring", I heard her sing it before and she does it justice. Will you let us use the hall for a few minutes to eat some cake and refreshments as a little get-together reception? I promise not to disturb anyone. Can you think of anything I forgot, Pastor Kefir?" Joy humbly asked.

Her voice was so sweet I wanted to kiss her right then, but did not. Pastor Kefir assured her she would not be disturbing anyone. He had a slightly deceiving look in his eyes, which accompanied his smile that was very unexplained, but warm. He placed his hand on each of our shoulders, bowed his head, and spoke a few words in a nice prayer for our happiness and understanding.

"You know, Joy, you have been in this church for quite a few years now, maybe twenty or more…you, and your fine mother and father. I buried them back there, but did you also know I married them right here, did you know that?" he asked softly.

"Yes, Mom once told me that she and pop were the first couple you had ever hitched," she spoke gleaming.

"Well, not really, but maybe the first couple I married here, I think. I was in a big church in Canada once, before coming here over twenty-five years ago. I think there are many people here who loved your mother and father and remember them still.

"However, they all know pretty Joyce Dixon though. Many fellow churchgoers saw me baptize you in your sixteenth year. Then, by our church laws, you were open to dating. Many young men asked me if it was okay to seek your hand, because you had no real living father to ask, but it was not my place, as in the old school religion.

"If it were, Greg, you would have had to have been baptized, also, before you could marry this lovely flower. However, now, times have changed. As long as you promise to love Joy forever, Greg, your union will be encouraged and honored. Never attempt divorce, which is strictly forbidden in our sect. Otherwise, I am afraid both of you will be looked down upon in our community forever. The church does not allow temporary separation, without the approval of the majority of our clan…and only in cases of ill health. It is only a simple "Yes, I promise" spoken by you both tomorrow that binds you. These are the words I will ask you both tomorrow. You must answer 'Yes, I promise'.

"Don't be surprised if one or two others show up unexpectedly tomorrow, since I took the liberty of putting Joy's upcoming betrothal in last Saturday's message, see this," he said, showing us the small, folded leaflet, made by a computer's programming.

"Oh, I hope I have enough cake," Joy said, very concerned.

"I'm prepared for any and all who come. Let's say that will be my gift, okay?"

"Oh, I couldn't ask you for that, Pastor…we asked Greg's parents to attend and they might unexpectedly bring along someone we don't know about."

"It's not your worry. Place your worries in the hands of Our Lord, Jesus Christ, and He shall provide," he reminded her. "Also, you and Martha come to my house early enough, around nine-thirty, and use it as your dressing room. I will not be there, of course. However, my wife Millie will be there to help assist you. I'll be trying to prevent our Greg here from skipping out the back door to sneak a peek, ha! No, just kidding, we'll be having a man to man talk, since I only met Greg momentarily, once before leaving our church," he said.

Joy immediately looked a bit confused. I guess I did not mention to her that I had attended one sermon on my own.

We left, feeling nervous, but so much in love we did not have time to worry anymore.

"Whatever happens just happens," I told Joy, who seemed overly concerned her wedding plans weren't sufficient…"after about noon, tomorrow, we will be Mr. and Mrs. Wetmore and then my worries can really begin," I joked. What I meant was from then on it was my responsibility to worry about problem solving, not Joy's.

Joy drew back her hand as to give me a loving judo chop, jokingly, but hesitated suddenly, in remembrance of the last time she did that and its consequences…no truck air horns this time.

"Am I always going to have to be alert to those judo chops?" I asked.

"Only if you piss me off a bunch, so don't," she laughed.

Joy had taken her two-week paid-vacation for readying for and after our marriage. She only had to get approval from Kurt, so that was nice. Our big day was approaching.

Chapter 9

Joy did not let me see her wedding dress, which she secretly obtained with Martha's help, after Martha came to pick her up. She didn't even allow me to talk much to her or even kiss her good-bye. She was a woman on a mission.

When I had asked Joy earlier if I should get a tuxedo, she peeked into my closet and saw only the gray.

"Nah! That one will do fine," she said, realizing it was my only suit. "You'll look super in that one and it will coordinate well with my dress."

Therefore, with Joy's understanding ways, I planned to wear my newest gray suit, my only suit, which fit well enough from graduation. It was hanging in my closet, recently cleaned, ready to wear, for any occasion.

I polished my once-worn, black Stacey Adams oxfords anyway, while I talked to Kurt on the phone. Kurt said he would gladly wear his grey suit, dark blue shirt and even a white tie to match mine. I asked him if that was okay, since it was an informal wedding, but all I really had to wear.

"It's your pick, I have so many suits, because of all those departmental meetings I'm required to attend. You'll need more suits as time passes," Kurt told me. "But today our ladies are the stars of the show, and all eyes will be on them. We cocks have to look good for our hens," Kurt chuckled. "You're a very lucky man, Greg, I hope you know it. Joy will make a wonderful wife and mother."

"You know, Kurt, I somehow came to that exact opinion very quickly. I am a very lucky guy, and I know it. In other crowds where I come from, she might have been high society with a little polish, but to me, that would only have diminished her wonderful personality…and, she chose me…that's what's so wonderful to me."

Time suddenly seemed to stand still in my anxiety. I found myself driving through a two-minute car wash to make certain my truck looked clean to waste time. Then I rushed out to Glenarm to meet with Pastor Kefir. He could see my worried look, as there were hundreds of trucks and cars parked around that little church when it was supposed to be just a small wedding.

I was shocked to say the least, and then I spotted two marines, both wearing dress uniforms. One was a captain who I did not recognize; the other was a marine staff sergeant who I did. It was Jill and her fiancé Captain William Char, pacing outside near the rear of the church waiting for me.

I shook Will's hand when he took off his white glove to make it more cordial. Then I hugged Jill long and hard and could not believe how she had changed physically and mentally. She was just amazing.

"Guess what, brother? Your wonderful future wife just asked us to be in the wedding party. I'm now a bridesmaid and Will is a groomsman, okay?"

"Oh, yes, I'm so very proud to have you both. We have so much to catch up. Did Mother and Dad come?"

"Yes, also Aunt Margaret. I want to explain something while there is a minute. We both have to leave to catch a flight out of Springfield to O'Hare at seven. In three days, we are being deployed to Iraq and have been called back to our units in San Diego. We wanted to get married in Vegas, but when I called Mother, she insisted on a church wedding. Here's my request. Would you allow Will and me to get married right after you two, in this church?" she asked almost pleading.

"Super, can Joy and I be in your wedding party?"

"Now how did you ever think of that?" she laughed, "Joy already approved."

As it turned out, Pastor Kefir joined us and announced a change in plans. Since there were so many present he was going to perform a double ceremony, so there would be less confusion.

"This way, gentleman, and marines," Pastor said, leading the way to the rear room behind his lectern.

We thanked him, again, just as we entered the rear of the church and the organ began. When Jill looked out upon the gathering in the pews, she whispered, "Are these the people they call Holy Rollers?"

"No, they're Mennonites, silly…they're some the finest people I've ever met."

I was temporarily set aback by her comment, but let it slide, since it was said in such an anxious moment.

"This is Joy's faith. They are Mennonites. These are some of the gentlest folk you've ever rubbed elbows with," I assured her.

"Sorry, I saw all that black out there and it struck me a bit unusual… look at Mom and Dad, ha…they're standing out like flag poles in that sea of black…but they sure flipped when they learned Will and I were here and in this, also," Jill said with satisfaction, as only Jill could.

"I thought you came with them."

"No, I was going to surprise them, but neither noticed us walking behind them, so we strolled on by to the rear of the church. When I saw Joy looking like a bride, we hurried over to her and introduced ourselves. She was a bit upset that anyone saw her, but she is so beautiful and kind that after she learned I was your sister and we were engaged, she invited us to get 'hitched', as she referred to it. We accepted, but told her we would ask you, also… thanks, brother. Then we found Mom and Dad, told them and they were in tears…isn't that great?"

Somehow, I suddenly felt Jill had not changed one bit. She seemed to be "for Jill" again. Nevertheless, it was always her way, so I was used to it. Jill left us to join Joy and Martha, just as Kurt rounded the corner with two boutonnières. He knew Will was being "hitched", also, and offered his flower. However, Will thanked Kurt, and then quickly explained it was not the custom of a military uniformed wedding, so he helped put Kurt's boutonnière on his lapel.

Pastor Kefir said, "It's time! Follow me, men…just stand on my left and try not to faint," he chuckled.

Everyone rose up upon Pastor Kefir's entrance. He stopped out in front of his pulpit, as we shuffled around him to our positions on his left. Will stood next to me, Kurt behind Will. Evidently, Kurt was both Will and my best man…it was confusing to say the least without a run through practice. Then Kurt walked down the aisle and disappeared.

The pastor turned and nodded to the organist, who began to play the bridal march. Mom was looking directly at me with tears in her eyes. I suppose this was not in her plans in life for how she envisioned her two children being married; in a strange church, in a strange town. Nevertheless, I knew she would adjust and still be her loving self. Then suddenly, voices of the crowd erupted with a spontaneous "Ohhhh! " sighed just as Joy entered in all her beauty.

When I saw Joy and only her, I could not take my eyes off her. She began her entrance on the arm of Kurt. Joy's dress was a wonderful blue satin, which must have been the custom of her faith. I had never seen a more beautiful woman in my entire life that used no makeup nor any special makeover hairstylist to build her beauty. Joy was already so gorgeous and only then did I really realize her hidden beauties of a model, when she made her entrance.

Then she slowly came to me. When Pastor Kefir joined our hands, my heart began pounding and my knees were weak. Suddenly I had this horrible thought, "What if she suddenly changes her mind?" Then I wanted the ceremony to expedite. Nevertheless, there was more delay to my self-righteousness.

Pastor Kefir motioned for Jill, who may have been a bit quick for being on Dad's arm. She seemed like she was marching to the beat of a Marine band. Maybe her marine training was shining through, as she made it to the alter and Will in double-time. I was rather pleased with her cadence to expedite.

It was a simple wedding. After Pastor Kefir joined Will with Jill, he openly then asked, "Who supports these couples in their marriage?"

Kurt and Dad said, "We do."

Then Dad sat down next to Mother, while Kurt came up beside the two of us as our best man.

Pastor Kefir then took all of our conjoined hands and placed them in his own, and asked Jesus to oversee our lives.

"Jesus, Our Savior, foresee the future of these, your children, and guide them through their lives."

"Persons of our Mennonite faith, relatives, friends, guests, you are welcomed here today to share with Joyce and Greg ...Will and Jill, who wish to share this, a very important moment, in their lives.

"Brought together by Jesus Christ, their love and understanding of each other

has grown and matured, and now they have decided to share their lives together as husbands and wives.

"Joyce Carol Dixon, Gregory Jonathon Wetmore, how do you say when I ask you both, until death do you part, will you both always promise to love, cherish and respect the other, without reservation, in sickness and otherwise, always obeying God's Commandments?"

"We promise!" Joy and I spoke in unison.

"Jillian Demeri Wetmore, William Franklin Char, how do you say when I ask you both, until death do you part, will you both always promise to love, cherish and respect the other, without reservation, in sickness and otherwise, always obeying God's Commandments?"

Jill and Will quickly snapped to military-like attention, almost comically, and spoke loudly in unison with their military jargon, "Sir, we promise, sir!"; quickly enough to make the good pastor retreat one step backward in surprise, then grin. Some in the crowd chuckled and Mom appeared to be as unexpectedly surprised as we were.

The Pastor then reached out and actually touched Will's and Jill's shoulders briefly, admiring their array of individual military medals and ribbons, then looking to them both, he said softly, "You both make us all very proud."

Then we stood by while one woman of the choir sang, "The Ring", our chosen ceremonial song. When she finished, she immediately took out a hand-written sheet of paper, scribbled out for her quickly by Will. She read out loud the four verses to the "Marine's Hymn" as best she could, still trying to sound as if it were being sung, still accompanied by a talented guitarist, who made it seem well rehearsed. It was really moving when we all realized the words and contributions our forefathers had made. It must have been strange to the gathered Mennonites, as it seemed a bit "gung ho". However, they were patriots as well, though a professed group of peace lovers.

When she finished, the entire congregation sang out "Hallelujah!" which echoed and rocked the little stone church.

The pastor nodded for our doubled-up, best man, Kurt, to hand over our rings. Kurt acted as if he did not have those rings, looked worried, patted himself all over continuing his very worried look upon his face, but still not finding them. It was all for the amusement and laughter of everyone, including the wedding party. Kurt even fooled me.

Shortly then, after the pastor raised his arms to quell the loud laughter,

Kurt surprisingly found the rings in his inside pocket to the delight of everyone. He handed them over and then turned to the congregation smiling brightly and making funny faces; his raised eyebrows, moving them up and down like Groucho Marx would have. This was not in our wedding plans, but it was funny. A noticeably relieved sigh could be heard among the laughing. Kurt was joking, of course.

I had seen intermittent flashes during the time we all faced the pastor. Apparently, Martha had moved back with her camera going to record some of the moments, including Kurt's performance.

Pastor Kefir then turned and asked each of us to place our rings upon our loved one's finger with these words, "With this ring, I thee wed."

I could not take my eyes from the lovely face of my betrothed.

When we each had delivered our offered ring to our intended, Pastor Kefir raised his arms above us, just as Charlton Heston had done portraying Moses in the Ten Commandments movie.

"What God hath joined together, let no man put asunder. Speak now, oh objectors and doubting, or forever hold thy peace. With the power invested to me by our Mennonite faith in Jesus Christ, our church, and the State of Illinois, I now pronounce you husbands and wives. You may kiss your brides," the pastor concluded.

We kissed as Mr. and Mrs. Greg Wetmore, officially. Jill hugged and kissed us and Will kissed Joy and we all hugged and shook hands with everybody else who extended their hand or offered their caress. We were all so happy.

When the church bells chimed out loudly, we were smothered in well-wishers. The wedding of five to ten had resulted in a humongous two-hundred-fifty, most strangers to Jill, Will, and me. Nevertheless, they knew Joy and greeted her with their love. Everyone moved next door to the big hall. Joy particularly was surprised that the women of the church had prepared for everyone's meals and had also baked and decorated an enormous, lovely wedding cake. There was more than enough for everyone.

Mom and Dad, with Aunt Margaret, all sat near us at a nice table arranged with fresh cut centerpieces and services. There was no dancing, no alcoholic beverages offered, or drank, just house tea. The guitarist played soft music continually while everyone dined. Overall, the people who loved my wife dearly, had very nicely conjured it up. It was their way of expressing much love for her.

Immediately after the meal, Jill and Will hugged Mom and Dad, then Joy and me good-bye. Jill thanked us for allowing Will and her to join our ceremony, and quickly they were headed off to the airport by taxi, to return to California and their military unit. It was the last time we saw Jill.

Before she left, Mom handed Jill and Will an envelope. I think it was their wedding gift, but Jill whispered something into her ear and forced Mom to keep it. I suppose they couldn't cash a check for that much money where they were headed. That was the first time in my entire life I saw Jill not accept a gift. Jill left us in a hurry with the love of her life, Will looked so in love and happy. I was thrilled for her as some young adults threw rice at them while leaving. I watched that taxi drive out of sight.

After Joy addressed everyone in her congregation with a little "thank you" speech, we hugged Mom and Dad, and received our gift envelope.

Joy then asked to be alone with me behind the church, as she took me by the hand and directed me to her parents' graves.

"Well, Mom and Pop, I know you were here today, cause I felt your love. Here's my husband, Greg, the guy that I've been telling you about every night in my prayers. He loves me and I love him, so you may rest in peace now. I know you waited for this...we're off now...good-bye," Joy spoke so openly that actually I thought there was something she saw.

However, when she closed her eyes and was then drawn up upon her toes, she appeared to have been hugged. I was aghast when I, too, felt I was being caressed lightly. Maybe it was the wind, but I am not so sure now if there isn't a hereafter. I looked at Joy and she just smiled sweetly looking very pleased.

"They love you, too!" she told me.

I took Joy's hand as we scurried past Pastor Kefir, wife Millie, Kurt and Martha and then through a gauntlet of rice and seeds being tossed at us on our way to Joy's Buick. I had to adjust the seat, before I could even slide inside and stood there being pelted by some vigorously thrown kernels, before we finally zoomed off to our apartment. We quickly began picking rice out of our hair between kisses.

"Wasn't that the nicest surprise wedding, Greg? All my friends came to see us hitched up...and Martha made this dress from my mother's gown, but you haven't said how I looked."

"I'm sorry, I thought you could hear my heart pounding, see my smile was so large it was hurting my cheeks, plus notice all the continuous drooling I did over you. I figured that would let you know, but if not, I think you're the most beautiful bride there ever was…I love you," I spoke to ease her of my unintentional inattentive way.

She just interrupted me and nervously rattled on like never before, "I love your Mom and Dad, but it was so sad for Jill and Will," she rattled off even more continuously. "We don't have to head up to Chicago. We can just relax, ha, ha, in our apartment. I'm exhausted already from the tension and maybe someday soon we can take a belated honeymoon vacation. Did you pay the Pastor? I wonder if everyone got the hall cleaned up. Maybe we better go back tonight and check…I promised to leave it clean…I…"

My hand was pushed away when I gently attempted to place my fingers softly to her lips to stop her talking so fast and silly, so then I leaned over and kissed her.

"Hush your sweet lips, and let me worry about everything…Chicago's only a few hours away and we can do and see a lot together there in a few days. Yes, later I'll take you on a real honeymoon, if you don't mind taking the kids, too," I said, looking at Joy, who was then seriously smiling, and also tried to kiss me back. She could not reach me, since I had seat-belted her in tightly. She tugged to get it loose.

"Leave it on, until we get home. I hope I'm not swerving all over," I said, looking at several cars backed up behind us in the rear view mirror.

I suppose they realized we were newlyweds, because many honked and waved while passing. Kurt had decorated the Buick with a "Just Married" sign, some crepe paper ribbons, and some old shoes tied to the rear bumper by twine.

In minutes, we were at our apartment. There was a surprise waiting for us upon our apartment door.

Chapter 10

"What's this?" Joy asked, thinking I had done some sort of honeymoon surprise.

Attached to our door by a piece of duct tape was a colorful envelope. Joy pulled it off, just as Joe Petito unexpectedly popped around the corner, and quickly told us it was a gift from Mr. Valero. Joe just wanted to know we got it, and be assured no one had stolen it, he laughed, and then took off after extending his own congratulations to us.

I scooped up my new wife into my arms and tried to carry her romantically across the threshold, but it was not quite as I had planned. Her sudden hard kiss blinded my vision. Joy accidentally bumped her head on the doorframe, while I twisted to get her and that beautiful satin gown she wore through untorn. I know it hurt. How clumsy could I have been on the most important day of our lives, I asked myself, as I set her down inside, closed the door, and attended to Joy's pain. I tried to kiss her pain away, as Mom used to do for me, but she backed off in pain.

"I'm okay, I'm okay…I'll live…that wasn't what I expected after I'd seen an old Doris Day movie with Rock Hudson doing this, but you gave it your all," she laughed, still rubbing her hand against a rather reddish ear.

I could have died regarding my clumsiness. Joy looked so beautiful, but slightly disheveled, until she pulled her hair ribbons loose and let them fall.

I had caused her big smile to leave, but she caused me to become aroused by her alluring sex appeal. Moreover, when she stretched her body around to relieve her stiffness, I got stiff.

Joy just kicked off her heels and wanted to get comfortable quickly. Therefore, we both headed into our bedroom and put on shorts and tees, in between kisses and a short "touchy-feely" session. We still had boxes on the floor, which held some of Joy's clothes and things, so we went back into the living room and both plopped down upon the couch, exhausted by our emotions.

I honestly thought Joy and I would head up to Chicago immediately and get a honeymoon suite at the Sheridan, where there were always available rooms. Then I would show her the night-lights of the big city. It would be just a simple, short, casually romantic honeymoon, since I had no accrued vacation due me at work to take off for any length of time.

Joy picked up and opened the envelope from Mom and Dad. Her eyes grew wide and they danced back and forth across the check when she saw the number of zeroes on the check. When her jaw dropped open, I looked at it, also. Even I could not have envisioned a present so enormous.

The check was written to Mr. & Mrs. Greg Jonathon Wetmore for one million dollars, with a loving note in Mother's handwriting, which read,

"This is our gift to Greg and Joy, may you always be in love and happy. It was your father's secret investment for a time just like this. We love you both and will expect visits on weekends, as soon as you two lovebirds come up for air. Love, Mom & Dad"

It was a bit of a surprise, I felt, considering Mother seemed too prudish to have written the note that way, but Joy thought it was wonderful. Maybe, I really had not known my mother well at all. Suddenly I realized, too, that all those times Pop was gone on business trips now seemed trivial. I then felt a bit of remorse for me ever criticizing him when I needed him and he was gone. He did it because he was thinking only of me, all the time, and that fatherly love had just shown through.

"Wooo-hoo-weee, are your parents that rich?" Joy shrieked out, 'joyfully', still staring hard at the check, unbelievably surprised as I was.

"I guess, there's proof…they wouldn't do it as an awful joke. I think Jill refused hers at the church. That's her style though…she probably gave her envelope back to Mother in protest for something they did to her long ago, I suppose, as she refused some gifts as a kid when she was pouting a disagreement between my parents and her. I really thought she had dramatically changed, matured," I said, a bit upset at my completely missing her maturing.

"Maybe not…maybe she told your mom to hang on to it until they got back…if they get back," Joy added very softly.

I did not know then how poignant those words were to become.

"Here, you open this bright one," Joy said, then handed me the colorful envelope that had been taped to our door. "Martha told me that there also were other gifts brought to the church for us and she would keep them at her house, until we came back. I think there were some handmade quilts. Remind me, Greg, I'll have to buy thank you notes."

At first, I could not believe this gift, and then remembered Doyle Valero really wanted me to join him at his casino to drain my brains. Besides the two plane tickets to Vegas and a week's free-stay-vacation at his casino-hotel, there also was money in hundred dollar bills, just like Doyle flashed my way before. A note said only, "Congratulations…there's more where this came from"…signed, scribbled with initials only of "DV".

I had to tell Joy the truth about that gift, before showing her the ten thousand dollars accompanying it.

After I told Joy about Doyle's offer, she simply said, "If you don't accept it, I won't mind one bit. Nevertheless, if you do not at least check it out, you will be wondering the rest of your life why you did not at least investigate the situation at his expense. If he really wants you that bad, and it's on the up and up, well, I'd at least look into it."

"I just finished a six-year's, cum laude degree, in five, propelled by my extra hard work to please my parents and self esteem. My only desire was getting to a job just like this. I can't just walk away…I won't even get a paycheck…oh, yeah, this," I said, and stopped short of exploding, when I realized I didn't even need the job with the gift my parents had just given us.

"Hold on, Greg…I didn't say that at all…what I said was only check it out," Joy repeated.

"I took time off myself and I'm almost sure the county will give you the time, especially if Kurt asks. Didn't you say Grub, their engineer, was in charge anyway?"

"Grub…is that his nickname? Humm, dare I ask how he was dubbed that?"

"Grub fit him well in high school. He was always filthy-dirty working with his daddy on machinery. His dad, Chub, was county commissioner back then…that's why he got his job. He only went two years to a community college drafting class when he got his job."

"Let's talk about this tonight," I suggested.

"Nope, tonight, stud, is for lovemaking…remember?" she said, so enticingly alluring to me that I could not resist her. One kiss led to many more and we did not hesitate to go into our bedroom. We came together consummating our vows. We were so in love, we two. I think Joy began praying, as she suddenly broke out whispering in my ear, "Oh God, oh God!"

For the very first time, while inside my apartment, I heard an overhead jet plane leaving Springfield Airport and my thoughts went to Jill and Will leaving to go back to their units in California, then sometime soon flying to Afghanistan. The news on our bedroom TV was about a major offensive push by US troops into Afghanistan. There were more casualties predicted to occur very soon. My inner worries began to sicken my thoughts. Joy noticed my deep thinking very quickly and hit the remote switch to "off", which turned me back on.

No one ever forgets his or her wedding day, especially if it was like ours. I will never forget how absolutely drawn together as one, like magnets, we were. We made love, true love, which only reached the highest heights we never could have attained until then, as man and wife.

When Joy released her passion, unafraid we were doing something wrong, we both blocked out the world around us. Our love for each other grew leaps and bounds, as her lips found mine and mine hers.

During a short interlude, right after a lengthy and rousing lovemaking bout that left us both gasping for air, both so satisfied; we sat up on our bed somewhat embarrassed, somewhat annoyed, when we overheard a voice from a nearby complex neighbor remark loudly, "They've finally stopped!" After that, we always knew the walls had ears.

Our play made us very hungry, so eventually that evening, before closing times, we looked in the phone directory and decided to slip out to one of the many steak houses that are so prominently located near the capital, because the government employees loved to spend their per diems there, Joy told me.

The featured lean, low-cholesterol, Black Angus beef steaks we ordered were every bit as good as advertised, except they were very expensive. Then again, we now could afford them. I just could not seem to adjust my budgetary ways that quickly. Joy then told me she would pay for our first meal together, therefore, I wised up to my miserly ways.

Our newfound, but temporary wealth had not sunk into my brain yet, because I personally was still operating on my college budget, which then I held firm to trying hard not to take advantage of my generous parents. I never imagined that I would reach this financial independence so soon in life. We returned to the apartment and discussed going to Vegas.

I called Joe to ask him what sort of complimentary tickets were the ones his brother-in-law had given us. I also asked how nice of a place was his.

"Hey, he did you right. Looks to me he gave you first class entertainment, a suite, Jacuzzi, full wet bar and threw in first class round trip plane tickets. Too bad he won't be there to show you around."

"What do you mean?" I questioned.

"The so-called big shot just got an invitation to testify before the Illinois House Assembly pertaining to permitting gambling in Chicago...his latest big investment. He thinks he will pull some strings and get permission to set up a Las Vegas-styled casino on the lakefront. Do you realize how lucrative that would be? I bet he greases some palms, huh?"

"I sure hope not. There's too much of that going around," I hesitated to mention to Joe since it was his in-law. I thanked Joe then hung up.

"Humm...maybe we could fly out there for a look-see on his offer after all. I have to get time off, but in the morning, I will call. The flight departure is at one already. Can we get ready by then, honey?" I asked Joy.

Her smile was radiating; her mind was, also.

"I like that honey part. It seems so intimate, yet somewhat domesticated, coming from my new husband. Call me that always. Anyway, sure, I can have our things packed, but I really need new luggage. Mine is so old and worn looking and yours are just duffle bags...I don't think I'd like to be seen with either, walking into a fancy hotel, would you?" she quipped.

"Not really, but there's no time to shop."

"Don't worry about calling Grub, I'll do that right now," she said, looking on her cell for his number, then calling him at home.

"Grub, sorry this is so late, but I need a favor," she asked.

"Who the hell is this at this hour?" he bellowed out, so loud, I could hear.

"This is Joy, silly. I know it's late…look, my new husband, Greg, needs time off this whole week from your project."

"Why? You've what, you're who?" he was confused by his 'Joy-ess' awakening.

"For our honeymoon, that's why, and who, what, where, and how! Yep, Greg and I…we got hitched-up today in Glenarm."

"I didn't know a thing about it…why didn't I get an invite?"

"Sorry, we thought it was only family, so we did not send out any invitations. The church surprised us with a house full."

"You got yourself pregnant, didn't ya?"

"No, stupid…I'm not knocked up!" she said, annoyed, but laughing. "You arrange this for me, got it? You owe me, Grub; you know that, so I'm calling in one of my IOUs. Get her done, son!" Joy told him demanding, yet jovial and then hung up to my complete amusement with a, "Later, bro!"

"What was that?" I asked.

"Grub is like my little bro. Went through school with him since kindergarten. We usually discuss everything. He always calls me at work, or home, and begs me to get things done for him; info on upcoming federal and state grants, applications, borrowing state equipment, those kinds of requests, all via the state, and I have. So now it's payback time…his turn to scratch my back, that's all. He'll do it; he better if he knows what's good for him," Joy told me, so arrogantly sounding.

As it turned out, everything fell into shape quickly using Joy's organizational skills. She called Lila for borrowing luggage, which she set outside her apartment's door, so I could pick it right up that night. Meantime, Joy sorted through our winter clothes but still found suitable clothes for Vegas inside her boxes and my drawers.

When I returned, I was simply amazed by Joy's judgment in clothes. They certainly looked like vacationers' attire; except she included my gray suit and a rather hot mini, and spiked heels that I had never seen her wear. The heels and mini and my suit, she said, were for the Wayne Newton show we now had tickets to attend. Nevertheless, that mini was drawing on my imagination already.

My lovely wife and I found ourselves staying up all night talking and planning. A taxi arrived to take us to the airport.

Come one o'clock, after an easy trek to the airport, we found our first class seats aboard Southwest Airlines, headed west out of Springfield. In only two hours, because we slept while we could, I vaguely heard the captain's voice announce we were arriving and asked everyone to please secure their seat belts. Joy still slept, and had not removed her restraint; I guess she still thought about my warnings.

Soon I felt the sudden sensation of our plane descending, so I nudged Joy to wake her up. She leaned over to kiss me, but then withdrew, trying to hide her breath. She looked for gum in her purse, and chewed it to freshen up her mouth just as we touched down; seemingly unbelieving we had already arrived.

"Oh, what's happening?" Joy sounded out a bit loud and frightened.

"We just landed, honey, dear," I over-emphasized to show her I hadn't forgotten her request.

"Whew! I just woke up…I imagined it was a nine-eleven thing…sorry," she said, as she looked around to other passengers staring at us then looking humiliated.

"Let's go, Osama!" I raised my voice, and then got one of those judo chops my wife was noted for…this time it hurt and the flight attendant asked us to please restrain ourselves.

"We're newlyweds," Joy told her smiling and very cocky. "Ever hear a happy Midwest babe screech like a real Midwest barn owl?" she asked her, and then screeched so loud, even I covered my ears. I could tell she was delighted we were down safely.

It was another "Joy-ess moment", as two U.S. Marshals came out of nowhere and escorted us off the plane. It happened so quickly, including them ordering our suitcases delivered on the double to a secured room to be quickly searched at the airport's police quarters, that we thought during our brisk walk past everyone standing in lines might be a way to expedite by-passing the future airport crowds. When the handcuffs tightened around our wrists, I tried to explain it was a harmless outburst by my happy new wife, not meant to harm anyone, but to no avail.

Instead, we were immediately taken to separate rooms and interrogated by police, both warned our actions weren't as amusing as we thought, but found not a threat to our country.

Nevertheless, the guy said we may be banded from our return trip home and possibly from flying again…all because of a little extra exuberance by my wife and me. We walked outside the airport's perimeter along a street, held on our arms by police officers who pointed to a taxi approaching almost a half-mile away. It was harsh, but after we thought about it a minute, we laughed.

We walked just a few more paces when we heard a commotion behind us. A zooming taxi had nearly hit our police escorts and they cussed him loudly. He wanted to get to us first for a quick fare, I assumed. The cops shook their fists, but did not pursue him as they were on foot. He kindly jumped out, grabbed our grip, and jumped back in very quickly, still looking for those cops to chase him.

"Here's where we wish to go, please," I told the rather foreign-looking cab driver, while holding up and pointing to the Diamond Casino's reservations through his safety glass divider, so he could read it. He had weird music blasting over a walkman earplug in one ear, limiting his hearing.

He glanced briefly at the reservations and just put up an "okay" sign with his fingers. We both fell back as we were whisked away in the back seat of his cab toward the Diamond Casino, and saw its grand marquee ahead in just minutes.

The casino was a huge place. As we approached I mentioned to Joy that I would hate to pay for even one electric bill. I tipped the weird looking driver and was met immediately by the real manager of Doyle's Diamond Casino, Mr. Zorn.

"Mr. Valero told me to expect you two honeymoon lovebirds," he greeted. "He also emphatically told me not once, but twice, I should not spare any expenses…so we'll roll out the Diamond Casino's best red carpet treatment, and hope you'll enjoy your stay and be very satisfied," he said, while also snapping his fingers to direct several baggage persons to haul our grip.

"Follow me, please, Mr. and Mrs. Greg Wetmore," he spoke, as if he were our luxury tour guide. The baggage haulers hustled onto another elevator as we alone rose to the top in another. Those same handlers had beaten us to our suite and had already laid our bags next to a big, colorful, heart-shaped bed. One man asked if he may remove the clothes to the drawers, but neither

Joy nor I wished to show our clothes. They refused any tip I offered them and left at the nod of Mr. Zorn.

I had noticed so much exquisite architecture after we stepped off the elevator, and before we entered our pent house suite, that had been reserved for our honeymoon. Doyle's taste for luxury had no end.

I, of course, looked not only to my lovely wife's wonderful smile concerning our suite; I just had to check out the structures of the entire theater-movie-like atmosphere, and its many structures and designs. It was schooled into me at UIC and I just could not resist asking Mr. Zorn who built the establishment.

"Do you mean the entire works, or original contactor, sir?" Mr. Zorn questioned. "If you mean the building, it was constructed by the Johnston Brothers; the insides have too many face lifts to even imagine one original atmosphere, since 1955."

"Then it was the Erechtheion, a copy of the multi-level, multi-use, ancient Greek temple. It was a fantastic sight to behold, especially in that decade," I told him to his amusement, since managers are subject to every patron's question. He might know that for the next time, I thought.

I had studied its categorization in classes and though not only was it elegantly appealing, it was long lasting, a quite safe building, as most of its kind. Then Zorn informed me with his knowledge.

"Casino owners always meet with much competition among us. It is our livelihood, all this fanfare for one's just share of that almighty dollar. Which I might add is very significant here, if I do say so myself.

"Therefore, Mr. Wetmore, you should not be surprised to learn that Vegas is always reinventing itself every few years. That is the norm. In its history, Vegas' outstanding fronts, which have all been imploded like the Aladdin, Sands, Dunes, Stardust, Landmark, Hacienda, El Rancho, and Desert Inn, are gone," he breathlessly rattled off. "The Moulin Rouge, our first racially motivated and integrated casino somehow burned down. Therefore, yes, there is an awful lot of architecture work ongoing here, constantly changing our faces."

It suddenly occurred to me how much talent was needed and how ever challenging it must be for the engineers here. I noticed several high tower cranes atop new construction. Then the pinch on my behind told me someone was not as enthralled by all this architecture as I was.

"Ouch!" I squealed out to a surprised Zorn.

"I hope you'll find everything to make your stay a 'Joy'," he said, smiling at my seemingly impatient wife.

Then a server entered our doorway with a meal for two, pheasant under-glass, and champagne on ice.

"I hope you won't mind that I took the privilege…enjoy!" Zorn said, while exiting backwards and closing the double doors behind him.

"What a wonderful place…those little cupids and the red hearts are carved into the wood… this bed's big enough for an orgy… but would you look at this meal…I thought he'd never leave," Joy spouted out quickly, as she slowly eased around the bed like a sexy temptress, crawled across the bed, then up to me.

To tease me, she reached out, pulling on my pant's zipper with a look of serious lust.

"I'm hungry, let's eat!" she shouted out laughing, at my downhearted frown and the bulge in my pants from anticipation. Then she kicked off her shoes.

"Come here, my baby doll…momma will fix everything once momma gets her tummy full," she spoke to me almost whimpering, as if I were her disappointed child. This was a side I had never seen of her, but it really turned me on.

I let things settle down before I managed to remove the food off the cart and trays and sat them on the dining room table.

"Why do you think that guy didn't have the server do that in the first place?" Joy asked.

"Because someone pinched me on the butt in front of him and he may have thought that meant he was intruding…so taking the hint, he left. I bet he comes back with more tickets though, because he had some in his hands. I bet he forgot."

"Well, I got Mr. Valero's gift tickets for Wayne Newton's Show on Tuesday, so what more can we use?"

"I think Marie Osmond would be a good show; I saw hers on one marquee. I saw one called "Sin City Bad Girls", also. I wonder what that's all about."

"Oh yeah, big stud! Well just wait until I finish this meal…then you'll know first-hand about that sin city bad girl stuff!" she told me, looking a bit miffed that I would want to see another woman's naked body except hers. She crunched down on a celery stick from a veggie dish so hard that I crossed my legs hoping she wasn't pretending that was mine.

I would have hated to have had to pay the bill for our meal, two fabulous, huge pheasants, but since it was on Doyle's tab, we cleaned up everything, including the wine. Joy got tipsy and had to pee just as she began to get frisky. She left me to go to the john, but hollered out to me so loudly that everyone in the hotel could probably hear her tell me that it was the most beautiful john in the world. I knew she was loosing it. She called me, "Come quick!"

I ran to her; she was still sitting down.

"What the heck is this I'm sitting on? It squirts me in the butt every time I sit down and now I have to go bad, but I'm afraid I sat on some kind of sink."

"Oh, you frightened me. That's a bidet. That is actually a French douche. Best go on that one, it's regular. You can let go on it, I think, but then pull that chain. It will flush, and then wash your behind, or even your pussy, but I don't know how to do that…can I watch?" I asked her laughing.

"Get out! Get out!" Joy begged, now feeling she could wait no longer. As I closed the bathroom door I heard her feet shuffle over to the toilet, go, then flush. Then she went back to the bidet. After a few minutes, Joy came out smiling.

"What's so grand?" I questioned.

"I want one of those things in our new house, someday. For once, I feel clean, inside and outside. Huh, those French think of everything, don't they? I love their French fries and French toast, too."

That conversation was so unsophisticated between the two of us, I felt somehow closer to her than ever. I was beginning to realize that Joy possessed Martha's unwitting, loving ways by living together. Neither Martha nor Joy doubted their man. That is what I liked the most. Then there was her fire!

She downright seduced me before she even touched me there. I was already so hot from her sudden advancing, gyrating foreplay moves, but when her perfume fragrance crossed my senses, I became much too excited. It was like an aphrodisiac. I could not help myself or restrain my strong loin feelings, even if I could have. I let go in only seconds, telling her it was her "Coffee!"

"Well, that was certainly quick! I knew you liked that perfume, but…I might not wear that again if I'm really horny next time," she teased.

"I'm sorry…I," I started to explain.

"I'm not...I'm still sore from last night and to tell you the truth, that bidet thing was a bit exciting," she laughed. "I'm going back now to use it again!" she told me unequivocally as she rose up and left me.

Never in my life would I have expected that to happen to me, but Joy was very captivating to me anyway, so just a soft spray of that perfume sent my senses into overdrive. I became ashamed that I even thought of that other woman. Joy was always bursting of womanly behavior that made my life exhilarating.

After her moment of freshening up, we lay across our bed, side by side, and both fell asleep while kissing.

A soft chime woke me up. It was the bedroom phone. I answered, and it was Mr. Zorn. He asked me if everything was fine, also, if he should send up our dinner. Otherwise, we could dine in the dining room. We chose one more secluded feast in our suite.

"Mr. Zorn, my wife and I are having an unforgettable time...thank you, and please give our compliments to your chef. Would you please use your expertise again to surprise us with a light dinner?" I asked, not knowing what to order, since Joy was asleep. I knew she would be very hungry after she awakened.

"Certainly! Aren't you really hungry?"

"Actually, a club sandwich and maybe a vegetable soup would suit my tastes well."

"I shall have the chef build your meals around that suggestion for six?"

"That would be fine, thank you," I told him.

Then he told me he would place a player's pass credit card for us under the napkin. "When you decide to leave your suite, please remove the 'do not disturb' sign to allow our house cleaners to freshen up your room. Good luck at the tables...everything you win is yours to keep...enjoy!"

Joy awoke sometime while I spoke with Mr. Zorn, but kept her eyes shut.

"You chose exactly right, Mr. Wetmore. That shows you have good taste."

"Marrying you shows I have excellent taste, honey," I emphasized to please her.

We began to play around a bit, we just could not get enough of each other's love it seemed, but we were interrupted by the server's knock with our meals. This time he set the dining table with fresh silverware and brought out nice club sandwiches served with bowls of shitake mushroom soup, not vegetable, and more tender garnished veggies.

For desert, key lime pie alamode or chocolate devils food cake. We feasted again, but subsequently Joy said we had to get out and walk, or she would absolutely burst from all the wonderful food we had eaten. We dressed in shorts and tees and ventured out into the casino.

"Let me see that credit card," Joy told me, then confronted a man looking like a security person on how to use the card.

"Lucky you! Just choose the game you wish to play and hand the card to the croupier. He'll keep track. At the slots just ask one of the girls for some quarters or halves…enjoy your stay," he told her.

"Boy, he was nice…they're all nice…which first?" Joy needed to know.

"I like the look of those slots," I said.

"Okay, let's go for it!"

We felt badly losing money right off, so we did not use that card very long. We had quickly racked up $4,000 in one hour's losing, thinking we could come back. Good thing it was at Doyle's expense. We could see some smiles of winners, but the later it got, those smiles seemed to turn to frowns of losers…big time losers.

Then Joy said we should see the city lights at nighttime during the week. She just wanted to rent a convertible and cruise. We gambled and drank fancy sounding gratuity drinks, which helped ease losses, but hurried them also as the first thing that goes with being intoxicated is your loss of judgment, next your morals.

We held our own, until midnight at black jack, and split money mostly. Next, we listened to a stage show comedian at the Diamond Casino's lounge. His inside jokes were based on his losses at the tables and that is why he said he had to work off his losses as a comedian, free, until he paid off his entire debt in four hundred years. That brought some laughs, but I think worries from many others. Yes, it was very lucrative to own a fancy casino, even the workers faired very well. Nevertheless, it was all those "once happy people" who left the casino with that horrible look on their faces of destitution that really got to me; and there were many.

Las Vegas never sleeps and every so often very unexpected things occur during those wee hours of the morning. After the older crowd leaves the ten o'clock shows and go to bed back at their hotels, it is much easier to navigate everywhere. We were walking the strip, enjoying the lights of the many marquees, holding each other close in the cool breeze, when Joy stopped several times to listen to music being sung loudly, but she couldn't tell from where. She seemed very happy.

The Gas House was a well-lit establishment that promoted country music songs sung by "wanna-be" singers, just like the karaoke joints back home, except they had live musicians, very capable of playing almost every country song. I guess that was why it was so appealing to the contestants, who were later voted as best of the evening by the crowd. They received one hundred dollars prize money, but also received a video clip of their performance. My Joy seemed to be tapping her feet and humming along, drawn to the beat of an old song by the Stattler Brothers called "Elvira".

"Gitty-up, um papa, mou mou"…she suddenly turned to walk backwards in front of me and began singing louder and punching me softly in the gut to the beat. Of course, I was thrilled, because I had never really heard her sing like that so openly before nor knew that she secretly always wanted to be a singer. Nevertheless, all these punches were causing wonder to me if she might be having second thoughts about being "hitched". I was wrong.

Joy just never had an opportunity like this or the guts, until one big Mai Tai from the bar inside the Gas House gave her all the fortitude she ever needed to step onto that stage. That big step suddenly led our honeymoon in a different direction.

The house spotlight had caught her dancing and singing out loudly to "Silver Threads and Golden Needles" being sung pretty well, but not great, by a contestant on stage. Joy was more or less committed to be next. Our social lives would never be the same.

The energized, yet challenging crowd's catcalls and shrieks coaxed Joy up there into the bright stage lights. The liquor pushed her over the edge, eliminating all of her fears, so she really cut loose. She was an immediate sensation, especially to the men. After just one rendition of her own-styled, "Midnight at the Oasis", not really country, but sung so softly and sexy, men moved closer to the stage. While I knew she only looked lovingly at me; a song like that which she knew well and then performed so arousing and sexy, even I was tempted to attack her; she became a star, literally.

After begs from many in the crowd for an encore, Joy sipped another

Mai Tai given her by the establishment, then told everyone she never liked to repeat herself, so she'd sing something else.

"Any requests?" she asked like a pro, while still sipping her free cocktail placed next to her on a tall stool. She held it gently and sipped, revealing her shapely figure as I had only seen it in the bedroom. That spot lighting was meant for highlighting singer's silhouettes and hers was more than just very appealing.

I was stunned and commenced to worry. After all, I had known Joy for such a short time. Could I have been wrong about her? No, I just could not have, I told myself. Were times like this going to happen continually? I moved closer to Joy.

Several dark-suited men had moved to the side of the stage and told the band to play a current hit, so they could better judge her talents. Joy was leery and moved away from them, until she spotted me near the front of the stage. She winked at me.

Thrilled when asked by those same men to sing them just one more song, Joy looked to me. I was all for that and shook my head yes. However, I thought they might be Mafia, talent agents, or the owners. She told them she might if she knew it.

For her, they chose "Jesus, Take the Wheel", by Carrie Underwood, if she could sing it. I knew she could pull that off, because I heard her do it in the shower, but then this was not the shower.

Joy moved around that stage and slayed them all, as if she owned them, and then left the stage with the crowd wanting more. Joy simply walked back up to the mike and said, "Next!" I think she had sobered up a bit.

Then she jumped right off that stage into my arms. I was the most envied man in the joint, they said. That is what the four men who followed us outside told me wanting to discuss business with Joy about her singing voice. They actually were local theatrical agents who booked lead-in singers to begin the real performances, killing time before the big star showed. I was thankful they were talent scouts, not the Mafia hit men that crossed my mind they might be. Joy was as brief as her stage exit denying them. It was a short, "No, thank you!" and we left.

They did not follow her this time, but hollered out several offers to her for Joy to be used only in certain best casinos, become her agent, and one offer assuring her that she would eventually get big money and become a big star.

Joy smiled from ear to ear, never answering nor looking back. She would later tell me it was the dream of her life to perform as she did. I hoped she would never stop smiling. She took my arm, held me closer and we both just kept walking back to the Diamond.

I think Joy's moment in the limelight was all she ever wanted. Just to be noticed and revered as a good singer.

"Greg, you'll never believe this, but as a kid after my parents were killed, I've danced with door handles singing to music, danced on the bed with a brush as my mike singing to music…pretending to be a star on stage to find any happiness from my loneliness. I knocked their socks off, didn't I?" she asked grinning.

"Mine, too, honey!" I added.

"Guess what, honey bun," she laughed. "No, I like Greg much better than honey bun…but it was for you only that I did it. I wanted you to see me, not as that secretary behind a desk you call at work to get things done, but someone else, a woman, a woman you find alluring and attractive…someone you'll love forever."

"Man, I must have been doing horrible in bed, huh? I was so hot looking at your bod and moves, because you are so hot. Where have you been? I couldn't love you more than ever…you succeeded."

"You know, you're not conceded or you'd realize how good looking you really are. I bet girls just fall at your feet, huh?"

"No, not a nerd like me…at least none ever fainted in front of me," I laughed. "But you…you are the only one that does everything for me," I assured her. Then I remembered a song. "I only have eyes for youoooo dearrr!" I sang off-key to Joy as part of a short romantic serenade.

It must have worked because she took my hand and placed it upon her heart.

"Feel that? That's what you do for me," Joy said, while also moving in to press her lips to mine. Yes, her heart was pounding, but so was mine; even faster, when her soft lips connected mine. It was a mutual admiration going on for sure.

We spent the early hours of our second day making each other feel very wanted. About noon, after only a few hours sleep, we awoke to an overhead jet taking off. That was the first we had even heard. We decided we had better look around this den of iniquity, since that was the "why" it was free and all this special attention given us. Therefore, when Mr. Zorn called to our room to ascertain if we needed anything, I asked him if someone would please show us around. He was delighted.

"I wondered if you might ask that. I have just the person; Monique is here and is very familiar with our organization. May I suggest one o'clock, so you beat the crowd?"

"Sure, what's her title?" I asked, because I wanted more than a tour. I wanted answers to every question that presented itself.

"She's my lovely wife," he reluctantly admitted. "She likes the stage and goes by her stage name Monique. Her real name is Shirley, but calls herself Monique. She dances at a friend's nightclub for her robotics exercise, she says. I like the way she keeps herself in top shape for a fifty's babe. Monique knows the inside-out of our organization. By the way, Mr. Valero just called and asked how you were doing. So, how do you like our palace so far?"

"As I told you last night, it's a wonderful gift to us for our honeymoon and we really are enjoying our stay. Ask me again after your wife clues us in."

It should have stirred my attention into having him define "organization" but it somehow slipped past. I assumed he meant their casino's operation. It would be most of my responsibility to make decisions based only on the logical knowledge I gained from Monique and our tour, I thought.

The lovely Monique met us in the lounge. She sat sipping on a yellow, frozen daiquiri, but left it on the bar to greet us. She wore black pants and silky-looking blouse that flared open at the top. She was trim, all right, and it showed that she worked out. Nevertheless, it became apparent the Nevada sun left deep wrinkles in her face when she wasn't smiling that she just could not hide. Or was it something else, like drugs? Joy, however, immediately told her how lovely she was and those two hit it off.

"Congratulations on your marriage. I hope this doesn't interrupt your schedule. Nevertheless, I think you might find this interesting enough to make you want to be a part of this place. Let's start with Tony here; he's in charge of fourteen bartenders, some on call part-time."

Tony smiled, but did not quit pouring the liquor to several customers I recognized as being there the night before.

It was a grand tour filled with offices, security cameras by the dozens and unexplained devices with monitors that I was afraid controlled certain equipment, such as roulette wheels.

Everything was high tech and out of my expertise, which I felt might influence Mr. Valero that I could be of no help to him. I was feeling pretty good and the girls were discussing their men. I hoped one was me.

Monique took us to a more quiet corner of the building which was filled with all sorts of contraptions…mostly boxes with hollow bottoms. Then she pushed that button of no return.

"I guess you know what you're here for," she told me stopping in front of a steel door about two-feet thick. It slid quietly open, revealing two armed men with AK-47s. They apparently were guarding the wealth of the business, I thought, and I expected a bank vault full of those one hundred dollar bills Mr. Valero threw at me, but stacked to the ceiling.

There was…Monique picked up several bundled hundred dollar stacks and dropped them back, showing us millions that were conveniently wire-tied onto pallets, maybe more. When Monique motioned for those same men to push another hidden button, a secret door opened for an elevator that took us down deep. It took several minutes it seemed, until Monique advised us, "Of course, this is where you make your final decision. If you deny, we need not look any further," she said, rather clandestine sounding. I noticed an old black and yellow, radioactive bomb shelter sign from the early fifties, placed high over a huge green door.

It was then I felt threatened and realized we could never be found so far beneath the Earth, if they had plans to do away with the both of us. I was certain, if I refused, we were dead. Nevertheless, I still could not figure why they even needed me. I knew nothing of electronics.

I decided to act very interested for the safety of my wife.

"Nothing is free," I whispered to remind myself, but Joy overheard it.

Then the big green door slid open. Exposed to my sight and burning nostrils was an underground factory full of a cloudy mist, very warm, with more armed guards overseeing people who appeared to be illegal alien workers. Everyone wore gas masks, but we had none. My skin crawled.

"You will see our operation is multi-faceted and making a plethora of drugs. The black shit is tar cocaine, the white is pure, the crystal is meth," Monique spoke fluently for the person I assumed was a Mexican bozo.

"What, no grass?" I laughed, which didn't amuse her one iota.

"We leave that to the amateurs," Monique smugly informed me, with a grimaced look.

I realized this was Doyle Valero's real so-called casino. Above was his cover-up for this, which was really making him filthy rich; tar cocaine and heroin, both unfamiliar substances to me. Everyone looked high and I was beginning to feel nauseous, so was Joy.

I then had to become an academy award winning actor, and Joy suffered through my roll playing, the roll of an enthusiastic future partner. I was in disbelief…I had been such a fool. Now what?

"Wonderful!" I began. "Slave trade going on for more profitability…okay, but we need more…say about thirty, all women, we can control them easier… to relieve the sick ones. We won't kill them. We will give them a hard cash retirement. Thirty thousand will shut them up and we'll start getting a run on the border to get here…production could rise thirty, fifty percent.

"And do away with electrical bulbs and get compact florescent lighting here…it's environmentally safe…let's go with solar from the roof and …solar cooling, also, it maintains a constant temperature, better for making good shit and giving our workers a happier place…happy workers make more product and more product means more money…got that down?" I said, turning to Monique.

I caught her off guard with my observations and demands, but she seemed delighted I was being more considerate of her fellow compatriots. I think my immediate observations averted any thought of hers to kill us any time soon. She thought I was very wise, but we were not out of the "deep shit" just yet.

"Doyle says you are an engineer, so I guess you're really in…you saw the packaging and mule boxes. He wants your input on more kinds, much more inventive; he wants engineering tricks to disguise and conceal the shit. We have run out of new ideas. We have been hit several times by DEA out on the roads delivering lately…he wants you to come up with a group of genius engineering ideas for concealable ways to transport," Monique told me ostensibly convinced I was in.

As she continued to clue me in about the operation, I remembered reading that down in Florida at an airport, police who were hired to watch for smugglers simply did not see anything when handed $50,000 just to turn their heads. I guess times had changed and I was getting a fortune to invent. Joy was getting very uneasy.

Monique was more heavily involved than I even imagined. She was in charge of this organization's receiving and distribution. Her brother, Rafael, was a drug cartel lord across the border. She was just one of his distributors in the states.

Doyle provided the storage below in his casino's convenient, once-used government's underground bomb shelter. He used it for his remanufacturing set-up, of cutting, mixing and diluting the product, to skim his share off the top. Those abducted aliens did it for him.

Most of Rafael's ill-gotten gains were being cut down to a lesser strength anyway. Doyle was first in line and offered a better quality, even though it was cut down. It was Doyle's idea to start up this factory here to avoid being caught nearer the border where Mexican officials and Mexican prisons meant certain death if caught. Apparently, it was working here in Vegas.

"I'll need time," I told Monique. "I will have to go back home and quit my job with the State of Illinois, so I won't draw any attention. I signed a binding contract."

"Doyle arranged for you to keep your job. He only needs your brainy ideas, he told me. He has plans for you later on Lake Michigan when his new casino is allowed."

When I saw my wife's fiery, blue eyes, opened to twice their size and her jaw dropped wide open in disbelief, I squeezed her hand and put my arm around her to prevent an outburst that was sure to erupt from her. Monique also noticed her discontent. I whispered to her to pretend that she liked it, right after I asked Monique how the ventilation worked and asked to get away because my nostril hairs were curling. She agreed to tell me outside the green door. We hurried outside.

"It's not very good in there, I agree. However, after awhile you get high, then it's not so bad. You can get a cheap high just watching those spics rolling up those packages," as she referred to them, herself of Mexican decent. "However, the boiling shit and the fuel oil smell here are so bad sometimes we lose one or two people a month."

"You mean they quit?" I unwisely asked.

"Yeah, they quit on life," she said, very derogatory about my ignorance.

"Here, take this money...you know as much as you need to know right now. Talk to Doyle...here, take this, it's yours," Monique said, again, when I was reluctant to accept anything. "I'll generate your suggestions right away. You will be figuring out the voltage necessary to run your ideas, won't you? I like it that you care for people. We are going to get along very well, you, Joyce, and me…here. Joyce, say something. You look sick."

When I looked at her, Joy was greenish around her lips and before we could move, she took three quick steps and then hurled into a nearby trash receptacle.

"Girl has style," Monique told me.

Monique pounded on a small door, opened it, and then she hollered out for someone to remove the trash immediately. Soon a very young boy came from that room to do it. He must have been about seven. As the door swung open, I could see other kids sitting and watching kids programs on a big screen TV.

"Who are they, rookie recruits?"

"Some are the workers' kids. Some are orphans of dead workers. I take good care of them."

"See that you do. They need sunshine and to play outside away from the smell."

"I guess, but I can't let them run free."

"Order some seven-foot tall cyclone fence from Sears…a hundred yards linier feet. They can install it quickly. Get some balls to kick around. And find them an old retired school teacher on pension who loves to teach kids."

Her eyes showed more satisfaction than Joy wanted to see from her.

"Look, Monique, if we're going to be good friends you'll have to know Greg is mine," Joy surprisingly blurted out in jealousy.

Monique smiled and told her she was happily married and that I was not her type anyway. Humm, it seems again I was told I was not another girl's type just not so long ago.

Monique led us upstairs via steps to show us one of the escape routes, just in case we were there when one of the mixes exploded, she told us. The steel spiral staircase went around and around, straight up, but was not bad…it might have been faster than the elevator. Then there was this tunnel, she said, but did not take us there, only pointed to it. It supposedly ran underground from a dried up old hand-pumped cistern well, several hundred yards out in a tumble-weed field.

"It's that old dry well over there, see it?" she pointed. "You grab the pump handle and lift. That opens up to a ten-foot drop, but there is a ladder. I have never used it because I never had to. There are rattlers and stickers out there, watch out. Some of the new workers come in with bites and scrapes. The spics come in that way sometimes. Inside the well is the entrance."

Then Monique led us back to the casino's bar and Mr. Zorn. She kissed him as he delivered up some iced rum and coke in glasses he thought would clear our heads, he told us. It was soothing to our thirsts, but did nothing for our skin's icky feeling and the smell of our clothes.

"So, that's your type," Joy told Monique, to her husband's complete confusion.

"Yep, he's my hombre. Are you going over to see Wayne tomorrow night?" Monique asked Joy to her surprise.

"I think so…we have tickets," Joy told her looking to me. "I'd really like to see some big country show while we're here," she added.

"Vamanos, let's go!" Monique shouted. "How about us treating you two to Rascal Flatts, at seven, por favor? You cannot get more southern gringo than that!" she squealed laughing.

"You got tickets?" Joy asked very excited.

"Ah chee wa-wa! Do I have tickets? Of course, senora…anything for the lovely senora and her handsome senor," she spoke, with a sudden turn to her Spanish heritage.

"How many times I got to tell you to be more refined and speak only English?" Mr. Zorn told Monique.

"Besa mi coola!" she replied angrily. "These are our new amigos, stupido!"

Up went his hands in surrender to his wife, and then he said somewhat angrily in reply, "She'll never learn…puta!"

I knew "puta" meant whore in Spanish somehow from Mexican students in college, so we excused ourselves and dashed off before a real rumble began.

"I'll call you!" Monique yelled to Joy, laughing then at our departure caused by them.

Our room was sparkling and there were several freshly cut bouquets of gorgeous flowers. There was a note. "Welcome aboard" and signed Doyle.

"Now how in the heck did Doyle know we were aboard so quickly?" I asked Joy.

"We're not!" she emphatically remarked.

"I know that, but they don't. I'm wondering how Doyle got my job stayed," I said first, while then opening the briefcase given to me.

"Holy shit, Mother…look at this!" I accidentally let out being stunned after seeing all the money in the case.

It must have been my salary for the whole year, I told Joy, who then grabbed it away from me, closed it, and sat on top of it on the bed without looking at it.

"Now, lookie-here, buster…I didn't marry a drug dealer…or, or a rotten crook," Joy said sounding shaken, shuddering in disgust. "We have to give this back and go home now."

"We can't…not because I don't want to, but we have to get to Doyle first and talk. Let's just use up our honeymoon stay and give it back to him in Springfield, where the climate is safer. I learned to never discuss business on your competitor's home ground."

My little darling turned her back on me and then quickly turned back to me.

"All right! Let's just enjoy our honeymoon, Greg, and when we get back to Springfield, we'll call the FBI and turn them all in."

I knew that was not a good idea, yet, but let it slide without objection. I decided I could not let that case out of my sight, so it went everywhere with me from then on.

The phone chimed and it was Homer Zorn. It was the first he mentioned his given name. He and Monique would be meeting us at 5PM for dinner in the dining room there in the casino. Then afterward we'd all be off to see a Rascal Flatts show, as we planned. Monique wanted to talk with Joy. They discussed what they would wear and Joy was glad she had her mini along. Somehow, the extreme tension we just experienced made us less playful. We both showered separately, before we caught some Zzzzs together on that big heart shaped bed. At four, we arose and got ready to meet the Zorns.

"Well, how do I look?" Joy asked me, after she stepped from the bathroom in her evening's attire. She looked magnificent in her silky blue blouse, high heels, and that mini.

"Next to that nightie you wore yesterday, this really turns me on. I don't know if I want all the eyes on you, except mine. I have to be the luckiest dude in Vegas," I said, and I meant it.

Joy looked so different in makeup; more city-like than the little Midwest church-going girl I first met and loved. I kept thinking we might have taken longer to get acquainted and eventually marry, because of all the sudden surprises Joy was constantly astonishing me with. Nevertheless, every one of those instances was so perfect; therefore, my mind was put at ease, as I now admired my excellent choice in women.

"Gosh, you didn't have much to say about my negligee, last night. I'm surprised if you even noticed it after I bought it just for you," Joy said seemingly bothered.

"Well, gosh yourself. Sometimes a guy is so bowled-over by beauty there are no words to describe his feelings…you were gorgeous…still are gorgeous…you'll always be gorgeous…it wasn't on you more than two seconds anyway," I chuckled.

"Okay…what color was it?" she asked, but I just could not accurately recall.

"Ah, it was red…no, black…dark!"

"It was pink…so how observant are you anyway?"

"The lights were off! Silly girl…I only felt its softness for those moments before your loving arms wrapped around me…wow! What a nice thought! Look, I think I'm getting hard just looking at you. Will you kiss me?" I asked to appease her obvious let down.

"The day you have to ask that is the day you'd better find another woman. I think it's going to be a long evening since I, too, have that feeling inside of me right now seeing you all decked out lookin' so handsome like this…you're a hunk, brother. Except for that ugly case you're carrying around when we go anywhere."

"I don't want to be your brother…that's called incest!" I told her.

"Then, boy, are we in trouble now," Joy laughed.

Then we quickly found each other's lips for a few strong moments of bliss.

"Stop! I don't have time to redress," Joy cautioned me, pushing me away, so I would not mess up her hair. "Oh why did we tell them we wanted to go out?" she moaned, whining as if she were a child not wanting to go to school.

"Rascal Flatts, remember? We'll have fifty years after tonight, hopefully with moments like this always. One day when we're old and gray we'll remember how we wanted to stay in our room tonight. I love you, my beautiful darling; I always will and when we get back here, look out!" I told her, as she backed away smiling from my advancing hands that were searching her body.

Joy was uncomfortably getting hotter with each loving touch and affectionate word I spoke to her. Her eyes were following my lips and I could see Joy felt the same way about me as I did about her. It was a match made in heaven, I thought.

Then my mind wandered to how I was going to get out of the mess with Doyle. Our emotions immediately cooled down when I bumped that money case and unconsciously mentioned his name in disgust, "Doyle!"

Her eyes closed and she turned her back on me. "You think we'll be all right?"

"I don't know. Never in my wildest dreams could I have dreamt this happening. I pictured us happily married with kids. How could this even happen? It never happens this way in the wildest movies. It is so bizarre. But, don't worry, God will guide us…I'm counting on Him," I told Joy to help her understand that I was not only sorry, but was never thinking I could become a criminal.

Chapter 11

Rascal Flatts was tremendous. The talent they had just flowed into the crowd and back again with the audience cheering and clapping to their music. Their performance was much too short for us, as they really were very entertaining. Our biggest surprise came when Monique took Joy and me backstage to meet them all. Joy got an autographed group picture with hugs.

Monique was acquainted with everyone who performed, only because she had access to everyone on the strip. Homer said he quit following Monique to those backstage sessions a long time ago, so he remained at our front row table. When we returned, Homer was plastered. I helped him out to the limo that waited for us and we settled in for a ride back to the Diamond.

With Homer almost passed out, I thought he was crowding us, but it was Monique who was pushing on my leg at every opportunity to let me know she was available and hot to trot. I figured that out when her toes ran up my pants leg, while Joy looked out at the many marquees still flashing on the strip. Finally, Monique gave up when I ignored her and we arrived at the casino.

The door to their apartment was just off the front desk in the lobby. Surprisingly, their home was smaller than our suite. I helped undress Homer down to his suit pants when he just fell face down on his bed and laid there passed out.

"He's out for the night. Hope you two had fun…sorry about him," she said while peering down over her shoulder at him.

Joy hugged Monique, as did I. However, Monique took a feel of my rump while Joy was still watching. Joy did not say anything until we got up to our room.

"That was uncalled for," Joy said, in an angry voice. "That woman is after you…she better stand clear or she'll feel my number six up her butt hole!" she continued irately.

"I have no clue what set you off like this…what the heavens are you talking about?"

"Why didn't you say something when she squeezed your behind?"

"It felt good!" I laughed, which brought out more of her ire, along with that old familiar judo chop of hers. This time I saw it coming.

I caught my girl's arm and after a near miss, we fell onto the bed haphazardly, tumbling around playfully, trying to get control of the other. Joy finally ended up on top of me, because I let her, of course, straddling my hips, trying to hold me down like a wrestler. I simply let Mother Nature take over as she saw through her own jealous tirade. We loved each other and it was all for naught, her sudden unhappiness, then she kissed me hard enough to know just that.

"Oh, well, she'll have to take seconds," Joy said firmly, but jokingly, rising up to begin frantically unbuttoning my shirt and tugging at my belt buckle.

"Wait!" I beckoned her, holding her back. "Let's neatly hang up our clothes, go shower, because I can still smell that gassy stuff in my nostrils, can't you? Then we'll come back here and set this bed on fire!" I said wildly, feeling her up to further entice her already aggressiveness.

Without so much as a word, we both jumped up to shower, but suddenly detoured to try the Jacuzzi. I stripped down almost as fast as Joy. When she bent over naked to ease into the bubbling hot water, I thought as a man, I had gone to heaven. I was wrong…it happened next in that Jacuzzi.

"How could you ever believe I would even look at another woman, if I had you to come home to?" I began.

"Shut up and take it like a man," my wife told me. It was that night we'd always remember for sure.

The morning came at three o'clock in the afternoon. Homer had not called to wake us up, nor had there been a knock on our door for breakfast or lunch. I thought my head wouldn't stop pounding. It was quite an eventful night and my wife lay sleeping curled up like a baby next to me. I stroked her body gently, until she began to be irritated by my touch. Then she had her little episode of trying to make me as jealous as she was.

Joy became restless in her sleep, apparently from my touching her there. Anyway, that's what she pretended.

"Oh, Clint, take me now, take me now!" she garbled, causing me concern; enough to push her can off the bed onto the rug. She rolled over laughing at my boyish mistrust and I saw my way of being jealous was just as ignorant as hers.

"Now we're even…I'm hungry enough to eat a cow!" Joy said, still sprawled out upon the floor. She was very alluring lying there naked and she wanted to be.

I slid down to her, placing my hands to brace her firm rear and we again used our honeymoon bedroom to its fullest. At six, we had filled all of our needs and were starving. I called down and a person I did not know took our dinner request.

"Is this for four or six people?" he needed to know for extra dinner service. I guess he didn't know just how hungry we had become. Anyway, it was suggested we place that case in the casino's vault and retain the receipt, which was a big relief.

We were a moment late getting a taxi to see Wayne's show. However, so was Wayne, as he himself had fallen behind in schedule. He had met with his best fan club members from Jersey and he could not disappoint them, so they all followed him to his show. It was jammed, but we still had our front-table cocktails poured right away. We were handed two handsomely signed autographed pictures of Wayne Newton as we were seated. I tipped the waiter for his superior promptness, however all I had time to say to him before he moved on so quickly was "Danke schon!" I spoke loudly then, over the beginning of the performance's music.

However, both Joy and I busted a gut laughing immediately when the waiter attended to the persons seated at the table right next to us. It was a couple from India; he looking sophisticated in his black suit and white turban and she, dressed to the nines, exposing a diamond dot between her dark eyebrows, as I suppose was their custom. When that same waiter had finished pouring their drinks, the man stood up, bowed ever so politely, and spoke to him in Indian lingo, no one could understand but his wife. He gave the waiter a small tip, and then said, as I had, but with gusto, "Donkey shit!"

That waiter, a foreign-looking person himself, was taken aback by the Indian's derogatory remark and small change tip. He stood there for a moment frowning with his hand still out, staring at the twenty-cent tip given to him. He quickly took back the pictures of Wayne, and stuck out his tongue at the Indian as he left.

After he questioned the waiter's anger, the Indian was told by others seated near him of exactly what he had spoken out so loudly to the waiter in English. That poor man eased way down into his seat, looking very embarrassed. His name was Hajji, I heard his wife call out to him in disgust.

It was around eleven when we returned to the Diamond Casino. I could not help but notice a black person wearing a bright chartreuse suit, seated at one slot machine. He was frantically pulling the hell out of that one-armed bandit as fast as he could. It was almost comical; until I found out that he had lost his lucky silver dollar to that machine and he just had to have it back.

"Please, Dear Lord, don't let me lose my daddy's last gift to me, please, Dear Lord, hear me," he kept repeating each time he'd pull that arm down and he hadn't won. It became depressing to me. "This machine took my father's last gift to me," he said to us, with tears in his eyes when we moved in closer. He took a deep breath and continued frantically.

I spotted Monique near a dice table and told Joy to come with me. When Monique saw us, she was thrilled.

"How are my two lovebirds tonight? I didn't think you two were coming up for air, ha?"

I couldn't wait to answer her…"Monique…see that guy over there…that black guy?"

"You mean the committed one?"

"What do you mean, 'the committed one'?"

"He needs to be committed if he thinks he's going to win. That's a highball machine, meaning the chance of winning is slim to none…for a purpose," she let me in on the secret.

"Poor guy needs help. Can we open it, and let him get his father's gift to him, so he doesn't spend all of his money…maybe he has kids who will go hungry? It's only one silver dollar."

"Are you for real?"

"Yes, it's the humane thing to do...please?" I begged.

Without moving away from her comfortable stool near that table, she looked up into a big mirror above everything and gave some kind of okay signal for slot sixty-two. "Watch this!" is all she said, turning back to look at the black person. We watched.

On his next silver dollar, maybe his last, lights lit up, sirens sounded, and silver dollars flowed out of that slot faster than the Colorado River. Girls with bags and security surrounded his winnings and began to bag it. Nevertheless, the first thing that man did was to drop to his knees searching for that special dollar and when he had found it he kissed it, then he hollered out, "Praise the Lord! Thank you, Jesus!"

I knew then my effort was truly valid and not in vain.

"You just cost us about $37, 000," Monique told me.

"You can tell that, too? Take it out of my cash in the case. I'll go get it right now out of the safe!" I said to her amusement.

"Yes, go get it, but don't leave it there overnight. If you have to carry it, our guards know to watch out for your welfare. We empty the safe every night just before we close about four, if the crowd has emptied. No personal belongings allowed over night, in case of a robbery.

"When you find out what really goes on here in the casino you won't understand why people gamble. No, that was chicken feed and he will be back to lose it all over again by next week. That one over there, number ninety-one, it has twice that. They will jerk it out, take it to the backroom, and empty it after tonight. Four old biddies from Missouri sat there all day trying to spend their social security and hit big. It's a week old, and the sensors tell us it's getting full. They just knew it had to hit eventually. I sent over lunch with red wine to keep them from starving. I do that every fucking day," she told us, this time not so eloquently.

I went to the cashier's vault to withdraw my case and they asked for my receipt. They gave it to me, this time with a light handcuff to strap to my wrist and two keys to open it. I thought that was smart thinking. That way I wouldn't just leave it somewhere, although I thought it might set me up for being a target for robbery.

After that Monique invited us into their apartment for a cocktail. Joy suddenly wanted to move to the other end of the casino to play some Texas Hold 'Em Poker, she called it. Monique was a bit offended, I could tell, when she was not invited, but wished us good luck anyway. She also reminded us we still had the casino's card and to use it.

When Joy hadn't had anything but bad luck at her seat, she told me to sit down there to fill in, while she went to pee. The croupier heard her and smiled, then stood up, stretched and yawned. He then asked if everyone was ready and began what was probably his one-thousandth deal that day, so far. He dealt two little deuces to me in the hole, but I didn't have faith in them, until he dealt a ten of spades, nine of diamonds and a deuce of hearts to go with my pair.

On the turn to bid, I just matched a man's pile of chips he offered. Two others threw their cards in and the last person raised the pot thirty-thousand, all I had showing. I just about quit, but for some reason, I slid it all in, thinking it was all or nothing. I figured I would just quit after I lost it all, maybe on this one hand.

"River!" spoke the dealer, as he so agilely flipped over another deuce; it was a club.

My poker face went sour, I guess. The person who had raised first, studied my face for at least five minutes through his dark glasses, making me edgy, then raised again. His final bid was… "All in", to bluff me out of the pot, I suppose. I was out of chips, but the dealer whispered I still had as much as I needed with the card.

Suddenly, I realized, also, that I still had that damned briefcase tied to my hand, which I was fearful to leave in the hotel room for it might be stolen. I unlocked it, reached inside and found wrapped paper ties of one hundred dollar bills to everyone's amazement, including my own, to try to match his bid. I kept reaching inside, pulling money out for the croupier to count, until I had matched his amount. There was much more where that came from, I could tell. Nevertheless, the case was considerably lighter. I felt lighter, too.

"Pot's right!" said the dealer.

"I call," I told him, feeling a bit shaky, until Joy moved into my sight. "Four deuces!" I told everyone, as I laid them down with their orphaned jack.

He needed that jack to fill out a straight that he held; however he just pitched his cards at the dealer's face with a derogatory expletive for the hand the dealer had dealt him. That was a no-no, and against house rules. He was then asked to leave the table to cool off, which he did on the arms of security men.

Without counting the loot, I grabbed up a fist full of chips and gave them to the dealer in appreciation. In turn, he quickly scooped up my winnings and gave me a credit of ninety-six thousand. Joy almost fainted, me too.

"Thank you, sir…shall I deposit your winnings and your cash into your account, Mr. Wetmore?" he politely asked looking to my name upon my card.

"Yes, please…that will be enough for tonight," I said, just taking one hundred fifty dollars out of the bundle and placing it into my wallet.

"You old show off hot dog, you," Joy told me laughing at my lucky hand. Then she hugged me and said, "We can keep this!"

"Unfortunately, no, honey. Everything belongs to Doyle. We do not want to owe him a thing when we make our exit. Maybe this extra money, not his, can make him a profit off us, so he won't feel gypped and want revenge."

"Get rid of that case, too. It's bruising my thighs," Joy mentioned, when I signed a $96,000 money deposit into my new casino account at one o'clock.

Monique, of course, knew about my Texas Hold 'Em luck and came over to congratulate me. I asked her to make an exception to their policy about leaving overnight personal possessions in their safe. She concurred. I left our plane tickets, also. Joy showed her thighs to Monique, and every man there, who was close when she lifted her dress to display her bruises.

"Those are big welts, senora. Looks like your hombre's own holding-on finger marks…maybe they're wedding night combat bruises," she laughingly told Joy. "She's got nice legs, your woman," she said turning to me.

I dare not piss Joy off by talking to Monique, so I just smiled.

We decided to use the stairs to our room for the added exercise. As soon as we began to ascend, we noticed that foul smell emitted from the factory below. It was intensifying, enough to kill us, and all those poor kids down in the old bomb shelter, if it continued very long. With all those people meandering around from place to place, you would have thought the DEA would have been there also…maybe they were, maybe they were, I hoped.

Joy and I opened our penthouse loft's curtains to the nighttime sky. The city was so beautiful late at nighttime, as were the millions of stars shown clearly in the sky. The moon had risen in the east and it was almost full. We held each other yawning continually, watching stoplights turning from green to red, and often police lights started up at several different locations. I closed the curtain and Joy and I watched the last house movie, off the selection, until I saw she was sleeping. I covered her with a sheet and snuggled up next to her.

Finally, I hoped, Joy would sleep the rest of the night. I, on the other hand, did not. I heard fireworks start up, lots of them, I thought. Why were they shooting them now, so late, or early? I rushed to the big curtain, but there was nothing in the sky. My mind went to thinking something may have gone wrong in the factory. I lay back down next to Joy.

I worried enough for the both of us. What if the dang thing caught fire and we were trapped up here? When more booms could be heard, I got up from our bed again to peer out of those skyline curtains, onto the nightlife below. Nothing was happening, so I sat there waiting for another burst of those booms.

I had time to think. I began first to ask my own question, which was "What if we are already dragged into this so deeply that we can't get out?" They will surely kill us if we departed without their blessing; here in Vegas or back in Springfield, it made little difference.

As I sat in a chair casually looking across the city lights and the casino's decorative grounds worrying, I became aware of an unusual movement just off one corner of our hotel room. I strained to see it, but could not. It appeared that an army was driving in on trucks. Behind that caravan, maybe a mile or more, it was so hard to tell, were more, many more. They slowly moved in unison up the streets that would eventually lead here. I counted twenty vehicles; some covered trucks, some vans, some cars, some motorcycles; all headed this way looking like a huge serpent, slithering down the winding streets in the wee hours.

Then it hit me. The DEA or the police were tailing the first caravan. I think my answer to the question, as to why someone, anyone, especially the police, had not detected what was really going on around here, was now forthcoming.

Without awakening Joy, or turning on the lights, I slipped out the door quietly. I put a morning gratuity newspaper between the locks of our door to keep it from banging shut or locking me out. Then I shuffled to the end of the hallway to look out the window there. That window was in line with the first incoming caravan.

I saw several trucks kicking up dust as they sped away, maybe three vehicles of the first caravan. Then, looking back as far as I could out near that old cistern pump, I saw armed individuals herding people off the backs of trucks. The people leaped off and were physically pushed down into that well hole. They moved very quickly and soon the last truck sped away and those armed people climbed down into that well, also and closed it up. It looked deserted again.

It all happened very quickly, as if a well-planned drill had just been executed. However, that second caravan was still creeping along closer and closer, moving ever so slowly towards this place and now without headlights. I feared my worst thoughts were about to come true. It was possibly a police raid forthcoming.

I suspected Monique had ordered those thirty or so more workers I told her the factory needed, as it also appeared many of those coming off the trucks were actually women. I became horrified I had ordered the probable deaths of all who were getting off those trucks. I was just sick inside and hustled back to our room. Joy was standing there, door cracked open, lights on and had seen me leave. She also saw me looking out the end window.

"What, you can't see enough from our big window?" she asked, as I jerked her back inside.

"Hey…!" she objected.

When I saw the elevator light come on and the numbers were rising, I feared the worst.

"We have to get out of here, right now," I told her holding her tightly and shaking her with both hands. "Turn out the lights quick…I think this joint is being raided by police…grab just enough clothes to wear and leave everything else behind…let's move!" I hollered to a very upset woman who could not see what she had selected to put on, nor could I. I cracked the door and that elevator was about to our floor.

I realized then we had just a few twenty dollar bills in my wallet. Because of my security concerns, I had deposited most of our money in the casino's safe, only hours before. We could not get out fast enough. I flipped over a chair in the cracked door's weak light and about fractured my noggin. I got up running. Joy actually was faster than I was and she stood at the door waiting for me, as I double-checked that I was not bleeding. I had to be certain we had not left anything behind that could identify us as being there.

"Let's get the heck out of here!" Joy frantically whispered to me when the elevator bell sounded at the other end.

We took the exit door and hustled down the stairs, almost killed ourselves stumbling several times over each other's feet, while putting on yesterday's clothes. They stunk!

"Whoa! Catch your breath," I said, as I stopped at the first floor's exit door. I opened it slowly, and peeked out. The joint was empty, except someone was banging against a slot machine with a sledgehammer, which surprised the hell out of me how he was getting away with that. Nevertheless, I had no time to care. His back was to us so everything was clear.

I grabbed Joy's hand, and as casually as we could, we strolled to the front doors and walked out. The person, consumed with his beating up on that slot machine, never quit.

I thought we had a stroke of luck when I spotted a cab parked nearby. Though it appeared the busy light was off and ready to hale, the cabby was curled up on the front seat sleeping. We immediately headed for him.

I pounded on his window and then we got the surprise of our lives. That cabby pulled out a 9mm automatic and stuck it in my face when I opened his driver's door to awaken him.

"Innn a rushhh...or were you going to rob me?" the man asked me with his gun cocked, pointed at my skull, and very angry looking. Then he noticed Joy...he looked back at me, back at Joy, then hard at me. "You're that newlywed couple I brought here the other day from the airport, are you not?"

When he said that, even in the darkness, I remembered his voice succinctly.

"Yes, sir! I am sorry I woke you up, but there's strange things happening inside there and we want to go back to the airport now! When I saw your cab..."

He stepped out of his cab and looked up; he looked down, around me to the west, then to the east... "I don't see anything unusual, my friends. You very certain you saw something? Or, I am thinking...are you some of those poorest gamblers who lost their shirts and stockings and you're both escaping your fate to pass away and no-one else absent on your present living hotel bill? Huh?"

"No sir, we received a call my mother is dying and we have to go, now!" I lied, but he began to sound absolutely hilarious.

"Okaaay, noooo resssst from the wickeeed…climbed your butts innn… did you good deal my…his, her ninety-five denar, ahhh, I put it to somebody to speak of your dollar for everyone's entrance fee? I do not learn by heart your country's speech rather very not well, almost, thank you, please," he told us with his hand out.

It was a bit exorbitant, and he was coo coo, but I gladly paid his premium at this moment in our lives. Joy and I jumped into his lighted back seat and away Hajji Majhi Resolii drove off. That is just what his lighted cab's ID card officially read.

"My God!" Joy let out in disbelief, which turned his head back to us. "You're that distinguished man seated next to us last night at Wayne's show!" she declared.

"Yessss…I am, maam, and, kindly sir," he spoke in a high-pitched tone, just as his Indian heritage allowed him.

"Where's that sexy turban?" Joy asked, and I elbowed her for her observations.

"Oh…itttt's at a homely persons…for another particularly imported occasions…I onnnly put it on my head in the public display, when I am romancing, you know," he told us smiling brightly to our amusement.

"Was that your lovely wife with you last night?" Joy asked him.

"Thank you kindly, yessss…she isss the love of my future dear life."

"How did you get here from…where are you really from, Mr. Hajji?" Joy wanted to know.

"I come from to you from my homeless land…India…Bombay, my glorious homeland, I think. Do you know of my Bombay on the Arabian Sea?" he said, seemingly proud.

"No, we've never been to your lovely country," I spoke to appease him.

"Oh…itttss not so loverly there…it is depresssed now. I come to your America on college scholarship visssa, by my represent, represent tiitttive…ah, a man who rules us…he sent me here…because I was concerned very much to be converted into your physician and someday return to help his people," he sounded a bit saddened.

"I'm sorry…what happened? I mean why are you not in school?" Joy interrupted.

"Oh, your own acquaintance Hajji graduated away from the institution of elevated edification…I was a medical doctor of the rectum, you know…but I like driving cabs much better…no confusion…just come and go," he explained, if you could call it that.

"You mean you are a real proctologist doctor?" I asked, a bit distastefully, but doubting if or how he passed any written tests.

"Oh yesss…but I do not treasure a goodly physician being verily much. I only get to gaze rightly up old people's butt holes…never a young girl's, so much fun it was not being."

"All right, Hajji, you're shittin' us, right?" I said, suspecting then he was not who he pretended.

"I know not of what you have spoken yet again!" he said, his face contorting to hold back his laughter.

"You're found out now, you phony. But you're very entertaining to say the least," I told him leaning up to get his truth.

"You have never heard of this Hajji?" he asked cheerfully, looking back to us. "I am a not so confidant comedian at the casinos. My wife helps me make a scene when I go into the floor shows as audience entertainment. That thing with the waiter was a skit just for you…I launch before the big tickets…not very good, yet, but I sure get a kick from all you westerners who think my speech is hilarious. In India, we laugh at westerners talking as you do, ha!" regulating his speech for us to better understand him.

"I practice my skits in my cab at night, but still like driving this cab though. The pay is good," he told us, as he zoomed his taxi through the airport entrance gates and up to the unattended, temporary unloading barricades, with a sudden braking screech of his taxi's tires.

"My taxi machine no longer can take you to any completed destination all over the place…farther…I picture…thank you for choosing AlQaeda Airlines," he hysterically spoke, which caused us both to laugh.

"Good luck and good-bye, Hajji!" we both said in farewell.

Joy and I stood on the outside of the receiving area. There were some others entering behind us, however, no guards or baggage haulers were present to check anybody's luggage. We also had no real difficulty walking inside and getting airline tickets aboard flight 662 to Chicago, except it was a bit uncomfortable looking grubby as we did.

"Oh, are you people from the Diamond?" she said, without much reason, so I just did not answer. "Only one way…that will be three-thousand, two-hundred dollars, and seventy cents, please. Do you have luggage over fifty pounds?" asked the rather talkative and very intrusive ticket agent. She looked hard at me, as I reached into my skinny wallet.

"None, we're traveling light tonight," I explained handing her my credit card, a bit embarrassed, as I felt we both looked untidy.

I badly needed to shave and Joy's hair looked a bit windswept in the airport lighting. Worse, was when she ran my new, unsigned credit card, it was limited-out to just two thousand, if it were valid. I had not used it before nor had I activated it by telephone, where I might have gotten a higher reserve. Now we were at her will.

"Apparently, you've gambled it all away, bet ya, huh? I have done that same thing, once or twice, actually, many good people come here with dreams of being big winners, but somehow leave here, broke just like you two. We do have a loan package, if you have a job's paycheck stub, that's good for two tickets, if you care to fill out this questionnaire.

"Many just like you come to me downhearted, just like you two. You'll heal," she assumed, when I searched further into my wallet and there was only sixty dollars in there. She and I both looked dumbfounded.

"Here!" Joy interrupted, easing around me, plopping down cash from her purse, which I didn't know she had. That quickly reversed the desk woman's pity speech.

"Oh, you were really the big winners. Pardon me looking at your stash. Congratulations…can I then upgrade your seats to first class?" she said, smiling with her hand extended for more money.

"No, thank you," Joy told her, grabbing the envelopes and giving her the evil eye.

She took my hand, and then led me like her little boy with our tickets in her hands. She was leading me quickly forward for our flight that was boarding now, just ten minutes from flying out to Chicago, announced the overhead speaker, informing everyone.

We would transfer and fly down to Springfield from O'Hare. The ticket person looked at us briefly, and then checked our tickets. Out onto the ramp we walked. I had no idea that our timing was lifesaving for us.

Many people, looking perhaps as ragged as we were, possibly Doyle's casino clientele, too, were shuffling their feet in front of us. They, unlike Joy and me conversely, held their carry-on baggage, walking in single file onto the plane. It was a quiet, sleepy group, who seemed to grab pillows right away and then eased back quickly to sleep in their seats.

"Thank God, we made it," Joy told me, as she eased into a narrowed passenger seat, because others had already lowered theirs to the sleeping positions, while reclining. I buckled Joy up immediately, then myself. My seat was next to Joy's. However, there was another person at the window who appeared to be using a pillow to hide her whimpering and tears. My lovely wife could not help herself, but to place her hand on the woman's arm and ask her if there was something wrong. The woman jerked her arm away and looked up. Her face was still wet with tears.

I almost had a heart attack, but that woman seemed as surprised as we were. It was Monique. The silence was deafening as none of us could speak. It was that intense, until we felt a jolt and the plane began to move, then accelerated, sending us back into our seats as it took off.

Still shocked, as the plane leveled out, Joy and Monique could not speak, but they both stared at one another, guessing what the other was thinking. It was surreal, until Monique spoke sobbing.

"How did you know? Were you warned or were you the ones?"

"What do you mean?" Joy asked very alarmed. "Why are you crying, Monique? Tell us!" she demanded, as only a friend might.

Monique still looked suspicious and kept sobbing. Then a flight attendant asked if we wanted to move, since she was aware Monique's husband had just died and she wanted to be alone, if at all possible.

"Oh no!" cried out Joy, who then put her arms about Monique to comfort her.

Monique raised her teary eyes to the flight attendant and told her it was okay. She sat up for a moment, wiping her eyes with a Kleenex that Joy offered her. She then began.

"You don't really know, do you?" she whimpered. "Well, that fucking bastard Doyle came into our home with a gun…behind him were more men I had never seen before…Doyle was screaming at my Homer and hitting him. He said my Homer was a traitor and had told the policia about the shelter. Someone shot at us with many rapid-firing guns through a window. Doyle just turned on my Homer and shot him, very bad, too. I jumped out the back window with only my purse, after I peeked out and saw my Homer laying there slaughtered in a pool of his own blood…Doyle saw me, then he came at me with his gun.

"I only had these clothes that I have on. I hid in the bushes, until I heard more shooting inside and outside, next to me. I think Doyle was killed, also…it was the policia…I ran more and more, until I caught a cab and got to here. My leg hurts," she then stopped and told Joy, pointing to her ankle and grimacing. It was swollen and blue.

"Miss!" Joy called to a flight attendant.

When the attendant came, Joy asked if she could have a bucket of ice. When the attendant looked suspicious, Joy lied again. "She tripped on the steps in the airport," Joy told her just to expedite service. "She'll be all right if she gets a cold compress on her ankle," Joy assured her.

Help came quickly. They gently moved Monique to the outside seat, propped her leg on a food cart, and locked it there. Then one asked if it was necessary to return to the terminal.

"No, no! I'm okay…please, please, keep it going!" she emphatically told him.

There wasn't much room to get past her leg sticking out, but everyone seemed to be sleeping anyway, it was a short flight, and the john was the other way down the aisle.

"Now, now…just lay back and we'll rest until we get to Chicago. I'll help you…we'll help you," Joy said, looking my way.

While immediately looking out the plane's window, I saw a bright orange hue, glowing off the horizon, which would have been near downtown Vegas and our hotel. When the plane banked against the wind a second time, after we had risen up higher to head back east, I was certain it was.

"Look, it might be our hotel down there, it's on fire…look at all those flashing lights down there!" I said a bit too loud, as others rose up to look out their own porthole windows and groaned at the sight.

I guess it was a huge fire caused by the raid, I thought to myself. We would have died. What about all those people in the basement? I was sick. Then it dawned on me what Monique told us; Doyle was killed, maybe. My concern was about to ruin our honeymoon…what honeymoon? I forgot about how wonderful my little wife could be and hoped our immediate future was not quite so exciting.

The ice apparently helped Monique in the two hours, or so, that we flew.

I had time for more thinking. Joy stayed next to Monique holding her all the way. They had bonded as friends, but I didn't like that since she was involved in the whole damn crime scheme. Nevertheless, I shut my mouth, until the plane set down at O'Hare.

Then, Monique let the cat out of the bag when Joy asked her to come home with us, and inquired if she could give her some of our money to live on.

"I must tell you, because you love me as a friend," Monique began to tell Joy. "The plan was just to free our people from Doyle. My brother Rafael, he sent word to kill him. However, someone gave the word to the policia...I know now it was our new bartender...he asked too many importante` questions. I hope he died, also."

Joy eased back then, knowing the truth about her new friend Monique. She was not innocent in any way.

"About my money...I have enough. In a locker, I have left for me a key and tickets...also enough to get to Costa Rica. There, I will meet Rafael. Do you hate me now? You look so unhappy."

"No, I don't hate you, Monique. I guess you think you have good reasons. Nevertheless, I have concerns, too, for all the people who died back there, innocent young people. You and your brother Rafael used them all making and selling your drugs to...kids, kids who get hooked and kill other kids in our ghettos. Your husband died because of that. Was it worth it?"

I thought my wife had responded wisely. I was proud of her. When Monique took it on the chin from Joy and seemed miffed, she just might have realized she was the one, the one who killed her own beloved husband Homer.

When we finally disembarked at O'Hare, Monique did not attempt to look back. Nevertheless, we did. Joy wanted to follow her for a moment to see if she indeed had that locker she told us about, before she boarded that outgoing plane south to Costa Rica.

Monique knew right where to go. Among the hundreds of locked airport lockers, she opened one. In seconds, she pulled a traveling bag from a locker and headed straight into the men's restroom of all places. Being a stripper, however, I guess it didn't bother her at all, it was just convenient.

We were simply amazed at her disregard, especially when Monique strolled back out of the men's john in a white pants suit, red, silky blouse, big bling, and looking Rio de Janeiro-ish. She now was wearing a very broad-brimmed, floppy Brazilian hat, a dark wig under that, red-spiked heels, and looking wonderful, as if she were a female rock star, but without tattoos.

If Monique noticed us, her dark glasses hid her eyes when she just continued past us, without hesitation onto her next plane. A man from the men's room came out frantically looking flustered by Monique's apparently being in there, while he was peeing, and he was still zipping up his pants. It was another "Joy-ess" moment.

"Hey, Monique…you're lipstick is smeared!" she hollered out, as loud as anyone could. She sounded like someone who was angry at an umpire's bad call in a losing Chicago Cubs' game. That yell caused many strange looks at Joy. Monique, however, came to an abrupt halt. She raised a mirror up to her face from her purse, and then raised her wiggling hand high as to wave back at Joy, without even turning around.

"Remember our last great adventure at an airport when you hollered?" I reminded my wife.

We laughed; Monique disappeared forever.

Chapter 12

"We're up here at O'Hare, Mom. Joy and I came home a bit early because the casino we booked burned down. Did you see it on the news?" I asked immediately when I called her.

"No, Greg, but I heard from Will and Jill...they flew off to Germany this evening and will head to Afghanistan from there. It sickens me with worry," she said sounding very distraught.

"Just hang in there. Jill can handle herself, Mom...she's a marine."

I told her that Joy and I would be there in a couple of hours, and then hung up. Joy had other plans.

"I thought we might get comfortable back in our apartment. We just cannot barge in on your parents. Heck, Greg, they put up with you for almost twenty-four years and thought all that was over. They gave us all their money to help you get out the door," she laughed. "Besides, look at us...especially me. I look like a streetwalker and you could pass for a bum. Let's go someplace and buy us some duds and at the very least look presentable."

"Okay, I think I've just the place downtown on Michigan. I wonder if it still sells clothing," I said reminiscing a bit. "Pop bought my first suit of clothes there and Mom used to work there. Dad actually proposed to Mom on bended knee there, also. No, Joy, that is not my parents' style. I will call

Mom later, though, and tell her we have booked into the Sheraton. Then run up tomorrow for a brief visit.

"Let's not go back home so quickly, just in case Doyle is still kicking. If he is dead, Joe will know. I will call him tomorrow if we cannot find anything on the news. We'll taxi to my parents' home and visit them," I said, then I haled down the next one that would stop.

From the taxi, I redialed Mother on my cell and told her there was a change in our plans and we could not get there until the next day. She was disappointed, but happy we were coming to visit. Mom said I always eased her anxiety over Jill's escapades.

Looking up to the cabby's ID while talking, I remembered Hajji with a smile.

"Say, bud, you do any comedy?" I asked.

"Well, bud…only to non-paying customers and smart asses, then only after I kick their royal butts…I do tell pretty good dirty jokes though…wanna hear some?" he let me know.

"Geeeze Louise…what brought that on?" Joy asked loudly. It was another "Joy-ess" moment.

"Oh, I was just remembering Hajji. I hope he has a good life. He seemed so fragile, so docile, so innocent, so funny."

"I think the word you're looking for is POLITE!" Joy said loudly enough so the rude cabby could relate to it. He just looked back, sneered at her, and then chuckled. His accent sounded as if he were from Brooklyn or New York City.

Joy refused to let me tip him with his hand still out, and the full cash amount still in my hand. She told him he had to apologize first for his rudeness…he did not, and pealed away angry. We heard his words, "Screw you, slut, and the horse you rode to town on, assholes!" he screamed out, fishtailing away.

I had to hold Joy back from throwing a picked-up handful of road chat at his vehicle.

"He wouldn't have said that if I didn't look like your whore," Joy remarked.

"But you are, you are!" I laughed. Then I braced for that familiar judo chop.

"Ouch, darn it, that time it hurt!"

"Serves you right...why don't you call the cab company and complain?"

"Just because."

"Because why?"

"Because you pissed him off, and made him so angry he just took off and forgot to grab his sixty dollar fare...I don't think he will be coming back, but if he does, let's step inside that deli and grab a bite on him," I told her, holding up the cash. "Then, we'll do some shopping on a full stomach," I told her.

We jokingly laughed at each other's shitty appearances. We brushed off some dust with our hands, and then tried to straighten out the other's wrinkles in our clothes. They had been long-pressed by sitting all night. We then kissed once before we entered the deli, hoping not to be mistaken for derelicts. Several sweet old women and a butcher behind the deli's meat case greeted us.

We stood in front of them for a moment, admiring everything in their huge display of very pricey meats and cheeses. There were many veggies and condiments of all kinds. The roasted chicken was tempting me, until I spotted what I really wanted.

"What may we serve you today?" one asked, looking at our messy clothes and my unshaven appearance. I think she thought we two might try to stiff them on the bill.

"We also have fresh chicken noodle soup for only three dollars...all you can eat, today," the woman told us after we sat down at their counter. "We make our own in-house noodles," she added.

I saw what I wanted on their numbered menu board and made my decision very quickly.

"We'll take two number sixes with two large glasses of number threes, please. Maybe we'll try some soup later, thank you."

The woman spoke to another and the butcher in a different language, even I hadn't heard for some time.

"What language are these ladies speaking to each other?" Joy questioned.

"I think it's a deli lingo of Jewish."

It was the first time Joy had ever eaten a delicious Chicago prosciutto sandwich, filled with avocado, roasted garlic havarti, spinach, tomatoes, and Grey Poupon. We both ordered seconds before completing the firsts. I also introduced her to buttermilk when she wasn't sure. She was game, but I had to finish hers after just one sip and got her a diet soda instead.

"These were my mainstay at UIC," I said biting into that sandwich.

"I can see why…but I wonder how I'll feel an hour from now?"

"Oh, maybe that's why I always had the shits!" I laughed to her sudden worried look.

Then afterward, arm in arm, Joy and I walked the Michigan Avenue storefronts, until we found that same store I remembered. I quickly explained to the first attendant who approached us hesitantly, who we were, and where we had come from, and why we looked the way we did. Most importantly, we had money in Joy's purse. Joy had not told me she hit $13,300 on a fifty-cent slot using only a single half-dollar, while I was sitting at the card table. My guess was Monique helped her win. I would have hoped she would have immediately told me and not kept it a secret. Nevertheless, I am glad she had not told me because that money saved the day in our run for our lives.

Robert, our young merchant, allowed Joy and I to shower together in their private facility. It was supposed to be used only for workers, but he stood outside the door to make certain no one walked in on us. I had to bribe him twenty bucks, and then another twenty because when it was my turn to use his razor it was dull, because Joy used it on her legs. I needed another blade.

"Suck it up like a real man," Joy told me when my 'ouches' became frequent.

After that quick cleanup, we bought our clothes, enough for a week's stay. That almost thousand-dollar sale made Robert very pleased he had trusted us.

We left our smelly old tropical clothes in their trash and came out of that store looking very well dressed and groomed.

"What are you looking for?" I asked Joy in another 'Joy-ess' moment.

"Oh, I was going to flip him the bird if I saw that cab driver, just to see if he could recognize me now all cleaned up," she said, still feeling insulted, I guess.

It seemed we never stopped laughing together nor ever stopped enjoying being around each other. I secretly thanked God for Joy, each and every night, before we went to bed.

We were close to the Sheraton so we continued to walk the Windy City Streets. The people minded their own business and it really was not very crowded, as I sometimes had seen it when I occasionally had to go downtown.

We watched and listened to the CTA's "el train" and its clackety-clack-clack overhead, strolled past a crowded Civic Center Building, The Play Boy Club, and later found a suite at the Sheraton, using some of Joy's winnings.

Later, we found ourselves enjoying each other's love in the midday, right after several superb glasses of red wine we shared together. That wine loosened Joy's tongue and for the first time she told me I was really good in bed. That wasn't hard to take. I told her the same. We ordered dinner from the room service menu , because I wanted to watch the news.

I scanned several news channels searching for some breaking news out of Las Vegas. Then on Fox News came the first story that multiple deaths had occurred in a DEA and local authorities' shootout and drug raid upon a noted casino. It was reported that no names of any wounded or death totals of deceased victims' names were being released on the tourists, police, or illegal aliens involved in the debacle. There were no facts given to substantiate the number of deaths or information that I felt could construe Doyle was actually killed. I thought they surely would have identified the owner of the casino.

Approximately two hours later, a representative of the DEA task force spoke publicly on TV. He stood at a podium placed out in front of the still-smoking scene, and in front of the scorched marquee that once shown brightly upon the now totally destroyed Diamond Casino. He gave a detailed account of their raid upon an immense drug manufacturing operation that used kidnapped aliens as slave labor. There were only ten arrested and all were previously known criminals, armed with high powered AK-47 rifles. The criminals had surrendered only after their place of hiding fell down around them burning, he reported.

An hour passed, when a list of fifty-five killed, either by fire or bullets, was given; two police officers, seven staff members of the casino, including sixty-year old Doyle Valero; the rest were apparently slave labor aliens, unnamed at this time pending identification, and killed in the resulting blaze. Mexican authorities were enroute to assist in identifications.

We both sat up at once when he said, "Also reported, but reported as missing only, are newlyweds, Greg and Joyce Wetmore, of Springfield, Illinois, who were registered to the hotel's newlywed penthouse suite, but not located as of yet. They became identified as missing, however, also persons of interest needed for questioning, he reported. Their money receipts had been found by crime scene investigators inside the casino's huge private fireproof safe; apparently along with millions of stored illicit cash. Foul play was suspected.

"In addition, also reported missing, and listed as wanted as a person of interest, was Monique M. Zorn, wife of the deceased hotel's manager whose body was found dead in the hotel fire debris. It is believed Monique is a major player in the casino's drug scheme. She has not been located. She is described as a thirty-eight year old Hispanic, five-feet six, dyed red hair, brown eyes. Anyone knowing the whereabouts of this woman is advised to call the DEA, or their local law enforcement."

"In other breaking news today…"

"That could have been us," was all I could say to Joy as I turned it off.

We were both very exhausted when the events of that week caught up with us, helped by the wine. We felt very safe, secure in our room then, and slept over nine hours.

We faced the morning with a much better frame of mind and it was prominent when Joy proclaimed she was sorry that she had been so vindictive to that taxi driver…that was her way always, finding fault in her own self to forgive others' transgressions.

"Joy, better call Martha and Kurt now just in case they saw this."

Without hesitation, Joy called Martha. When Joy began explaining to her what had happened, I realized they had not watched the news piece and knew nothing about the fire. Shortly, Joy hung up and told me the same.

"Nope, they didn't see or hear a thing, but Kurt said for you to come back to work Monday morning at the shed. I guess we're back together again… think we can secretly get it on sometimes in your john, boss number two?" she said grinning, looking for a rise out of me.

"Only if you can take 'dick-tation' in those cramped quarters, when boss number 1's not there, and the work crowd's gone, too," I told her, returning her suddenly sexual-pun-humor with my own. If that could be construed as humor.

We were joking around today, because we both knew we had been delivered safely from the tremendous mental strain of the entire bad casino scene. It was odd to believe our lives had gone through such a rigorous challenge, just hours before, and which we apparently had no real control over after we decided to honeymoon there. Someone solved it all for us.

"Thank you, Jesus," was all we both could resolve when we briefly discussed our relief.

However, new worry concerns developed as to why I was meeting Kurt on Monday, and that part of the Fox News report, which repeated several times on their morning show that authorities still wanted our whereabouts; those mysterious people who left thousands of dollars.

In addition, leads had surfaced through airport authorities that Joy and I had boarded a plane to Chicago shortly after the raid, as did Monique. I wondered if they now assumed we were involved in everything with her.

I did not have long to wait. Father called me and wanted more information. He was very upset, wanted the truth, and nothing but the absolute truth with no stone unturned by me. He said he was immediately setting up a defense team to defend us.

After I objected to his concern and involvement, and saw my refusal was futile, I began as he told me, from the beginning, since the moment I left UIC to go to Springfield. He wanted names and telephone numbers, from every one of those people who could verify I was in their presence at any time to show I could not have been in cahoots in Vegas. It would have taken lots of time away from Chicago and my classes to have been a part of that organization. My cum laude certificate might attest to that.

When I gave Professor Max Davis' name to Dad as my first verification and that I attended every one of his classes, without missing a single session, he took notice immediately.

Dad asked, "Who did you say? Did you say Max Davis? That person was a close friend of your mother's…oh well, that was long ago. Next name, and spell it."

He seemed shocked that Max was my main instructor. He did not know that. Nevertheless, when he learned I lived at Donald Stuart's condominium, eventually free of charge, he had a dramatic moment off the phone with Mother. I could tell he had placed his hand over the receiver, but when Dad became loud and demanding answers from Mother as to why she allowed me to be with those ex boyfriends, he came back mumbling to himself with a few little expletives.

"I guess I don't know your mother as well as I thought," he spouted.

"Well I do, Dad, and you might be ashamed when I tell you that they vaguely remembered her. What they did remember, was you. They both said you were the Casanova who took her away, not from them, just away. I guess you could verify that, huh? Mother never knew they were there at the college.

It was only when each learned that I was your son that they told me you took her out of circulation, away somewhere and they never saw her again."

"Really? Well, that makes me feel better. Your acquaintances were just as coincidental as I hope to prove about your association with what's his name, ah; let me see here, it says he went by his middle, American name, which was Doyle; his full name was, Dominic Doyle Calandro Valero. If there are any charges or if it ever goes to trial we must be prepared well in advance."

Dad grilled me as only a pro of his caliber could, very thoroughly, asking me to be very concise. He made me repeat things many times after I had already spoken it ten minutes before. I think he thought if I was making it up, he could tell by my giving him a different version. He would not stand for that at all.

Though it had taken a while, and I had explained everything repeatedly, only then, after he was satisfied his son was innocent and we should be completely exonerated, did he tell me authorities had already come to his home, requesting our whereabouts. He learned quickly that they had already entered our apartment in Springfield with a search warrant.

"Greg, you and Joy stay available. I'm calling some acquaintances and maybe you two might have to go in for questioning. There is a DEA office in the Civic Center. I will see if we can meet the officials handling this case there. I will call you as soon as I know. I believe you, son, one hundred percent. I love you, son," he told me and I was proud.

"I love you, too, Dad. Thanks for believing in me. This is only a big misunderstanding, but I can understand their concern. I just hope it is not why I have to report to my work place Monday. I'll be on my cellular, thanks again, Dad."

The recurring worry caused me to want to take a walk. The cool breezes off the lake beckoned me to get out even more. Joy pulled out her new running shoes and sports bra from her soft luggage she bought on our shopping spree.

"You know, Lila's going to be pissed I lost her nice luggage. Maybe I can find some like it," Joy said getting ready as we exited the back parking lot.

We both took off jogging near the harbor docks and along the city park's beautiful shaded trails on the lakefront. We had run our two miles along the shoreline, where local anglers also fished for Coho salmon from the bank.

After I felt I was about limited out running, we crashed on a shaded park bench. Below us, a man jumped up reeling in a fish; his pole bent in half, caused by that huge fish he had hooked. Joy stood up next to me to watch, as others took notice.

My cell's ring tone sounded, so I sat back on the bench. It was Dad, who caught me out of breath from our jogging when I answered out of breath.

"Hello!"

"Greg, this is Dad…what's wrong…sounds as if I called at one of those honeymoon moments…call me back when it's over, okay?" he chuckled. "You're a tiger."

I laughed, because Dad actually imagined he had interrupted Joy and I having sex when he heard my exhausted breathing and was embarrassed. I guess he thought we were locked up in a sex act.

"No, Dad, you're not interrupting anything," I said, as I continued to try to catch my breath.

It's really hard to catch your breath and speak, too, I found out. Nevertheless, when Joy stood next to me and hollered, "That's a really big one, Greg!" Dad hung up.

I could not help but laugh again, and dialed him up right back. Joy was curiously listening.

"Dad, it's Greg…Joy and I are at the lake front running. We just jogged our two miles when you called, really! I'm regaining my breath, go ahead, and tell me what you want."

"What was all that 'You've got a really big one', I heard Joy tell you, or whatever that was? You're a chip off the old block, son…can't fool me," he laughed.

"A guy hooked a fifteen pound Coho off the riprap and Joy got excited when he pulled it ashore. Maybe we should try fishing now that you're close to retirement. Shoot!"

"Okay, here's the scoop. You and Joy will meet with me tonight at ten in room 1700. It's late, but they want to get the ball rolling. They'll ask you both some questions in my presence. I think they really got suspicious, because of your financial status. They verified I gave you one million as a wedding present. A croupier, John Aspen, verified you beat a man known to them as a house shark name Montero Munier, at Texas Hold 'Em. He said you took him at the card table with four deuces. Is that true?"

"Yes, I left it in the house safe with our plane tickets, since we were staying several days longer and I was afraid it might get stolen. I was going to give it to Mr. Valero to get out of him not killing us when I said no…I told you that."

"Yes, but you didn't mention it was $96,000."

"Sorry, but you didn't ask."

"They tracked you to the airport by those plane tickets, or else they might have thought you burned up in the fire. Now, what about all of Joy's money?"

"Well, I didn't even know she won that money, ah, $13,300 something on a slot machine. She won it while I sat at the card table. Ha, I took her place at the table, so she could go take a pee. I won that money right away before she got back."

"Okay, that's what you first told me, but what about her six million in the bank, in only her name?"

"What?" I thought he was joking. "Are you sure? My money is her money, but we don't have that kind of total."

"There's a Joyce Carol Dixon registered in the Second State Bank in Springfield with a savings account drawing interest for a fat six million. There's also listed Kurt and Martha Rakers as beneficiaries. Who are they?"

"Dad, Kurt was my best man and is my boss. He was that humorous guy with our lost wedding rings prank, remember? You met him, didn't you?"

"I can't remember, really, because of Jill and Will suddenly showing up. I had to cut her a wedding check not covered yet, because I took only yours out of the savings we had planned for you. We had savings for her, too, but hers was not cashed in yet, because she surprised everyone. I was a bit relieved she told Mom to hang onto it. But it's there."

"Well, let's ask Joy."

"Look, you're covered. Let me talk with Joy in person when I get there. I will have to get ready soon and drive down. See you at the Civic Center, room 1700. I think it's the US Marshal's office, not the DEA. Got it?"

"Okay, Dad, got it. We will be there at ten. It's just a short walk from the Sheraton. Thanks!"

"Wait for me before Joy talks to anyone," Dad advised, as he hung up.

I turned to Joy, who had curled up next to me on the bench, and was chilled. Her perspiration met the lake breeze. I had nothing to give her, but suggested we run back.

"Beat ya!" Joy yelled, darting away down the jogging path. It took us about eighteen minutes to get back to our Sheraton room.

"Joy, why didn't you tell me you were rich?"

"I'm not. That's why I apparently got lucky marrying you, ha!"

"My father told me the investigators discovered there's a Joyce Carol Dixon, Glenarm, with a six million dollar savings account in the Second State Bank," I said, looking into her eyes for a flinch or something, but nothing.

"I hope to heck it's mine, because I don't know anything about any money. Maybe there's another girl with my name, or I have hers," Joy said, then looked like she might have thought of something. "Except, Greg…I do remember Kurt telling me several months ago there was a settlement about to take place with my parents' death suit after all these years. You see, that trucker who killed them tested as being on drugs and there was a question about how fast he was going. It has been locked up in civil court for years. I just figured Pop made a mistake. Lawyers and Kurt took care of it. I wasn't there remember? I don't know…maybe it settled."

"I thank God you weren't there!" I said, thinking of how I would have missed loving her and being her husband now. "Did I mention to you when we were together after the ceremony out by your mom and dad's graves that I felt something odd happening, like someone put their arms around me, not once, but twice?"

Joy stared at me… "Really?"

I just shook my head yes and then held her close. "You know…you must have had some great parents."

"I did, Greg. I had Mom, Dad, Martha, and Kurt. I was very lucky."

We showered and dressed, then took off walking towards the Civic Center. However, we heard a honk and it was Dad driving toward us. He decided to see if we were walking, since it was only five blocks away.

"Hi, Joy…please sit in the front and Greg climb in back. I want to talk to my new daughter-in-law. Joy, tell me what you know about Dominic Doyle."

"I don't know a Dominic Doyle."

"Excuse me…Doyle Valero."

"Well, he offered Greg a job as his thinker, because Greg is so smart. He gave us a free honeymoon to check out his business. I don't think he meant for Monique to show us their drug factory…she just did. Doyle was in

Springfield, I think he told Greg, getting some congressional representatives to help vote on getting his new casino in Chicago…I guess somewhere nearby here. We were going to call the FBI just as soon as we got back."

"Where is Monique Zorn?"

"I believe she flew on to Costa Rica after we landed at O'Hare to be with her brother, she told us. She had clothes in a locker at the airport waiting for her. She changed clothes and her appearance inside a men's john, from a red head to a dark brown-haired person in a white pants suit. I really don't know much more except she was very nice to me and…and she was a strip tease dancer at a nightclub."

Dad had a recorder going and wrote everything down Joy told him, also.

"Good…that coincides with Greg's story entirely. Don't worry…what you kids did isn't prosecutable in my opinion, maybe a bit reckless. I'll discuss this with the interrogators first. When we get there, mum is the word, unless I advise you to speak, right? We might settle this yet tonight."

My father never looked so important to me before then. I took his work casually and accepted his absence. Nevertheless, I now had the deepest respect for the career choice that took him away from us to provide a good living for our family. We all took the elevator up to the seventeenth floor and met with several men, all armed. Dad sat us down and went inside another room, then came out.

"Greg and Joy come inside and tell the officers what you know about Joe Petito and his wife Angelina."

Joy walked inside and just stood in front of the agent and rattled off everything we knew without even being asked, and without stopping to take a breath. Her words were also recorded. After she quit, the agent said she was very helpful and he was satisfied ours was just a coincidental acquaintance. He thanked her especially for the added info on Monique. Then Joy was shaken by his words.

"We're going after Monique with extradition and murder warrants, if those authorities of jurisdiction nab her and her brother Rafael. They were responsible for all those poor aliens captured and used as slave labor. They should get the gas chamber if Mexico prosecutes."

"Thank you, Jim," Dad said to the agent.

"No, thank you, Jon, you made my job a lot easier. My wife will be glad I get home tonight," he spoke shaking Dad's hand. "Oh, yes, call headquarters for that money in the vault," he added.

"Let's go home, kids," Dad said, with his arms around us both like a protective father.

Joy looked up at Dad being so tall and compared his stature to my shorter frame.

"Boy, are you certain Greg is your son?" she just let loose asking.

That really caught Dad off guard to say the least, but he would grow used to her frankness. That was nothing like what he was going to learn straight out a few months later when she told him he and Mom were to become grandparents.

As it turned out, upon our return to Springfield, we found our home in disarray and personal things strewn about out of their boxes. I went to see Joe about repairing our door, because a drill, not a key, had damaged the lock. I soon learned Joe and his family had disappeared according to Looney Laura, who was drunk, sitting on the side of the pool.

The note on Joe's apartment door was written in scribbled green crayon to everyone. Joe wrote it and stated not to expect his return anytime soon, and that everyone should fend for himself or herself concerning repairs and requests. I don't know when he left, but looking at the green algae that Looney Laura was dangling her toes in, it must have been several days.

I simply went to the unlocked chemical shed and got some chlorine tabs and filled the in-line chemical feeder. There wasn't a big supply left. I found some algaecide and threw in two gallons into the skimmer to be shot back out the returns. That was all I could do, except turn on the pool's pump to filter and see if it helped.

Kurt called to see if we had arrived home safely. He only wanted me to report to the shed Monday morning because the DEA investigator told him he wanted to question me. We cleared that up in Chicago, I told him, but he also asked us to another dinner that night to give Joy her surprise check from that substantial civil suit. I knew nothing about it, but Kurt seemed terribly jovial about it.

When Martha and Kurt explained to Joy their involvement with a civil suit about her parents' untimely death, she listened holding my hand. It was a great deal of money written upon the check and it was hers. The suit was settled out of court.

My Joy did not hesitate. She just went to her purse, got out a pen, endorsed the back, and handed it back to Kurt and Martha. She wanted them to have it. There wasn't a more unselfish moment in her life than then. Joy was thanking them both for saving her life by taking her in. Nevertheless, after many tears of thanks, Kurt and Martha would not accept it. Joy turned to me.

"Greg, it's six million dollars…it's up to you, but I'm for giving it all to the church then. I don't want that money, though I thank both of you," turning to them. " Somehow, it doesn't seem to help ease missing my parents and I never knew anything about what you did."

"Joyce, the suit was filed in your behalf because you were a minor. I dare not mention it to you, since the young attorney who approached me to take on the case, for only a win he got paid or lose-nothing proposal at his own asking, and was working only for ten percent of any settlement. He collected his fee first, because he won. We just did it for you…it's yours, it didn't cost Martha nor me a single dime."

"It's yours, sweetheart," Martha reiterated.

"It's your call, Joy," I ,too, spoke.

"Settled then, we'll drop it in the offering Sunday and wait for old Pastor Kefir to faint!" she laughed. "He's always been so great to everyone, especially to me. I bet he builds us a new church!" she said, as we all hugged on her decision.

Funny, that next Sunday during the offering, a hallelujah sounded out so loud I thought the steeple might collapse in our little stone church. Joy decided not to drop it in the plate, but while the organ music played, she walked up and handed to the good pastor that check as her parents' offering.

"Here, Pastor Kefir, this is from my parents to the church, they loved you, also."

"Hallelujah, praise the Lord!"

The good pastor then stood there recovering from the shock, looking dumbfounded at the enormous check made out to his church, then finally came out and spoke trembling, "Fellow parishioners, God has brought us a gift from Darrell and Jewell Dixon. Will all the Elders please meet with me in the big hall after this service? I think I better stop now, because I forgot my sermon," he chuckled. "Be good to one another, let the light of Jesus Christ shine down upon you, but don't forget to come back next Saturday for probable announcements of construction beginning on our new church facilities…Amen!"

Then he sat down flustered, but quickly realized his duty to greet his flock, while exiting. He hugged both Joy and I while in tears. He was more than thankful for the money. His first thought was the granite cornerstone to place in the church foundation inscribed with their names…"Hallelujah!" Joy added.

"It was the perfect choice, my dear, the pastor was overcome with joy," I said to her leaving Glenarm. Her face was beaming and I could tell her heart was always in the right place.

The next few weeks were busy. I went out to my work's project daily, where Grub became my friend. We seemed to work together well, except he kept asking to know more about our honeymoon escapade that he'd heard about.

Grub had started the project using my calculations and his very small crew was good, but slow. Soon, in about two months including rain delays, that roadway was completed, elevated higher than the flood plain. Installed was a huge ten-foot corrugated whistle culvert running completely under and through it for floodwater passage. A by-pass was constructed thereafter. It was a good design.

It was time to bring in the big machinery to construct the bridge pillar forms, which held straight the concrete piles for the pile drivers to sink them to their rest on the hard pan stone layer, pounding continually, until sixteen feet below ground level.

Also, it was time to order delivery of concrete, made at 7% air-mix , and the steel rebar at 26' lengths brought onto the site to begin the actual bridge construction. Ironworkers and more laborers from the local union halls were hired to help complete the project. It was taking shape.

Planned as a one hundred-seventy feet, two-lane, high-railed, fifty-ton bridge crossing, it was simple, but adequate for the service it was to render. When the weather held, I was able to go home happily every evening to my lovely Joy, who by the way always told me about her day, even if I didn't ask. The project was about to be completed a month ahead of schedule, and below estimates. It finished in only eleven months.

It was on Memorial Day weekend that Joy and I ventured up to my parents' home in Northfield. Joy got carsick on the way and unfortunately had to have me stop the car, as she bolted out onto the shoulder of I-55 to hurl. I jumped out to assist her, but she told me then she was getting used to it. That surprised me. I imagined she was hiding an illness from me, but she told me she was going to a gynecologist and she had given her diagnosis.

"It's nothing infectious, Greg. I will discuss this later when I feel better. I'm going to sleep now, wake me when we get there," was her only reply to my concerns. Then she went right to sleep.

I continued to keep an eye on her very closely as I drove. I became ill myself thinking she was going to tell me she was dying or had something and was taking the heroine route 'sucking it up' as she often advised me to do when I was with headache or minor sunburn pain from the job. I drove into my parents' drive after three hours of worry. However, when Mother met us waiting at the door, I somehow felt relieved.

It was another 'Joy-ess' moment after Mom led us to the dining table and we saw her delicious meal there waiting for us. Dad was seated already, reading his Wall Street Journal paper. I noticed the Tribune had been already read, and placed loosely on an armchair near him. Then he grumbled a bit why we took so long. He was very hungry.

"Your son knocked me up! I had morning sickness on the way," Joy delightfully informed him, even before we had begun the meal. It was my surprise also.

Mother squealed with excitement and Father told us he was thrilled, forgot the meal and said he was starting another savings account. When Mom realized her great meal was cooling, she asked us to say our prayer and eat before she had to pitch it out. I was never so worried, then relieved and elated in my entire life.

My lovely wife said grace in her special way, which touched all of our hearts with her straightforward take on her good fortune of now having my parents as hers also. She never quit being so humble. Because of her, we all felt blessed. I was proud, too.

Time passes quickly when you are having fun and soon Joy was showing her pregnancy. I returned to the state shed from a small road project completion to begin helping Kurt. He was in the draft planning stages for a section of a huge bridge that was to cross the mighty Mississippi River from St. Louis to its namesake western Illinois sister city.

If accepted by the Missouri lawmakers and the Illinois Assembly, it would become a major three to four year project. It was coming, Kurt said, whenever the money flowed. I pulled out all of my instruments and rolled up my sleeves very happily. Now, I thought to myself, this was finally the kind of project I had always envisioned that all the hard work in college and of my expertise was needed.

Joy took a leave of absence when the baby was due in six weeks. Sheena decided to stay long before that. She assumed she had a good chance going on to the fall semester in the next year of community college working through the winter, spring, and summer for Joy and staying with the state in her secretarial job.

Everything seemed to be running smoothly. Until one afternoon I felt this strangeness come over me, which I could not explain, as if it was gloom. It lasted for several days and I just couldn't shake it. Looking back, I wonder now if it was her spirit calling to me in her last hours.

As if a cold, numbing, icy-chilled-feeling was seeping into my soul, although my face seemed hot, came the news I received one night with a midnight call from Dad. The message he delivered sent more chills down my spine. Jill was reported missing in Kandahar, Afghanistan. It happened when her marine unit went into an enemy city on a night raid, Taliban-sweep, four days prior, he said.

The good news was she was not confirmed dead, nevertheless she may be held hostage and tortured. We both were aware of the past actions of the Taliban. They often slaughtered our soldiers and cut off their heads, only to be kicked around in the sand like a soccer ball and this might have become her fate.

Jill's commander had called them personally on Jill's own cell, because every soldier was required to surrender their personal phones before going out into the field in case of being captured. The commander tried to explain the situation as to why Jill was still unaccounted for, as were some others. In a firefight that strong, one basically had to cover the other's back and if your backside went down one was left vulnerable and had to fend for oneself. She could be in hiding in the city.

Though the commander and a task force had regained the attack area, they found but one alive, near-death soldier. Her unit had been under heavy fire and Jill was assigned to her support group, which was called in reserve to help, but her unit was met by a well-planned ambush. That was the first report he received.

Dad called the Char family to see if they had been alerted, or heard any encouraging news, but they had not.

More calls came, which all upset us each time, as if it were torture. Then the Chars called back. No survivors of any of the attacks were located, Will's commander had sadly told them. Nevertheless, when Jill's body had not been found, it was presumed she was captured with several others. But they still had no news other than Will was missing also.

Dad said Jill's commander sobbed and said she was sorry to Dad, but Dad told her Jill had found her place in life by her husband's side, fighting for our country, doing what she could do best.

Dad could not accept Jill's commander's expressed guilt of feeling responsible, if something happened bad to Jill; it was not her fault. Dad could only share the pain her body was feeling. It was a long sickening night with little sleep. It was so hard to imagine as a kid something so horrendous and courageous would come from Jill.

Fox News reported the casualties of the incident in the morning, even before the war department officially notified Father and Mother later in the day their child was killed. Jill's name was among the list of three killed from the Chicago area. Will's name came across in the other listed casualties. We had lost them both.

Dad, choked up and crying, called immediately when he saw the news report and found us crying also. My sister and her husband who had died possibly in the same hour, both paid the ultimate sacrifice for our country. Although we never actually knew what occurred over there, nevertheless, we were proud to know Jill and her husband, Will Char, had served their country with honor.

Jill's mutilated remains were sent home aboard a cargo plane with several other valiant soldiers. Will was laid to rest in Rancho Rio Grande, California, his home, at the request of his relatives we had never met. We just wanted Jill back home. Father called to express his condolences to the Char family, but they were not so receptive, saying Will died because he tried to save Jill. Dad hung up on them. We never heard from them again.

That sealed coffin came draped in our US flag; Jill's body too disfigured to display. Her coffin was accompanied by a Captain and six pallbearer marines.

We buried Jill in the Northfield cemetery two weeks later, with full military proceedings. Mother accepted the commemorative US flag, the only memory left from Jill.

Then weeks later came the combat story accompanying a Congressional Medal of Honor, Bronze Star, with Purple Heart medals concerning Jill's marine group theater event.

As described by a dispersed soldier, who managed to escape the wrath alive, apparently, his legs were shot out from under him, and Jill was mortally wounded in the first barrage of a Taliban ambush. However, when everyone thought they had expired, he and Jill lay bleeding, but conscious, he was paralyzed.

Suddenly on the approach of the enemy, Jill arose bloody and torn apart and managed to lob her last three grenades into the advancing groups that came to desecrate the soldiers' bodies, as they usually do.

Jill killed seven or more, the overlooked, helplessly wounded soldier related in his report, then watched as Jill stood her ground defenseless, her firearm without bullets.

Basically unarmed then, she struggled to her feet, still severely bleeding, searching for a weapon to arm herself, as a Taliban machine gunner finished her life. She had been valiant in her obvious face of death.

With the passing of Jill and Will, Mother never regained her family happiness again. Dad did not retire as planned, and they each seemed to blame the other for not being there to teach Jill ways that were more feminine to keep her out of the service. They became angry with the Marines for their poor treatment carrying out Jill's death notification, among other problems. It was not as pleasant visiting them as it had been. With Jill's passing so abruptly, it seemed to me as if someone had taken an eraser to my chalkboard-life and erased part of it forever.

Then Joy delivered our first child in the dead of winter nearing Christmas Eve. She insisted we name our newborn daughter, Jillian Martha Wetmore, after my sister and Martha. Joy had refused my presence in the birthing process. She said I would never look at her the same, if I witnessed the contortions her body went through and the pain she suffered then. It was a place for womanhood and doctors only, Joy insisted.

Joy was mostly correct, however shortly after the nurses laid Jillian in her arms and invited me into her room, I thought she was more beautiful then, than ever before as a mother. I was proud when I held Jillian for the first time. She looked like me, I think, even with her eyes still closed. Everyone sees him or herself in every baby, but luckily, Jillian began to look more like Joy as months passed.

Jillian's birth was as if a healing wand had passed over my parents. Suddenly they came down regularly to Springfield to visit their grandchild, who had little resemblance of their own daughter, but it was a chance to make lady-like their granddaughter. Jillian got all their attention along with Martha and Kurt's.

"You can spoil a child with presents, but not with parental love," Dad told us, contrary to his arms bearing gifts of love he said were for our Jillian every single time he and Mother walked through our front door.

Jillian possessed a good nature, just like her mother, and was an easy baby to love and raise. She was also very alert when her home schooling began, about as soon as she had begun teething at six months. I remember how Joy often read to her. She bought Sesame Street flash cards for beginning her first reading lessons.

After Joy's gift to the church, we learned that her contribution was to serve many people so well. Kurt and I both offered ideas for its design. The tall steeple stood as a monument to Joy's parents in that little prairie state village. We managed to purchase and level that tavern and made its place a nice parking lot.

It never dawned on me why the Rakers had no children of their own. I guess God planned for Joy to be Martha's only child, since physically she could have none of her own.

By her baptism, Jillian recognized His religious picture and spoke the word "Jesus" very readily. When Jillian spoke His name 'Jesus' out so clearly during her actual baptism celebration, anointed with purification waters by Pastor Kefir, it was apparently a remarkable child who exited our church, everyone told us. We were so proud.

When I look back upon my life, knowing Joy's, Kurt and Martha's, Mom and Dad's, I wonder at His scheme of things to bring us all together in his new church that Sunday morning to witness Jillian's baptism; she was just turning two and the first child ever to be christened in the newly completed, one-week old church. The pastor's flock had grown to well over six hundred on news of a better place to worship, the largest sect of Mennonite faith in Illinois.

The Pastor Kefir had baptized our daughter only one week before my father fell ill with a heart condition at age fifty-nine. Doctors told Dad his work life had to be curtailed. He decided to sell his interest in his practice and finally retire.

Though the hospitals of Chicago and its suburbs were large, arranging swift help seemed much delayed. Both Dad and Mother decided to move to Springfield to be closer to Springfield's famous heart hospital, Prairie Heart Institute of St. John's Hospital. Also, they would be closer to their granddaughter.

As a result of his lawyer's lifestyle ending, Mother and Dad sold their lovely home and bought a much smaller home that became available near Springfield Lake.

Shortly after they moved in, Dad went into by-pass surgery to unclog arteries; it was a triple by-pass procedure. Dad was in the hospital for only three days and walked out on his own. The surgery left scars, but along with his prescribed exercise program of he and Mother walking around on the big lake's walking paths, it saved his life. They soon became healthier and happier and closer than each could remember as a result.

Mom, of course, refused to allow any other babysitter for Jillian, just in case Joy and I needed alone time. Dad always came, too, and sometimes it was a foursome when Kurt and Martha also showed up. Those four became the best of friends, always going to church and socializing together.

It did not take very long for Joy and me to realize we needed more space. We had the full payment, which helped us decide. Joy saw Danby's farm up for auction. She told me that she knew them well. I did not even know that.

On a whim, we attended that land auction one Saturday morning. Joy just kept bidding higher. She really wanted old Mr. Danby's lovely 640-acre farm with that state-built, five acre lake that I helped survey off for him. He had taken good care of his family's homestead and it showed, allowing for a premium which not many could afford.

The gavel went down on our bid and we had spent a lot of money. Danby was satisfied with our purchase, especially because I told him he was welcome to fish any time, except when Joy and I were skinny-dippin', which suddenly made his wife Minnie blush. I guess they had tried that out themselves a time or two.

Unfortunately, Mr. Danby had become ill, just like my father, and had to adjust his lifestyle, too, although his heart troubles stemmed because he labored his heart too hard, too many times.

We agreed we had bought the most wonderful piece of property and probably the only gently rolling hills on the big prairie within twenty miles of Springfield. Our wedding gift from Mom and Dad had taken a big hit, but we were still in there for our retirement package IRAs.

After we moved into the farmhouse, I started plans for our own with Joy's help. We offered Dad and Mom, Kurt and Martha to come out to live there, anywhere and select home sites free of their own choosing. However, they told us, although they all were appreciative, they were too old to start over again.

With Dad available to golf, suddenly Kurt decided it was his time to take his state pension, retire, and learn the game, too. The state was beginning to show signs of depression spending, he mentioned, and I would have to deal with it.

Kurt bought a great set of clubs and he and Dad began to take lessons together from the club pro. Two peas in a pod they were then. Joy and I were happy everything was working out for us all.

Kurt and Dad bought memberships to the Springfield Golf Club where they told us our congressional representatives spent too much time. Each man bought three wheeled bikes for themselves and their women to use on the trails for added exercise. They bought the best New Balance walking shoes together and a big Ranger bass boat for fishing out on Springfield Lake together, while Martha showed Mom how to quilt and can their fresh veggies. Mom gave Martha a makeover, which Kurt could not stand and had Martha get a perm the way she had done since they first met. Nevertheless, everything else worked wonders for their now "brotherly love friendship".

However, it was that damn custom golf cart they bought together that caused consternation. It was a replica of a new Dodge Ram, like Kurt's truck at work, which Kurt had always desired to personally own and bought it without Dad knowing. Though Dad agreed afterwards to put up his half, as he had with the expensive Ranger Bass boat that cost ten times more, Kurt considered the cart his. He even used it at his home to retrieve his mail left in his mailbox. It was his favorite toy.

Their sharing stopped when Kurt always hustled out to be the cart's driver every time they visited the course. Dad offered to drive, but Kurt would not have it. Therefore, Dad bet Kurt the keys to their fancy golf cart, at their next outing one day, just to settle their friction once and for all. Dad won and Kurt became angry. Before we knew it, they were no longer friends.

Like two old farts quibbling, eventually father time healed their forgetful memories. On an outing to our lake where Joy was teaching Jillian to swim, they were each invited, not knowing the other would be there. It was our Jillian, who shouted out after her first successful swim from mommy to the shore.

"Look, grandpas, I can swim!"

They each stood looking at the other when Jillian slipped upon the bank, flopped on her behind, and they both hustled to pick her up. Dad allowed Kurt to hold the happy Jillian as a peace offering. It was a simple lawyer's trick of not getting himself covered in mud, but Kurt took it as an apology. Kurt and Dad grew up and buried their silly hatchet sharing our daughter, while Mom and Martha watched their boys being boys.

Though I was considered for Kurt's retired position, his job was put in the hands of a person who had much more time with the state than me and her political connection was in power. I knew my time would come eventually and I was glad to accept second fiddle, because I still did not have to attend all of those boring outside meetings and travel away from home, as Kurt had.

However, that person turned out to be an obnoxious female, named Clara Turner, a woman who evidently thought she was supervising an army patrol, and gave orders like a drill sergeant.

Clara Turner was a fifty-ish aged woman, tall, about six feet, trim, with long black hair and witchy eyebrows that caused one to stare at her long Italian nose. She smoked incessantly in the office, though it was illegal in any state building. She was someone who had never married and I could understand the reason why, very quickly, after having spoken with her the very first time.

Clara laid the law down. Whatever she said was our team's goal…she might not always be right, but she was always the boss. She would be the one with her tit in the wringer if something ever went wrong, she told me. Therefore, she expected me to follow her instructions explicitly, whatever they were, if I approved or not. That was the only way we could get the job done. I was dizzy.

Then Miss Turner began by telling me about all of her credentials. Why she had to explain them to me was ludicrous, but she did. She had graduated from South Dakota State. Her major was business management with a minor in kinesiology. She played basketball on the girls' team. They won their conference. How that related in any manner to her being a highway engineer supervisor and considered over me was not understandable. I was beside myself.

The state construction jobs were coming to a halt, I could soon tell. I highly considered quitting, until she finally spoke with some sincerity in her speech.

"Mr. Wetmore. I will need all your help. Our state's highway budget is a disaster and in the toilet. They do not need someone like you, a talented engineer out of Chicago. They need someone like me, who is ruthless and willing to eek out a workable plan to save the state millions of dollars at any cost, cut from our already fleeting monetary highway budget.

"Yes, there will be some construction and building from time to time when necessary. Work will be minimal for quite some time. Therefore, as I work over the budget, maul it, would be a better description, you will do the actual work, while I will get the credit. Nevertheless, if I tell you that you have to lay off people, cut short a job, or anything else, you have to comply... you must."

"Am I going to take over this job just because of political reasons? Are you the Turners from Chicago, the so called 'family' Turners?"

She stared hard at me then asked me how I knew of the Turners.

"My father was a corporate lawyer. He mentioned the Turner Family from time to time in the same breath as Capone, Baby Face Nelson and Mrs. O'Leary," I said, meaning to insult her.

She did not reply, but held her ire by biting her lower lip.

"Your concern is only to do your job. When the state gets back on its feet, I will have done my job and you will probably get my posted job. Until then, you must be prudent to my plight."

Her mumbo-jumbo was making me sick. Sarcastically, I then asked if my salary would be cut also. She said she had not considered that, but the thought was a good idea and she would work something out. I shut my mouth. Therefore, she assumed I was with her.

My first order of business was to meet with the union reps and tell them I was releasing almost everyone there. In two weeks, I would recall a select skeleton crew to be available for projects. Snowplow drivers were exempt. That left about fifty total shed personnel, me included. Nothing made sense. My indigestion began.

Next, I was to start delaying payments to state vendors, until they made their third request for payment, which usually meant ninety days, or send something, if they charged a major interest charge. If they threatened court action, send partial payment. It was delay, delay, and delay. I wondered what Miss Turner was doing, since it seemed I was doing exactly what she was hired to do.

The wretchedness of telling someone they were without a job was devastating to me. I knew most of these people as ordinary, hard working, men and women. Unfortunately, I took my work home with me and my irritability crossed the line with Joy. I was cussing mad.

Joy was even more ruthless than Turner was, if it meant yelling obscenities in front of our daughter watching TV. Joy grabbed my ear and led me outside dancing to the quick step in much pain, and immediately sorry for my outbursts.

"I'm only going to say this once, husband of mine. Don't you ever take the Lord's name in vain in my presence or Jillian's, or I will pull this ear off and start on the other like a wild momma bobcat. Now, I understand your problems, but from now on leave them there at work! Understand me?"

Jillian called out, "Momma!" right then, and saved her daddy's ear.

Joy immediately left me to go to our daughter. I sat on the porch swing thinking…just thinking…well, I was rubbing my poor ear a bit, too.

I got up from the swing and decided to go inside to apologize to my little family. Joy was tight-lipped, arms crossed, and sitting on the couch watching Jillian up and dancing to the music about a hotdog, excited also about Mickey Mouse and his friends on a windmill. It was amusing to me how The Mickey Mouse Club show had evolved into an educational program, and still had its cartoon humor.

Joy did not look at me, actually she tried hard not to, until I crashed next to my daughter and told her that her daddy talked like Donald Duck. That got her attention. I gave her my rendition of, "Halloo, I'm Donald Duck!", which made her giggle and ask me to do more. Therefore, with the best I could muster, squeezing that air through my gritted teeth and cheeks, I said, "I'm worry sorreey, sweeet heart! Daddddy was a wooorrrrry baddddd boooyy!" Though Jillian wasn't sure why I said that, someone else was.

It worked, because very quickly I had two lovely girls rolling all over me on the floor and one was on top of me tickling extra hard. I begged to have her quit, but that made Jillian laugh hard and it was so cute when she reached out, working the fingers of her one hand, pretending to tickle her daddy. Though she did not quite touch me, I screamed out laughter as if I could not stand it anymore. It lasted until I almost got hoarse faking it. When the newness wore off, Jillian went back to watching Mickey and Joy and I lay beside her on the rug.

"You know. All that fun made me feel much better. Although, I don't think I can hear very well out of my one ear, but this one is good," I complained, realizing Joy was a bit sorry too.

"You're very lucky, Mr., after your cussing outburst your daughter saved you…your ear was my second choice to grab onto, this was the first!" she laughed, grabbing me below the belt playfully, causing Jillian to jump onto us.

We three frolicked on the floor wrestling, until right before it was eight, Jillian's bedtime. We all knew what that meant. After her bath, our little darling knelt down beside her little bed in her pajamas next to Mommy. I did too. Then together, we asked Jesus to receive us in Heaven. Jillian blessed her grandmas and grandpas, mommy and daddy and Mickey, too…Amen. Then Jillian took little time crawling into her bed and asking her mommy to read her a story.

"Tonight, Daddy wants to read to you, dear…pick one, Daddy," Joy said, offering up a handful of children's books for me to select one.

I chose the thinnest, little book about the "Mean Old Witch Who Tried to Steal the Schoolhouse". It had pop-ups and I must have done well reading to her, because our little girl soon was sound asleep. We both kissed her goodnight trying not to wake her and quietly backed out of her room and turned off her light.

"I have been elevated to cartoon status," I told Joy later. "Maybe that's what we need to do every time I have a bad day at work," I joked.

Joy had better ideas as how to relieve my stress, and hers. It was another one of those short nights before dawn that we shared many more times in our lives.

Chapter 13

Spring had sprung, which usually meant our crews would be out patching roadways and mowing right-of-ways along the state highways. Instead, few workers were in line to punch-in and most were distressed by what they were reading on the bulletin board. It was from Miss Turner and it was not good news.

"That bitch is going to get hers!" screamed Sheena at me, when I walked into the office one Monday morning.

"What's wrong now?" I asked.

"My name is on the lay-off list. My uncle is going to hear about this!"

"I better check myself. Is she going to completely obliterate our department?"

"That will be enough!" came loud words from behind me.

It was that wicked witch from the west side of Springfield; the workers had rightly dubbed her. She came in fiery mad and slammed her things down upon her desk.

"I told you two that nobody was safe. I could not help it, Sheena. You don't have anything to do here, since we don't have anything going on. I can't keep you and lay off one of the field personnel. I just can't."

For a moment, I thought I saw a bit of remorse from Miss Turner. I also noticed the dark circles under her eyes, which I assumed was drugs, booze, or lack of sleep or all of them. I was wrong, she was on the rag, and there is nothing worse for a man in my position when he sees his boss reach into her purse and grab that little Tampax and two Motrin and head off to the john. I was in for one hell of a bad day.

Sheena was on the phone to her uncle faster than slick snot. "Unk, I got fired!" she screamed. "What am I going to do with my new car payment?" she said, seated next to me at my desk. She was using my phone.

"Honey, don't get upset. I will talk to Miss Turner. I know her and she knows me. It's just a misunderstanding," is what I heard him tell her over the phone. "Just do whatever she says and let me handle it my way…love you…got to go…don't worry."

Sheena still looked worried and apologized for using my phone. Nevertheless, I got something out of her rage more than she knew. Though I was the happiest married man in the world, Sheena wore that fragrance that jarred my mind and my senses.

"You're wearing that Coffee perfume, aren't you?" I suggested, inhaling. "It does something to me I can not explain," I added.

"Well, thanks…it's Lila's…we share. What am I going to do?"

"Hey…you haven't a choice. Leave today, when the phones start ringing, about noon, maybe she will reconsider. I wish I had some paperwork for you, but I don't. I'm probably next."

"Thanks, but what could she do without you? I saw you have to do all the serious hard work…my eyes are on it."

"You still here?" the voice sounded.

Without backtalk, Sheena locked up her desk and told Miss Turner she would be back to pick up her things, after she had some juice in the lounge.

"I get credit for today, don't I? I did drive in and there's a show-up rule clause in the contract, if you don't know that!" she said, as the phone rang.

"Then answer the phone. That's why I pay you."

"Listen, lady, you don't pay anyone…the taxpayers do. I'm a taxpayer, too."

I thought there was going to be fisticuffs or a wrestling match on the office floor, so I moved between the two and managed to pick up the ringing phone at the same time.

"State shed, Wetmore speaking," I told the caller. It was the congressman.

"Oh, Greg Wetmore…Sheena has told me how you have taken over and helped her. Thanks…is my niece there?"

"It's for you, Sheena…it's your uncle."

Sheena took the phone and listened. Her face grew grim and she licked her lips looking hard at Miss Turner. Then she hung up and began removing her things from her desk.

"Good-bye, Greg…see you around," was all she said with no explanation as she turned and walked out.

"Better punch out!" Turner yelled. However, Sheena just exited the door without further ado. Then Miss Turner walked over, found Sheena's punch card, and punched her out herself.

The phone continued to ring and I became the secretary. Miss Turner left carrying plenty of folders and told me she was going to be in a meeting with personnel bosses. Apparently, the unions were on her back and she had to deal with it herself. I received a call from the governor's office for Miss Turner and transferred it upstairs to their switchboard. That was probably Sheena's Chi-town congressman uncle pulling strings to get Sheena back on the job.

I needed to go to the restroom, but could not as suddenly people were calling in non-stop, complaining about the grass along several highways too overgrown, unsafe for cross traffickers. Additionally, the road potholes were so huge that they could swallow up a school bus. The complaints covered every avenue we handled from our shed.

I tried to explain the financial predicament our state was in, leaving us short on funds, but met opposition that I should grab up a sickle and get out there myself, because the caller was unemployed himself.

"Tough shit, buddy!" the caller said, while slamming the receiver down hard.

I was in a no-win situation. That last caller's voice sounded vaguely familiar, as if it could have been Clint. Then I realized with all those calls coming in simultaneously, it was the recently laid off workers complaining to get something done that could bring them back. I wished I could.

Miss Turner almost ran in and went straight to the john to smoke, I guess. I could smell the smoke from nearly thirty feet away with the door closed. Then I decided to ask when Clara returned if I could just move out of our office to Sheena's desk, away from her. I got up and then answered the next caller from Sheena's desk. I heard someone coming down the stairs very fast.

Turner returned a bit winded and breathing as if she had just been jogging. Her face looked very pale.

"Greg, get Sheena's number…and call her back. Don't ask why, just do it. Her uncle is a nice person and pushed more money our way. Using our seniority list, call back twenty workers and all the mechanics to start up the tractors mowing. I think…I think…we can get by for…now.

"Anyway, you can start doing…what…what you do…best. Here…this is a release let on your next project," she told me, fumbling her folders breathless-sounding…handing over a project's release to me. Suddenly Clara looked odd. Maybe her presentation was just too much for her or her period had caused this tormenting look on her face. I thought she had cramps. Nevertheless, she suddenly seemed to catch a second wind.

"Kurt Rakers had started this huge project on that bridge across the Mississippi down at East Saint Louis. Somehow, they have dickered a deal with Missouri and now it is moving again. I…I'm going for some air…I think I need another smoke," she said, again fumbling aimlessly while opening her purse and finally getting out a pack of Winston filtered cigarettes and her lighter, and two more Motrin. She had it bad.

I was very surprised how quickly Clara Turner got the ball rolling and even reconsidered my negative opinion about her taking over. Actually, she was the best at doing her job. Even that afternoon some mechanics, who had left hours before, came back into the shed to service tractors and get them out on the road. The phones stopped ringing as much, but Clara was nowhere to be found. She left me with no word how to reach her.

Sheena did not come back by quitting time; however, everything around the shed seemed almost normal with more workers leaving after punching out on the time clock. Their demeanor was now better as they were getting their paychecks after all.

The life of a secretary was more crap than I imagined. I had to admire my wife's previous expertise much more now that I had walked a day in her shoes. I had long decided that my workday happenings would stay right here as I locked up to go home. Then I got the surprise of my life. Why I glanced up I'll never know.

As I started to back up my truck to head out, something strange caught my eye. Behind our office, next to the huge winter salt storage bin was the figure of a female's body lying on the ground. I drove up to find it was Clara lying face down. I first thought she had been raped or beaten. Her hair was bloody and when I gently rolled her over, she was unconscious and barely breathing.

Looking harder at her, her face was almost black. I tried to awaken her, however I then knew something was seriously wrong. I ran over to my state truck and found the radio worked just by turning it on, even without the key and pushed the intercom button to key the police radio.

"Any police unit, this is the IDOT state shed. I have an emergency…go ahead…"

Immediately, the state police answered and asked my position. I retold them I was at the IDOT shed, and I had found an unconscious woman near the winter salt bins… "Please send EMTs and police. She might have been attacked," I said, realizing then I sounded desperate.

My thoughts immediately went to a retaliation attack by some furious worker laid off that day.

It was only a few minutes, but it seemed like more. My cell phone buzzed and it was Joy. I suddenly could not believe in my nervousness I had forgotten it was there to dial 911, but I had gotten direct communication anyway and help was summoned, I told Joy quickly. I explained what had happened and I would be late, and then hung up.

The EMTs drove through the gates and saw me waving. One jumped out running and carrying his medical kit. With just a glance at Clara, he announced to the other that Clara had had a stroke. He placed an oxygen mask over her face, elevated her feet, and began to monitor her vital signs as quickly as he could rattle them off through his portable radio. He made contact with a doctor at St. John's Hospital immediately, called in her stats, and then started asking me questions that I did not know any answer to, except she went missing about one thirty and she was a heavy smoker.

It was amazing how they performed and when additional help arrived, they had put an IV in her arm and readied her to transport. In less than ten minutes, Clara was whisked away in the emergency unit with sirens wailing. The two young men had given Clara a chance to survive.

When a police officer arrived, he found where Clara had hit her head when falling against the salt bin. There were incredible amounts of cigarette butts, scattered around, as if she had used this place to hide her smoking habit for some time. I really did not know Clara's full name or age and address but I saw her car.

I showed the police officer her car. He called in the license plate number, and it was registered to Clara Turner, but still in Skokie, Illinois. The officer received all that information in seconds from his dispatcher to give to the EMTs, who had not arrived at the hospital yet.

Eventually, when I closed and locked the gates, my energy was spent. I was so exhausted I barely made it home. I sat in my drive, until I had time to catch up with my feelings. I guess the suddenness of finding Clara lying there bloody, looking as if she had been assaulted, was a bit traumatic and drew upon all of my adrenalin, leaving me weak. Nevertheless, I was thankful I could help her.

I decided to tell Joy everything was okay and the doctors had Clara now. I did not bring my worry home, though Joy would have listened. I called Kurt to tell him about his replacement for the first time, but called him really to tell him his work on the Mississippi Bridge was approved and construction work had begun on the Missouri side. He offered his knowledge and told me to remember everything I approved might come back to haunt me twenty-five years later, so make certain everything, every single thing I approved, was correct and safe, before I signed off on it. Then Jillian wanted to talk to Kurt and Martha, so I said good-bye and ate my supper late. I felt much stronger afterward.

"You know…see that guitar over there…well, I'm going to learn how to play it and my girls can practice their singing, while I play" I told Joy, thinking she would like that.

I picked up the Gibson that Joe Petito had given me and strummed the strings. I put it back down and thought I'd search the internet for books that taught how to begin playing the guitar. I was surprised then that Joy had picked it up, and actually played a beautiful little church song for Jillian and me called "Faith, Hope and Charity". It was an electric guitar, so it was not very loud, but I heard my wife being a little girl again. I decided to buy an amp and a mike, maybe two, off the Ebay site. I envisioned the making of a star as Jillian kept singing, "The Bible tells me soooo."

"Here, it's now yours," I said, giving it to Joy after she sang but stopped strumming. "Why didn't you tell me you could play? I knew you could sing."

"I guess you never asked me," she said, smiling and strumming soft cords.

That was the beginning of more happiness in our family as Jillian acted as if she wanted to play it and sang every song mommy knew. Life was good, I thought to myself. I hoped Clara had pulled through, too.

Later, I called into the hospital. They told me the only thing they were allowed to tell someone who was not a family member; Clara was admitted. Joy said she would send flowers in everyone's name in the morning and being a former secretary she knew exactly what to do.

Day after day at work, memos came down concerning our boss's health. To make everyone aware of new help in dealing with stroke victims, the information we received about Clara surviving her stroke may have been because doctors administered a new drug. It could completely dissolve most blood clot stoppages in the brain. The medication was useful, if done within about four hours from the beginning of a stroke, we learned in a bulletin.

Clara would survive, they told us, although her returning to work was doubtful. She would be placed on workman's comp leave, while she regained use of her limbs. I wonder now, why I had noticed her at all, since I usually just swung my truck around and took off, never looking to the area where she was laying unconscious. I guess the Good Lord wanted me to see Clara.

I learned to account for everyone before I closed those gates after that. I was then put in charge of the shed operations along with my engineering duties, but my pay remained the same on probationary-observation for one year. I was okay with that, except I did not want to go on any out of state meetings.

The summer brought us much fun around our big place. I kept it well manicured when I purchased a new John Deere tractor and brush hog. I used them to mow around our lake and along the dirt roads that led to planted fields where we walked. For the fun of it, I also bought an old hay wagon and filled it with straw from time to time for our whole family to enjoy riding on hayrides, going out to the lake for weenie and marshmallow roasts. We made it there, with everyone singing and Joy accompanying us, playing her new louder Martin acoustic guitar she wanted.

Eventually, via cruising slowly down our field roads, looking at the grazing deer and an occasional bunny jumping out from the roadside, we all arrived there safely. I built some portable steps, using scrap wood used as concrete forms that were to be burned at the shed, so the grandparents could climb up easier. I had noticed they hesitated on how to climb aboard that wagon.

I decided to cut down some young trees that had grown along our creek to make firewood; instead, Joy wanted me to make a little log cabin for Jillian's playhouse out of them. More or less, I just wanted to get out and get even more exercise out in the open air. However, with Grandpa Kurt's help, we made the best little log cabin playhouse since Abe Lincoln. In fact, I got my ideas from photographs taken of Joy, Jillian, and I visiting there.

My job was sedentary mostly and I could see my youthful trimness fading at twenty-nine. I always tanned in the summers and lost ten pounds, but turned white in the Illinois cold winters and gained ten back. I felt good now and Joy liked what she saw.

Joy and Jillian swam at Springfield Lake beach regularly because there were lifeguards. It was right near my parents' new place, and they, too, were tanned and healthier looking. Grandma Wetmore got out there with them on that beach and she was enjoying the time of her life, while Dad and Kurt still putted around on the golf course, sharing that fancy cart. Martha, however, chose to stay home most of the times to knit afghans or quilted colorful blankets for church raffles. Mom did not enjoy that as much.

Years before, after the farm was ours, I had been approached by other wishful bidding farmers wanting me to cash-rent them my dormant fields for their planting. However, I sadly refused them and put them in the government's CRP program that allowed the fields to sit unplowed, because I had no equipment. Therefore, unplowed, the fields became overgrown with weeds and sometimes small trees the first years. I was not a very good steward of the land one farmer told me, so I looked again for someone I felt I could rely upon to be fair and do a good job.

Actually, being from the city, I had no real farm knowledge and was pleasantly surprised how much money just one acre could normally be rented. I then put out the word I was open to someone farming my fields. The normal procedure was to poison the weeds and plow them under, most applicants proposed, however I was not going to allow that because during that time farmers sprayed their fields with herbicide, correlated to the spring birthing of many creatures in those fields, like the cotton tailed rabbit, fox and any small living animal. Even box turtles died when they came into contact and waterways such as my own lake we swam in were subject to run offs in wet weather and posed a hazard to our health.

When a young man named Denny Donaldson, who worked part-time at the state shed as one of our highway mowers, found out I owned the former Danby farm he came to me with a proposition to sharecrop my land. However, Denny did not have the money to pay the normal $275 per acre rent on almost six hundred acres I had available. He wanted to give me a third of his profits contract, if there were any. Denny explained that he and his brother had total use of his father's farm equipment.

Denny projected a better return than the cash rent, provided our weather permitted him and his brother getting into the fields on time. He said if I mowed those weeds, he would control burn them as they dried in a week, thus sparing thousands in chemicals and putting nitrogen back into the soil from the burn. Animals might die, however at least they could run away and return afterwards. With chemicals, it was always their misfortune to come into contact.

Therefore, when he convinced me to burn, not poison, that is what I did every night after work for almost two weeks. It worked. In retrospect, it proved a good move as his first harvest of soybeans yielded a higher return to us both. From then on, I contracted Denny and his brother Jordan Donaldson.

During the planting and harvest times, Joy would prepare the renters noon lunches and evening suppers at our home. Their clothes always remained farm-dirty, so she served them outside on the porch, so the boys could wash up and eat there and return to the fields. They loved her cooking as much as I did. And, they often cooled down with a quick swim after work, sometimes almost nearing midnight. They worked as hard as anyone could.

When the manager of our local feed mill issued checks for our harvest, I got my one third. The total was determined purely upon the weight of the truck loads of grain hauled into his granary. The truck was weighed fully loaded when the driver got out and witnessed the scale's reading, thus minus the driver. The grain was then tested for its moisture when a helper thrust his fluted prong deep into the pile of grain and extracted a sample. He dumped that drawn out sample into a pan and placed it directly into a moisture testing machine. The results soon showed its market value based on its dryness, right then and there. This was done to every load of our soybeans, corn, or winter wheat. A nearly "dry" result paid the best premium and went to the best bin for storage.

Weighed grain was then dumped into his underground drill elevator by lifting the entire front end of that truck by a hoist. Upon opening the rear hatch of the truck's bed that grain flowed down into a pit; it was pushed up from there into the top of one or more of his several hundred-thousand bushel bins by several long, corkscrew elevators to store it with other farmers' harvested bounty in the bins.

We took the elevator owner's company check right then for the daily market's fair trade value of the grain. However, he sometimes speculated on the future market price going up, and then dumped it all on the market for even a larger profit. It was good for everyone, but I could do the same if I had my own bins.

I personally dumped most of that grain money into Jillian's future college fund, with some going for our vacation fund. I earned three weeks vacation with pay, ten paid holidays, and I got tenure after my probationary time was up. My life was blessed and our family was about to grow again when Joy announced she was with child. Jillian was then four.

His name would be Tom, Joy first told me, and he was to be born the next spring. Joy and I figured out it was that romantic moonlit night in August at our lake skinny dippin', when Jillian stayed with Martha and Kurt to go to the St. Louis Zoo, that his life had begun. What a night that was!

The winter at the shed was routine and the weather held off being snow less, right up until approaching Christmas. That saved the state hundreds of thousands in salt product and overtime pay for some snowplow drivers, who sometimes relied on that stipend for added Christmas money.

However, as usual, those second two weeks of January through February made up for it. Then the following month the sun grew warmer and the rains developed across the prairie in April. It was time to get ready for planting all over again. The price of fuel, seed, weed killers and fertilizers, some liming, plus the necessary time in man hours to plow, disk and cultivate before even combining the harvest, if there was one, was enormous.

However, I had sowed my oats a bit early. Thomas was early; I was late. Though I had planned to be back in Springfield a few days before Joy's due date, I was stuck out in Sacramento, California on business, learning their newest contribution to their California highway system.

They had experimented much with road-usage tests. Their department came up with a long-wearing, rubberized asphalt they had tested, implementing old truck and car tires, shredded and boiled into the hot asphalt. The seven-year test proved its superiority, stability, and performance qualities they hoped for, which helped solve several other problems, besides its holding up physically on heavy truck traffic lanes.

The make up was 75 % asphalt and 25% rubber. This cured out hard, yet flexible and vehicle road noise was reduced dramatically, while vehicle-stopping performance doubled over smooth asphalt or concrete.

I wanted to fly back with their samples having my own calculations ready to set up statewide tire collection stations. I had to quantify the best I could for a necessary tax needed to be imposed on tires to support the drop offs that cause dealers to dispose of them to selected road building companies. I knew though, the highest bidder was not always selected, but that is what congress did. I just gave them my genius.

My mind was on my work when I passed through the x-ray portal. I emptied my pocket change, then my pens and walked cleanly through, after also removing all my jewelry and putting them all in a container.

ZAP!

"Shit!" I spoke, when the metal detector at LAX airport sounded off on my carry-on, which immediately caused the security personnel checking carry-on baggage to confront me. They took me by the arm and led me to their interrogation room to ascertain what substance I was carrying on board in my bag. I explained its purpose and consistency and they believed me. It looked and smelled like a rubberized asphalt road patch.

Authorities ran my name through the computers and I was cleared there, too. I convinced them also by showing all of my official credentials with State of Illinois identification. However, it took so long to get an answer from the California Airport Authority to get my release that I missed my flight. They were sorry, but they were just doing their job. Nevertheless, my Thomas was born that morning without his father there, also.

"Greg! You are the proud poppa of a healthy seven-pound boy! He looks just like me! Joy is doing fine and Mom and Martha are with Jillian in her room. Joy wants to know if you're okay, so what happened?" Dad asked me excitedly, as soon as he could call me after the event.

"Dad, I missed my plane and I'm headed out to the next plane now. Will you pick me up at twelve twenty-two, according to the flight schedule, after I transfer at Midway?"

"Sure, son…we'll talk tonight, bye now!" he said, then hanging up.

The four-hour flight to Chicago Midway went smoothly and I slept. The transfer was twenty-minutes delayed, so I called Dad to see if everything was still fine with Joy. Then it was touchdown in Springfield. I was walking down the disembarking lane when I spotted them. It was Lila, Joy's old roommate, and Sheena my secretary was beside her.

"Hey, you…what's happening, boss!" Sheena called out cheerfully.

I was in a hurry to get to Dad, but Lila insisted I clue her in on Joy's life. I quickly explained I was rushing home to greet my newborn son of that very day and Joy was enjoying being a stay-at-home mommy.

"Man, you sure filled out nicely…married life is doin' you good, bro. You're almost looking like a brother with that dark tan," Lila told me.

"Thanks, I've been working out in the fields and chopping wood and regularly getting some sun and exercise."

"That's evidently not all you're regularly gettin' done according to Sheena here," she giggled.

"Congratulations, boss!" Sheena interrupted quickly. "I went by to see Joy and your son after work and he looks just like you."

Sheena looked embarrassed, as if she'd been telling Lila about me from our working together.

"Well, you're going to have to do without me for two weeks…we're going out to Vegas and play those slots and some guys, too," Sheena continued loosely.

"You could have saved most your expenses by hitting the River Queen Casino down in East Saint Louis. I saw it while I looked around at the site of that new bridge. You could then donate all your losses to help paying our salaries," I said jokingly.

Our conversations were innocent, but Sheena seemed a bit friendlier around me with Lila there and actually gave me a peck on the cheek good-bye, as if I were her dearest friend. I overlooked it because it meant nothing. Nevertheless, Dad approached and saw Sheena kiss my cheek and grew very suspicious. I said good-bye and told them that I would wire plane tickets if they got in trouble as we did. Then I went to Dad.

"Who were those black girls?" he immediately wanted to know. I think he actually suspected they had come home with me on the plane and I was a philanderer.

"The tall one is Joy's ex-roommate, Lila; the other girl is Sheena, my secretary."

That did it. Dad turned his back on me, spun around and then turned back, stammering and mumbling to himself, shaking his head back and forth, "no" looking hard at me, frowning, and acted very disturbed.

"Dad! Stop it! You have jumped to conclusions that never happened. Those girls are headed to Las Vegas and if you don't believe me, there they are, headed onto their Vegas Southwest Airlines flight."

"Oh, good…I about had another attack. I once got in trouble like that with your mother and it took years for her to forgive me," he said, shocking the heck out of me.

"So?"

"So, I just thought you were a chip off the old block about women. Don't ever think of doing that to Joy or I'll ring your neck," he declared, very uncharacteristically of him. "Oh, here, I bought these flowers and candy for you to give to Joy."

"Dad…believe me…that never, ever, has crossed my mind…thanks, but let's go see my new son," I told him while accepting the gifts for his thoughtful considerations, but still a bit disturbed by his tactless accusations.

I kept looking to Dad while he drove for some understanding. He did not bother to elaborate and I really did not want to hear about his infidelity. It just could not be that simple.

"Thomas Darrel Wetmore," Joy announced. "This is your daddy," she said, kissing me while sitting on the edge of her hospital bed, holding Tom in her arms. "What's this?"

"Flowers and candy for my sweet, my sweet…compliments of your father-in-law who thoughtfully bought them just so I could give them to you," I said, to a staring Joy.

"No, what's that!" she stared.

"What's what?"

"Buster, if that's lipstick on your collar, you're gonna need a doctor fairly quickly."

"Oh, that must be Sheena's," I answered, pulling my collar out to look.

"Sheena's!" Joy blurted out.

"Hold it! Listen…I was just getting off the plane, when I ran into Lila and Sheena headed out on vacation to Vegas. Sheena just kissed my cheek to congratulate me on Tom, that's it! She said she was here. Sheena never did anything like that before today, honest."

"She was here…earlier…I don't like it when secretaries fall for their handsome bosses."

"You did," I said smiling.

"Isn't he something?" Joy asked, changing the subject. "Look at all that hair and those long fingers."

When I eased Tom into my arms from Joy, he never even opened his eyes, so I could not tell what color they were. I looked around and everyone looked gloomy-faced, including Mom and Martha, as if I was a guilty person. It was as if I had cheated on them all.

Dad, I guess, feeling guilty of his past indiscretions, but not wanting to rekindle any flames reminding Mother, finally told Joy he saw it all. He assured her it was just a friendly gestured smooch, which eased some doubt. However, I do not think Mom took it very well.

Kurt came in and started his kidding. "Why he's the handsomest boy ever. I think he looks just like your UPS driver," he joked to Joy and me.

Kurt was met with a healthy elbow in his side from Martha that almost doubled him over and received silly frowns from Mom and Dad. Kurt shut up a bit embarrassed, "Just kiddin' folks! I think he really looks more like the milkman."

"Now stop that, you old fart! Oops!" Martha surprisingly spouted, and then put her fingers over her mouth embarrassed by her outburst. None of us had ever heard her use anger in her words, never. Kurt was surprised, too, and quickly behaved himself. Nevertheless, we all knew our Kurt brought laughter with him always and we loved both him and Martha dearly.

Soon Tom began to howl. It was feeding time, Joy told us. The hospital's visiting hours were now ending and the chime alerted us that we had to go. Everyone lined up to kiss Tom good-bye, including Jillian, who was very quiet the whole time. She had asked Mommy to stay with Kurt and Martha, to their delight. Mommy said it was okay, thank God. I hoped she would love her new brother and wondered if she would treat him better than Jill had me. Only time would tell.

I stayed a moment to talk with Joy. I kissed her and then kissed my Tom, who still had his eyes shut, but was now searching hard with his mouth to find Joy's nipple to be breast-fed. He was content when he found one, and then opened his dark eyes.

"Look, his eyes just opened!" I told Joy.

"Don't get excited, because he can't see you yet, or focus. The color will change too," she told me, looking so tired, but beautiful.

Then I told Joy she had done a marvelous job and reminded her to believe me that it was a big misunderstanding. She said that she did…that was always her way.

I was south bound on I-55 when red lights and sirens came screaming by me in the form of fire trucks. I did not imagine I was headed in the same direction as they were. When finally I saw the huge flames above the trees in my yard, I knew it was too late to get worried then, because our house was already too far gone in fire destruction.

I drove down our lane and around the fire trucks to the little tractor shed. I intended to get the tractor out and away. However, the doors to the shed were opened; the tractor was not on fire. Someone had pried off the Master Lock, which I had put on the arm bar for security reasons. A thief or thieves had siphoned its gas, as I could see the gas cap from the tractor and a hose were lying next to the tractor. I think the perpetrators had used my own gas to burn down my house for some reason.

I was so tired from my long drawn out trip, my dad's clumsy insinuations, and meeting my new son, I did not have the energy to get more stressed. Instead of getting sick, or cursing, I quietly whispered a prayer of thanks that none of my family was inside. What if God had not chosen this day, this time, to remove them all while I was away? "Oh thank you, Lord!" I spoke loudly enough to have the fire chief get suspicious of me.

I had good Farm Insurance; I told him, when the Fire Chief came to me and began questioning about the fire. I showed him the hose, the gas cap, and the damaged doors and lock on the shed's dirt floor. He noticed footprints in the dust and said they needed to be cast, and then immediately called for the State Fire Marshal in Springfield.

He told me he was sorry, but our house was too far-gone when they got here as I had also arrived then. His men were only hosing it down and containing it. Everything we owned was gone up in flames in a matter of an hour.

"That's the hottest doggone fire we've had in some time," he began. "The last time something like this happened, it was your neighbor, what's his name...ah, darn. I'm getting too old to remember," said the chief. "Norm!" he hollered out to his assistant chief. "What is the name of the family down by Richland Creek? Their place was lit up like this by burglars about six months ago."

"That was the Donaldson farm," answered the assistant chief. "It was suspected arson, but it wasn't proven, because it burned all night, until there was nothing...only ashes. No one called it in until the next day. It burned by an accelerant, too. The family said they were at the fair with their hogs and cattle at the barns all night. Nobody could confirm or deny that."

"The Donaldson's are my ground rent tenants. They're both hard working young men and they do a really good job for me."

"Humm...I have to ask you this...where were you late this afternoon... more precisely, about say...two, three hours ago?"

"I understand. I was in the Los Angeles LAX airport, until about nine this morning...flew to Midway, transferred there to Springfield, and then my dad drove me to the hospital...St. Henry's. I got 2,800 air miles today."

He suspiciously stepped backwards to get a better look at me to see if I had somehow burned myself setting the blaze.

"Why'd you go to the hospital? What was wrong with ya?" he said, looking me up and down.

"I went to see my newborn son, Tom, and my wife, Joy. She delivered earlier this morning."

"You must be Greg Wetmore!" he said, putting aside his notepad that he was taking down my info on and extended his hand. "I know you...darn it; I should have recognized ya...you got married with your sister about four or five years ago in our church. My daughter sang in your wedding, remember Helen...Helen Renfro? I'm her daddy John. Say, Joy didn't deliver already did she?"

"Yes, this morning. And your daughter did a splendid job, too."

"Norm, come over here...I want you to meet Joy Dixon's husband, Greg Wetmore," the chief called out and Norm came running, boots flopping.

"I know you! You put that new bridge on Richland Creek and opened up my field. I used to farm there, but I decided that a steady income being a firefighter was more stable. Glad to meet ya, Greg. I'm Norm Dennison."

The scene went from a crime scene to a buddy-buddy meeting and back to a crime scene, as soon as the fire marshal came wheeling up in his red SUV with blue lights flashing. He was an elderly gent with a white goatee and beard.

"Damn hot fire to do that…the fire's not very old…who lit it?" he asked.

"That's why we called you, Jed. The only thing we found was that his tractor shed was broken into and there's the gas cap and hose someone used to siphon off the accelerant to burn his place down."

"You know this man's whereabouts prior the fire, John?" he immediately asked.

"Do I? Do I? He was with Joy Dixon…Joy had his baby."

"I thought she married some engineer guy. Did they get divorced?"

"Nope, I'm her husband," I said interrupting the conversation before things got whacky.

"Awe, he's okay…he was in the hospital with Joy's newborn baby. He's Joy's husband," injected the chief.

The marshal immediately went to work, first with his camera, his tape recorder, and plaster of Paris poured into the footprints for capturing the characteristics of those footprints. He dusted the tractor and found nothing, but the chrome gas cap yielded several good fingerprints. They were good enough to convict someone, he told us, however first we had to find that someone.

The fire marshal told the fire chief he wanted someone to stay at the fire all night to guard it. When he said he could not spare anyone, I volunteered. I had no place to go anyway. He hesitated, then handed me his business card to call him if necessary, but also asked me where I was going to sleep.

"I'll just have to roll up in the bed of the truck. The front seat is too short and that consol makes it impossible…I'll take off tomorrow."

"Wait…I've got a bedroll that's fresh out of the washer I use to go out bow hunting. I'll get it back from you tomorrow, if you want it. First, just to eliminate you from the mix, why don't I fingerprint you right here on the fender so I can later compare your prints to the ones off the gas cap. Yours are probably on there, too. When did you last fill the tank?"

"Ah, last Saturday morning, I think."

He pulled out the bedroll and handed it to me. He also had his finger print card ready. He rolled my fingers on an inkpad and in a few minutes, he had my fingerprints. Then, the whole fire crew got a call for a grease fire at the Ramada Inn's kitchen.

Off in a glory of road dust went everyone, including the fire marshal. I was alone and my fingers were still black with ink. I was so darn beat I didn't care and climbed into the truck bed with the bedroll and eased up against the windward side of the truck bed. It wasn't comfortable one bit, but I was out like a light in a minute. I should have called Kurt and Dad, but my mind was so bogged-down tired, I just had to close my eyes.

The clattering whine of that Dodge diesel woke me up and I was afraid the approaching truck would not see my truck parked there before it smacked into the rear. I had parked my truck before dark without lights and went to sleep. It was close, but Kurt just missed my truck in the late night.

"God dang, that was too damn close! Are you okay?" Kurt hollered, while running back to me after blowing my doors off and skidding sideways to a halt. "I heard about your fire on the eleven o'clock news and hurried over to see if you were hurt. Why didn't you call? They didn't give any particulars… what the hell happened?" Kurt asked, very upset that he almost crashed into me and even more upset after he got a closer look at our house in ashes that was not there any more.

"Arson…some SOB lit it up. I guess we will never know what was stolen. Luckily, I do have a fire safe in that rubble somewhere that has my important papers and insurance info. The fire marshal was out here and got some good prints, he thinks, but we have to have a suspect first to check them against his. He'll be back in the morning."

"Did you tell Joy?"

"No, and I dread it. She will be devastated, because not only did she love this old house, she had all of her parents' memories in her scrapbooks including yours…they are gone. The fire marshal asked me to stay here to guard the place."

"Well, son, you can climb in the back of my big Ram cab and stretch out instead of that steel bed. Pull out my old in-the-field sleeping bag. There is a blanket and the little pillow in the back of the seat. I used it to sleep on the job overnight when we did downstate work to eliminate travel, and other times, when I wanted to catch thieves stealing from the job site.

"Just pull the latch forward; it might be dusty behind there. In addition,

I think there just might be an old full bottle of Southern Comfort for the night chill, still back there rolled up in it, if I recall correctly. I'll curl up in the front with the pillow and I'll keep you company tonight, just as soon as I text Martha like I told her I would."

"You...you can text? When did you learn that?"

"Your daughter, my granddaughter, showed me, that's how," he said very proudly, lifting his cell phone up and started punching keys. "Martha said to just text her so that the ringing wouldn't awaken Jillian. Jillian's sleeping with Martha tonight."

After Kurt texted Martha, I was all right. We both might have had too many sips on that old bottle. Kurt soon was back to his old self, telling his corny jokes. Only Kurt could lighten my sadness that night. He turned the interior light on and leaned up over the front seat to hand me the whiskey bottle and then tell me another tale.

"You know...my brother Charles once told me the best piece of ass he ever had was just five minutes after his baby was born," he disgustingly told me.

"Yuck! You mean he actually made his wife have sex with him right after. I bet that hurt her."

"No, silly, it was the nurse!" ahh, ha, ha, he laughed uncontrollably at my surprised look, and could not stop with his silly laughter. That made me laugh too and we kept making each other laugh like that for five minutes, until we both had tears in our eyes. I guess he tried to make me feel better, because Kurt knew how depressed I would be in the morning when everything sunk in at dawn.

That morning sun peeked through the truck's windows and we had not slept a wink. We only managed to kill the bottle. The embers in the ashes glowed all night and then started up with fire at dawn. I could see the aftermath clearly. The upstairs had fallen into the basement and Joy's fruits and vegetables packed in canning jars had burst their seals in the heat. Kurt eased up, reached in with his gloves, and grabbed several blue jars. We dined on peaches and pears for breakfast. It was our only consolation. The heat from the embers were still blowing hot winds.

"Better let the upstairs know you're not going to be there today," Kurt whispered to me at five-thirty. "Old Johnsey will be there sweeping up already and he'll answer the phone. Good old Johnsey...hell, let me tell him for you. I like talking to him," he said, dialing on his cell.

Kurt recalled Johnsey as being a janitor with a brain. He would write it down on the upstairs secretary's pad and I'd be logged out. I never knew that, or knew of Johnsey. Maybe, I thought Clara Turner had laid him off too. He was there.

At eight in the morning, I took a deep breath and called Joy in her hospital room. She answered immediately without me beginning..."Martha told me everything and that you are safe, staying out there with Kurt."

Her words took the chill out of me. Martha already had done her motherly job, much better than I could have ever explained, because she had told Joy in the only way a mother could break bad news...with love.

Martha was always so believable and understanding in dark situations. That is what rubbed off on my Joy. Relieved, I began to sob thinking how Joy really was "sucking it up" as she often told me to do even though she would be very upset, also. However, I was hung-over and that made me weak.

"Looky here, Mr...stop that! Now you just have to build me that new log cabin I have been hintin' about to ya for years now. We will build down by the lake, this time, with a walk-out patio, just like I wanted...got it! In the meantime, Granny Martha is inviting us to stay with them, so if you get hold of Carl Hopkins, he can start the ball rolling with our insurance. And Martha says keep Kurt away from that whiskey bottle behind the seat."

"Oops!" I let out.

"Oh, too late...I thought so. You've been drinkin' already, too, huh...I can tell. You're gonna be sick...better get straightened up because we have lots to do. I'm getting' out of here before noon and your mom and dad are picking me up. If they don't know anything it's because they're early to bed, early to rise, and seldom watch the news anymore since Jill's...," Then she stopped short. "I'll tell them...get what you think needs to be done, then call me. Heck, I'll call Carl, you start making a list what you can remember we had insured and was ruined."

Joy was organized, always.

"Honey, everything...everything is gone...in a big heap of ashes...nothing is left...except, I can tell you with Kurt's endorsement that your peaches and pears were the best."

Joy actually laughed when she learned there were still a few jars cooling in the rubble. Only my Joy would be strong enough for the two of us. Her attitude was God wanted us to have a better place to live and we could not cry over spilt milk. Nevertheless, she was determined to find out who did it to us and she had her suspicions.

I saw Kurt coming out of the old outhouse looking uncomfortable. Apparently, he discovered we did not ever use it and there was no toilet paper in there.

"What did you use for God's sake?" I asked Kurt, feeling queasy about him going in that thing anyway without something with which to wipe. I planned to destroy it long before now.

"When ya gotta go, you gotta go! I owe you a few pages from the 1968 Sears catalog," he said smiling, looking squirrelly, then chuckled. "Boy things were cheap back then," he quipped.

Now that made me laugh. Was there no end to Kurt's jovial behavior? I soon realized, again, he was worth his trouble, then again, he was never trouble.

"Okay, now that that's over, let's get started with a list of everything missing. I'll get out my old clip board I now use to store my golf cards…the good ones that is," he smiled.

I guess we sat in Kurt's truck, almost until noon, had about three hundred different things listed, but no fire marshal came. I called his office using his business card. His office told me he was supposed to already be here. I pretended that was good and hung up. I became a little irritated, but eventually we saw his SUV coming down our long lane.

"Good morning! Kurt, well how in the heck are you?" the fire marshal greeted him with a vigorous handshake.

Kurt looked at his wristwatch, and then asked, "What took you so long, Jed?"

"Sorry, I had some work to finish up on this morning at the inn. Those chefs at the inn sure can cook, but they never get that grease off the grill into the disposal right. They get in a hurry and slop it all over…that's why it flared up out of control. Did six-thousand in damages…gave them a lesson this morning…a ticket…that woke them up. It just changed hands…they had never worked there before."

"Can we get going with this?"

"What do you mean, 'we'?"

"Okay, Jed, I know you've got that sneaky-snake look on your face. How'd those prints turn out?"

"Possibilities, possibilities, but if I tell you, you'll be smarter than me, ha. It will take a little time, but I'll get 'em, if not now, the next one. Same prints on a fire down at Litchfield three weeks ago at a grocery store. Took the till and dumped it on a county road. They are probably amateurs, I say that, because one man was physically unable to move that safe alone, and because they left prints galore. Computer can tie them into this one and maybe others soon."

"You learned all that since last night?" I questioned.

"Yep, that's what they sent me to fire marshal's school for and pay me so little for," he mused, looking at my home, or lack there of one.

"You've got good insurance with old Carl. Now let me tell ya, cause he's worked with me many times. I'm clearing this one, though it's arson, because you couldn't have done it and I know the character of Joyce Dixon, ah, your wife. He'll piss and moan trying to scale down your losses, especially without the paperwork and try to get you to sign off on a lower estimate."

"I have a fire safe in there someplace and it's guaranteed for twenty-five hundred degrees. All of our important papers, including the insurance are in there."

"Nevertheless, it's recorded and you should break about even on your $300,000 policy."

"You checked our insurance, too? Why?"

"Everything gets checked that we can to find out why this happened. By the way, did Kurt here tell you about your UPS driver?"

"Which UPS driver now?"

"Yep, he already did…I thought so. He used that same yarn on me, and my son, when my son had his first kid. I knew right away he was joshin' him, because Kurt doesn't have a brother, only a sis, ha! I know because I remembered she possessed that terrible disease."

I looked at Kurt for his response, but he was tight-lipped. "What terrible disease?" I questioned very cautiously.

"Poor thing…she's got that disfiguring "zakly disease."

Still cautious, I told him, "I have never heard of that disease. I'm sorry, Kurt, I didn't know," looking up at his grim face. "What was her prognosis? Can it be cured?"

"No, it's a terrible lifetime predicament…will last her forever was the doctor's say so…see, she looked "zakly like Kurt!" he laughed, and Kurt joined in. They both were goofy.

Two tractors started down our lane, one with a large disk and the other a plow. They stopped and one driver went back to talk to the other. It was my tenant brothers and they apparently hadn't heard about the fire. They stopped there probably wondering where the farm house went. Then they came forward and both climbed down to talk to me. Jeb looked at Kurt, both with curious eyes on them.

"These are my land tenants, Denny and Jordan Donaldson," I told Kurt and Jed.

"Who burned down your house?" Denny suddenly asked me, which brought a strange look and a comment from the fire marshal.

"That's what we'd like to know…got any ideas?" he said, getting a closer look at them both. "You know I hear criminals always return to the scene of their crime…strange, huh?"

"Ah, yes, I guess…we've got fields to plow," Denny told us as both turned away to go get back on their tractors.

Then Jordan asked, "We still got a deal?"

"Yes, we still have a deal, except you'll have to bring your own lunches, because Joy had a baby boy yesterday and won't be coming here for a while and you don't want my campfire cookin'."

"That's okay, Mr. Wetmore. Congratulations on your new son…well, let's get going, brother, we're burning daylight."

They took off to the winter wheat stubble fields in high gear. One followed the other as they began tilling the soil, making it ready for a late corn crop.

"Nice hard working guys," I told Kurt and Jeb, but neither replied.

Then my cell chimed and it was Joy. She asked how things were and if I was coming home with Kurt. I asked Kurt and he already knew I was living with them for a while.

"Well, I guess since you won't be mowing your grass here you can stay in practice on mine," he chuckled.

That would be the least I could do, I told him.

We left the scene while Jeb said he was staying. He wanted to do some tests for insurance purposes, he said. Kurt and I left, both feeling hung-over with hunger pangs.

Chapter 14

Wednesday morning, I kissed Joy, Jillian, and Tom good-bye for the day. I returned to work from Kurt and Martha's house, after having been awake several hours earlier holding Tom, who wanted his warm bottle of milk, not Joy's breast. It happens sometimes that the mother's milk fails to adequately nourish the baby, until the breast is fully ready to produce. Joy had started a breast pump to have Tom get his immunities from her milk.

I was extra busy those next few days of the week, since Sheena left with Lila to go to Vegas. She was due back in two weeks on the following Monday. Nevertheless, on Friday when I came in Sheena was back, busy putting files away, in their right order this time.

"Sheena…I thought you took two weeks…weren't due back until a week from Monday. Did you girls get cleaned out even before the week was over?"

"Kind of…I canceled my second week of vacation…but Lila got wild and crazy the very first night, actually in only a few hours, and took off with a guy she met."

"You mean she ran off with a guy in only hours after she met him?"

"No, she knew him, alright. He was from Chicago and they went to school together, I thought she said. It was very inconsiderate just to walk away like she did, but we both said if we met that certain guy it would be okay to separate. I didn't imagine it would be that quick. The brother had lots going for him, too old for me, but Lila's age."

"So what did you do then?"

"I put on my best threads and headed to the slots…won a few dollars, but there's no young guys my age hanging around those one armed bandits. I moved to the Texas Hold 'Em area and to a table needing a player. There were several brothers looking interested. I plopped my whole three hundred down when the dealer turned up my third six. Out of five players, mine was lowest. One friggin' game…that's all I got to play.

"Ya can't play without money, so I just stayed in my room. Then, looking at the plane ticket, I saw that it read I could use it at anytime provided I called ahead and there was a seat available. Therefore, I hooked up with this strange foreign taxi driver on the way to the airport. He was outrageously funny; the only fun I had at all, and on the way out to the airport. So, here I am," she said miserably.

I knew she had met Hajji by the way she later described him. Then she said she was headed out to the Harness Club after work to meet some friends. I had a few programs to present upstairs, so when I came back late, Sheena had gone home for the weekend. I decided to take Joy and everyone out to the Country Kitchen for supper and called ahead. Joy said Tom was not feeling well and might not enjoy his outing.

However, by the time I arrived at Kurt's, everyone had decided my idea was a good one. Kurt drove with Jillian between him and Martha, and Joy had buckled Tom's safety seat between us in the rear. Unfortunately, there was that empty bottle of Southern Comfort stuck up between the seats and jabbing her butt. Joy held it up and frowned. No wonder I was uncomfortable all night.

The restaurant wasn't crowded then, but Joy insisted upon a larger table. As the girls and Jillian slipped over to the salad bar. Kurt ordered our steaks, while I held Tom. He was such a good boy. It was good for Joy to get out and she mentioned she'd like to start walking or jogging to lose her flabby baby-weight gain. I suggested we buy a baby stroller used for jogging and we all could go together.

Then, to my surprise, Mom and Dad came in. Apparently, Joy had told them to come dine with us and they were pleased to join our happy little group; thus the reason for the larger table Joy wanted. After Kurt said the prayer, Martha suggested Mom and Dad could come over the next weekend and play cards and help baby-sit Tom and Jillian, while Joy and I went out on a date. That was surprising, and I thought a very kind gesture. Joy said it was up to Tom.

The dinner went well. Afterwards, Kurt wanted, no he demanded, that we all go out to the fairgrounds right then as the state fair had just begun and he had a surprise for us all. He said he had tickets for George Strait's Show at seven-thirty.

Martha bumped me and said, "Darn fool thinks he really knows George Strait. I hope he doesn't make a jackass out of himself," she whispered. It was another surprise coming from our mild-mannered granny.

"What makes him think that?"

"I have no clue. He once said he knew Leo 'The Lip' Durocher, too, but he died in 1991…that was long ago."

Kurt was savvy to the fairgrounds being overcrowded and parking was at a premium. Men stood waving their signs out in the streets, which were painted "park here". They made big bucks packing in cars onto their own front lawns and their backyards, also, at twenty dollars a pop for the night.

Therefore Kurt said, "Give 'em to me…the gate keys."

Kurt was holding out his hand to me as he drove us up to the shed's front gates. Looking my way, he said, "I guess the boss won't mind me, a retired old fart…will he…parking here again, like I've done for thirty years. We can walk right over to the corner and pick up the shuttle that's headed to the race track."

"That's where they have the big-named shows," Joy told me.

I had never been there during the state fair week. I couldn't believe how much there was to see as we passed by the crowds. I saw games, food venders, the many rides, water slides, carousels, gigantic Ferris wheels and tent music shows; and especially amusing was all the thousands of people trying to get through the gates. It was exciting. Just as Kurt said, the shuttle stopped for him on the corner.

"Thanks, Grady!" was all he said to the driver, as we all got a ride through gate six into the interior of the speedway's racetrack. I spotted several employees I knew walking with their families; some pushing strollers, some with babies like ours.

We all got off the shuttle walking quickly behind Kurt. He went straight up to the huge colorful buses of the performing stars, which were parked side-by-side in the interior of the track.

There was George Strait's fabulous bus with its fancy artwork, which was a sight to behold. Joy was thrilled. We were quickly met with friendly smiles of two men who were the star performer's liaisons and backed by Illinois State Troopers, as security.

"No, sir, Mr. Strait is getting dressed for his performance and can't see anyone. No, sir, immediately after his last number the bus is out of here to Branson, Missouri, according to his schedule. Sorry, sir, but if you are his personal friend, and I see you are by your complimentary tickets, please also understand everyone who gets those are his personal friends. I will give him a note, if you want to leave a message though. He'll get it, I promise."

"Mom, you have any paper and pen?" Kurt asked, seemingly very dejected. He scribbled a note and handed it to the man.

"Well, I tried…let's go find our darn table way up there in the restaurant above the grand stands. At least we'll be in the air conditioning."

Off we trudged, marching in line, something like a mother hen and her chicks behind Kurt. I held Tom, while Kurt held Jillian's hand.

The pushing and pulling through the big crowd ended with our turn getting onto the elevator, up to the restaurant. Not many had those kinds of seats. It felt good inside with air conditioning, but Tom was wet. Joy took him to the restroom to change him. I was relieved, because my arm had about gone to sleep and the blanket was extra warmth. Nevertheless, the dejected look on Kurt's face told us he was very disappointed and he kept rubbing his left arm as if it was sore.

As soon as the music began, we all turned our eyes down to the stage. Soon through the shooting fireworks and smoke came our superstar. It was wonderful non-stop country music, about ten hit songs, when George finally raised his hands to his crowd and asked everyone to please listen up. The crowd quieted down.

"I have been handed a note here from one of my very good friends. He's retired now…we met a long time ago when I was broke and headed here to one of my first shows. We've kept in touch all this time. I can't see you up there, but Kurt, hope to see you the next time in and we can talk then. Until then, thank you for coming and bye, y'all!"

The big star removed his big, white Stetson and waved to his admiring, applauding, standing-ovation crowd. Then he hustled off to the back of that stage and we actually saw from up top his buses take off immediately behind the red lights of the state police escort. Out of the race track they went and he was gone.

We were very impressed, though Kurt was modest. "He's one hell of a good singer, isn't he?"

Martha just said, "I'll be damned…oops!" she sounded out.

"One of the things I miss most," Joy began to tell us, "are my guitars. Jillian misses them, too, because she had begun to sing very well and I was teaching her the F,G,C,D cords on the frets. Oh, that reminds me…guess what, Greg? I had rubbed some varnish off that old Gibson and guess what? I meant to tell ya…guess what?" she anxiously wanted me to guess.

"It was really clean?" I laughed.

"No, silly, believe it or not, there was a name carved into the back…it was E-L-V-I-S, believe it or not."

"Elvis who? Oh, The King, Elvis? Why didn't you tell me it meant that much? I'd have gone out and gotten another."

"Not anything like that one. It had character, real character, but we had no amp for an electric guitar, remember?"

"That's okay, just tell old Carl it was a big, pretty expensive one you lost," Kurt joked. "He'll pay for one through the nose!" he laughed.

"Nope, I know you don't really mean that, Dad," she said. "Anyway, no use frettin' over the loss, cause I've still got…oops, no I don't…I forgot my new Martin was in there, also," she sighed.

I looked over and Kurt had tears in his eyes.

"What's wrong, Kurt?" I asked.

"Joy just called me her dad!"

"She calls me mom and granny all the time, so there," a suddenly bit of unsympathetic Martha sang out.

I wondered if being kept up all night with Tom was affecting her. Martha was holding both Jillian and Tom and refused to let anyone help.

"Darn, it wasn't supposed to make you cry…I say it to show you both how much I love you for everything you've done for me, as a kid, and now with my own kids."

Then Joy kissed his cheek and hugged Kurt.

It got very quiet, until Kurt spoke. "We might just know who stole your things, kids, and lit up your house. But I can't say right now. Maybe, just maybe now, those youngins' ain't very smart," was all he spoke.

"Yes, but really with no evidence, except gas cap fingerprints from ours and no idea who's they could be, or could have done it, we'll probably just have to settle on Carl," I added. "Anyway, you're birthday is nearing, dearest, so I have a hint on your next gift…acoustic or electric?" I asked, smiling at my lovely wife.

"Shoot! I want a big, long expensive log cabin house where we all can live!" her shrill voice sang out.

We mingled through the crowd, buying snow cones and cotton candies. Dad bought tickets to the kiddy merry-go-round, swings, and those circling, up and down little airplanes for Jillian. Mom took pictures of us all and Dad blew kisses or clapped every time Jillian came around to us. Then, mosquitoes began their intermittent biting, so we hopped a passing shuttle and headed home. It was a very good day.

We decided to drive by our place to let everyone see the aftermath of the fire. As we passed my fields, I noticed that the Donaldson boys had finished off one eighty-acre field and half of another. I was happy, because the weather was holding and they had chores and field work of their own, at their father's place, I mentioned to Kurt.

"Son, have you ever been over to their place?" Kurt began. "Unless they've bought some land I don't know about, they only farm about seventy acres and it's really poor ground…never been fertilized, just burned off. The foxtail weeds are taking over their place. I don't even know how they get along financially."

"Maybe it's farming for others. I got my one third of their $90,000 from last year."

Kurt remained unusually quiet and still seemed to have difficulty with his arm as he moved it up and down to limber it up. "Gettin' old," he said.

That seemed a bit unusual though, considering the huge new equipment that must have cost hundreds of thousands that they drove over to my fields. I decided right then to look up their homestead and drive by there.

We still hadn't gotten our big safe out of the rubble. A week later the debris still smoldered, so I got help. Some guys I knew who demolished homes for the state and filled in fire holes like ours, came out on the next Saturday.

After their backhoe driver found the safe lying on its side, he gently scooped it out and placed it up on the gravel road right-side up. Then, he and his partner began bulldozing dirt over the house. They did a wonderful job, but it also appeared all was not lost, as they also, at my request, scooped up seventy-five more fruit jars of Joy's 'fixings'. She had done three hundred with Martha's help and she was giving Martha and Mom some. They deposited them, also, gently in a pile next to the side of the safe.

With the big yard now smoothed over, it added three acres to my available farming ground then, so I asked them to look at my future site of our planned home.

"We're here! You got your surveyor equipment?"

"No, it's at work."

"Stake it off anyway, we'll do some of it now, and after your final figures, we'll go to work filling or expanding. Give you a deal today, since we're here already with no place to go next."

It was normal for people with huge equipment to let their machinery sit at a finished site a short while, until the next job. It was all part of the understanding to help out the contractor. Out there on my farm security seemed no problem at all. We drove to the lake and they looked at my plan, which I had quickly worked out using just my pencil and paper. I showed them the hill I wanted to dig into to have Joy's walk-out basement to a patio below her new six bedroom log cabin with long veranda overlooking the property.

With no real plans, they suggested digging the basement wider by four feet, which would allow for tarring the sides of the concrete walls against the dirt with asphalt sealer. Good idea. We worked together, until they said it was quitting time, and they were headed to the fair. It was the second to last day and they were headed to livestock judging. They were both official judges, which surprised me.

I, on the other hand had a date, too. I promised Joy we'd go out to the Harness Club for some karaoke music and enjoy ourselves. Maybe I'd get Joy to sing and later have a little romance thrown in, too, I hoped.

I stopped and bought three-dozen yellow roses, Joy's favorite, from a florist and brought them back to Kurt's. Joy still had her hair up in a towel and was wearing her robe, but kissed me right in front of everyone for the flowers.

"Expecting something extra special tonight, are ya?" she bravely spoke in front of the women.

Martha and Mom kept their heads down, but I saw their smiles and elbows bumping each other after that message. Soon, they had Tom and Jillian together reading nursery rhymes to them. It was heartwarming to say the least.

I shaved, showered and got a wonderful surprise. My Joy was really in the mood, because she had on her tight fitting jeans, a rhinestone cowgirl shirt and boots. Best of all she sprayed on my favorite fragrance, Coffee. This time, I could only think of her charms. Joy's beauty had surmounted any I could have imagined with "what's her name". I still had it bad for Joy. We kissed our babies good-bye and "head 'em up, move 'em out, rawhide!" we were out of there.

The Harness Club's parking lot was filling, but we were a bit early. When we walked inside, I had no idea the furnishings had changed and it was under new management. Tonight was musicians' night. No karaoke, just live band and people wanting to show off their live talents, using their instruments and singing, too, mostly guitars, violins and the piano. It all worked for us. We hadn't been there for a while and everything was a bit different and new.

There was dancing now on a wooden floor with sawdust strewn about to make our feet glide across the dance floor. Whenever the on-stage person sang or played country music, Joy especially demanded I join her in the Texas Two-Step, which she taught me just that night. It was easy, foot-stompin' fun.

The rum and coke drinks we drank made me happy and Joy loosey-goosey. I just knew she was dying to get up there on that new stage and sing and play a guitar. I talked to a guy who was more than willing to lend her his guitar, so I took it to her about midnight. She stroked a few warm-up cords, whispered the song she was going to sing in the emcee's ear, then nodded to the emcee that she was ready, just like a bull rider to have them open the gate.

"Get out your clean handkerchiefs guys and hand it to your best girl, cause ladies and gents, this little girl is tuggin' at our heart strings with Carrie Underwood's 'Jesus, Take the Wheel!' Let's give it up for Glenarm's own Joyce Wetmore!"

She sang to the crowd and moved around that stage like she owned it, singing her heart out, making weaker hearts cry. I was thrilled, and had cold chills; she was that great. The applause was deafening when my lady finished her rendition.

Then when the crowd hollered out for more, Joy just hit them with another of Carrie Underwood's songs called "Un Do It". Boy, Joy really un did it! Afterward, Joy was so relieved and happy, because she wasn't too tipsy to hit those singing notes and her guitar strings and cords all at the same time. I was proud.

Even over an hour later, after she had sung so well, several patrons came over to congratulate Joy and asked her for her autograph, saying to her mostly that she was going to be a really big star someday and they wanted her autograph now.

"Why thank you, but I already am a big star…I got him, and two little sweethearts at home…that's all I need, thank you."

Joy sounded loaded and even curt, but scribbled her name anyway in their little books with a smile. She began to worry me. Others offered her more free drinks, but she had had too many already. Therefore, I thanked them all for their kind gestures.

"You know…if I were a drunkard and had a really good voice, geeeze, I could get really plastered here every night," was her inebriated spoken thought.

"Yes, dear, but you wouldn't have me or Jillian, or Tom, now, would you?" I said, to make her confusing thoughts better.

More drunken singers got up when their liquor hit them and I could see why the owner was raking in the dough. I was more than ready to leave, but Joy was not.

Joy's eyes had become focused upon the next two shirtless, tight-jeaned, suntanned, well muscled young men wearing dark sunglasses, and dressed as cowboys, big belt buckles and all. They were about to perform as a duet. I thought she was staring at them only because she thought they were sexy, just as any well-intoxicated, old married woman might, right in front of her adoring husband, who couldn't compete with those young bodies.

Out of the blue, after those two cowboy studs got up on stage to strum their guitars and sing a song called, "Indian Outlaw", Joy stood up like a banshee and hollered out just like John Wayne in 'True Grit'…"You sons of a bitches! Arm yourselves cause you're the bastards who stole my guitars!"

Away Joy went with a chair from our table, raised high above her head.

Before anyone could have suspected she would be hostile, that chair crashed over the head of one man…it was Jordan Donaldson. His brother, Denny, caught a chair leg, too, on the next swing and there they both lay sprawled out cold by a fired up woman. Sure enough, those guitars were Joy's, so I summoned the police on my cell and took up the guitars myself.

I was worried, because Jordan was still out cold and was clearly in need of a doctor and Denny had a bloody gash on his noggin, too. The owner came with security and surrounded us all, because Joy had discarded the chair, but now had her fists up to box, daring either to come get her.

I had to defend my wife's honor when a big bouncer put his hands on my wife. I only told him to let go of her. That blackjack sap he used on my head sure can change one's demeanor. If I would have been sober it would really have hurt badly. When I awoke to a stinging sensation on my brow from the EMTs attention, I had blood in my eyes, and was a bit stunned and dizzy. I was thankful the cops were there.

Joy knew the policemen and EMTs who were attending to me and both Donaldson boys. They were not nearly as hurt as I thought. They also had hand cuffs on them.

When the owner came with a piece of paper for me to sign, relieving him, his club, and his bouncer of using excessive force upon an unarmed me, I didn't sign, thinking there was time for that later, after we cleared up this fiasco. We all went to the sheriff's office to sign complaints and give statements.

As it all turned out, Jordan voluntarily sat down with Joy and several detectives after he was given his Miranda Rights, and admitted to them that he and Denny had set fire to our home, not because they hated us, but because they needed things to resell. They had taken lots of saleable items, like Joy's jewelry, our TVs and VCRs.

They thought they could take my safe, too, their first objective, but it didn't budge, since I had it bolted to the floor in concrete. Yes, they also had stolen the gas and tools from the tractor's tool box and they took the guitars at the last moment, before Dennis decided to burn the house to eliminate their fingerprints. They both did it to help pay for their expensive farm machinery and a recent purchase of additional land.

The Donaldson brothers left with jail personnel to be booked and charged.

It was seriously life-changing for them both. Eventually, that escapade solved several lingering burglary and arson files, perpetrated by my former tenants.

As an added test for Joy to identify the guitars as being hers, and because there were many guitars in this world similar to hers, the interviewer told her he wanted something, a bill of sale, serial number, anything to establish they were in fact hers, especially that Gibson, even though Jordan admitted stealing it from our home.

I told him it was a gift to me from the brother-in-law of a former Las Vegas casino owner. I didn't mention Doyle. That seemed to correlate for him.

Additionally, Joy asked him to look-see if there wasn't the word "Elvis" carved into the back of that Gibson and the name "Jillian Wetmore" written on a little card inside the big Martin. Joy had put that card in there just in case something happened to her, I guess. It was still there.

The detective had had experiences with stolen Gibson guitars before, both fake, and original and had done some research. Before he conceded they were Joy's, he put the feel of the Gibson across his lap, as if to hold it just one more time before giving it up. Then he began to give us a little bit of history he had obtained, while strumming some soft cords he knew.

"I learned this is an original Gibson, probably given by "The King" himself to someone in his audience after one of his performances in Vegas or Nashville," he explained. "It was not reported stolen, but checking the serial number on the back here, with the Gibson Guitar Corporation in Nashville, Tennessee, this truly was one Elvis ordered and received in the early sixties, and most likely he used it.

"Elvis had all kinds of guitars, many of them personal gifts to him by guitar makers or even borrowed ones that he learned to like. He had lots of big Martin guitars that he liked, too, and strummed some of those in his movies. Don't you miss him? They're yours all right," he told her. "Now for my report…their value?"

According to Joy, remembering the bill of sale she had gotten with the guitar, the Martin's value for his report was $2,700 plus tax. However, the old Gibson Super 400, made in the early sixties, and probably used in one of Elvis's many shows, though scratched and worn, was priceless, said the interviewer.

"It will be our son, Tom's, after I teach him to play," Joy told him.

Then he handed over the guitars and Joy signed his official receipt. We left the station and immediately felt that muggy Midwest humidity and heat.

It all eventually became a "Joy-ess" moment.

Joy began her incessant talking…"Well, old Carl will be happy we found those guitars, so the insurance company doesn't have to pay up, huh?" she expressed, still a bit tipsy and holding both guitars in her lap in the back seat. "I'm glad that detective was so resourceful to discover some facts about my Gibby. I always thought it had character," Joy spoke, rubbing the front gently. "You know what? Did you ever go skinny-dippin' on a hot summer's night, like tonight. I bet we could find a cool lake made for swimmin' that is about five acres, quiet, and secluded, and add one heck of a finish to this date, don't you think, darlin'?" she affectionately hinted.

Our romantic evening had not been stolen away by cops and thieves; not put on hold after all. We were quiet slipping into Kurt and Martha's at six that morning, still dripping wet, because we had no towels. We had only left the lake, because anyone passing by on I-55 could have easily seen naked people, if they swam nude during the daylight. However, we didn't get caught and my Joy was very happy…so was I.

Chapter 15

"Daddy! Mommy!" Jillian yelled as she ran barefooted across the hardwood floor to us. It was bright and early, less than an hour after we had laid down exhausted upon our soft bed, which once had been Joy's.

"Good morning, sunshine! Were you a good girl for Granny and Grandpa last night?" Joy asked, hugging Jillian.

"Yes, Mommy, I'm always a good girl, like you tell me to be."

"Where's Tom?"

"He's still sleeping in his crib. Grandma went into the kitchen to get Tom his breakfast, mine, too. He is a very good child. However, I will be so glad when he no longer wears diapers," Jillian spoke, so adult-like, told to her mommy. "Daddy, are you still asleep?"

"No, sugar…come give your daddy a big hug…big enough to squeeze out all that bad night air," I said, to make her really hug me tightly.

"No rest for the wicked," Joy said, crawling out of bed, pinching my behind, headed to get Tom.

She took Jillian by the hand to get her little brother and had left me alone.

That scream, I will never forget. The horror, sorrowful sadness, and shock all coming out of her all at once was chilling. Joy's wonderful foster dad, Kurt, had died in his sleep. I rushed to her. In his crib, our son Tom was visibly shaken by Joy's sudden scream. He didn't cry, it just looked as if he were kicking, riding a bicycle upside down, non-stop, when I picked him up.

Afraid something terrible had happened to her husband of forty-seven years, Martha came into the room cautiously. She went to his side and called out, "Kurt!", but realized he was gone. Then she slumped down beside him.

Martha, who had gotten up to prepare a warm bottle of mother's milk for Tom, had not noticed anything unusual from Kurt when she awoke, except said he was unusually tired before he went to sleep and had yawned excessively.

Martha had petitioned off their king-sized bed with extra pillows to separate her from Jillian, because Jillian had restless legs. Tom slept beside Martha in his crib moving and kicking, but was quiet then, she told us, while still sitting next to Kurt.

Somehow, after only a few moments of uncontrolled sobbing by Joy and Martha, then one last kiss upon her husband's lips, Martha let go of Kurt's hand saying, "Farewell, my sweet prince…good-bye," she said, letting his hand down gently.

Then she backed up very wobbly into a chair, helped by Joy and me. Martha sat looking at his still figure. Joy covered him with a sheet, because he was obviously deceased.

"Better call the coroner, Joy," Martha told her sadly.

That coroner, an old friend of the Rakers family, arrived to examine and observe Kurt, as did EMTs, and a county sheriff…all of whom knew Kurt. The EMTs immediately made no attempt to check further than his vitals. There were none, and he had rigor mortis beginning. He had been dead for about five to six hours, sometime shortly after midnight, it was determined.

Kurt had expired at age sixty-seven. In his medicine cabinet, where the coroner asked to look, Kurt had only vitamins, aspirin and some laxatives, no prescriptions whatsoever. He never seemed ill or had never so much as taken a real sick day from work in his entire life, according to what Martha told the coroner.

"Unofficially Kurt died of natural causes," began the coroner. "Kurt apparently had had a heart attack, also known as a myocardial infarction. That is a rapid death of heart muscle from the sudden blockage of a coronary artery thrombosis, a blood clot heart failure. The dark bluish tint around his mouth is a strong indication. God bless his soul," he spoke.

The coroner reiterated that Kurt had passed so quickly that he probably had expired without even knowing pain in his sleep. It was a peaceful retreat from life and that was comforting to us all.

Jillian had experienced the whole incident. In her child's way she had one thing to add.

"I guess my grandpa is with Jesus now, Momma. Will we put him behind the church to wait for us?"

"Yes, honey…next to my mommy and daddy Dixon."

"Are they waiting for you and Daddy?" Jillian asked.

"I suppose so, but it might be a while, honey, before then, we have to find you a handsome knight in shining armor first, just like your father."

"Then I won't look for one."

I had my own tears flowing and turned away on that one.

When Mom and Dad arrived they rushed over to comfort Martha and said they would help make the arrangements with Joy's guidance. Dad was an elegant writer and began the task of an adequate obituary for Kurt's life that was ample enough for a kind man such as Kurt. Kurt's long obituary was sent to the Springfield papers and I called Sheena to tap our flower fund.

There was no mortuary in Glenarm. Therefore, after the coroner removed Kurt's body, arrangements were made to deliver him embalmed, dressed in his favorite suit, early Monday in a chosen casket to the church. It was done. A Springfield mortuary completed the tasks.

On Monday afternoon, Kurt was laid to rest in the old cemetery near the Dixon graves. There were many visitors and Pastor Kefir gave Kurt's eulogy, written by Dad and Joy, inside the church he had helped design and build.

"Kurt was God's kind of man," Pastor concluded his eulogy.

We all went home solemnly and felt the absence of Kurt's spirit.

I later contacted a builder, who told me he could move onto my selected site and have our dream home log cabin up and livable in less than three weeks. All I needed was the land, one of the designs they made, and lots of money. His price tag for a six bedroom, six bath, and with everything Joy insisted being in there, was a healthy $450,000 completely erected, fully equipped. I told him, yes, but on my wife's concurrence. Joy was thrilled and said yes.

At the office Sheena was very quiet, until I mentioned the Harness Club incident. Surprisingly, she was there, but only saw us arrested, she said. I guess she was too embarrassed to ask. After I told her what made Joy get up and attack that guy, she was relieved.

"What bothers me most, is she said she'd do the same to any woman who tried to take me away from her. Think that means she's a jealous woman, or what?" I laughed.

Sheena was uneasy and said she was all for that.

"What ever happened to Lila?" I asked, after I finally thought about her roommate.

"Oh, she got remarried, I think…who knows? That guy was her first husband, Cabell something…straight out of prison in Utah. He was sentenced to twenty years for armed robbery…served seven. That's why he was so buff, I guess.

"They just showed up at the apartment late one night…she got some things put in her boxes and cases and said I'd hear from her, but I haven't yet. I don't know what to do, because her half of everything is overdue now, and I'm stuck. Her boss called and I think she's fired ,too, and if I don't come up with the utilities, Springfield will cut me off after only fifteen days over due."

"Well, maybe I can loan you a couple thousand to prevent that. How long is your lease?"

"Lila had eighteen months left on hers when I sub-leased. I never saw my papers. I think I have about three months' payments left, times two."

"How much is all that?"

"About…what, all three months?"

"Yep…if you fail to pay, that won't look good for you or Joy. How much? Use your math."

"Gee thanks…$2,700, by my figures. You mean you'd loan me that much?"

"I did hear you say 'loan', correct? That means you intend to pay it all back, right?"

"Well, yes, thank you very much, but…"

"Then it's settled. Here, it's good…and when you can…," I said, handing her the check.

"Now, has anything come in on the IL-MO bridge project?"

"Yes, here it is, and notice that it's unopened. It says here on the front, and I quote, 'To be opened by addressee only'," she told me in a much happier, spirited voice.

I opened one letter concerning the results of a financial evaluation meeting I had attended and it was good news. The project had begun on target. It would employ an estimated 1,599 workers, from the Illinois side. Basically, I was finished for the next project. And there was one, but it was deferred to another committee. It was a casino project on the Lake Michigan waterfront. I guess Doyle Valero got his word in before he died. I wondered just who would sponsor the bill. He was apparently a crook, too.

Then came a surprise. Resurfacing orders for I-90 on both east-west lanes, six full lanes, plus median and emergency lanes, with new guardrails running continuously through the adjacent Chicago suburbs of Hillside, Maywood and Oak Park, up to the Chicago city limits at Central Avenue; a piece of cake for the boys in the Windy City District #3. I confirmed the submitted plans and was satisfied it could be brought in on the fourteen million dollar budget estimates.

It was finally lunchtime. Sheena insisted it was her treat. She went to the workers' canteen machine, which served up two tuna fish sandwiches, chips, and diet cokes for both of us to split. I guess she thought that was dietary. After the desire to go back for seconds left me, we went back to work, but I was waiting for supper time to arrive. It's not good to work on a full stomach nor a half-empty one.

I called George Morley, the District#3 engineer in Chicago, and gave him the go ahead. He was waiting for my call with another project. He wanted my expertise on a new I-94 overhead and clover leaf at Illinois 58.

"Another piece of cake," I told him. "Tack it on to this already appropriated one and resubmit them both. Three or four years from now, it may be called up again."

He got the message, sounded a bit downhearted, but I told him to fax his info and I'd look at it. Sometimes I had a love-hate relationship with the other district supervisors who thought I had too much say-so. I just kind of inherited that with Kurt's leaving and being close to the people who paid for everything. The legislative body naturally submitted construction proposals through me, which I calculated and reaffirmed at their requests. Somehow through time, my word was good enough for them.

Maybe, too, it was the respect that Kurt earned and placed on his decisions that carried over to my office. I had lots of review work and practically none of my own. It seemed if a senator or representative hit a pot hole enroute to the capital, it was appropriated for immediate repair. Thus, there were more small insignificant jobs than huge construction projects, but they kept the personnel humping in the shed.

Then, I read a letter for the reinstatement of Clara Turner, my ex-boss of only a month, until she experienced that stroke. It read she had gone through her required therapy and was released to return. However, her new position was now in the Office of Public Acquisitions. I guess that was where she could do her best. At least our paths would not rub. Nevertheless, I was glad she made it through, and more so at our four o'clock quitting time.

I stopped by Mom and Dad's to wish Dad happy birthday, his sixty-seventh. It made me think of how he could leave us at any time, like Kurt, but only God knew when. I had bought him a pair of New Balance, American made, golfing shoes, with a promise that I would go golfing with him.

Martha had told Dad to keep that fancy golf car, but Dad had no one he liked to golf with, so I volunteered. I was good competition for his style, because I had never golfed before, so Martha also gave Kurt's clubs to me.

Then Mom handed me an envelope from the both of them. "This is from your father and me."

"What's this, my adoption papers?" I laughed.

It was unsealed when I opened it; it was Jill's part of the savings, which she and Dad decided should now be mine.

Would there ever be a more needed time, I said, after I thanked and kissed them both. When I told them of our planned replacement home, they said that they already knew, because Dad went fishing and asked why the big opening was near the water. A construction boss told him they were going to put up a log cabin and showed him a picture of it as it might look completed with yard work from one of his former clients.

"Dad took his brochure and brought it home for me to see. They circled the one just like you're getting. Then I called Joy to tell her it was magnificent," Mom told me. "Joy decided to come by and pick me up so we saw the construction, too. They had the basement floor and walls poured already, but it rained."

Joy had told Mom the final insurance offer covered only up to 80% of the home's value, and unfortunately, due to the recession re-evaluations, its value had fallen considerably just that year; good for paying real estate taxes, bad for resale. The fair market value of our personal belongings was pro-rated really low, too, to thirty thousand. Joy nor I were big dressers.

"Gosh, Dad, here I came over to ask you both out tonight and you do this. I thought a trip to the Country Kitchen would be nice, since our birthday boy here gets to blow out the candles on the cake and eat ice cream, too. You want to meet us or I'll be back here in thirty minutes."

"No, no, no, just pick up Joy and Martha and my grandbabies. We'll meet you all there," Dad told me.

I left and drove straight home. Joy handed me a towel to shower. That quick two-minute rinse off, two-minute beard touch up felt good. We were dressed and on our way in twenty-minutes. We beat Mom and Dad, but Jillian spotted their big dark blue Buick headed our way.

At dinner it was I who took over the prayer duties from that moment. I got everyone's steak ordered, except Jillian always wanted a burger. The meal was great and then it was dessert time. The birthday boy was feeling pretty excited about the cake with a toilet seat on top brought in by Sugar. We had not seen her for quite some time. It wasn't what I'd call a very loving gesture, but more like comically-funny. It read, "We don't give a shit that you're an old fart!"

I wondered who thought that up. It was Mother.

Mom could not stop laughing at the words and sounded out, "Really, dear, your family loves you a lot! Ah, ha, ha, ha, ha, ha!" with tears forming. She had seen it in a magazine.

Mom's laughter made everyone begin to wail, even Dad, until he blew his uppers onto the table.

"Oh, my God!" Martha let out to Dad's extreme embarrassment, as he covered his toothless mouth.

I never knew he had dentures. I grabbed them up pronto inside a napkin and stood next to Dad to block everyone's view, while he reloaded. When he looked back at us, he just started laughing right where he had left off. Jillian right away wanted another look at him without his teeth, but Joy told her some other time. Dad was a good sport about it. I only wish I had known it would be his last birthday shared with us.

The economy began its upturn, as it always had after a long recession. It was then our congressional members got careless with their constituents' money. Projects flowed across my desk faster than I could sign off and return them approved or needed work.

It seemed the car industry dictated the mood of our country, because they employed so many people who in turn helped assemble different types of manufacturers' products. I even bought two late model, end of the year trucks, on their 72 month, no interest plan. Joy and I had our own choices, she a Ford 150 crew cab pickup, me a Chevy Tahoe SUV.

Both vehicles were very useful in our Midwestern blizzards when our long drive got blowing snow drifts four-feet high across the fields. I used to hit them with my pedal down and the drifts would explode into the air. Jillian just loved to tell me how pretty those looked when I got home.

"Oh my, it's simply gorgeous," Martha told Mom and Dad looking up, viewing the big lighted chandelier that Joy had wanted suspended from the high ceiling.

We had our log home completed and furnished to show them. Jillian, of course, was anxious for everyone to see her new bedroom, "It is all my own and Tom has one, too," she informed Martha, Mom and Dad.

However, up once, was enough, because all the bedrooms were upstairs, something which Mom said we might not like so much when we reached their ages. But Joy had a surprise for them. Out back, built next to the lake with an overhanging wooden deck-patio, was the guest house. It was two bedrooms, two baths, nice and cozy for them to stay permanently, if they so chose.

"Hey, that deck's right over my favorite fishing spot. I can sit in my lawn chair and fish, have a cocktail, and watch the Cubs play, too…wonderful!" he said, so enthusiastically.

I wondered if Dad thought somehow his saving that money for his kids was worth it. He could have done this same building for himself and Mom long ago and enjoyed his life and retired sooner. I told him often how grateful Joy, the kids and I were, that's why we wanted them near.

As it turned out, neither Martha, Mom, or Dad wanted to move into our lake cabin permanently, instead, wanted to stay put and visit as much as they could. I had invested in the extra cabin, hoping that they would.

Nevertheless, Joy gave us all fun times there. From time to time, we all gathered onto that deck above the water to picnic and barbeque. Joy sang to us using her guitar or played for Jillian as she sang to us. Eventually Tom joined in with them in a surprise song of "Old MacDonald".

Dad kept his pole in the water during those times and swore fishing was best with everyone singing. He proved it one night in late August, by catching and landing a whopping eight-pound channel catfish, one of many I had added to the lake's mix to control an overabundant population of stunted blue gills.

We took his picture holding up his trophy catch, right before he decided not to throw it back in, but clean the damned thing for a fish fry. Nobody, except Dad, approved.

I thought Dad was very knowledgeable about cleaning cats. He had done it before, he told me. He had his own fish cleaning table beside the dock that made it simple to discard the skins and guts. We watched him go there and stick that fish, which made it flop. Unfortunately, Dad struggled so hard to kill the big thing, he had a heart attack. When I saw him fall, we all rushed to his side and he was getting up on his own.

Mom called 911 anyway and summoned help right away. Dad left the fish lying on the ground flopping. He was smiling as we helped him up to the cabin, assuring us he was all right, only a bit dizzy. Then he asked me to finish cleaning that big cat. I just kicked the big lunker back into the lake, scars and all, and cleaned myself up in case I had to follow the emergency vehicle.

When the EMTs arrived they were cautious and gentle with Dad. He was still dizzy, he mentioned, so they hooked him up quickly to their equipment. They talked to a doctor and he ordered an IV and some kind of medication. They had to get Dad's system stable first, before transporting him. His heart beats were irregular and his skin was clammy, I heard one report to the doctor via their radio system. They took the necessary time with moving Dad off to St. John's Hospital.

When the emergency crew finally drove away in their vehicle with Dad aboard, it was without lights or siren. I assumed they were confident in his condition. However, half-way down our lane to the highway, Joy alerted us to the fact the emergency vehicle's lights suddenly came on and they had sped up out of sight.

Mom began to weep and I felt that deep, sickening feeling I had felt when Jill passed. I sped to the hospital and saw the emergency vehicle, still with its lights flashing next to the emergency doors. I ran through the doors and was met by Doctor Korman, who delivered the bad news. Dad was DOA and had suffered a second attack enroute, although the EMTs had administered the normal precautionary medication, and the electrical shock program. Nothing worked.

The doctor inquired about the incident leading up to his occurrence. When I told him Dad had decided to clean a really big catfish he'd caught in my pond, he said that explained much. Apparently, the doctor told me, Dad was stabbed twice, once in the hand and once in his side, by one of the big cat's fins. Those pointed thorn-like fins extruded a venom, not normally causing such a violent reaction. Maybe, because it was so huge, it expelled more venom, he told me.

Dad had first suffered aphaeretic shock, caused by his intense allergic reaction to the sting of that catfish, which initiated his extreme body distress. Hence, the heart attack began and aphaeretic shock continued unnoticed by the hidden punctures. An anti-venom serum was available had it been known sooner.

My father had passed and I didn't get to tell him I loved him that time. The doctor took me alone into the emergency room where a nurse handed me his valuables. I heard a nurse asking for someone to sign papers for his release and bill payment. I found that a bit distasteful, but that's just the way life works. Mom went in for just a moment, but thought Dad was too exposed with needles still inserted in him and patches stuck to him and came right back out.

I told Joy to take Mom and Martha home and that I would take care of all the arrangements. Mom and Martha spent the night at the lake house, because our bedrooms were upstairs and their legs couldn't stand the climb.

Mom told me to make arrangements for a Northfield mortuary to pick up Dad and he would be laid to rest, next to Jill, in our family plot. The arrangements were made and the funeral was to be that Wednesday. We all drove up and stayed at a hotel nearby. It was tough on Joy with the kids.

Dad looked himself, lying inside his casket. The funeral director had dressed him in his best Italian business suit, and looked just as though he had fallen asleep. I kept wanting to say something, but all I whispered was , "I loved you, Dad," as we gave our last good-bye.

It was a warm, clear day and Mom put some of Dad's flowers over on Jill's grave. She took her loss well, but I saw the pain of a real dignified wife, being a lady. Many professional people, who were Dad's closest friends, came to offer their condolences. Somehow, Mom always looked her best in black, and that time was no exception.

When it was time to leave, we drove straight home on I-55. Only Jillian could have lightened up our day, and when she just started singing out, "Jesus Loves Me" Joy began to sing softly with her. Then Tom joined in. There was solace to our sorrow.

Mom remained too quiet about her loss of her husband and that bothered me. I wanted to cry, but so many tears can fall, until you become insensitive and distraught with dry eyes. Anyway, that happened to me. Maybe it affected Mom that way, too.

Joy asked Martha and Mom to reconsider staying with us on our farm, in the lake home. Joy promised to be near always and asked if they might share babysitting duties so that she could return to work. This time, that did the trick, although it struck me as being odd. I think she never planned returning to work, it was said to them just to get them both into our home.

Joy's request convinced the other to ask if the other surely could try hard to get along together. I knew they could and I liked having them close to our kids. However, I did not understand Joy's sudden desire for employment. I found a realtor who had lookers for their homes and both Martha and Mom were financially set. It would be terrific with us all being together.

Joy again came to me with her idea of her coming back to work for me. It wasn't as if we needed any money. Somehow I surmised Joy must need a work- life to give her something more meaningful to do. But what could ever be more meaningful than a good mother to our children? I said, "Sorry!"

I think this was where Joy knew something was going to happen to her. As months passed, she began to tell me about the unusual dreams she was having. At first I laughed at her, innocently, but Joy clammed up, seemingly hurt, so I apologized.

The dreams were nutty, screwy, and always stemmed around the deaths of her parents. This continued on for more than a month and both Mom and Martha became concerned with Joy's mental health and behavior. She complained of stiffness in her legs, too often had headaches, and she had trouble watching TV very long. I feared a brain tumor could be the cause.

Mom suggested a doctor of psychology. I think she also feared Joy was losing it. Joy seemingly had everything to live for; her children, and me, a husband who needed her and loved her dearly. I was her lover and she was my best friend, but we suddenly moved apart, caused by her anxiety attacks and pains. She began seeing things in a different light.

I eventually told Sheena of Joy's sudden behavioral changes. She said sometimes drugs affected some people she knew that way, who suddenly went off the deep end.

"No, I'd know if Joy was hitting on something...and that's not her way at all."

"Well, she could have a chemical imbalance. I read about that in health classes. It seems some people lose their direction and it's simply because there is a body chemical imbalance. There's medication for that. Take her to the doctor, for God's sake...make her go," Sheena was adamant.

"I suggested that but she turns away from me. My Jillian said she saw her mommy crying more than once...once is too much. I think you're right. Would you please look up a good physician for me who might deal with mental disorders like Joy's?"

"I just told you. It's not a mental disorder, just the sudden chemical imbalance in her body."

Sheena was helpful and I hoped she was right. Her prognosis was simple, again, I hoped she was correct.

I was pleasantly surprised Joy's appointment was at five in the afternoon the very next day. It was made by Sheena, with Jennifer Wilkin M.D., who was a wonderful physician. I had to literally drag my wife into her office to meet the doctor and had tricked Joy into being there. Realizing Joy's tension, the doctor casually offered Joy a small drink, which she accepted. It helped relax her.

The doctor quickly examined Joy, first physically, then questioning her feelings and if there were any physical pains. She was very thorough and then she assured Joy that she could help her. Joy seemed very relieved.

Doctor Wilkin made immediate arrangements for within the hour at the hospital. I suppose she was in a hurry, because Joy showed no objection and felt substantially better under the medication's influence. I called home and told Martha we were at the hospital for tests and would eat out. The kids were busy watching TV and presented no problem for her.

Doctor Wilkin ordered a complete blood-testing and an MRI for Joy and gave her a prescription for some medication for depression. There was immediate betterment, in Joy's own words, and I wanted to kiss Sheena for her brilliant insight that led me to Doctor Wilkin.

After the hospital blood-testing in the lab and x-ray, Joy seemed eager for us to dine and we ate at a Western Sizzler before going home. That very night Joy slept soundly the entire time and for the first time in weeks. I did also.

The next day at work, Doctor Wilkin followed up on her examination through me. She called during a meeting and I excused myself. The doctor asked me immediately if I was aware Joy had MS. That floored me, and I told her no.

"The results indicated she is suffering some major discomfort from the disease and I feel she must know this already, because the symptoms are not manageable without a doctor's supervision. Has she complained about eyestrain or headaches in one eye?"

"Yes, she has, but she once told me it was from her secretarial duties."

"MS can be hereditary, do you know anything about her parents?"

"No…but look…I know someone you might call and get everything you need to know. It's her foster mom, Martha Rakers. She lives with us and raised Joy, until she graduated from high school," I advised.

"These questions are very personal, so I'm going to ask you to inquire from her foster parent for me. The laws prohibit me asking or disclosing her private health, these days. Unfortunately, there's little known about MS, but we can ease some of her pain. MS usually sneaks up on young people early in life. But sometimes they might already know. I fear that it has caused mild depression in Joy and it can get worse if left unattended. I must tell you it's an uphill road from here on out."

"I'll get back with you tomorrow, doctor. I'll have to talk with Martha in Joy's absence."

If someone had hit me between the eyes with a sledge hammer I wouldn't have even felt that. My worry was overwhelming and I had to tell someone at work. I began to lean on Sheena. At home it was Martha. Mom could not handle our situation.

"Joy's mother definitely had MS, I'm afraid," Martha privately told me that night after supper.

Martha had much to offer. I learned that Joy, beginning about age seven, had taken good care of her mother. When her mother's reoccurring setbacks returned, Joy was always there beside her. Nevertheless, the symptoms seemed to go away for months, and she was almost normal; then suddenly the pain and disruption in her life unexpectedly returned. She must have told Joy something about it being hereditary.

"As a matter of fact, now that you reminded me," Martha spoke, "Jewell, Joy's mother, had pains that last week and Darrel began to drive her. That's when they were in the accident," she said remembering.

I then assumed Joy had suspected or known of her MS for some time. Was it her love for me that she had not told me? That night, I spoke to Joy and told her I knew everything and told her together we could get through this with God's help.

"You never should have taken on this burden alone. I married you for better or worse and nothing could dim the better we've shared. I love you, darling, and you must be strong for me and the kids. You're our pillar," I told her.

Then, she burst out crying in my arms and hit me with more sadness. She told me that Jillian was having the same symptoms, at seven, as Joy began in her early twenties right after we married. That is what Joy was so miserable about all this time, and it deeply depressed her.

I held her tightly and felt her body trembling. Her tears flowed off her cheeks onto my shoulder. When I told her again we could get through this together, she sobbed heavily saying, "I just can't stand to see our Jillian suffer so young in life," then, she cried and cried some more.

I guess I could have said it better. I hated myself for not knowing how. I would have done anything to relieve my Joy's worries and without doubt would have taken a bullet through my heart to save my lovely wife and daughter. I never saw her inner-thinking or anticipated her next move.

I called Doctor Wilkin early the next morning to tell her of Joy's mother's MS affliction. She said Joy would need special care now to bring her out of her present condition, however, she felt we could dramatically delay her pains up into her older years with a designed program of exercise, good nutrition and medications. When I told her Joy also thought Jillian had the beginning of the disease she said, "Oh, God help us!"

I never knew of any physician relate to God in any way, so I knew her thoughts were grave. I made advanced appointments at her suggestion for the next six months, beginning that next week to assure Joy's scheduled medications could be monitored, as well as her mental attitude. I could schedule my work around most of the appointments, and then there was Martha and Mother.

While sitting on my lap at home, I noticed Jillian rubbing her eyes.

"What's wrong, honey, do you have something in your eye?" I questioned her continued rubbing.

"Daddy, they itch and sometimes I get a headache in one eye. Momma says she will know what to do after she sees her doctor again. I hope she hurries up…it hurts, Daddy."

I then saw what Joy meant about Jillian and it scared the hell out of me. I immediately began to wonder what I had done to the Lord to have him punish me this way. I thought I had been a good Christian my entire life and Joy was nearer being an angel than anyone…why us?

Sheena was a friend and really helped me through my coming weeks. She read every article she could lay her hands upon and tried to give me encouragement.

"Jerry's kids!" Sheena told me was about to begin that Labor Day. Jerry's weekend-long MS marathon was on and I planned to learn as much as I could. Unfortunately, Joy accompanied me on the sofa and it depressed her badly seeing a little girl the age of our Jillian in a wheelchair.

Joy didn't cry the next time her pains began. She just stayed in bed daily and left things that were household chores to Martha and Mom. Joy refused my sexual advances that I meant to make her happy and assure her I loved her. There was reason for her confused worry, except she was getting mentally ill, also.

The first three weeks of one day sessions with Doctor Wilkin, worked wonders and Joy realized less pain, but still was lethargic at home and especially around the kids. It was when I had to fly out to Los Angeles on a week's interstate meeting, that Joy fell more ill. She missed her doctor's appointment.

Martha called me on Pacific Coast time at six in the morning. She told me Joy had told her life was not worth living and she was very worried. I asked if Joy had taken her medication on schedule, but she didn't know. Martha did say Joy lost her balance and had accidentally destroyed the Gibson when she stumbled and fell with it and Tom in her arms. Joy let Tom fall upon her tummy, but Joy fell atop the guitar. She lay there and couldn't get up for some time. Joy became violent when Mom tried to call for medical help.

Joy demanded of them to just let her die there, but she was all right. Mom cried then, thinking Joy's back was broken. However, Martha found her medication and made her take it. Joy soon crawled onto the couch, but stayed there.

My world was plummeting around me and I had no way to stop the fall. I flew home immediately to the dismay of several congressmen from Illinois who also were there at the conferences.

Joy looked like a wild woman with her beautiful hair straggly and just hanging uncombed. I took her brush from her vanity and began to stroke her beautiful hair as she sat on the edge of our bed. Joy began rocking back and forth mumbling, then singing words to a verse that always ended with, "Why, Momma?" I was helpless and I thought she imagined I was her mother.

I left Joy momentarily to call Doctor Wilkin. When I told her of Joy's peculiar behavior she recommended a psychiatrist in a local rest home that she knew and believed I had better not hesitate to call him. I did, and he told me to bring Joy to New Salem, where his facility was.

The facility was huge and sprawled out on the countryside, east of town. I never knew it was there and yet it looked promising when Joy had no objections visiting there, until she found out she was admitted to stay there. Then she wanted to leave, but the doctor gave her a sedative shot which zonked her. I accompanied Joy to her private room and they put her to bed.

After we settled the financial questions, they asked me to bring her some casual clothes and pictures and things of the family for her to be reminded she had another place.

As I left Joy sleeping, I saw many residents there, male and female, being attended to and freely moving around with some supervision. They seemed to be content and I felt good that Joy was safe and getting treatment that would bring her back to us. I drove on home.

Martha helped me collect Joy's things and put them in two suitcases. Then she handed me Joy's Martin guitar thinking Joy might find time to play it. That was a great idea, I thought.

When Mom walked into the room with her bags, also, I was surprised. She had her bags packed and advised Martha and me that she was calling a taxi, then heading up to the airport, and flying to Chicago to go visit family. I told her no taxi would come out here in the country and that I would take her. That way, I could take clothes back for Joy. I loaded up Joy's and Mom's things as Mom hugged the kids and Martha good-bye.

I supposed Mom was not nearly as strong as Martha in dire situations like ours and had lost her courage to stay with Joy, me, and the kids, since Dad passed. I accepted her tormented feelings of being here, as I, too, wished I could just pack up and run away from it all.

I took Mom to her scheduled flight and kissed her good-bye. She then said she was sorry and I told her to visit as often as she could, because my kids needed to know their grandmother. I waved good-bye at the airport and tried my best to smile...she did her best, also.

It was late, a non-visiting time that I arrived at Crimson Sky Rest Home. I wanted to take Joy's clothes and personal things to her myself, however, I was denied.

"But no one said there would be restrictions on seeing my own wife," I told them with some sarcasm attached to my voice.

When I demanded to see Joy, eventually a discontented doctor came to escort me to her room.

"The reason for our concern with you being here at this time, unannounced, is this is the sedation period for Joy and she may not respond to even knowing you are here. Her medication is strong and is meant to relax the brain...sort of a vacation from thinking too much, or in most cases, worrying too much. You'll understand," he said as he unlocked Joy's door.

It was like a prison with no way out, I thought at first. But then I found my lovely lady looking quite peaceful. Joy was dressed in a new night gown and soundly sleeping. She didn't move a muscle, even when I accidentally dropped one suitcase to avoid dropping the guitar. I set them inside her closet, then walked over to her and kissed her lips and whispered good-night. I was satisfied Joy was being cared for and noticed her room was very clean and had 24/7 monitoring cameras, also, to observe her.

"Thank you, doctor, I'm satisfied my wife is where she can get good help," I told him.

"The absolute best help," he then added.

I drove home feeling lonely and empty inside, longing for my wife's sweet voice to comfort me, but that did not happen.

Later at home, I told Martha I wish I could wake up from this and discover it all was a bad dream, but it was real, and I was in it.

Chapter 16

The road to Crimson Sky became well traveled for the next eight months after work, rain, snow, or shine, but still the florist told me I was his best customer. The kids cried for their momma continually, but the doctor, nor I, wanted them to see Joy that way. Martha did her best comforting them, and eventually they grew callused to their wanting pains. They still asked me, when, every time I came from Joy?

In one of her better moments, Joy had discussed Jillian's condition with Doctor Metz, but he said to her, as he had told me, her own health was foremost. Without her, Jillian couldn't make it either and there was time for Jillian. It was to stimulate Joy's desires to help herself get healthy for Jillian.

The thought of Jillian's future deterioration, apparently kept Joy unstable and suddenly wanting to end it all. I knew that was not my Joy. But this time mentally, she just couldn't suck it up to be there for Jillian, bless her heart.

Joy got much worse then before she got better mentally, and sometimes I could not see her at all. One day, I did get to see her un-medicated and quite comprehending and told her Jillian was doing just great, was normal, and soon would be starring in the school's play. I guess because of her condition, Joy suspected Jillian had fallen ill, also, and her mind played tricks on her thinking. She seemed surprised and elated. Medications were eased and she continually progressed.

She had reversed her thinking, as one day Joy welcomed my arrival just as a new spring had sprung, seemingly returning to very normal, and glad to see me. She asked to have the kids come to see her, too. I got the doctor's approval.

"If you don't bring our youngin's here to see me pretty soon, I'll jail break and go to them," Joy laughed, but then turned away looking a bit sad. "How long have I been this way, anyway?"

"Too long, sweetheart, but you're coming along just fine," I told her.

I knew she was confused, but I also felt it was good that she wanted them near her. We talked a lot about the new renters of our ground and I told her I was going to learn everything and take over their duties when I someday retired.

Joy then told me she liked to harrow and disk. She once had a neighbor boy that she thought she had a crush on and rode on his tractor sometimes, out in the fields. He let her drive once or twice and she disked so well, his father paid her just to disk behind the plow to expedite planting.

"Grub? His dad, Chub?" I then surmised.

Embarrassed by my accurate guess, Joy couldn't lie and reluctantly admitted she discovered her knight in shining armor wasn't so gallant after all.

"You know, I was never so sick in my life, as when I saw Grub stand up on his big John Deere tractor, while I was disking behind him on that little red Farmall, and he would blow big strings of snot out of his nose, without so much as a handkerchief…and then he wiped his nose on his sleeve. That did it for me. I still disked, but I stayed way behind him, so I couldn't see his misgivings. And believe you me, I never ever let him put his snotty arms around me ever again. So there, you now know if you're going to plow in front of me, you'd better buy some handkerchiefs first."

"I just want to plow you," I said, beginning to get romantic, since Joy seemed so "back to normal" where we would sit together and she'd keep talking non-stop. My life had a little light at the end of that long tunnel.

"When you coming home?" I asked.

"What? And give up all this wonderful maid service?" she laughed. "You just bring me Jillian and Tom and I'll consider coming home," she said smiling, then kissed me.

The door opened unexpectedly, and untimely, as a nurse leaned in to tell me to kiss Joy again good-bye for the evening.

"Doctor Metz, Joy's doctor is here, and wants to speak with you now, please," she informed me after I left Joy's room and had kissed Joy good-bye.

She led me to the doctor's office and he seemed very knowledgeable and encouraging about Joy's progress.

"I hope your visit with your wife was a pleasant one. Let me give you the facts. Joy still and always will suffer from MS, but she's overcome with fears she can't handle and it's hard to isolate. Especially, if she thinks Jillian, your daughter, is afflicted.

"At Joy's age, I think we can delay its total affects by many years. It's your daughter's welfare that she can't handle. I've explained that medicine has made tremendous advances in MS and maybe by the time Jillian begins to experience her problems with this disease there might be a cure."

"Sir, I know you are the learned one, but my daughter already shows those signs and has pains, Doctor Metz," I told him. "However, Joy became happier once when I explained Jillian was acting very normal and was in her school play. She seemed to doubt me.

"I think Joy thought Jillian's condition had digressed as quickly as hers. She seems much better now after I told her. I encourage you to tell her that Jillian's alright. I believe that is her best medicine for getting her mental health back. I'll deal with it at home. My kids will help me, and I have her mom to assist her."

"Unfortunately, I'm only here to focus on giving Joy back her life now. She's progressed, but I need her to become stronger in handling what she ultimately must face when she returns home, as you both will. MS doesn't get better. But, we can ease some of the pain to make victims' lives more tolerable. Maybe a time at home may snap her out of this.

"My treatment included corticosteroids, drugs that help keep the immune system from attacking the body, and drugs to relieve symptoms. From now on this is where you come in for extra support and to comfort her.

"You might want to hire someone extra you can trust and afford to be a full time 24/7 live-in. There are some nurses who do that for a living. This way she can receive the medications on time and be under medical supervision and surveillance, as needed, while you're at work.

"I understand you are a state engineer and your job can support them. You'll have to dig deeper, not only into your pocketbook, but your intestinal fortitude. Your lives will change, have already changed, but it doesn't have to end. Do you understand what I'm telling you?"

"Yes, Doctor, I already have done that, and because I truly love my wife I can withstand anything, anything. But I'm not certain if she could have before right now. She's had a difficult life and now the bad is continuing. How long can she hold up?"

"I suppose that's up to the one who said 'forever', I guess," he said, meaning me.

I left the good doctor knowing what to expect and what to do. I couldn't just let Martha do the tasks necessary for Joy, Jillian and Tom, although she wanted to. Bless her heart, she was old and soon would be incapable herself. No, I had to find someone I could trust. The search began.

At work, I asked Sheena if she knew of any reputable service person or nurse who performed the duties I needed. It would be basically a whole-house maid with some knowledge of Joy's needs. I called the hospital and was told about Visiting Nurses Association, but for now they only performed medical services in the home for doctor directed services. It was way beyond thinking that I could ever afford their continued service for years, even from my own wallet.

Therefore, after much thought, I asked Sheena if she would type up an ad suitable to attract an honorable female for the position I offered.

"What kind of salary are you going to put with the ad?" Sheena asked, as she quickly copied another ad's wording.

"Let's see…room and board in your private home. That would be our vacant visitor's log house on the lake, now that Martha moved into the spare bedroom we made downstairs for her out of the utility room…all utilities paid…wow…put $3,000 a month," I told her. "I already pay that at Crimson Sky."

"You shittin' me? Oops…sorry, boss, you told me never to swear, but for that dough I'll take that job myself! I'm getting nowhere in this state job, really, and I certainly don't like being a secretary all my life…I wouldn't even be one if it weren't for you making things so comfortable with no big demands…but I'm thinking of learning to become a domestic, like some of my aunts and uncles. They've all loved their lives. With little overhead and few worries, they all saved up their extra money and now live the high life in retirement. No need for a taxed retirement plan."

"No, no, you're needed here. Besides, I can't offer you a retirement plan, too. You've got a retirement building up here and health insurance. I can't offer those. Besides, what could you know medically?"

"Just listen this time, please…I can buy my own insurance through Cobra here. The money I save up is my retirement plan. And how much medical knowledge does it take to hand out pills from the doctor? I'll learn as I go…I can certainly do that and I'm a great housekeeper, too…it runs in our family and I love Joy and your kids. I'm practically family already; and, I'll just charge you $700 a week. How's that?"

"No, I'm sorry, but I just couldn't. Who's going to replace you? You make me look better than I am. No, you've got security here with me. Joy trained you."

"Oh yeah?" Sheena said sarcastically, as she handed me an official inner-office memo, which showed that "due to her advanced skills" Sheena Johnson was needed and moving upstairs where the big wigs sat.

"They can't do that to me!" I said, reaching for the phone to call upstairs to complain.

Sheena's hand held down the receiver and she just pointed for me to look behind me.

I turned around to see this very attractive young thing, slightly more than a girl out of puberty staring me in the face.

"May I help you?" I asked.

"Hello, I'm Twila!"

The girl smiled and told me she was my new temp secretary for Sheena. If she worked out the state might offer her Sheena's position. She had worked in the filing department in Clara Turner's office. I suppose Clara wanted to get rid of her. I sat down and looked at Sheena.

"Are you sure? Don't you have a lease, too?"

"Pardon me…hey…I'm looking for a place!" the girl inserted abruptly. "Is yours available?" Twila asked Sheena anxiously.

"Yes, I split, $950 plus utilities, no extras…share with a white girl who's about your age. Two bedroom, two bath, no pets, no drugs or strange sex inside…the usual. Her name is Donna."

"That sounds good to me. I'll take it sight-unseen."

"It's no dump, honey," Sheena told her.

"That's settled then…or, better yet, you two settle it," I injected.

"Okay then…when can I start?" Sheena asked, with her biggest smile.

"As soon as you can, after Joy returns home…get Twila here, broken in quickly…I hope very soon. I have to tell Martha and the kids you'll be moving into the lake house. They'll be very happy…need help moving?"

"No…I have brothers and family."

"Okay…then it's a deal at $700 a week, as I stated, right?"

"Right, boss!"

"Okay, young lady, let's see what you can do," I said, to the young newcomer. "Sheena, will you begin with…oh, what's your name again?" I asked.

"Twila Donaldson, sir."

"Donaldson? Are you related to Dennis and Jordan Donaldson, by chance?"

"Yes, I know you know them. I'm their little sister, but that was them, this is me…I'm not like that."

"Small world, huh? Okay then, let's get to work. First…oh, heck, Sheena will clue you in," I advised her looking at my watch. "I have a one-thirty upstairs on a personnel budget recall meeting and I'm almost late. Be out in two hours, Sheena."

"Okay, boss…drop the hint I'm not moving upstairs, will ya?"

"Yep, might make someone sad…glad it's them, not me."

I finished the day, as did Sheena and Twila. However, Sheena stayed over to tell me that since Twila was already someone's secretary, she knew almost everything, plus lap dictation.

"What's lap dictation?" I asked.

"You didn't hear this from me, but rumor mill has it her last boss got caught with his pants down and she was on his lap. Clara put her out of her office, is the word from the canteen. She's union, so they couldn't fire her, only suspend or transfer her. They wanted her gone. She's basically got this job. I think she's a nympho the way she talks about her constant need."

"Oh my Gosh! Now what am I gonna do with someone like that?"

"You'll think of something…you'd better think of something…you just hired her."

"Where's Clint? I need Clint Edwards. He's just like her and they'll be good together. Call him into the office and tell him he won a door prize at the Harness Club…here's fifty. Give it to him in an envelope tomorrow at punch-in time and make sure you tell what's her name, he likes her looks. She'll hopefully take it from there, if she's that sex-crazed. Oh, God, I hope this works!"

"I never saw you so uptight like this, boss. You afraid of a little extra curricular activity after hours?" Sheena teased and laughed. "Or, is it because you have guilty thoughts about her already?" she continued teasing, I hoped.

"No, as long as it's my wife you're talking about. Here, run off a hundred of these. Schedule this; two sessions for tomorrow morning, two in the afternoon, also, and everyone will attend, unless they're dead…then I want a hand-written excuse!" I said, handing Sheena a state employee policy pamphlet, attached to two videos from down deep in my junk drawer. "Use upstairs', room 2A…please, you better run it, okay? It will be all day, so break whenever you need to…thanks. I'm counting on you, again."

I was never so upset before about my employer-employee relationship, possibly ruining my job, my marriage, and my life over one dizzy girl, who looked so young and naive. But the more I saw of Twila, the more she disturbed my thinking that no one would ever believe me if she got caught on my lap. I was frantic. I was angry with myself for even looking at her body that seemed perfect…firm and voluptuous…I needed relief in the worst way. I was also very horny.

"Darn that Clara, I saved her life and she did this to me?" I sounded off.

I had Sheena post up morning and afternoon scheduling to accommodate everyone. It was a mandatory shed employee meeting, with films, upstairs on "Sex in the Work Place" and "What is, and What is not, Sexual Harassment".

They also had to sign off with Sheena that they attended one session. We were overdue for re-schooling anyway. What would I ever do without Sheena? She was as efficient as my Joy was in her day.

I left work and headed straight to Crimson Sky and room #97, my wife's.

"Hi, honey, how was your day?" I asked my lovely wife, who glowed when she smiled at me.

"Guess what I did? I sang and played my guitar for the residents here."

"Well that's great. I expect to be your biggest fan and hear about your album coming out next spring, 'Joy to the World,' let's call it."

"Funny, but not bad, not bad. How about, 'I'm comin' home, I've done my time!'"

At first I didn't get it, and said I liked mine better, because hers was a verse from "Tie a Yellow Ribbon". Then it sank in.

"Oh! Oh, you mean you're done here and you're coming home?"

"Yep, this Saturday, after I re-interview with Doctor Metz. Will you come pick me up?"

"Oh, honey, yes, the kids will be so happy and me, especially. Doctor Metz is a great doctor. He told me to get you a live-in maid, so when Sheena became available and wanted the job, I gave it to her. I'll tell her to move in Saturday, too. What? What's wrong now?" Joy's face was stern and not happy-faced smiling anymore.

"I don't like someone living in our house who's not family."

"That's good…Sheena will live in the lake house and do all the cooking and washing and clean up. It will be easier on you, dearest, and you can spend time teaching the kids," I rattled off so she would accept the situation. "We can easily afford her and she loves you and the kids."

"Sheena, huh? You don't have something going on between you two, now do ya?"

"Don't you ever say such a thing again or I'll take your sweet little ass over my knee and spank you blue!" I said pissed.

"You ain't big enough, buster!" she retaliated, standing up to me for another "Joy-ess" moment.

Soon we were very close, longingly looking into each other's face, when I kissed her; she kissed me, and our clothes flew off as fast as we could shake them loose. We made hot passionate love and brought some entertainment to that rest home. Unfortunately, it was time for Doctor Metz to make his evening rounds and he popped in the door.

"Oops!" he said, and then right back out he went.

"Well, if he didn't see you naked before, he has now," I told Joy.

"No, he saw your big butt, not mine!"

Then we laughed together, I got off and locked the door. We made love trying to hang on to Joy's single bed. I didn't leave, until after the chimes let us know it was visitors' leaving time.

"Thanks, I really, really needed that," I said, to my loving wife who returned to be my lover.

"It should be me, thanking you. I needed it, too. It was just like the first time."

"The very first time? The very first time you said I was done too fast."

"This time I beat you…twice," Joy said brazenly, which built my ego.

"I can't wait to get you onto our king and have no one to interrupt us," I told her trying to tell her how much I desired her love and missed her.

The knock on the door was Nurse Fritz who yelled to us, "The honeymoon's over, kids!"

We laughed again, but then we looked up.

"You think they saw everything on that damn camera?" I asked.

"I'm sure of it," Joy whispered.

"Damn! I forgot about that thing, didn't you?"

"I forgot about everything…it was wonderful…who cares! YOU PERVERTS!" Joy yelled up at the camera and then stuck her tongue out at it.

"Hush, damn it! They might decide to keep you here," I whispered, then got up quickly and tippy-toed over to turn off the light.

We both heard the faint sounds of laughter and applause coming from down the hallway, obviously from the crowded nurses' station. I straightened up, got dressed in the darkness, and Joy let me out. I gave her one last peck and she slipped me her tongue, just to remind me what I was missing. I already knew that.

I quickly stepped out and looked straight ahead, while walking past the nurses' station, but received one, "You've really got it going for ya, Mr. Wetmore!" jeering, and some chuckles.

The kids were excited when I got home, as was Martha, who said she best start dusting and cleaning, before Joy came home. Then I told her, "No, never again!"

I meant it with all my love and appreciation for her taking over for Joy. I then told them all about Sheena's coming to be our live-in housemaid. The kids cheered, but there was a frown.

"What does Joy say about that?" Martha grimly asked.

"Now look. . .Doctor Metz says I must get extra help for Mommy and someone who can go up and down those stairs ten times a day. Martha, you just kick back and teach Jillian how to knit and pearl, or quilt. . .woman things. I'll take charge of Tom and we'll all let Sheena pick up after us like kings and queens. Joy thinks it's a marvelous idea and you two can spend the good days shopping or whatever makes you both happy.

"Now, there will be some times when Mommy gets a bit under the weather, because she is still ill. We have to help her through her bad times. But, Mommy's comin' home to us, so I want you all dressed Saturday afternoon in your finest, because this family is going out to eat and celebrate. . .got it?"

"YEAH!" the kids screamed.

I showered and readied for bed. I said a silent prayer that what I had done with Sheena was going to work out. I dreaded the next morning, but the sun rose as always from the east.

"What day is this?" I asked Martha.

Unfortunately, Martha stopped short of delivering my eggs and bacon breakfast, looking a bit confused. When she hesitated too long, thinking hard, I took the plate from her and looked across at the calendar. It was Wednesday. It was seven-thirty at work, and as far as I was concerned it was "d-day". By now, Sheena would have slipped the money to Clint Edwards and introduced him to our new secretary Twila.

I drove to the shed with some trepidation. I entered the office and saw no one. Then I remembered the films and headed upstairs to room 2A and peeked inside. I was happy to see it full of attentive employees. Sheena, who was handling the video presentation looked my way and signaled an "a-ok" with her fingers, therefore I returned downstairs to check mail and answer the phone. No one called, so I read the complicated reviews of several projects.

An hour later, I heard rumbling and some laughter as employees came down the stairs to visit the canteen with those pamphlets. It was the ten o'clock break. Clint Edwards and other hardhat employees came down jovial and seemed to take the films in stride. Instead of entering the canteen they met with Ted, their road supervisor, and headed out to a job site.

Ted waved to me and said, "Thanks. . .now I might be late coming in on the culvert project today! Remember today!" he said, I think sarcastically.

"Sheena!" I called to her, as she came down the stairs. She saw me and left the other women who were also headed into the canteen.

"Well?"

"Well, what?"

"Did you get done what I asked?"

"Well, yes and no…I gave Clint Edwards his fictitious fifty dollar prize and he hit on me, not Twila."

"Oh darn, where's Twila?"

"I don't know. She was at the films…maybe she's in the john."

"Okay…did you tell her about Clint? Keep an eye on her…did she see the film?"

"I just said, yes, to you, boss, simmer down…I'm going to pee in my panties now, if I don't grab my coffee and hit the john before that next big show upstairs at ten-thirty…see ya!" Sheena said, a little perturbed as if she thought I thought that she failed me.

"Good news!" I hollered out to her, trying to regain her spirits. "Joy is coming home Saturday, and you can move in any time now."

"Well that's really good news…thanks," Sheena said, less enthusiastically than I imagined. I guess she was still perturbed or had to pee badly… women!

I couldn't begin to believe the trucks full of furniture that were headed up our drive the next evening. Sheena didn't tell me a thing about it. It was Sheena's family with Sheena's furniture, then some. Sheena, I learned had six brothers and two sisters, some with different fathers, but they all intended to reside in the guest house with Sheena for a while. They all said how happy they were to move here; I panicked big time.

"Sheena! Sheena!" I called out to no avail.

"My sister went to the store to get us some foods…Are youins' her kind new boss?" one cute little girl in pigtails and cornrows asked.

"And what did your big sister tell you, sweetheart?"

"She say we all gonna be together again for a little while."

My real worries began when I finally caught up with Sheena driving past our house. Her car was loaded down with at least ten bags of groceries. A relative seated in the back and called Moombie was introduced to me by Sheena, then she got out to talk.

I politely asked her what was going on, because her entire family had moved into the guest house. She told me she promised them just a few weeks' stay for helping her move and they would be out of there by the next month.

They had all been victims of a house fire and had no place to go. I could relate to that. So, Sheena had to help them.

"Sheena! We never made arrangements like this...just you were supposed to move in."

"I know, I know, but picture this...a fire from lightning destroys your house the same week the Detroit car manufacturing factories lay off the entire lot of male providers from one large family; you have to eat, your family has to eat, and you need a roof over the head of your babies and you absolutely have no extra money...that was three months ago...we sisters and brothers lend a helping hand to one another, if we can. Thanks to your kindness, I hope, I won't have to put twelve people including four children and two pregnant sisters out in the street. Now what?"

"Wow, that is sad. Okay...whatever it takes...I think I can give them a few maintenance mowing jobs down near Litchfield and at the weigh stations, up north of Springfield, until they can find good jobs. There haven't been many applicants, there's six or seven men still needed. It pays state minimum, but it's work and together by them sharing rides and money, it might be enough. Anybody skilled?"

"They're all skilled...they're top mechanics, painters, assemblers, tire men, brakemen...you name it. They're not looking for a handout...they're looking for work...real work."

"Okay, understand me... besides me and the kids there's Martha. She's your boss, too. I hold you responsible for keeping both my home place and the lake house in tip top order, dusting, windows, cooking, ironing, scrubbing... the whole nine yards, and especially looking out for Joy and our kids. She's fine now, but the doctor said she'll have her difficult times. I think she's going to be surprised as I am, but if anyone will understand, it's my Joy."

"I know Martha, Joy and the kids...man, you'd think I was a nigger comin' in to harvest your cotton!"

I realized my social prejudice was showing and I felt really bad. I asked Sheena to forgive me and promised we'd try to work this out together.

"I'm ashamed of myself, Sheena. Believe me, with so much on my mind I have to be a fool not to blow my brains out right now. Sorry...give me a hug, so I know you're not really pissed," I said extending my arms.

"You better not touch that girl, brother, or I'll come out and kick you ass right here and now!" came the ranting from Moombie, the woman in the back seat.

Sheena rushed to shush her and said to behave. However, that look of Moombie's at me could stop a clock and I'd have dreams of that face for some time. It appeared her mouth was overflowing with banana and I could see five or six skins scattered all over.

"Sheena, tell the boys, ah, the men, to be ready in the morning, dressed for work…when I'm ready to leave to take them along to the shed."

"No, they can use my car and follow you," Sheena told me. "My job starts here at six, and I intend to cook you the best breakfast first, and then the family's. I can play it by ear from then on. Martha can tell me. "

"Super, I knew we could work together if we put out heads together. Oh, the boom boxes stop at eight, that's Jillian's and Tom's bedtime, got it?"

"You're the boss," Sheena spoke.

Surprisingly, everything changed when Sheena arrived at the guest house with the food and orders. The boom boxes stopped booming, and lowered to an almost silent sounding. I could tell the radios were still playing, because three young guys were dancing together on the old fishing dock Danby had built. I hoped it held up. They walked away with several fish and I knew that would help with feeding them. All in all, only Martha was scared, but she knew Sheena.

Morning came, only after I peeked out the window to see if the new residents had gone to sleep. They all packed it in, inside on the floors, and camped out upon the deck in small tents. Everything was peaceful, until dawn when I awoke and looked outside for the umpteenth time. The guys were up early, out in the lake taking baths naked, soaping up in the water. When I heard pots and pans rattling downstairs, I rushed to shower and shave, but met Martha shuffling out of the bathroom like she had been up to pee and back again. She was supposed to sleep downstairs in her new room.

"Morning, Martha!" I said, but she just continued her shuffling walk and closed Jill's door. She said nothing. I thought she might be mad at me for having Sheena move in. Maybe she was sleepwalking, I thought, and she didn't realize it. She could tumble down the stairs and kill herself, because it was the first night she slept upstairs in quite a while. So I peeked in on her.

"Martha! What are you doing?"

There Martha was, standing on a chair, using my binoculars to watch the naked bathers. Embarrassed, she played it very cagey like a coyote caught in the hen house. What could she say?

"You know, I could get used to this! But what the ladies say about black men isn't really true. My Kurt was more endowed and I'm not at all impressed."

I could have died. This woman, who I symbolized as a near saint, our Martha, had turned about-face in her ever so religious ways and was now a sinner. Imagine that? I had scared her, and when she became wobbly, I managed to catch her fall.

"Where am I?" she said, acting sound asleep, but very, very embarrassed. I could tell by the flushed cheeks.

"Now, Martha, you'll just have to control yourself. Go out to the veranda, it's a better view," I laughed.

"Oh, Greg, forgive me...please don't tell Joy," she moaned sadly.

"Martha, everyone enjoys a fling, now and again...Jesus met Mary Magdalene by the well...did that make him bad? Think on it!" I said, to give her comfort, but left laughing inside at her...she reminded me of Granny Clampet on the Beverly Hillbillies. I went to have breakfast.

"Ummm, that's delicious, Sheena. What is it?" I said of the tall cool fruit drink she made with the blender we had never really used.

"It's a health drink, don't ask me what's in it, it just tastes too darn good to advertise. My auntie told me her secret. It's like an aphrodisiac with lemon, orange juice, shake of Peppermint Schnapps, cinnamon, mint and juleps, grape juice and a touch of rum, well lots of rum. You get drunk and you fall in love, ha!"

"I won't need anything like that...I might walk around with a hard on all day?" I laughed. "No alcohol before work...remember Smoke? It does taste mighty good, but I'll just have coffee...but thanks for being inventive."

"Man, you sure must have gotten some good sleep. I had those radios turned off and everyone who's working today in their beds by nine," she said walking over and drinking my juice drink.

"By the way...you might have the guys bathe farther down the bank, maybe down by the dock. You know...when Joy comes home. But Martha thinks it's great."

"Daddy!" came the voices of my kids in their pajamas to jump on me and kiss me. "Those people are still out there in our other house," Tom spoke.

"Those people are Sheena's family and they'll be with us for a while. Their house burned down and they need our help. What do good Christians do?" I asked. "Huh?"

"We share our broken bread," Tom said, to my surprise.

"That's right and we're going to be good Christians and share. Right?"

"Right!" Jillian said.

Kids say the darnest things, but they seem to tell their true feelings. I finished my breakfast and headed outside. Sheena's car was full of guys willing to work, so I went over and introduced myself.

"Hi, fellas, I'm Greg. I hope I can help getting you all temporary work today. Anybody here got a criminal record? None, good. Do you have IDs? Everyone, good…follow me," I said.

They followed me to the shed and waited for me to tell them to get out. Most of the employees had already punched in and headed out to their work sites. Then, I saw old Smoke standing near Twila's desk with papers of reinstatement in his hands. I went over to talk to Smoke. I learned he had been through rehab, was cured, and asked if he could return. He would do anything.

"Smoke, I'm proud of you. Have you ever been a supervisor of the mowing crew?"

"Sure enough…when I first got my promotion, I was a supervisor."

"Think you could supervise these fine six men and show them the ropes. I need a crew for mowing around the bridges, the truck weighing scales, around the center dividers at overpasses, and here around the shed when you run out of things to mow, all the way from Litchfield to the North Sangamon County line at Saline Creek. Think you can handle that?"

"You can count on me."

"I am. And if you show that you're always on time and don't drink, I'll see you get your job on the road crew back…that goes for everyone. Okay, sit down with Twila here…she needs your IDs and use my address, Twila. These men are staying with me. Their house burned down, so try to bend with them as much as you can.

"They're grade one…Smoke is grade three…he used to work here not so long ago, but he has experience for this job. Give them truck #31 the crew cab, and the #3 tractor and the utility flatbed to haul it and three self-propelled hand mowers. Have them head out to Litchfield, Smoke, and do a good job for me, will you?"

"You have my best, Mr. Wetmore," he said putting on a red supervisors hardhat, as required.

"All right, men, let's get started," Smoke said, as he and his men sat down with Twila for paperwork and were out in twenty minutes, headed for Litchfield.

I read my mail.

"Damn, damn, double-damn!"

I had an order to attend another California seminar. This time it was in Sacramento and on Monday next.

I called upstairs to see if anyone would go in my stead to California. I told Frank Little, the head of our Department of Public Building Construction, that Joy was coming home and I hoped to be with her.

"I heard about Joy. She used to be in my wife's class at Pawnee High. My wife cherished Joy when she lost her parents in that wreck. I guess I can find someone who wants to fly out to be away from their wives for a couple of days. Say, where'd you find those mowers?"

"They are Sheena's relatives from Detroit. They're laid-off car workers and their house burned down. They really need these jobs."

"Okay, Greg…I'll let you know on the California trip. They do have some remarkable advances in engineering that might benefit you in your decisions…oh hell…I will get someone, even if I go myself. That's in Sacramento, right?"

"Yes, next Monday."

"I almost forgot to tell you. You got a promotion. You stay where you are, but the assembly has come up with a big problem concerning the East Saint Louis Bridge project. For insurance purposes, get this, you are now our new Director of Geotechnical Services."

"When did they come up with that, Frank?"

"We looked on everyone's resume and saw you delved into structures that could fail during an earthquake…let me see here…you inspected the Chicago Police station and found fault in their buildings and they were later condemned. Your professor wrote you were very intuitive about that area and offered you a position to study under him, but you refused."

"Yes, because I had this job waiting."

"Well, you were the closest person to elevate and it was unanimous. You get a pay grade and a company car, or truck, which you already have, but you can take it home, because you'll have to start a survey of the geothermal something or other on the Illinois and Missouri side. Got any idea what that is?"

"Yes, I'd be interested in that. It's really interesting to me. A geotech studies and uses instruments to analyze foundational sub-surfaces capable of withstanding a shift or not withstanding a geological physical shift...that's an earthquake."

"Looks like we picked the best man. Okay, I'll go out to Cal myself. It's nice out there and Schwarzenegger owes me lunch anyway from last time. I'll send down your new guidelines with my secretary Joann now, and you'll have to tweak them to fit as soon as possible. Tell Joy I said hi," he said hanging up.

The secretary wasted no time in delivering my guidelines, rules, regulations and responsibilities galore...I loved it. I picked up the introduction and immediately read. My mind went into high gear with the thoughts of what I could study, had studied, and remembered. I researched this in college.

I learned an Illinois Geotechnical Engineer was to provide statewide guidance on geotechnical engineering and engineering geology products and services for the department. This included soil and rock field investigations, geotechnical earthquake engineering...my immediate concern, exploratory drilling, geophysics, and the development of foundation recommendations for structures, which would be the underlayment surfaces at the Mississippi River Bridge's banks, including design and construction support.

This was also to provide policy for emergency response to landslides, rockfall, bridge scour and earthquake damage and getting a new accredited geotechnical laboratory approved and built. It was an enormous go-ahead.

My new geotechnical services department was to provide statewide policy, standards, procedure and guidance for geotechnical engineering and engineering geology products and services. It would serve as the department's liaison to professional groups involved in soil and geologic investigations, design and construction. I was now in hog heaven. It was a piece of cake.

I spent little time getting in some updated reading on siezmic charts data and saw that present day concern existed mainly for a major destructive earthquake in the New Madrid seismic zone.

Way back in the 1800's a huge quake rocked the area. It was said the earth opened up for thousands of feet and fell, causing the Mississippi River to flow backwards for days. Untold casualties were never even counted.

Many structures in Memphis, Tenn., St. Louis, Mo., and other communities in the central Mississippi River Valley region are vulnerable and at risk from severe ground shaking. This assessment was based on decades of research on New Madrid earthquakes and related phenomena by dozens of federal, university, state, and consulting earth scientists.

One such great scientist worked hard to discover and chart out the possibilities of a huge Midwest quake. His name was Browning, and when he predicted the exact date, people took notice. Afraid and uninformed, some citizens fled the New Madrid area, while others held him accountable for its failure to take place with ridicule.

He had certainly done one important thing, he had awakened interest in many federal and state agencies in their disaster preparedness. Thus, I was one of his beneficiaries of science and engineering.

However, there is also educated evidence to the contrary on the New Madrid zone that it had lessened activity for some time, over a decade. I had to deal with both issues down at East St. Louis.

I had so much going on in my life when I got hit on the chin again. My long time renters had not told me in advance that they were not renewing their contract, because the costs of fuel and fertilizer emergents were too high. I had to respect their decision and I even considered farming on my own, but I wasn't able to dedicate that kind of time in the spring and summer, my engineering and IDOT high activity times. But from my past experience, I wasn't going to be accused of not being a "good steward of the land" again.

The only thing that really mattered to me was my wife's return in good spirit. Joy was beaming again when I, Martha, and the kids picked her up at Crimson Sky, almost nine months from the time she was admitted. I hoped this nightmare was ending. We whisked her away with the blessings of Doctor Metz who also said he wished us well. It was only then that I had to tell her of Sheena's guests and waited for her divine direction.

"I don't see a problem. God wants us to help out our brothers and sisters. I'm okay with that. He evidently guided them to us, don't you agree?"

"They're good swimmers!" chirped Martha suddenly.

I about shot snot out my nose with Martha's blurted-out comment, holding back, trying not to laugh out loud.

We ate out in Springfield that Saturday afternoon and even had time to go to Lincoln's Tomb for the kids to see. Tom was a bit shy, held closely to his mother, but when he saw girls his age going inside, he didn't hesitate any longer, and hustled inside beside Jillian, Joy, and me. I don't know if he liked little girls already, or if he was embarrassed they were not afraid to go right in as he was. Anyway he went in and came out asking questions only a child could ask.

"Daddy, why does Mr. Lincoln stay in that box? I couldn't see him. Does he ever come out?"

"Well, son, he was shot by a man and died. It's a place like Grandpa Kurt and Grandpa and Grandma Dixon stay, only a little fancier, because he was our sixteenth president."

"Do you think he's really in there?"

"I hope so, because there would be a lot of people fooled, huh?"

"You betcha!" he let out, sounding just like Joy.

I drove through the Burger King drive-thru, ordered ice cream and sodas, because everyone wanted drinks. Jillian just leaned over from the back seat on her mother's shoulder, hugging her, showing how she missed her. Joy stroked Jillian's hair and kissed her head softly. I didn't tell her to put her seatbelt back on that time. Tom was next to Martha fiddling with a trinket that came in the food bag. We were going home together again.

It was dark by the time we were nearing home. I could see our house was lighted and surprisingly the driveway's edges had been mowed by someone all the way to the highway. It seems Smoke heard about the good fishing in my lake from Sheena's brothers and brought them all to my place after work on the way to the shed. They decided to spruce up our place.

One of the brothers voluntarily trimmed the weeds using state mowing equipment. That was nice of him, but it wasn't kosher or permissible, when state employees did work with state equipment, possibly on state-paid time, or not, and for personal reasons. I was a bit upset, but waited to explain to them. Up until now they were more than satisfactory tenants.

Sheena was there to greet us as she and Joy immediately hugged.

"What's that fabulous aroma? Look how nice our home looks, Greg," Joy said, whirling around looking in every direction. "Even the chandelier is shiny and has been dusted. My, Sheena, you really worked your behind off, didn't you?"

"Well, I knew you were a comin' so I baked a cake, baked a cake…you know, Joy…got a little prime rib roast goin', with some mashed potatoes, gravy, carrots, salad greens and that special chocolate cake for your dessert. I tried to keep your dinner warm, but no one told me you'd be so late.

"I think we better get more of a schedule going between you and me, Joy, and that way I won't have to ruin any meals. Are you guys hungry, I hope?"

Not to make Sheena upset, we all said we were starved, though we had eaten light at Burger King right after our visit to New Salem and Lincoln's Tomb.

"What's that green stuff?" I questioned Sheena on her huge meal.

"It's my salad…I spotted some poke weed growing out by the lake, near a fence. Try it, you'll love it. I used one of my auntie's recipes, again, but added creamed corn and cheddar," she told me.

Then Sheena stirred it for Joy to see its consistency. Joy sampled it, also, then raved over its flavor, then asked for a copy of the recipe. We all took a smidgen, but Tom really liked it, and asked for more. Before long, that serving dish was scraped clean.

"And here I used to mow it down…what was I thinking?" I told everyone.

"When you say that," Sheena told us, "it makes a girl feel good about making extra special. I'll get the dishes later…your beds are turned down, and it's past Jillian's and Tom's bedtime. Okay, kids, upstairs and into the shower, pronto!" Sheena told them, as they hurried upstairs together without a sign of complaint.

"I could learn to love this," Joy said, which eased all my worries about Sheena's abilities and staying here.

Martha actually hiccup-burped, excused herself, and said she wanted to help Sheena with the dishes anyway, since she had the kids cleaning up. Martha and Joy started gathering the few leftovers. I had bought a fold-up, mobile serving tray on wheels that was never used and got it out. I stacked up all the dishes and realized I had thought ahead for when Joy could no longer do anything like that.

Sheena came down and was surprised we had done the dishes and thanked us, but warned not to spoil her.

"We're all family now," Joy began. "We'll have to help each other out when we can. Does your family have enough food? If not, please give them the extra roast. It's delicious, but we just couldn't possibly finish that off in a week, it's so big. But, if you see any more of that poke growing by the fence, I'll send Greg out to get more…that is really good!"

Sheena smiled and said, "As long as you really liked it."

It was a restful night after we all retired. With Joy in my arms and no work in the morning, we picked up where we left off in room #97. It was coming Sunday, also Sheena's day off, therefore we might sleep in. My lovely wife was finally back home and everyone was happy again.

Surprisingly, Sunday morning arrived earlier than expected. I got up and looked out across the lake and saw the complete area around the lake had been mowed, too. However, the trailer was still there and the mowers were cinched down tight on it for road travel.

While my lovely wife still slept, I ventured out for some morning air around the lake. Fish were jumping, birds were skimming across the water scooping a drink and catching mosquitoes. That warm sun felt good on my back.

I noticed an occasional fish's loud splashing, which made me think to grab my rod and reel. I had no bait, but I used grasshoppers anyway on a hook, under a cork, and there were lots of hoppers that year to catch in the grass.

I quickly caught several grasshoppers and stuck two extras in my pocket. They tickled me, squirming, biting and clawing, especially with their prickly-spiked back legs inside my jeans. I stabbed one onto my hook, right behind his collar so he couldn't shake loose. He was grabbing onto my fingers and spitting out his tobacco-like juice onto my hands and staining them. But he was a feisty, excellent, big one for cats. I threw my line way out in the middle, hoping to catch a whopper.

I saw Joe fishing on the bank, so I moved along the now nicely mown edge of the lake and then sat down a few yards from him and his two willow poles. He had made them from the willows that grew near the dock.

Then he just got up and wanted to talk, so did I. I recognized that he was one of the men I had just hired to mow, but never once had I talked face to face with him. I asked him who's idea was it to mow around the lake, a bit embarrassed I had to have some one do it for me. He seemed a tad taken aback, but said they all did it together to show their appreciation to Joy and me and to have it nice when she returned. Sheena had kept them up to date and that Joy was coming home today.

I thanked him and tried to explain politely that it was against state policy to do that with state-owned equipment, but I was very thankful. I did not tell him that I would have to report myself to my superiors on Monday, but I was in no real trouble if I reported it and paid the actual costs.

"Okay," was all he said to that, but then yelled out, "You've got a good bite!" pointing to my cork, which was taking off across the water, as if it might be a big one on the grasshopper.

As soon as I set the hook, that big cat wanted his freedom and took out ten yards of line in a split second. Then he played hard to get. It took a little finesse, and about ten minutes of me following him down the bank fifty-feet or so; walking behind it, pulling back on him to tire him out, but trying not to break the line. He kept bending my rod in half, again and again.

Then sometimes he'd take me on another long run. Nevertheless, suddenly it was over as quickly as it started as that big old cat stopped, out of energy, floated to the surface, and turned his white belly up. I knew he was spent. When he gave it up, Joe was there with his fishnet to haul him in for me, when I reeled his big carcass near the shore.

"Eight pounds!" Joe estimated, lifting it out of the water in his net.

"You want him?" I asked.

"Sure, and I'll invite you all to our fish fry this afternoon. Boy that is the best color of fish."

"You mean that greenish-gray color of his skin?"

"No, sir, he, he," he chuckled. "It be his flour-coated, lip-smackin', crispy-brown color comin' out from my deep fryer, he, he, he!"

We laughed and somehow Joe Teller immediately became my closest friend of the group, besides Sheena, of course. Then I learned he was actually her father, with a different name. Sheena had her mother's name of Johnson.

"You know, Joe," I said, just to make conversation, while laying back waiting for another bite. "I know there are millions of people named Johnson, but I once knew a fine lady in Chicago named Alberta Johnson. Come to think of it, she looked a lot like Sheena does now. Alberta was tall and shapely...hard worker, too. I wondered when I first saw Sheena, if they were possibly related someway," I spoke out, not really expecting any reply because it was so far fetched.

"If she was as tough as nails and was a cleaning lady, also, that might be her."

"You're kidding! She told me her husband was a no-count, a gamblin' man, a drug dealer, and a cheater who was sent off to the penitentiary," I said, not even looking his way.

"Dat's her all right!"

"You must be joking…then how did you get hired? Why did you lie when I asked if anyone had a record back then?"

"Listen, I need this job, and I've changed my way after fourteen years in Statesville. No more carousing, drugs, and no more gamblin'. Now I'm Joe Teller, not that Joe Johnson anymore…Teller was my deceased cellmate. I took his identity. I ain't gonna hurt no one, honest. I just leave everybody alone and they leaves me to myself, too. I'm sorry I lied, but I gots to, to feed my babies."

"If Joe Teller was in the slammer, he had to have a record, also. Didn't you think of that?"

"He was only a kid, first-timer, hung himself with only a one year, and one day sentence…he was a loser, in for petty burglary. When he died so did his record…I was in for murder."

That about made me swallow my tongue. "But you didn't do it, right?"

"Yes, I killed, but he was a murderer, too, and we shot it out after a bad drug deal. He got me first, but I got lucky…hit him in the head…aimed for his balls. Must have pulled that trigger ten times before I nailed his black ass."

Now I was really worried about my family, until Joe spoke again.

"In Luke 6 verse 37, I think, it say, 'judge not thy neighbor, nor condemn him and you will be forgiven' and elsewhere it say, 'let those not guilty cast the first stone', or something like dat, also. I knows this was seriouser… but, well, I'm asking you to accept me the way I am, now, not back them twenty years ago. I gots out, stayed clean, and gots a good job in Detroit as a union painter…and now they don't make cars there anymore. What can I do at my age? On paper, Joe Teller is fifty years old…I recollects I'm a bit older."

"I know your daughter, Sheena, very well. She is responsible for you being here and she wouldn't have helped you get here if you weren't straight. Forget it, Joe Teller, we can still be friends.

"You've done good work everywhere for our crew. Now, when are we going to fry up that big cat?" I said, to comfort his thoughts of my firing him. "Watch those spikes on the sides and on top. They'll kill ya!" I said without really thinking.

"Oh, I knows that… fryin' him up…I'd say 'bout noon. I still have to clean him up and season it…throw him in with the others we caught. There's twelve of us, you know, is eatin'."

"That's enough fish. We're not big fish eaters…just like to catch them. I'd like to personally meet all your family. I think Sheena would like for me to do that, too, after all this time. You know, my wife said something that meant a lot…she once said about the same as you, but that God had guided you here.

"Joy's a Mennonite and holds her faith dearly. I have come to like it, also, but I was Lutheran in Chicago. Anyway, I saw the guys dancing on the dock and my wife is in need of a captive audience to sing for…care if I sneak over with her guitar and ask her to play for everyone?"

"Shucks, no! That would be good…we could all sing together."

"Okay, we'll be over about the time I see you pulling out those golden brown chunks from the fryer."

Joe left his fishing poles there, but stuck willow forks into the ground to stay the poles from being pulled into the lake by a big one, like mine. I went back to the house.

Everyone was up and eating breakfast cereal that Martha had served.

"Good morning, everyone!" I greeted. Joy kissed me and looked fresh and happy in her white terrycloth robe.

"Guess who caught an eight pound monster catfish on a grasshopper? Me! Guess what, too? I met Sheena's father…and Sheena, as it turns out, is the daughter of my former maid up in Chicago, at UIC," I spoke looking for a surprised look.

"You mean you actually had a damn maid at college, too? Damn! Oops, sorry children. I don't know what's come over me lately," Martha said much embarrassed.

"It's those swimmers," I insinuated guardedly.

"Joy, kids, Martha…we're invited to a fish fry at Joe's. Joe is Sheena's father. He wants us over about noon, or so, after he's done frying. What say?"

"Did you already accept?" Joy inquired.

"Yes, but if you don't really want to go, I'll understand."

"Kids, get your jeans on, no shorts, and no sandals…real shoes. I don't want you getting bit up by bugs and chiggers. I'll spray you down with Off first. Maybe we can swim, if the water is warm enough two hours later. You have to always wait two hours after eating or you'll get cramps and drown," she informed them. I could see Martha's parental education coming forward in Joy.

"Mom, Tom and I just wade on the edge," Jillian advised.

"Well, if I'm with you it might be okay then," looking up at Martha.

Everyone wanted to go fishing, Tom, especially. Martha said to bring along some lawn chairs, because she wasn't going farther than the dock.

"You could kick off your shoes and dangle your feet in the water. Never can tell, one of those swimmers might happen by," I said to kid her.

The fish fry smelled good as our family caught the scent of Joe's cooking, walking over to the guesthouse. Martha and Joy made a big bowl of potato salad and I brought along a case of beer and a case of mixed soda in a cooler, all hauled on Tom's Western Flyer wagon. I had Joy's Martin guitar hidden in its case under extra lawn chairs and blankets for sunning. It was going to be a real hoedown day.

Everyone introduced themselves, then sat themselves down to eat Joe's deep-fried fish, onion rings and poke salad made to his liking, until we could eat no more. They all enjoyed Joy and Martha's potato salad, too, and there was none left over.

Some guys grabbed a beer or two and their willow poles and went to fish for more. All the ladies, including Jillian, cleaned up the bones and scraps. I dug a hole and buried them in some weeds. When I found worms there, I also yelled for an old can. Before long, the guys were digging for worms everywhere. I must have dug in an old feed lot because there were millions. The others dug up a huge plot and saved every worm in three five gallon cans.

"That's just what I've been praying for…a place suitable for a garden. Let's get the seed!" Martha told us.

It was Sunday, but she still called her friend who owned the hardware store in Glenarm to see if she could get turnip seed and pumpkin seeds.

"For turnip and pumpkin seed planting it's the fifteenth of July, wet or dry!" Martha declared. It would be done right then, while the garden was turned, she insisted. I therefore drove her there and back in a half hour. Martha took over with sticks and strings to line up the planting. The care those helpers took in making a really good seed bed made me think. I wondered how good they really were. When they finished, they wanted to take a dip in the lake to cool off.

But before I could talk to Joe about farming, Joy, Sheena, and several of her sisters came out in their bikinis to wade and get cooled off. Immediately, they were getting "Whoa, brothers!" from the admiring young boys in the crowd. Jillian was out there, too, with Tom, then Martha finally came out strutting in hers, also.

"Oh, God!" I couldn't help saying, when she spread out her blanket between Sheena and Joy's, then lay down beside them with her snow white varicose veined body. I closed my eyes and looked for Joe. He was cleaning on the fryer still and pouring the good grease into a gallon jar, made for pickles.

"Joe, that was the absolute best fish I've ever tasted."

"Learned from my daddy down in Tupelo. He and my Uncle Ferd had a tavern. On weekdays, when they wasn't hard at work in the fields, they fished with hoop nets and gigs in the river and creeks. They caught frogs till there were no more to be had along the creeks with flashlights at night and put them in a gunny sack. Sold them as extras on their plate dinners.

"On weekends they sold whole fish along the mail road to any passersby."

"How old were you then?"

"Oh, 'bout thirteen."

"What did you do?" I asked.

"I worked in the fields like the others, plowin', diskin', plantin', then weedin' till harvestin' time come."

"Did you ever have your own farm?" I asked Joe who seemed then to look up into the blue sky to remember.

"Once did. Dad had twenty-five acres deeded to him, paid fair and clean. Worked it until the crops got too good. The greedy men wanted that farm, but it always pay for it's own…but then the rains came one year bad and we gots flooded out…bank wouldn't rent money for seed planting and we went under after a flood. They took our farm at a sheriff's sale. We started walking north, until we got wind of hiring in Detroit. All of us got jobs, then…"

Joe stopped speaking and had that far away look in his eyes.

"Then what?"

"Then I had money in my pocket…a good wife and a habit I couldn't control. I messed around and lost my wife and kilt that nigger."

"It's over now," I said.

"Is it really over?"

"Yes…I had an idea that maybe we all could make money…will you listen?"

"Will you trust me?" his voice was low.

"I have to. Listen, I've got over six hundred acres out there going to waste. I need someone, lots of someones, to take over the planting, and everything next spring…it's too late now. But next spring you and I and the rest can share crop my farm and we'll split…fifty-fifty. I'll buy the seed and I'll have to get more tractors and plows at a farm sale, or something. At least let's give it a try…what say you? Think you can do as great a job farming as your pop and frying fish?"

Joe sat there, got back up and looked at everyone out by the lake.

"You'd have to accept them all and me, too. An honest day's work I promise you."

"Okay, let's get together tonight and figure out what we need now and how we're going to do this. I've seen the tenants do it, but I never have farmed."

We shook hands and Joe's big hands covered mine. I mentioned that he probably could palm a basketball, but he said he never learned to even dribble…didn't have time.

Then everyone started coming up to the guesthouse, wet, to dry off. It was time to pull out my surprise. Martha had brought her homemade ice cream maker and had it just about finished with all the kids taking turns spinning that crank for everyone's enjoyment. The other ladies were very quiet, until I announced my wife was going to play her guitar and sing us a song.

"My husband loves me, but I'm not in the mood to make a big fool out of myself tonight, sorry."

Then the ladies seemed to come alive and started humming church songs together that they all knew and asked Joy to play along. Four of them, including Sheena, came together like a quartet and began singing their songs.

It was marvelous and Sheena turned out to be the lead singer. She had an amazing voice and when several guys chipped in on melody and bass, it was awesome. They rocked the deck and you know how voices carry over water... we started seeing people we knew from Glenarm stopping up on the exit ramp. They actually got out to sit on their hoods and listen. I guess they might have walked on over, except for the frontage fences blocked them.

"Look-see up there, Martha...those people really like this music," Joy told her.

"Yeah, they're passing by, coming and going to summer church. They're experiencing this week and Sunday school, too, all week long. We haven't been going regularly and we really should. You should be going."

"Mom, after we donated that church, everyone kept thanking me and they should have been thanking the Lord. I just quit, again."

"Some daughter I raised. Kurt and I thought we were missing you on Saturday, so we went on Sunday, too, and you never showed. Then it was your illness, but you have no excuse now."

Joy smiled, then hugged Martha. Then she let go on that guitar like I had never heard her play. The others picked right up on her song and boy they rocked the joint big time. First song was "Oh Happy Day" and everyone knew it. The guys picked up on the harmony and it was amazingly beautiful.

Ten cars had parked illegally on the exit ramp and began to honk after every song. It must have lasted an hour, until the mosquitoes started biting and we had to quit. The horns honked for more, but the curtain went down.

Before we left, Joe and I stood together and told everyone about our plans to farm in the spring.

"You can't wait until spring, honey. You gots to bury those weeds under now so they won't sprout back, come next summer," a woman informed me.

"That's Shirley. She used to farm and knows a bunch," Joe spoke.

We all thought we could farm it, except two young fellas said they got recalled back to Detroit. Joe said they were going back to make big mistakes as he had, because they were lying. He could not or would not try to stop them.

"I thought that was a marvelous time, didn't you, honey?" Joy related her thoughts to me as our family walked back to our house. "Your old friend down the road was talking at the grocery store that he was selling out and headed to Florida to a retirement community. He has good farming equipment and four hundred pretty good acres. Might as well dicker a deal on the whole thing.

Kurt told me when you first came to work that you had a silver tongue…use your charm," Joy suggested.

I had to think hard about taking on more ground, six hundred was plenty.

"Honey, I have a deal for you I've been contemplating for a while."

"No, you're not getting a vasectomy, I won't hear of it!"

"What, what made you think of that?"

"I don't know. Maybe it's that yearning, puppy dog look in your eyes and the way that you kept me awake last night has something to cause me to think that way."

"I must admit it makes sense, but that's not it. I thought you all sounded so wonderful together, I'd like to hear you singing in church with Sheena and all the rest. I might even want to become a Mennonite, if you'll say yes. Imagine how you could rock that church," I told her.

"Mom wants me to return to church. I think I'm ready to return now. Okay, buster, I'll have to ask them. They're Baptists, you know. But if we sing, you have to join the church and join me and the kids every weekend you're not called away, promise?"

"I promise…now about getting that vasectomy? Ouch!" she gave me one of her loving judo chops. "You promised not to do that again, remember?"

"Aw, let mommy kiss it then and make it better, little Gregory, baby."

I must have been convincing, because I saw them all rehearsing "Standing on the Rock" and "Give Me That Old Time Religion" and many others.

Back at work that week, and without Sheena, I avoided talking casually to Twila, but she wasn't hesitant to be herself, though I ignored her mostly.

"So, what'd ya do over the last weekend. Get your wife back?"

"Yes, I really missed her badly. How was your last weekend?"

"Sheena living with you now?" she asked, avoiding my question.

"As a matter of fact, yes, she lives in our guest home and helps my wife when she's ill."

"Oh, that sounds cozy…does that include everything?"

"Now what do you mean by 'everything'?"

"You know…sex?"

"No, my wife and I don't need any of that kind of help from anyone, anytime, anywhere."

"Sounds as if you're doubting yourself."

"Look…my personal sex life is none of your damn business!" I said, rather emphatically.

Twila threw the mail down on the desk and sarcastically said, "This is yours."

Then she walked over to her desk, picked up her purse, got out a nail file and started filing her nails. She sat atop her desk, exposing her legs up to her mini. She didn't give up easily.

She wasn't making a very good impression, I mentioned to stop her. She stuck her tongue out and scooted down to her seat exposing her thigh. I knew I could not fire her for that.

"It's been raining all morning, could you see if you can locate Clinton Edwards in the shed. I don't think the crew went out. They're probably cleaning up the equipment. And call in Smoke, too. Use the intercom. Tell them to please come to see me," I ordered her.

I had her call Clint Edwards into a meeting at my desk. From time to time a good boss asks his people under him how they liked their job and if there could be improvements. It was just routine good management skills. I hoped he had lots of ideas, or got some looking at Twila. As far as Smoke, I had to reprimand him for leaving the equipment at my house. Both came at once, so I summoned Smoke first to give Clint time to operate.

"Smoke…what happened. Why did you leave the mowers and trailer at my place?"

"Boss, it wasn't my fault. First, I cut my arm on a sign, then the truck started missin' out comin' home from Litchfield pulling that trailer."

"Hang tight."

I called the Litchfield scale to see how well the job he supervised was done.

"Oh, yes, those bastards really worked hard. Where'd you find them? They even washed the fucking big window and I can see the tare again," the weigh master related of Smoke and his crew. I hung up.

"Okay, Smoke…in the future, please call me and let me know if things like this happen. Where is the truck?"

"Oh, young Gene tinkered with it and found a fuel pump was bad. Used some wire to fix it and I limped it back here. It wouldn't pull the trailer, so I left it at your place. Gene came back with me to get their car, then left. It's got a new one now and runnin' just fine. Say, they didn't steal anything did they?"

"No, no, but they used the mowers to mow my yard. That's a no, no. I called upstairs and reported it. I owed for gas and time. It was worth the Two-fifty."

I looked over at Clint and he had Twila working.

"Smoke, keep up the good work. That weigh master was more than pleased."

"Wish I had a cushy job like that weigh master's."

"Hey, I'll watch for a retirement. How old are you, Smoke, anyway?"

He looked around and then whispered, "sixty-two."

"I think it's time we found a place off the roadway…maybe as a janitor?"

"No…I like what I'm doin' now, thank you."

"Okay, then hang in there and keep up the good work. Hit those underpasses well, because two tractors have already scraped up their fenders trying to get too close…see ya!"

The phone rang and I had to pick it up, because Twila was too busy with Clint. It was a woman who related she was an investigator for the Disabled Americans Society and she wanted action.

"We checked your state's call boxes and we found there's no deaf access on route forty-one. I've submitted our reports to your governor and you've been warned."

"That certainly concerns everyone, but when did we have call boxes on Route one? That's in Indiana, this is Illinois…who are you?" I asked the caller who refused to tell me her name before she abruptly hung up.

It wasn't all for naught. I began to research our state's call boxes later that day.

Clint was still making time with Twila. They seemed to really hit it off, like two refrigerator picture magnets. I continued with my own work and reviewed my report to IDOT and MODOT on the bridge requirements and expectations.

The expected lane closures on the Illinois side were much more worrisome than Missouri's side. Significantly more vehicles entered Missouri than Illinois in the normal beginning working hours. We had to have advance notices, both visually and written to other department agencies that would be affected.

The extra expenses expected to be included; twenty-four hour security, video progress reports, additional land acquisitions, demolitions, road rerouting, photo work on main beams and connectors, power source supplied costs from Illinois Power and Amron Electric, in Missouri. And not least of all, was my next study of the geological sub surfaces concerning earthquake stability. That was just the beginning, but I was up for everything, if I had the time.

Then I laughed at the additional instructions meant for me to begin a real-time earthquake publication that had no funding. Now how in the heck could that have been approved. It came out of Clara Turner's office. I decided to call the old gal. I couldn't find my new reading glasses, anywhere, but by squinting hard, I found Clara's number in the phone book. I dialed her.

"Hello!"

"Clara! This is your hated friend, Greg Wetmore. How are you? I smell smoke…are you smoking again against your doctor's orders?"

" Who is this? How in the hell did you know that?" she sounded upset.

"I didn't…once a smoker, always a smoker. Anyway, your girl came here and I want to give her back."

"I bet you do…tough shit…what girl?"

"Twila, she is about to report you to the officials on your habitual, unlawful smoking. You're in a public building. It's because you reported her little pecker-sucking fiasco on the guy's lap. You know what that means? You'll be on the governor's carpet to answer for unsupervised carelessness," I said, trying to fool her.

"What? The governor?"

"Skip the crap. Ask for her back and she'll drop the suit."

"Suit! You got to be shittin' me, buster. Who was sucking a little pecker when she was caught here?"

I thought I now had the edge on Clara Turner, but I saw the two lovebirds go down and disappear.

"By God, I think she's doing it again…CLINT! TWILA!" I hollered, but they were out of control and couldn't hear me.

They had slipped back behind the rolling caster file cabinets and the files moved under their pressure and I saw them. I grabbed my cell, put Clara on hold and started clicking pictures off as fast as Verizon allowed. I moved in for close-ups so they could be identified.

"Get up and get out of my sight!" I screamed.

Clint flipped upside-down over the trash receptacle and hobbled into the john pulling on his pants about his ankles. Twila ran for cover out into the shed behind a snow plow truck, but left her thong panties on the floor. I laughed my ass off. She had a tattoo of Popeye on her butt. I wasn't going to pursue either, so I quickly checked back with Clara Turner.

"Clara, Clara, still there? I think you are cleared. I just caught the little nympho with a bigger pecker in her mouth."

"Well, she's improving anyway…now who in the hell are you again, buster?"

"Clara, this is Greg Wetmore…IDOT!"

"I don't know any idiot named George Weitzman, or whatever your name is."

"Is this 254-3535?" I asked confused.

"No, this phone is in Clara's Tavern in Pawnee, bud. Do take a flyin' leap!" Then she angrily slammed the receiver down.

"Oh my!" I said, doing a hard Curly Joe noggin thump, pounding my hand to my head. I quickly found my glasses. They were still pushed up on top of my head. I rechecked my misdialed number and felt very stupid. It was a Clara's Tavern that I had called.

"Oh, shit…that wasn't good," I thought.

I hoped she didn't have caller ID. But anyway, those oversexed frolickers were gone from sight and forever beholding to my every command. I couldn't fire them, but I sure could blackmail them with sultry pictures posted on the internet upstairs. I leaned back in my chair exuberant about the lovebirds, but worried about my call.

The lunch bell in the shed rang to have the canteen ready with sandwiches and hot soups divvied out faster by outside commercial cafeteria personnel. They came here once a day and stayed from eleven until one to serve the normal count of two hundred building personnel. I was going to lunch with mission accomplished…a job well done, I hoped.

I did wonder though what Clara at her Pawnee Tavern was going to tell her customers at the bar about the dumb ass who had just called her…oh well.

I later researched disabled and handicapped call box access and realized Kurt had installed those years ago, so I began to read up on earthquake zones and it appeared that St.Louis Bridge might be going up right in the middle of a possible catastrophic area from the Saint Madrid Fault in south Missouri.

No wonder they pushed it off on me. Now I would be responsible for possibly hundreds, thousands, even millions of human deaths should a seven or eight magnitude quake hit that bridge, if I didn't get every department prepared for the worst. Plus, my responsibilities didn't halt there. I had to organize and coordinate every survival unit responding to the event, if the big one hit; train them, help equip them and fund them to a certain extent.

I straightened up and received data that was too old. Additionally, all I had access to was outdated materials from the Department of Homeland Security used in case of mass attack. So I called what I surmised were the people most likely to have the best current info on seismic activity.

I called Sacramento, California and spoke with their chief geotechnical service supervisor.

"You just missed one. We have lots of seismic activity…just had a 3.2 magnitude twenty minutes ago, which is nothing these days. Californians are used to those. They just rattle the windows. If we ever get a seven plus though, I fear we will be with Davy Jones out in the Pacific, because the San Andreas Fault runs through the valley and we're next door and we could just slip into the ocean like Atlantis.

"The plates are moving almost a meter a year here and that's a lot of pressure building. If you recall our Parkfield six-point quake, the bridges fell and buildings crumbled in 2004 at its epicenter. You better hope that bridge is built right down on the hard pan floor and anchored deep.

"I will fax you some recent quick-study facts for construction info. I just received the conclusionary report from USC on their building study requirements to withstand a six. Nevertheless, Greg, I can tell you this personally, if there's a direct seven or better hits, bend over and kiss your butts good-bye, especially with your Mississippi River acting as a channel of energy.

"Good luck with your big bridge, Greg, nice talking to you. Call me anytime… I'm glad to assist," he said hanging up.

It was surprisingly quiet in the office and I locked up without seeing Clint or Twila again that day.

Jillian held my hand while Tom held Martha's, as we made our way up to the front row of our church. Pastor Kefir was already at his pulpit and began to tell everyone of his new choir, headed up by Joy Wetmore, that would perform one song for their enjoyment, breaking the normal custom. Afterward, the elders would vote with their private decisions in the big hall.

There was a rumbling of the crowd as they saw Joy leading in all our black tenants, men and women, who had dawned choir robes to perform for them that day. I don't know what happened to those Mennonites, but when Joy and Sheena sang out loud with "Give Me That Old Time Religion" those people left their seats and began stomping and dancing in the aisle.

The black hats flew off, bonnets too, and the dresses were pulled up not to be stepped upon as they whirled and twirled. The house was officially rocked. Then, as if a sudden calm had caused them to regain their composures, they put their hats on and pulled their hemlines down and again sat like petrified wood, erect in their seats.

Pastor saw this great coming together of his flock and called a meeting of the elders immediately after the service to discuss whether or not to allow this new generation to perform every Sunday or not.

The resolve after their meeting and vote by the elders was unanimous 12-0 in favor. Attendance almost doubled when the word of that new choir got out among the flock. I was committed into becoming their faith. That scene was repeated at several more Sundays that were not in harvest times.

Chapter 17

It was the beginning of September, I awoke, to find that Joy had left the bed. I heard both Jillian and Tom crying. I hurriedly went downstairs and saw Sheena had two breakfasts made.

Had I overslept? I had to look at my calendar watch to see if it was Sunday, but it was Thursday, so why was Jillian all dressed up and crying, I asked Joy. Joy had tears in her eyes, also. It was one of those "Joy-ess" moments.

"What's going on? Did something happen to Martha?" I asked my tear-faced wife, who was down on her knees in the middle of the kitchen floor hugging Jillian.

"Our daughter has her first day of school today…and she doesn't want to leave her mommy."

I looked over at Sheena and her big brown eyes rolled up, then she quickly turned around and went back to making breakfast. Tom clung to the back of his mommy, as if he wasn't going either, but of course, he wasn't.

I hadn't even realized my daughter was already school age. It just seemed like yesterday I was holding a baby…I guess that was Tom.

"Maybe, honey, if you stop crying, it won't be so traumatic for Jillian," I said moving down to my daughter to convince her she'd love school.

"You should love the chance of being in school, you'll be learning new things every single day, meeting new friends, having a nice teacher…what's wrong sweetheart…won't you be a big girl for daddy?"

"Father! It's not me…Mommy won't let go of my hand!" she complained so adult-like, which started me laughing so hard it set the mood.

"I…forgot…to…buy…film for…the camera!" Joy sobbed loudly. "I have to have this moment in her life…whoo, whoo, whoo,…to put it in her scrapbook, and now I've ruined everything!" Joy bawled out.

I then realized how traumatic it was for Joy, because she had begun to regress in health in just these last few days and was feeling poorly. I raised her up and sat her down at the kitchen table. Then I tried to lighten things up a bit.

"Aw, sweetheart, here, let the master-thinker ease your mind."

I simply ran upstairs and retrieved my reliable Verizon cell off my desk, came back down with some pants on this time, and then asked Jillian to stand next to her mommy with Tom and smile.

"Click, click, click…that's done…except, Mommy, you didn't smile," I mentioned.

"Then take another," Joy lightened us up with a big smile. "You too, Sheena…get in here," she said, very relieved. "Twenty years from now when her fiancé or boyfriend comes calling, I'll show him this day."

"Honey, Jillian will be twenty-seven then, that's a little bit late, don't you think? A beautiful girl like her mother…well I give her only ten," I said, tickling Jillian to make her smile, too.

"I just saw a big yellow school bus turn off the exit and it's comin' down the frontage road. Who's going to get her to the end of the drive…I am…I'm the only one dressed…come on, Jillian, get in my car," Sheena to the rescue shouted.

Jillian never had any qualms about listening to Sheena at all and gladly took her hand and out to her car they went. The bus arrived about the same time Sheena got Jillian to the bus steps, but there was a moment we all couldn't see. Sheena took Jillian's picture getting on and waving on her cell phone and sent it to my cell.

When my cell sounded its vibrato, I opened it up to see a perfect picture of Jillian smiling, very suitable for framing, I noted. Joy smiled at that picture, then collapsed. Her sickness was overcoming her strength. I scooped her off the floor and took her to the recliner in our living room. Then I called 911.

Sheena came walking inside saying, "Did you get it?" But she stopped short and came over to Joy. She rushed to the kitchen sink and grabbed two paper towels and returned with them wet and rubbed Joy's face and hands to revive her. It worked as Joy aroused, but looked very weak and sleepy.

In five minutes, the first responders came down our long drive. I invited them inside and explained I panicked when Joy fainted, but she had come to. They wanted to see her and checked her vitals and asked her a few questions. Then the EMT wanted to talk to me outside.

"Mr. Wetmore, I think your wife is all right now. But talking to her, well, does she have any other difficulty of some sort besides MS. Could she be pregnant?"

That really floored me.

"She does seem to have gained some weight, but I thought it was our wonderful cook's fault," I told him, looking over to Sheena. "Joy does have to pee a lot lately and her illness seems to come on rather quickly, and go away rather suddenly, too, like morning sickness. We have two children. She does have MS and I thought it was that."

"I think it's time for her to see her gynecologist," she said. "She acts just like I did in my first three months," she told me pulling back her EMT jacket, exposing her bulging stomach from pregnancy.

"Are you supposed to be working if you're pregnant?" I questioned, trying not to insult her.

"Hey, I'm only six months along. I'll quit when I feel the knock on the door, if you know what I mean. Want us to take your little lady into the hospital? Got a gynecologist you used for the other two?"

"Yes, Doctor Maxwell."

"She's my doc, too. Say, let me take her with me now into the hospital for a check up at Doctor Maxwell's office, and I can get a check up, too. I'll call you before she needs picking up."

"I'll pick up Joy," Sheena told us loudly. "Martha can watch Tom for an hour. You, Mr., are going to be late, get dressed, your breakfast will be waiting on the table…just cereal this morning. This is girls' stuff and I think we can handle it. Worst comes to worse, I'll call you…you might have to pick up Jillian when she gets off the bus at one; it's only a half-day of school, but we should be back by then.

"By the way, this happens every day from now on. Why not build a shelter with a bench seat down near the road and get Jillian a bicycle and teach her to ride? She can get down there on dry days by herself...good exercise. Stop by Wal-Mart...they got lots of pretty bikes...make hers a pretty pink one with a basket for her school supplies and a blue low-rider one so Tom knows which is which. His birthday is tomorrow...so is Joy's."

"Oh my gosh, I forgot," I told Sheena. "Where has the time flown? My mind is slipping...twice this month. I haven't remembered to call Mother on Wednesdays either."

"You need a vacation," Sheena wisely suggested. I concurred.

I had skipped all of my own birthdays, purposely, but now it was Joy's and Tom's, also? I didn't realize that either...the same birthday? Joy's had to be a special present. Tom would love a bike.

Her amazing organizational skills were second to none. Sheena had the makings of a presidential secretary, but I was glad she was ours. Her ideas were always great and I listened.

I allowed the EMTs to take Joy, because I felt Joy was too sick. I wanted the very best for my Joy and I could not beat having two doctors double-checking her out completely.

I kissed her good luck, but she threw up on me. The EMTs wiped her face then put something under her chin and away they went, as if it were a dire emergency. They didn't say so, which was unsettling.

I saw the work guys headed out behind the emergency vehicle and I was reminded that they were all favorably doing their jobs and I looked for ways to keep them, I had told Sheena. She smiled, but Tom came running to me.

I was upset, and then Tom really began wailing loudly seeing Joy leave. Surprisingly, when Martha came out she had unbelievably slept through all the commotion, even the sirens. Martha then took Tom upstairs to get him dressed for the day. I grabbed a paper towel, but Sheena took it away and began wiping the residue off my tee shirt, then pulled it off up over my head.

"I really appreciate how you've just come out and accepted my family," she told me up close and personal, while cleaning up my tee, then took it to the clothes hamper. "I'll be washing the whites after while."

It was already eight o'clock when I decided to take one of my personal days and to call into the office. Every employee received three days. I was surprised at the prompt pick-up and her kind voice saying, "This is Greg Wetmore's office, how may I help you?"

"Who is this?"

"Oh, hi, Greg, this is Joann Stallings from upstairs. I took over as your new secretary. Your little misfit, Twila, got a real promotion...you know how that goes with terrible employees...anyway, she got herself transferred to Statesville, effective yesterday...not as a prisoner, but the new warden's secretary...think she'll like that?"

"No, there's too many men...she might get dizzy looking...Oh, sorry...hi, Joann...that's super. We'll get along fine. You're at my desk all day delivering those referendums anyway. Say, I need a personal day today. Will you paper me out?"

"Anything you say, boss. Will you return tomorrow, or shall I burn all the nonsense mail the postal mail lady stacked up on your desk?"

"Really...just leave it, please. Nice to have you aboard, Joann. I'll see you in the morning. You're in charge...I have my hands full today."

"Is it Joy?"

"Yes, she's on the way to the hospital...they think she's pregnant."

"Oh!" was all that Joann spoke, before I hung up.

"What next?" I said, to myself as I plopped down sadly at the kitchen table.

Suddenly, I felt the aggressive touch of Sheena's fingers massaging my neck and shoulders.

"Oh, my God, I think I'll have an orgasm," I moaned, looking up at her laughing, because of her wonderful touching.

Sheena, on the other hand, jumped back and said that was it. She quit.

"I was just fooling, Sheena. Joy does that to me and I joke with her. I needed that, it's okay, I love that, thanks."

Sheena quickly returned to me as I was still seated, but this time when she began again, she was more gentle. After a while, she moved up to rubbing her fingers and long nails into my hair; she let her body lean in against mine. I closed my eyes and then inhaled deeply. I could smell her alluring perfume, not so unlike the Coffee perfume that I once enjoyed, which also served to stimulate my senses.

I let her touch me, almost everywhere, knowing some of it wasn't right. I think she was enjoying it. I was getting warm...I was weakening, but I needed the tension released and enjoyed that. Then she hugged me gently from behind and I felt the fullness of her breasts held against me. She was about to begin loving me, too, I thought.

When I felt I was drawn from within to turn and kiss her, instead, I regained my emotions and quickly got up, and headed straight upstairs, not before I looked back at her standing there so invitingly. What were we both thinking? I hurriedly took a cold shower, dressed, and came back down.

"I'm headed to the hospital, Sheena and Martha. Thanks for everything, really," looking directly to Sheena who stood stone-faced. "I'll wait to pick up Joy, if you three will watch for Jillian. It's just a half-day today, I forgot," I told them as Sheena poured milk into Tom's glass. "Make Martha drink hers also, will you, please, Sheena?

"And, happy birthday, Tom," I told him, kissing his cheek. "I'll be back as soon as I can, Martha," I said, leaving as quickly as I could, without again looking Sheena directly in her brown eyes.

I drove up our lane searching for a nice spot to build a little shed to shelter the new bike that I intended to buy for Jillian. It would be handy for her to be by a road culvert of a field entrance to be out of the way. I then continued.

I drove into the hospital parking lot. I read signs for everyone to turn off all electronics before entering, so I guess that meant my cell, also.

At the admissions desk, I found out Joy had been admitted to a room, so I took the elevator up to the fifth floor and walked past everyone to her room. I knocked, but a strange woman's voice told me to come in. I entered.

"Is this Joyce Wetmore's room?" I casually asked, leaning in and seeing only one elderly person.

"I don't know the young lady's name, but they took her someplace quick… maybe back to emergency or x-ray…did she fall?"

"Thanks!" I said, worried, backing out with a fake smile and ran to the nurses' station.

The nurses were busy, but one came to inquire of my need, seeing my very worried face.

"Yes, my wife, Joyce Wetmore was just brought in by the emergency crew. May I see her?"

The nurse looked over her shoulder and spoke, "Her husband's here!"

A doctor, dressed in a green emergency room frock, carrying a clipboard, came forward and asked me to come sit with him on the hallway's couch; I panicked and my heart started pounding. He sat down close to me and put his arm around my shoulder.

Then he softly whispered to me, "We did all we could do."

I was horrified and stunned and everything else at once. Here I came to see Joy's face smiling and now I find out my Joy was dead? I couldn't believe it.

"I want to see her right now!" I demanded, standing up scowl-faced at the physician, still misbelieving. I became numb when he unobjectionably took my arm and led me through the near-by emergency room double doors.

I saw a light green sheet covering a person's torso who lay prone upon a gurney. Scattered medical paper coverings, torn open, contents removed, lay randomly all over the floor, as if many people had tried to administer drugs, IVs, the shocker, and more. The doctor gently removed the sheet down off the face. There was a bare-breasted woman, covered with too many stick-on patches, red pricked places where needles had been inserted, laying face up, her eyes closed, her body very white, breathless, and cold.

It was my Joy. I began to weep, as I bent down to her and asked her what had happened. The doctor and a nurse sat me down in a chair next to her and the nurse tried to put one of those blood pressure cuffs on my arm, but I told her no. She stopped immediately.

Who knows how anyone can handle such a traumatic intrusion thrust upon our lives; the horror and the guilt I had for not expecting this violent outcome from an apparent minor symptom overwhelmed me.

"Why?" I asked the doctor. "I thought she only had morning sickness."

"We don't know for certain. Maybe there was a hidden coronary problem, maybe a drug interaction…I just don't know yet. I followed the rules and regulations, as did everyone. She went into cardiac arrest taking her into her room and her system attack was so permanent we couldn't find a life structure at all by the time we rushed her here. She died, instantly brain dead, and that was it. No delay, just death. I've never seen this, ever," the doctor assured me.

"Does that mean they will have an autopsy?"

"Yes, it's the law."

"Okay, I hate that…I guess it has to be…let me know what happened to her. I can't understand it. She's a wonderful woman and I love her."

I got up with very weak knees, helped by both the nurse and doctor. They led me outside, and down the hall to a little room where they said I had to do some paperwork first. I couldn't resist and did what they told me, but turned on my cell phone to call home. I remembered I had turned it off after entering the hospital after reading the warning directions of the signs posted.

Then my cell buzzed and it was Sheena crying. She asked me where I was.

"Sheena, Joy died, and I'm at the hospital. You've got to help me keep it together at home…I hear crying, you're crying, did someone call you?"

I couldn't understand Sheena's sobbing voice, only that someone had called her from the hospital and she had told Martha already and she would be there at home for both Martha and the kids.

As I sat there at the desk, I spotted Pastor Kefir hurriedly coming down the hallway with Bible in hand. When he saw me, he came in and hugged me. We prayed for my wife, then talked something about my courage, the everlasting life, and about God's will, all of the things I'd forgotten in my busy work life. But now they weren't registering either in my mind.

Pastor Kefir was more than Joy's pastor, he was her dear friend. I saw how hard it was on him, as he tried to hide his own sorrow and tears, all the while trying hard to comfort me.

The pastor asked me if I wanted him to help with the funeral arrangements, as he had with Kurt. I thanked him, shook his kind hand and tried to write him an advanced check. However, he said this was not the time nor place and I must go to my children and comfort them.

I was in a state of open-eyed unconsciousness. I saw and heard, but I didn't comprehend. And worst of all, I became aimlessly selfish, feeling sorry for myself only, when of course, my kids were really the ones who were going to need me most.

After they released Joy's body to a funeral home from Springfield, I heard the coroner say he would schedule his autopsy for five o'clock, at their mortuary. I cringed at the thought of someone tearing open Joy's body and probing her organs to find the reason of her death. But, it had to be done.

I don't know how long it was, but Mother called on my cell phone. Martha had notified her. She was enroute already, and driving on her own. I never knew her to drive anywhere. But still I could only say, "Okay."

When I suddenly found our mailbox staring me in the face through my driver's window, I couldn't understand how I had driven all that way seemingly instinctively. The name on our mailbox's banner was Mr. & Mrs. Greg Wetmore & family. That was a cold awakening, as I looked at the cars parked at my house and I knew mourners and friends had come already.

I didn't want to face anyone, but I gathered the mail anyway from within the box. I noticed a yellowish envelope that was thick and bulky. It was from the mail-in photo company and held new film and newly developed pictures Martha had taken of us all at the fish fry. I knew there were some pictures of Joy in her bikini in there.

I opened the envelope and found them. She looked so alive and so happy, especially the ones Martha had snuck up on her and taken, while she was playing that guitar. There was one where she was kissing me, too, and I almost lost it right there. But, I heard a car horn honk going by, as I was stopped, partially blocking the road, so I pulled into my drive and stopped.

I tucked the pictures into my shirt pocket next to my heart and closed up the seal. I wanted only my eyes to see her lying there looking so sexy in her bikini. I drove on to the house and saw the guesthouse was full also. I took a deep breath, and then I told myself I had to be the strongest person I had ever been for my kids.

I walked inside and there was Jillian, who dashed into my arms crying. Tom stayed with Martha. Sheena looked haggard from having to deal with this as I did. I held Jillian and told her what her mother had told me just before she passed, which was a white lie.

"Mommy was so sick the doctors could not help her, honey. But Mommy told me before she went to sleep that she loved you and Tom, and me, so much…but she knew God was calling her and she was afraid by her leaving so unexpectedly, that her little girl would not be strong enough to keep us together, or remember all the things she taught you. You're the woman of the house now.

"Mommy asked me to tell you to always help your brother and Granny Martha, and Sheena, until we all can be together again. She wants you to read and study and be a good student and a very smart girl, too. She wanted to know how your first day of school went and do you like your teacher? Mommy gave me this big kiss to give to you and Tom and it will not only last forever, you can come back any time you need a kiss from Mommy.

"Here," I said, then kissed my daughter who was writhing in pain, but believed me, so she gently kissed my lips, as if they were her mother's.

"I love you, Mommy," Jillian surprisingly said to my lips.

Then Martha brought Tom to me. She took Jillian's hand and sat beside her.

"Tom, Mommy told me to wish you a happy birthday and that she loves you and is proud of you, too. Mommy said she will always be near and you should come to Daddy when you need her. Mommy has a surprise for you, but I have it hidden at my work place and have to go get it, since I didn't go to work today. Mommy said to tell you that someday in heaven she will bake you a big cake and help you blow out your candles, too. She said to tell you, also, to be a helper here, and here's Mommy's kiss to you," I told him and then kissed him. He was unsure what was happening; I guess he was too young.

Mom arrived later. She immediately ran to me and began holding onto me, crying in so much grief when we embraced, that she drew more hurting out of me. I hadn't even seen her cry for my father that openly. It was telling her everything over again that broke my courage. I thought I might join my Joy right then. My reasons to live without her were diminishing.

Nevertheless, when my Tom clung to my pants leg, and told me to stop crying, because he said his mommy didn't like it, I stood there looking at my wife telling me to suck it up. I knew Joy's spirit was there with us. Tom's words saved my life. Mom and I both quit wailing and I hugged my son as my mother had always hugged me when I needed her tender touch as a boy.

"We'll be all right now, son. Mommy is here with us. You can kiss me now for her."

"I did as you told me, Mommy. Dad will be good now. I love you, Mommy. This is for you."

Then Tom's thin little lips pressed hard against mine and I saw my wife there in his face. That warm inner peace began inside of me and I held that kiss, until Tom said, "Mommy says good-bye."

I whispered, "Good-bye, my love."

I couldn't sleep that night and sat up drinking coffee with Martha, Mom, and Sheena. Mom sat very close and told me I would survive for my kids and be the extra love radiating from Joy.

Mom was bonding closely with my feelings for the first time in my life. Before this nightmare, we had only seemed to talk of inconsequential things. She said after everything was done, she wanted to move back here with me. I ,of course, said yes.

It was three when I finally fell onto my pillow. The fragrance of Joy's pillow was gone, but I put it against my face and kissed it, searching for one last grasp of her being.

Joann called at seven-thirty in the morning and said she was sorry, but she just had to have some papers that were locked inside my drawer.

"You know my wife died yesterday?" there was silence. "Joann!"

"Oh, my God, I didn't know, Greg, I'm dreadfully sorry…forgive me, please."

"That's all right. I'll have to come in and get some things settled anyway today. Give me twenty-thirty minutes to straighten up. You tell the big wigs my plight and…well, you know…bye."

I looked up and it was Sheena in my doorway. "You need breakfast, or just more coffee?"

"Coffee, thanks," I told her, as she went downstairs into the kitchen. She had slept with Jillian to give her peace.

I rushed my shower and shaved, then dressed like I was on a mission. I was considering quitting my job, but as minutes passed I realized I could not for my children's sake. If I were childless, I would have just walked away and tried to farm this place, not caring how things went. My whole aim in life had tarnished.

Mom was up and Martha was brushing her false teeth. I sipped my coffee and looked at the newspaper to see if something about Joy was in there. There wasn't, so I headed out for the state shed.

When I got there, I unlocked my desk and handed Joann my extra key. She grabbed a needed file and was headed quickly upstairs, but I stopped her.

"Okay, there's another key in the file cabinet under "K" for keys. I forgot until now that Joy put it there for me. I want to get back to my home, but I have to find my son a bike for his birthday. His mom died on his birthday, but I don't think he understands. Where's a good place to buy that bike?"

"I guess, Wal-Mart, Greg. Get him one of those kind with training wheels that are mini motorcycles. My sister's boys got those last Christmas."

"Thanks, Joann."

I left headed out to Wal-Mart and found one of those bikes. It was pretty cool all right, I think it was a bit too big for Tom, then, but he got that present from his mom. That was the important thing.

I bought him his first baseball glove, a pro model Rawlings that he'd have to grow into, autographed by Albert Pujols…that was my gift. I knew Sheena or Martha would bake a cake in the next few days. My trip home left me time to talk to my wife and I told her how wonderful she had been and I'd always love her. I think she knew that anyway, but if her spirit was beside me, I tried to feel that too.

The church was filled with people and flowers, too many for one person. But I wasn't complaining, that was said by someone seated behind me in a pew. The pastor had said Joy's eulogy and everyone bowed their heads during his farewell prayer.

Then the funeral director came forward with his son and thanked everyone on behalf of the bereaved family. Next he asked our family to come to the front for a private, final viewing. This was the hardest thing I ever did so far.

The kids and I were last in line and when the director handed me the contents of Joy's coroner's estate bag, her diamond rings and watch, I was a bit upset. However Mother moved in beside me and held my arm. She picked up Tom to look at his mother and say good-bye. Tom didn't know any better and just reached out his hand and touched her. He quickly jerked it back and said, "Mommy is cold…give her a coat."

Jillian was almost spent. "Bye, Mother…I love you," she said, as she passed by, not wanting to look. Then she stopped, turned around on her own, and ran back and looked at her mother and spoke. "Mom, I'm going to be that good girl you want me to be…I promise…bye."

Then she darted off back to Martha. Mom and Martha led them both away, so they would not see the casket being closed on their mother. It was my turn.

"How about a kiss, honey?" I said, as if she were really alive. I bent down and kissed her cold lips, but I knew it was my last chance. I stared closely at her beautiful face, so I'd never forget her beauty, but then my tear fell upon her face.

"They gave me your ring back, honey, don't tell anyone, but I'm putting it back on your finger, right now. With this ring, I will always to thee be wed… you'll always be my girl," I said, crying as I slipped that ring back onto her finger; that ring which she herself had once chosen. Thinking that now I was still all alone, I kissed her good-bye once more and turned to get the pastor.

Then, the very same moving sensation happened around me, which I had felt the day we were "hitched". Joy had taken me to the rear of the old church to introduce me to her parents. She told her mom and dad out loud at their graves that we had gotten married and wanted them to meet me.

Back then, I had felt as if someone had hugged me. This time, I actually felt that my Joy had put her loving arms around me and my lips felt something touch them, ever so softly, so I kissed back, though I knew Joy was lying still in her coffin.

I knew then, it truly was Joy's spirit, and she'd always be there, always.

"That was very nice, honey...do it again." I didn't get that second experience, but only looks from that funeral director's son who had suddenly peeked in to see if I had finished. He ducked back out.

From that day forward, though I never professed it happened, I knew right then and there, absolutely, there was an everlasting life for those who believed. Joy made me believe. I finally understood what the pastor had told me at the hospital and I had a wonderful warm feeling of inner peace.

Somehow, inside of me came the words Joy had once told me to say if I ever wanted God to hear me, "Jesus, I need your help, save me."

I listened and watched as the director, who was watching my unusual talking and movements, came to me. Then he asked if I wanted to stay, while he closed the casket. I nodded my head, yes. Then he unlatched the latch and sealed the little door that closed upon my entire life.

"Let's go see your parents and Kurt, honey," I said to Joy in her casket, with a worried-looking funeral director staring strangely at me.

I had requested only myself and the pastor attend the actual interment.

The pastor said his final words that gave me peace and allowed me to let go of my wife to a better place of homecoming. I had something to say to the good pastor.

"Pastor, I want to be baptized in the name of Jesus Christ."

Then I asked if I could be completely alone before they lowered the casket. The pastor and funeral director obliged.

"Well, honey, I just wanted to say, 'hey' to your mom and dad, again, and to Kurt. You just convinced me you were right...you were always right. Now I really know you guys can hear me, but I wanted to tell Kurt that Martha will always be cared for in our home and I wanted to see if I could get your hand shake, Kurt, to thank you for being there for us…so here," I spoke over his grave expecting to feel his hand, something, anything touch mine.

"Whoop!" I yelled out, feeling as if I had just been goosed. "Thanks, Kurt, you just can't give it up, can you?" I told him laughing.

"Well, good bye…see you all soon, I hope. Take good care of my sweetheart."

I finally turned and walked past a very startled director.

"She's all yours."

That Sunday, Tom and I both accepted Jesus Christ as our savior and we became baptized Mennonites…you know, those funny-looking men in long beards and black brimmed hats. Well, we kind of modernized the clan, but it took a while.

That next day, we all ate Sheena's baked and decorated, belated birthday cake for Tom. He had several gifts other than mine, and his mother's bike. The bike was still in the box, unassembled, because I didn't have time to put it together. Criticized by my mother for not doing so, I told her it would be his first lesson to learn to let the girls read the instructions first, and that would be Jillian's job.

Jillian had knitted Tom a very fancy winter hat with Martha's help. Tom looked debonair in it, but wanted to take it off right away.

Sheena gave Tom reading books that Joy had once told her she wanted for Jillian, to begin reading earlier.

Martha gave to my Tom, Kurt's old baseball collector's cards, some of which were old rookie cards, all signed by George Herman "Babe" Ruth, Mickey Mantle, Willie Mays, Ted Williams, Joe DiMaggio, Roberto Clemente, and a host of others. While a young boy Kurt visited Wrigley Field often and met them all in person, and later as state engineer. They were priceless, but had been meant to be given to Joy one day.

Mom gave Jillian and Tom their first savings accounts to build upon, she thought. It was a paltry fifty-thousand dollars each for their college funds. I didn't tell her I had accounts for them started already, because money was her way of giving up her love. I didn't want to ever diminish her feelings for them.

We all celebrated Tom's fourth birthday, but I could tell he kept looking around for his mommy to appear as a surprise.

Chapter 18

Our lives had changed drastically with the loss of my Joy. I couldn't sleep nights, my work was behind schedule constantly; I almost gave up. The men in the guest house decided to become my tenants in farming and I luckily did make a farm sale. I didn't buy the farm, just the equipment I needed. That farm equipment was not only in excellent condition, but very cheap because of the economy and the overabundance of farmers quitting farming.

I received a call from the coroner concerning Joy's autopsy. He had determined that my lady with a heart of gold had a hole in her heart as big as a quarter. It was a birth defect, maybe a result of MS, but he was not certain. Anyway, that was his conclusion and he was sending me that report with five copies of her death certificate. I thanked him and told him I hoped never to see him anytime soon. He understood.

We had a moderate winter, because of El Nina, the weatherman kept repeating. Planting season was delayed by spring rains, but nearing the end of April the men had gotten into the fields and worked diligently on weekends and after-work hours. Joe announced planting was done on six hundred twenty-five acres of corn and soybeans and, of course, Martha's vegetable patch, which had grown considerably to five acres. First planted were watermelon, squash, spinach, cucumbers and melons in one area.

This time Martha had lots of help with the women planting, too. They needed to feed their family and babies good food. They added sweet corn, beets, and asparagus, brussel sprouts, potatoes, all in long rows the length of the lake fence, ready to be irrigated from the lake, if needed. There were leeks, bok choy, collard, cabbage, Swiss chard, carrots, radishes, several kinds of tomatoes and green peppers all for everyone's use. Martha even searched, but couldn't find, poke seed for Sheena's salads.

Apparently, after they quit laughing at her inquiry to purchase the weed seed, she found out it was poisonous, if not cooked properly, and an illegal plant to cultivate in several states. Everyone, including Joy loved the salads Sheena was encouraged to prepare for our meals. They told Martha that if she really had to have some, look along uncut fence rows or around old barns that were left unmown. Martha wasn't going to do that, so she watched the small crop that grew wild on our ground slowly disappear.

The women decided quickly, after they saw their overabundance of vegetables growing strong, that they could set up a roadside stand to sell their bounty for extra income. They decided to locate it on the interstate. I told them that idea was not only dangerous, but it was illegal for anyone even to walk upon an interstate.

Alternatively, I suggested the frontage road to Glenarm where lots of vehicles drove past. I said that I would even donate a war surplus tent to operate from, which I saw for sale in Springfield. I began to see how hard and industrious these folks were. They worked their tails off and everyone showed lots of promise.

Unfortunately, there was an overabundance of foxtail weed growing on the rest of the fields, because the controlled burns did not kill the foxtail seeds. The next season I would have to invest in weed killers.

My most exciting time came in late May, when Jillian was promoted to the second grade and Tom was admitted to pre-school for half-days in Pawnee. My kids went to both Saturday and Sunday schools to learn the Lord's way, not because I demanded, but they wanted to be like their wonderful mother.

I, too, had been extraordinarily busy keeping up with construction of the new St. Louis bridge. I wore a path down I-55 and I-70 to the East St. Louis City Hall, where I met with other supervisors and ordered their construction materials daily. When I heard I was allowed to acquire another assistant, I called Professor Davis, at UIC, and asked for his recommendation. He had the man for me.

"I see all that studying you did certainly paid off, Mr. Wetmore. I congratulate you. Having that much work placed upon your shoulders with so much responsibility has to be trying at times.

"I have a graduate student here who I've been fond of and I'll suggest he sends his résumé to you quickly. He's the type of person who takes his work seriously, yet searches for additional knowledge...remind you of anyone?" he asked, to insinuate he was a lot like me.

"By the way, did Gen say when she was returning to Chicago?"

I almost died. Apparently Mother had looked him up after Father's death and never mentioned one word. Maybe it was an accidental meeting.

"Please, Professor Davis, call me Greg. I don't know, but I bet if you called her she would talk with you."

"Certainly...thank you. Please, then call me Max. I was sorry that you lost your father, so young was he. May I extend my belated condolences, Greg. I'm certain he was very proud of you. Say hello for me to your wonderful mother. Gen still looks as beautiful as ever.

"Well, it's class time, and you know how I demand promptness. Going to open a new chapter this week on bituminous coal additives used in construction. It's very interesting to me how when one avenue closes, like prohibiting sulfur coal to be mined in Illinois, they suddenly have this miracle of miracles new use as the new road rage for our highways. I've seen the studies and the wear factor is impressive...almost twice that of the rubber mixture. Might read up on it yourself, Greg. Got to go, good day, son!"

What did he say...son? I hope he was exaggerating about his relationship with Mom as I had during my time searching for...Amanda, that was her name.

I called out to Ferd Little in Sacramento for any new developments in seismic activity there. I also told him of the bituminous issue. I thanked him for his faxed report that opened my eyes as to what may be forthcoming for the Prairie State.

Their entire state was serviced by strategically placed seismographs, which Illinois had few. He had several unused machines, but I didn't have anyone who could operate them so I chose to send Eddie Kunnemann out to

California to learn from Ferd, whenever he got here. Ferd and I had become good friends over the phone. I actually had not even visited him.

The crops were in the fields, the corn was "knee high by the Fourth of July" and I had help. His name was Edward Kunnemann, not Eddie, a fine young engineer. He was so advanced at his age that he took over my office duties easily and kept me informed daily on assembly-approved projects, while I turned all my attentions to the bridge.

My burden was lifted, so that I could feel good about allowing the Missouri group to supervise my side of the river, as I had often done for them. They had more money than Illinois and more engineers working.

I realized that I needed a long overdue vacation, after I continually came home exhausted every Friday night. One Friday after work, I discovered Mom and Martha had taken Jillian and Tom to buy new school clothes. Later, they also had planned to take in a movie at Springfield. Then the kids were promised a visit to McDonald's afterwards.

"Sheena, have you ever dreamed of a place so pretty that you just had to go visit there, but never had the time or money to go there?"

"Sure, lots of times…everyday. But you don't ever go anywhere yourself."

"That's just it. I don't want to go by myself. Jillian and Tom liked Disneyland and Six Flags, sure, but that's not for me. I thought of Italy, an African safari or Australia's Barrier Reef…maybe Alaska, on a camp out, horseback fishing-hunting trip. I've never done any those ever."

"No fish or bears for me, uhh, uhh…I'd like to go to Bora Bora, or Tahiti…maybe Jamaica, Puerto Rico, or even Costa Rica, even Brazil where there are oceans and warm breezes and the beaches are white, no pun intended, but there are no black sands, or I'd go there!" she laughed. "I've seen all the pictures and I can get lost in dreams doing your dishes every day."

"I once liked the thought of Sicily, too, but you just drive around and around there on that island…not much there but lots of sheep and green grass and I really go for those architectural places. I'm hard French, anyway my ancestor's were. Ha, can't speak a word of French myself, except l'amour."

"Oh, I know that word. Spoken in Hawaiian, where my ancestor folks came from on Maui that word means Me-lack-en-a-lotta-nooky."

"Really? That's a hard word to pronounce meaning love."

"No, silly, sound it out, it's an old joke, hint, hint."

"Sound it out? Ah…Me lack en a lotta nooky…Me Lack en a lotta nooky. Ha, I heard that before…that's cute, Sheena. Got any other words or stories? It's nice sitting here with you this way enjoying each other's dreams."

"Did I ever tell you the story about a girl that was so horny her pants caught fire?"

"Hey, you got something to say, speak up, or forever hold your peace."

"Dat's just what dis here nigger is been doin' all dis time, boss man, it ain't got her no place, no how!" she spoke like a degenerate, and it tarnished my opinion of her.

"Why would you stoop so low as to talk like that? I don't like you doing that. That's talk from the sixties…eighteen sixties."

"I'm sorry…it's you and me in an empty house…I thought we could get together, just as friends…you know, you scratch my back, I'll scratch yours… nothing serious, just a little release of tension."

"What do you want me to do?"

"Fuck me, dummy!"

"Oh, Sheena…I'm still married to my Joy…forever. You know that…I think our arrangement might have to end now. And I loved you as my dearest friend…really, I feel like crying this happened."

"Okay, I was weak, I apologize…don't go gettin' so uptight. But if you can forget I ever said this, it will never ever happen that I throw myself at you again. But in case you don't forgive me and send me packing…I…I have to say I think I've secretly loved you for the longest time," she said, with tears forming in her brown eyes.

I saw this girl voluntarily come from my office into my home and make me and my family very happy, many times over. Sheena had left a good, secure job with retirement, and I just couldn't fire her for liking me. My kids needed her, and she was really good with them. I decided to ease her worry about my personal life situation, because she deserved more than me loving her. So I got up and fixed us both a mixed drink and watched her squirm around nervously, then sat down next to her. But then I thought of Eddie.

"Look, I just can't do this in Joy's house or in Joy's bed. School is starting after Labor Day. Let's both go on separate vacations, now…I'll pay for yours. That's the least I can do. You go wherever you want. Then I want you to come visit me at the shed one day to meet someone, someone I think you'll really like.

"I'm in desperate need of finding myself, because my job has driven me half nuts. I can handle everything, but up until now, I thought I was the only engineer that could do my job. I have help now, his name is Eddie Kunnemann. He's your age and a nice guy. I want you to meet him, because he's the type of guy that a wonderful girl like you needs to look for. I promise you'll adore him and throw rocks at me for you ever thinking I could be your man. Once, maybe, but not now after Joy."

Sheena sat up looking angry, and began stretching, flaunting her gorgeous body before me that really was too irresistible, if I were so inclined.

"Okay, I understand, though it's been over a year now. Mum's the word, you lose me by trying to push me off on someone else, when I can get any nigger I want to want me. I'll behave, and try to be a better housemaid... anything else, Massa?"

"Damn you, woman," I said, taking her hand and pulling her to me, then kissing her hard and going down on her. We stripped, she wanted me, and took my all. It lasted only until she gasped saying, "I love you," then clung to me.

"Are you all right?" I whispered.

"Better, Mr. Wetmore."

"Why only better? Miss Johnson."

"Because it could have lasted forever...this was your one and only time. I'm temporarily cured, but you're not. I can see it in you eyes right now you want more of me...but you couldn't say to me that you loved me, though I did."

"It takes time. You're talking in circles, Sheena. Didn't you enjoy it?"

"Didn't you feel me tighten up? Hell, yes, you're good, but I'll just wait until you beg me to be yours. I know you want me as much as I want you, but you're hung up on a dead girl, also maybe the color-mix between you and me, I'm not sure yet. You don't feel it yet, but at night, remembering this moment, you'll come to me one day.

"When you beg to be inside me, you'll be mine and I'll be yours. Until then, I can stay dry. After all, it's been years already waiting for you to come home free. It's that taste of honey I just gave you, baby, pure honey. You know you won't be satisfied without loving me deep."

"Wow! You know how to turn on a guy's burners, but you evidently don't know that I already feel that way about you, I just can't. Not just for sex...for everything that's good about you. I'm feeling I'm not good enough for you, nothing to do with I'm white and you're black.

"Go on your little vacation, Sheena, then come by to my office afterwards, and meet Eddie. If nothing happens for you...we can talk about this, okay? I've lost my Joy to your love tonight, once is all that counts, and I can't undo it. I can't forgive myself, now can I?"

"Until death do us part," Sheena quoted.

"I don't know. It hasn't been that long. But if I were wanting someone, I hope you'd be wanting me then."

We heard a car drive up and it was the family. We jumped into high gear and dressed. I went to my favorite chair and Sheena got out a rag to start dusting the window sills. That might have been a giveaway, since that woman had no dust in her house at all, anywhere.

Suddenly I noticed the sweet taste of Sheena was on my lips and I smelled of her sweet fragrance. I got up and headed to my upstairs bathroom and splashed on some cologne and gargled Listerine. I went back down as they all came in, excited about the movie and their new school clothes.

No one looked suspicious towards me, though I felt that I wore that guilty-look expression on my face.

Everyone understood my desires to go on vacation, but not when I said I was going alone. Again, I just couldn't do it alone and we all decided Sheena must go along, too, to help with the kids, since she didn't have plans.

We finally decided on Branson. Branson, Missouri, the Midwest's largest entertainment attraction had everything a family would want. Besides the live on-stage country and western stars calling Branson their home, there was great fishing nearby on the huge lakes, like Table Rock and Bull Shoals. Fun time entertainment was at Silver Dollar City, somewhat like Six Flags there for the younger set. Branson had it all.

Branson is just a short four-hour drive south of St. Louis, about six hours one-way south from near Springfield, but when I read that we all could fly into Branson, landing at their new airport and leaving from Springfield, I bought passage and eliminated the driving. Then I had to get a rental car there...no problem.

Two weeks later, on Monday morning, an hour after everyone swallowed their Dramamine for air sickness, we all boarded our plane very excited. When the airport announcer advised everyone to make certain we had our carry-on bags ready for boarding, I immediately put my arms through Mom's and Martha's. Mom thought that wasn't funny at all, but laughed anyway.

"Old bags are we?" Mom said, looking at my firm grip and leading them onto the boarding ramp.

Sheena had the kids, hand-in-hand.

It was a first-time-flyers-flight for the kids and Martha. We were up and away, and then down again, before Martha and Mom could even hit the potty. Our rental was a Dodge Caravan and we had lots of room on the way to our three adjoining rooms at Holiday Inn Express which was close to all the action.

Excited about their front row tickets, Mom and Martha both said there was little time to waste for us all to get to the opening of Daniel O'Donnell, at seven. They jumped at the chance when they got their senior discount offers.

Apparently this boyish-looking, Irish tenor learned the old songs of their era, not sung much these days in America. He was handsome and debonair and swooned those old ladies into a hot panting lather, almost.

After his two hour performance, jet lag struck us all back at the Express. Rather than fight the traffic to go out to eat, we ate in. Mom and Martha conked out at nine. It was a long day, however the kids didn't really enjoy the musical show, and slept through most of it, and then were wide awake at bedtime.

Sheena had on her bikini and walked around appeasing the kids' appetites. I didn't want to get caught with my eyes gawking at her curves, so I casually asked her what she was doing in her bikini.

"If I can get control of the kids, I'm going to relax in that huge hot tub they have going... I'm really cramped up...want to go along?"

"What about the kids?"

"Kids, your father and I want to go use the hot tub. You can't come. Do you want to watch Shrek, Harry Potter or Batman? That's the only kids' DVDs I had from home you haven't seen yet. If you keep it down, you won't wake up your grannies who are sleeping next to you, right through that door...and... we're on vacation so you can stay up late tonight. How's that?"

"Yippees!" sounded out, as they lay on their beds when Sheena selected Shrek first. When the movie started they were glued to the TV. I came out in my swim trunks and they didn't even notice. Sheena turned on the bathroom light, left the door open, then threw out a bag of Doritos to snack on.

"Now, when Shrek is over, in about two hours from now," Sheena told them looking at her wristwatch, "push this button and put in Batman or Harry Potter. Got it!"

They didn't answer.

"They've changed them before back home on ours when I let them, but I'm certain when we come back they'll be zonked out like our grannies, ha! Let's go."

I couldn't help noticing those married guys being pinched by their wives when they got caught watching Sheena pass by strutting her stuff down the hallways. She just walked way out in front of me, headed to the elevators to go down to the pool and hot tub area. I personally noticed the swing on her back porch and was a bit dizzy watching her gyrate so smoothly, with just a little jiggle to entice my thoughts. I knew she had planned it that way. She had done a lot to attract my attention the past week or two, anyway, that's when I first noticed her, mostly. I guess I was getting lonesome again.

No one was in the hot tub at that hour and we were surprised. We slipped into the big hot tub which could have held twenty people, I think. Sheena went to the opposite side from me and we both just lay back in the curved seats and began to let the bubbling hot water sooth our tensions. I actually fell asleep and I guess that irked Sheena.

Suddenly she flicked water on me and woke me up. She was much closer and I could smell her warm body's fragrance over the chlorine. She looked around and then removed her top. I guess she thought it was safe because the white bubbles obscured other's visions of her, except mine. She was tormenting my yearning and I knew it.

I saw the pool was empty, so I decided to just get away before my brain told my arms to pull her to me and kiss her. It would have been so easy to do. Sheena was truly a very beautiful woman, especially all wet and half naked.

My plunge into the deeper end of the pool was much chillier and my emotions seemed to settle down in my body. I decided to swim a few laps then go back to my room and crash. That hot tub took a lot of energy out of me.

When I arose out of the pool, Sheena was doing her own workout in the hot tub. She was doing leg lifts and reverse kicks, which I suppose kept her rear and stomach so firm. Her body didn't have any fat at all, but she was full- figured that was certain.

"Sheena, I'm going back. Are you going to be in here very long?"

She gave me a look as if I was the stupidest jerk alive leaving such a magnificent woman, without so much as touching her lips. It was hard not to, but the sudden thought that Joy might be there deadened my desires. I wish I had brought Joy here, for this night would have been much different. I grabbed my towel and left alone.

When I slid the room card quietly into the slot, the door lock clicked loudly. However, the TV was on with the Children's Channel and cartoons, a bit loud. My kids were neatly tucked between the sheets and sound asleep. I turned it off and went to my adjoining room. I showered and put on my clean underwear. I liked to sleep with as few clothes on as possible and decided just a tee and boxers. I hit the sack.

Sheena was to sleep with Jillian and I heard her come in, before I fell asleep. I slept until I heard the service carts rattling in the hallway. I got up and my Jillian had the TV on, almost without sound. Jillian waved across the room with a big smile. Tom was still curled up with his pillow and Sheena was face down on hers, next to Tom. Apparently, Jillian was still a restless-leg sleeper.

Then Mom peeked inside from her room and asked what they should wear today. I told her we'd play it by ear, so dress casually. I picked up the gratuity Branson newspaper on the continental breakfast tray that was sitting outside our doors…all three of them. I grabbed a cup of black coffee and a Danish and told Jillian to drink the juice and eat something. Mom and Martha came in and got theirs and returned to their rooms, but they both noticed Sheena still sacked out in Tom's bed in only panties and was braless.

I saw a professional guide listed for $300 a day fee and thought I'd enjoy going out on Table Rock in his boat and catch smallmouth bass. His ad pictured one of his past customers holding a long stringer of fish. Suddenly, it seemed unimportant to me when I looked at my kids, and when I noticed a shuttle headed out to Silver Dollar City, I told everyone to, "Rise and shine!"

We all got dressed quickly and headed out as the maid service came in to clean up. Although, Sheena had everything straightened already, just like a mother would.

I seriously had been thinking about us, but something in my heart told me my Joy would have forgiven me, once, and I had another chance to be true to my word the rest of my life.

So, I bent again, as a good father should, and after breakfast we shuttled over to Silver Dollar City. My kids were having lots of fun and Sheena went on every ride, and participated in every game event with my kids. She even did the go carts over and over for Tom's enjoyment.

Mom and Martha found their enjoyment in the frontier part of the city and watched a man carve a log into a huge male figure with a tyrannical face. They browsed through the many shops and bought souvenirs. I bought a wood duck carving for my desk. I don't think either woman had had this experience as they were just as giddy as the kids and Sheena.

We dined that afternoon at a Steak & Shake restaurant before going to see the singing and joking "Bald Knobbers" perform. The kids giggled as Mom and Martha laughed out hard at all their skits, but I kept noticing Sheena was constantly looking hard at me. I think she might have given up trying to rush me and then decided to change her stratagem on enticing me into marriage.

Our first comments coming out of "The Bald Knobbers" were we would buy advanced tickets before we ever returned, as almost every show was sold out.

The kids wanted adventure. Therefore, I rented a big three-bedroom houseboat, filled it with foods and beverages and we cruised out onto the waters for two full days. I let everyone pilot, until we discovered the sweetest little sand bar to swim from, when I ran aground. It was nice there, so I didn't even try to dislodge it, though I think I could have. It stabilized the boat nicely for barbecuing and swimming.

I even got to catch blue gills, but the kids kept jumping off into Sheena's arms from the on-board water slide and scared the fish. I had then anchored permanently on a sand bar to stay the night and began to barbecue steaks and hot dogs, when suddenly I noticed Mom wasn't with us. I called out for her and heard nothing. Everyone took notice and came aboard.

"Damn it," I said frightened. "She was here ten minutes ago…she was dog paddling near you kids, didn't you see her?" I asked.

When I could not see Mom anyplace in the water around the boat, I ran inside to the john to see if she was there. She wasn't. I dove into the shallow water where I had last seen Mom and hit bottom. I began walking around, reaching out and feeling.

The sudden horror of coming against a lifeless body underwater can chill anyone's soul. But I knew it was my mother's body and I raised her up quickly. Apparently she had stepped out into deeper water and had drowned with not so much as a sound. I had a hard time getting her body aboard the boat by myself, but did so because the kids, Martha and Sheena were all screaming bloody murder.

I waved frantically and hollered at other boaters passing, but they just waved and hollered back something and did not stop. I tried CPR, though I never had any such instruction, just examples shown at work seminars and maybe on TV of how to do that.

However, after ten long minutes of counting and compressing her chest and attempting to breathe for Mom, doing mouth to mouth respiration by myself, I could get no response. I checked several times, but there was no breathing nor did I see her chest rise after I quit blowing in air, or get any pulse. I knew it was over. Mom's eyes were glazed over. She had that whitish death-look on her open-mouthed, blank-staring face, and I knew I was doing her no good. She was dead.

"Get the kids in the bedroom and keep them there, Sheena," I said, as I went to drag Mom onto a blanket and cover her. "Sorry, Mother, I didn't see it happen. I don't know why you didn't put on a life jacket when you made the kids do it," I said, getting up crying and feeling guilty as hell for not making her wear a life vest.

There were several extra vests on the boat, but she was just wading up to her waist near the kids, who had theirs on. I waved and hollered at more boaters but they just waved and hollered back and did not stop in their speeding boats.

I finally was able to remember my cell phone. I had dived in and it went under with me, but it still worked after being under water, as well as on land so I dialed 911.

I had a hard time explaining where I was, but the person on the other end decided she knew exactly where we were. She herself had been on that sand bar to swim.

I sat with Mom, as a patrol boat pulled along side. Four men came aboard.

One was an EMT and was quick to her but after he checked Mom with his stethoscope, he said Mom was gone and covered her back up.

Again, I had to answer too many questions and sign papers, even before the coroner came to pronounce her deceased. It was an obvious drowning, but there was going to be an autopsy, anyway, since no one really witnessed anything.

I asked if Martha, Sheena, and the kids, could get off and I'd pay for someone to take them back to the inn, but they, too, were interviewed right there.

Afterwards, I piloted the boat back to its dock. The owner had already heard of the incident and extended his condolences and told me he'd take it from there when I gave him the keys. Sheena held the kids' hands and I supported the now very wobbly-kneed Martha, who seemed to have gone her last mile too.

This death of Mother's would take its toll on Martha and she wanted to leave right then. I finagled our return flight that evening by paying through the nose to get aboard. It didn't matter, I was in no mood to complain. Most airlines that I had been on would have offered to exchange tickets to accommodate their passengers with illnesses or deaths.

Mom's body was flown into Chicago four days later and met by the same funeral director we used for Dad. We placed her beside him and I felt very old and alone then, as just Sheena, the kids, and I left the cemetery.

Before I left Chicago, I called Mom's attorney, because she had left with me an "If I die, do this" small, note-letter, directing me to open only after she had passed. She gave it to me after Dad died, but I never opened it. I had it folded tightly in my wallet. I did it then in our hotel room.

So, as per instructions, it read I was to contact her attorney immediately. When I did, he was very fraught with cases, but assured me I could expect an inheritance of six million, as soon as he received the death certificates and it cleared probate court. I was really surprised by the amount. I trusted him, ha!

"Sheena, Martha is going to need our help," I told her that night. "I could see how dejected she immediately became over this when we first got home. We have to watch her," I tried to explain.

"Martha's stronger than any of us. She'll want to be with the kids as long as she lives. She will be there knitting when we arrive, I'm certain."

We all flew into Springfield and our arriving home was not quite the same. Martha greeted us and asked about the funeral. We retired early and Martha slept downstairs as usual.

Thereafter, she spent most of her time with the tenant women cultivating, picking and then selling their veggies to the public. I think Martha was an inspiration to us all who needed faith in life and ourselves.

I couldn't believe how much money they made selling all those vegetables along the roadways. The garden vegetables were much better quality than any in the local stores and one store owner bought regularly, well up into September, before the first frosts came. Then everyone got out spades and went out to salvage what we could.

We picked everything out of the garden, ripe, or not, just to save them from ruin, even the green tomatoes were picked off the vine, when the weatherman predicted a low of 28* one night. The men pulled up the plants and put them to dry on a burn pile. Then they brought in a tractor and plow and turned the garden soil. It was all ready for next year.

Martha taught the women how to preserve and can their harvest bounty. I came home from work one day and found all the women in my kitchen boiling and sealing jars of fruits and vegetables by the hundreds.

It seems that back on my property, where an old homestead used to stand, an orchard grew still and the men had harvested the pears and apples. The apples looked rough, but put into apple butter it made no difference. I think Jillian learned her cooking skills that year and Tom finally asked me to play catch.

All along, Sheena refused to meet Ed, which he settled for instead of Eddie or Edward. Therefore, when I saw how lonesome this handsome, well educated, eligible bachelor was; him so happy being one and alone, but sometimes slacking off on Mondays after a joyful weekend with wild women, I decided to ask him out to supper.

My intentions were for him to meet Sheena, because I had lingered too long, thinking I might just start dating her and then marry her. I wasn't in love with Sheena, as with Joy. Sheena was purely lust and somehow the more she advanced the more I retreated, until it came to this.

"Man, you have nice digs here," the young engineer told me. "Wish I had a place just like this. You say you farm, too?" Ed asked, whirling around, looking up at the structured log ceiling, as any good engineer would, to assess its stability and practicality. Then he looked out over the big lake and saw the guesthouse and the occupants. He seemed stunned and concerned something wrong was going on.

"What are those people doing over there? There's two guys fishing…hey, that's Joe Teller, isn't it?"

"What do you mean, 'Those people?' Those people live there, and are my land tenants and close friends. They farm my acreage, which I couldn't do one-tenth as well as they can. We split the harvest money. Yep, that's Joe," I said, seeing his slow, gaited-walk headed our way. "I split with them on the harvest."

"What, a third? You give them a third?" Ed questioned, looking at everyone coming in from the fields with grain wagons and pickups, after combining the soybeans.

"No, even-up, at fifty-fifty," I explained to his curious mind. "They're all headed here for supper," I told Ed. "Looks like a bumper crop this year. I had the men put up two large twenty-thousand bushel grain bins this summer to store our grain. And after supper, they will use an elevator to put the soybeans off the wagons inside the bins.

"We turn on fans to dry the moisture out of the beans, not all of it, just enough to get the best price and their best weight, when we decide to sell. This has been an exceptional season and I think we'll have about twenty-some thousand bushels this year, but for beans the price is down to seven-sixty-two per bushel this morning. It will go up near nine dollars by February and we'll dump them on the market then with a phone call."

I could see Ed's eyes looking up; his mind was figuring up the money to be made.

The women had varnished the interior logs on one wall of the bedrooms and asked if they could eat here tonight, also, because now the fumes were sickening them.

Martha and Sheena had invited them all for the night and we could make-shift the couches for them to sleep on. I told them to open the windows and let it air out and come on over. I was glad to talk to Joe anyway, since he was always either at work or home farming. Joe was really a soft spoken guy and I grew kind of attached to his slow ways.

The women and Martha conspired with me and were making a big pot roast with all the trimmings at my direction, just to impress the bachelor, who they knew needed a good home cooked meal. All done without the suspicion of Sheena. I hoped they might make that long overdue connection. Those canned garden veggies came in handy.

I couldn't help notice that Ed couldn't take his eyes off Sheena. She looked so domesticated in her apron and her still-floured-face cheeks, from making homemade rolls.

Sheena really didn't notice Ed much, until she had to pass him the greens twice and when he said hers were the best rolls he'd ever eaten. Then she held the greens dish and looked hard. I think she liked what she saw and though I was a bit jealous. I saw I had started something.

I bumped Joe and then Martha when Ed got up to help Sheena with her chair every time someone asked if there was more roast or greens or potatoes. Once, during the many obvious gentlemanly get-ups to seat Sheena, she looked over at me smiling with Ed at her back, and winked.

To make everyone laugh at Ed's being obviously smitten with Sheena, I asked, "Oh, Ed, did I formally introduce you to my daughter, Sheena?"

Ed straightened up, looked at Sheena, then me, and then looking suspicious, he began, "I need to talk to you about that, Greg…have you ever heard the word 'propaganda'?

"Well, before you answer, let me tell everyone a story I learned all about this kindly, well-educated reverend, who every Sunday spoke to his flock with a high-toned, highly-verbalized speech…which happened to be far above the learning power and understandings of his flock…therefore, they all had one heck of a time understanding some of his sermons.

"One Sunday after his sermon, as he was standing at the exit shaking hands to thank his parishioners for attending, one of his flock members stopped to ask him why he spoke so many high-fla-lootin' words he couldn't rightly understand…to which the kindly reverend immediately returned his question as to what words he didn't fully comprehend.

"Well, reverend, he say, how about that word propaganda? What do it mean…you said it ten times, if not more speakin' 'bout our government."

"Well, I can explain it this way," the reverend began. "You know that pretty little Sally Brown who lives by the river?"

"Sure nuff do, she's a fine lady," he tells him back.

"You noticed then how dark skinned she is, or did you not?" the reverend asked.

"Yes, sir, her folks must sure be close comin' out of Africa."

"Dat's right, dat's right…now what about her husband, Will Brown… he's really dark, too, ain't he?"

"Yes, sir, never seen a darker nigger than old Will Brown, that's right."

"Say now, what about their son, little Willy? Now he's a real light-skinned boy, isn't he?"

"Hummm…I always did think that was strange…he being so light and his parents so dark…humm, but what dat gots to do with propaganda?" he asked rubbing his chin.

"Well, I'll tell ya, I'll tell ya…is just goes to prove, Sally is the proper 'Mother Goose', but old Will ain't the 'proper gander'!" Ed finished, making everyone burst out laughing.

I couldn't help thinking Ed sure had a good personality, but if I had told that same racially-tainted joke, I'd have been chastised. I guess that kind of talk was acceptable among their own crowd, but certainly not when spoken by white bread.

Then, walking around the supper table, still wanting more laughs, and while coming to look hard at me, Ed said, "Uhh, uhh, never happened…you ain't the proper gander!"

That caused more laughter and when Ed asked Sheena to go for a walk by saying, "May I please take your daughter for a moonlight stroll around the lake," I almost said no, but Sheena was up, ready, and smiling brightly to everyone's taunts for them not to stay out too late or they'd both get mosquito bites on their bare behinds. Then they left us holding hands.

Though I felt the jealousy twinge, again, I knew this was the way it was meant to be. An hour later, we all got the surprise of our lives.

Martha and the women had cleared up the dinner mess and everyone had settled down in a place where they were going to sleep. When Tyrone and Thelma were struggling with making Thelma more comfortable, because she was eight months pregnant and she could lay but one way on her back, I said I'd sleep on the floor and they could have my bed.

Tyrone and Thelma had a young daughter named Ponchey, though everyone called her Poncho, and she went to sleep with them. That made room for me in my favorite chair and next to Joe, who had remained quiet all night. I asked him that very question.

"Joe, you're so quiet, what's wrong?"

"My boy was killed, Greg. He was in the army and got killed ten days ago. I gots the letter today. There's nothing to send home, so after they buried what's left of him there in Afghanistan, they just sent me a letter. I hadn't seen him for seven years, since he was in the service. He was going to write or call but I guess when the house burned he couldn't find me."

"I'm sorry, Joe," I told him, as I put my hand upon his bent shoulder. "I lost my sister and her husband there also…eight years ago now."

Joe raised up his head and said, "And you lost your Joy, your momma and daddy, Martha's Kurt, and now your spirit, too, like me. I can see it in your eyes. You and I, we sure have suffered our losses together lately, haven't we? But I learned as a youngin' from bein' in church that the Good Lord has His plans and there ain't no disputin' His word. He may not always be there when you need him, but He's never late. I guess he saw my boy was a good soldier like his poppa and wanted him near."

We both fell asleep talking about James, Joe's oldest son from Detroit. James was Sheena's half-brother that she had never met, and now never would.

I heard a car door slam and Ed's car drive away at two in the morning. Boy was I going to kid him at work. In the morning, I had to submit my Southern Illinois Earthquake Disaster Plans to Ed. I had copied the California plans and adopted them, then tweaked the overlay to fit our area.

Then I heard Sheena tippy-toe in. I told her just to go to bed, because everyone had already gone to bed and that Thelma and Tyrone and Poncho were sleeping in my bed. She said nothing, but I saw a light come on from a bathroom. I sat up and looked up to see Sheena there brushing her hair.

"Do you think you did right by her? I think she loved you," Joe whispered.

I didn't answer, because I really didn't know his answer. I was confused, but wouldn't try to rectify that, because of my pride.

The next morning I was alone with Joann in the office, because Ed called in for a personal day off.

"I may have started something last night," I told Joann. "Ed has found Sheena and I think Sheena has found Ed," I chuckled.

"Well, poor girl, it's about time. Now you didn't hear this from me, well sure you did…I'm going to tell you anyway now, because you really need a woman…Sheena told me long ago she had the hots for you…years ago."

"Oh, I do, huh? Why do all you ladies feel a man without a woman is so bad off?"

"Because I'm a woman and I know how I'd feel without a man…we need one another…it's God's design," she told me.

"God, huh? I had the best and he took her away from me."

Joann had no response for that and she went to her computer.

"It's all right, Joann. I think I'm too old now to meet someone comparable to my Joy. But if another woman would actually show up and be as wonderful as Joy, I guess I'd have to reconsider. My pastor told me I was a good man and I had too long a life ahead of me to be alone and I needed to share it with someone. I told him I had two wonderful kids to share my life with. He said no more about it."

Our discussion ended when I left to go to the Capital Building to appear before the Assembly. I delivered my report on the geological standpoint and preparedness program. I proposed to them if an earthquake of magnitude seven or greater hit the designated areas around or near the new bridge at East St. Louis, it would be extremely disastrous.

I had prepared films to coincide with similar catastrophes from California that Ferd had sent me. They all were convinced money needed to be appropriated to continue with some of my suggestions.

My first suggestion was to re-train all the state, county, and city police and fireman in mass trauma situations. After the initial occurrence there possibly would be great losses of life in the bigger cities, subsequently, there would be aftershocks hindering the first responders. Mobile command centers had to be set up and triage centers and temp hospitals would have to serve if the real hospitals were destroyed. I told my theory and plans to a captive audience and was applauded at my closure for my foresight and meticulous planning. I was assured by those legislators they would act promptly. I left hoping they were not just politicians.

As luck would have it, only three days later, a 3.5 quake struck near Poplar Bluff, Missouri and was felt in St. Louis and all through Southern Illinois. That alone prompted the assembly to go forward quickly with my first phase. Additionally, soon everyone had to go to see films I had gotten free from Ferd in Sacramento. I made five copies before sending them back.

I was again promoted, but relieved of my shed responsibilities. They were given to Ed at my suggestion and approval. After all, he was an alumnus of my alma mater and I trusted his good judgment.

I was away a lot in the field doing interviews with police and fire heads throughout our state, often overnight. As weeks passed I was certain the good men in our departments had bonded to make a state-wide effort to assist one another, not withstanding city or county boundaries and would act as one big unit.

Then I received communications from the Illinois State Police Command, Red Cross, Salvation Army and Illinois National Guard that they, too, had initiated response zones and would be available on a moments notice as first responders. They had been fully informed and trained with the knowledge that was presented to them.

It was looking like a great plan was coming together. However, three years passed without even another rumble and the light dimmed in the support I had received from the Assembly. No funding came and my program was slipping away into oblivion. I decided to take all of my personal time and go see Ferd as a preliminary of leaving my unnecessary job permanently.

Ferd said he knew me by my voice when I walked into his office. Surprisingly, he ,too, was leaving his duties behind, because of El Nina. He believed the random forest fires there were set by American-born Al-Qaeda members attacking where they could.

The removal of his department's funding caused by a weakened California economy, and the money it took to fight those random forest fires, had left a 'big fat crack' in earthquake studies, he punned.

Ferd said, "To hell with this, let's go deep-sea fishing, Greg." Ferd was older, I'd say late fifties, and had no family that I knew of. He owned a big offshore rig he lived upon, docked near Vallejo, but ready to take out anywhere at his leisure. He took me out that afternoon for an "all-nighter", is what he told me, and out into the Pacific's deep shelf. I caught some of my first big monster fish with him.

I thought I had found a real friend, until Ferd came to my cabin that night nude, and then crawled into my bunk with me. He was worse than Sheena. I fought him off, and ordered him to the dock, while I held him at bay with a ten foot, fish gaff point. Upon arrival to the dock, I left immediately, telling him, "Thanks for your help with earthquakes, but no thanks." I never told anyone about that escapade or saw or heard from ol' Ferd again.

I flew back to my home in Springfield, but before going home, I stopped off at Ed's desk with my signed resignation in quadruplicate. I told him I could go into private life anytime, but had learned of my mother's last will and testament, but only after her Chicago attorney apparently thought I had discovered his foul play.

When my bank called his, it was noted that interest had been paid to him through his power of attorney. My bank told them that was in error and had anticipated receiving all of it. They contacted the lawyer.

The crooked lawyer was retaining my inheritance and skimming the interest off the top monthly, on its deposit in my name, with his power of attorney. I would never have known without my bank's inquiry.

Sure, I'd get my inheritance in full, but he kept it long enough to receive thousands of dollars in non-traceable, tax free interest. It was wired in total directly to my bank account in Springfield. I had learned all this only when I had called my bank to inquire of its deposit showing up on my statement.

Joe Teller became despondent. He suddenly got off a tractor, stopped working in the fields one afternoon, came home and laid down. That day Sheena found him in his bed, dead. Joe Tecumseh Johnson-Teller was eighty-nine. Up until the death of James, his son, he actually looked fifty.

After the tenants returned Joe to Mississippi to bury him next to his own real father's grave, of 1864, near Tupelo, only three persons came back. Apparently their seven-year stay in farming had grown as old as my job.

Without Joe's supervision, they quit all farming and thought Sheena would allow them to stay. No, she would not, so they moved on. All Sheena told me was that they headed back to their roots.

It was nearing that time, when I said Sheena and Ed, when married, could buy that guest home. I would take over her household duties. It was the Coup de grace for our once romantic friendship.

In all that time my kids were excellent students, being tutored by Martha and Sheena at home. They both attended Glenarm's newly built grade school. Jillian graduated grade school and was valedictorian of her class. Then she wanted to join their chorus and asked to learn the piano, all on her own.

After I bought a grand piano, I arranged for a piano teacher to come to our place to give Jillian lessons. She had begun her life change from a child into puberty, with padded bras and her cycle beginning, and behaved accordingly.

But I liked the way Jillian was becoming strong, determined; she had dreams and direction at a very young age. She was developing into a very fine little lady like her mother wanted her to become. I think it just came naturally.

I was thankful that Martha was still around to be available for Jillian. But Jillian was demanding and no longer wanted her little brother Tom tagging along. She had many friends who came over to visit her from her school.

However, that suited Tom. I bought a small backstop for the garage door that allowed Tom, as a single player, to bounce balls off the rubberized surface, catch it, and return it. It sharpened his skills considerably.

Soon I couldn't stand the continuous racket and decided it was less noisy to just go out and play catch with Tom. He had a great arm and great movement to the ball. It wasn't long before I knew Tom could be good…very, very good at baseball one day.

During one summer, Tom picked up that expensive leather Rawlings, a once too large pro baseball glove I had bought for his fourth or fifth birthday. Soon thereafter, Tom became a proficient shortstop for the city league's green team, Prairie Land Creamery, the sponsor of his baseball team. Later Tom played for his grade school, also. I was proud of both my children's developments.

Sheena became Tom's pal and coach when I was gone. She liked playing catch and regularly hit Tom ground balls at the grade school's ball diamond; as much as Tom could stand. Sheena had him hustling right, then left, always charging the ball, and catching pop flies constantly. If he slacked off, she made him run around the bases as fast as he could run; all fundamentals she learned as a young player, which had made her so good, and made Tom much more agile.

Tom showed a lot of natural ability and speed, Sheena told him, which made him try even harder. She was an outstanding softball player and quite the fast pitch softball pitcher in her high school days and she taught him everything she knew. But that was still girls' stuff…a great starting point.

As he grew older, which seemed so quickly, Tom then was proud to challenge me in whiffle ball games, so that he could get used to curve balls being thrown at him.

For hitting improvement, I had an idea to have him stand against that garage door's pad using a real baseball bat. However he had to use a really heavy bat to connect on that dipping, zipping, flighty, plastic ball.

Nevertheless it worked wonders. It developed his hand-eye coordination, which was why after he actually got his eye and swing together, he hit the crap out of it, sometimes splitting its seams. Therefore, in a real game with kids throwing a baseball, they couldn't get one past him.

He became known by his peers as "Tom Terrific", which was the opposite of his dad's moniker "Gregor the Terrible" attached to my abilities as a kid. I began to enjoy the times spent with Tom and Jillian more and more at a near adult level. I didn't need anything else in my life except them. I hadn't considered dating a woman in years.

Sheena was still dating Ed Kunnemann regularly, but didn't skip her duties or dedication to my family one iota. Ed was doing very well, also, in charge at the shed. I'm certain he tasted her fruits, because of their late-night hours. But Ed hadn't talked about tying the knot, until I asked him one day of his intentions. He said he loved her, and I said it was time to step up to the plate to make an honest woman of my best friend.

When he balked, I told him I wanted Sheena for my own and he should never come back. He sat up and listened then, as I told him of her many attributes and why I wanted her. I know I did some good; like it was a real eye opener for the nerd.

That evening, I saw Sheena constantly on her cell phone, but only heard one reply, as I peeped over my newspaper, just hours later. It was an "Are you sure?" question, followed with a smile. I smiled, too.

Then, as they had secretly planned, Ed drove up to my farm, but parked a few hundred feet from our house, so I couldn't hear his loud-mufflered Mustang. It was about four in the morning; I guess he thought I would be asleep and he and Sheena could make their move.

Ed and Sheena eloped that very weekend, by flying out to Reno, Nevada. Because their decision was so sudden, Sheena had to return to tell me for the kids' sake and mine. They snuck back to my home on Monday, as if their tails were between their legs, like two pups who had to face me. I then knew I had been much too nosey and much too overbearing, but it worked.

Sheena, feeling some guilt I suppose, actually knocked at our door. I greeted their news with much excited joy. I hugged them both. Especially when seeing Sheena's big diamond on her finger, as she extended her hand.

Somehow though, there was this mutual look into each other's eyes then that seemed haunting. It might have been our farewell look of final concurrence, only we understood as friends. Or, she might have been saying to me that I had missed something really good in life. I had to put on a happy face.

Nevertheless, Ed was so surprised to find I wasn't fighting angry that he had stolen my dream girl that he asked to buy the guesthouse, not rent it. He only had moments to decide his fate and lived in a very small, downtown bachelor pad in Springfield, unsuitable for them both. They needed a nest.

Doing a little UIC math, I surmised I could allow them to rent the place to own, but only after both Jillian and Tom were in college, if they were so inclined. I would give them a deal they couldn't refuse. When I learned that Sheena still wanted her job here, the guesthouse was still free with her salary as we contracted before. It all worked out fine after all, for all of us.

"That's some big debt I'd have to take on, if we bought it, but I certainly would try to figure out some way to buy it, Greg, not lease. I loved this place the first time I walked in, remember?" Ed said, holding Sheena's hand.

"Yes, I remember, but you loved something else that day the moment you saw her, too. You were the most chivalrous guy we had ever seen," I said laughing.

"Well good...I don't think I would someday want to come back here, because I've left my heart in no-man's land. I just don't feel the same way now that I felt buying this place with Joy. If my Joy were still along side of me, I wouldn't consider selling. If I could have forgotten her, and I never will, Ed, I would have been in your place instead, long ago," I told him, then looked briefly at Sheena to make her understand.

"You know, in the back of my mind, as a civil engineer, I often thought why I hadn't already built a huge, gated, retirement complex on this property out there. It's the old people that have accumulated money. Think about this project, Ed and Sheena. Elderly people don't want steep rolling hills, it's too strenuous for them in the waning years. They appreciate flat, more gently rolling land like ours.

"Imagine all the bike and foot trails that one could meander through, like the woods, along the cool, shaded creek...it's almost three miles with some deep holes, then sprinkle in some multi-complexes, not side-by-side, but spaced out to give each one a character of its own...and named accordingly...

like Blue Sky Mansion or Queen's Castle or Dream's End. Silly names, but yet young names to give the occupants' homes identity.

"I can vision there are places out there for tennis courts, shuffle board, swimming pools, this lake and the creek for fishing, and I'd build a championship golf course, right in the center of everything to allow access to everyone by cart, but keep it open to the public at certain times to pay for maintenance. They say there will never be enough golf courses built.

"This place could be a fun land for the feeble minded…one big circled walkway, with stores for shopping and groceries, so no matter how old or lost they might get from dementia, if one just kept walking the walk, in this planned circle, someone would eventually see them pass by, ha.

"Now, you being a brilliant civil engineer, also, but young with forethought and foresight and with a better mind than I, it should tickle your fancy. Got any investors in mind, Ed?" I spoke to get his mind stirring.

"We can do it!" Sheena told him seemingly excited by my visions.

"That's exactly what my wife would have told me, exactly, if she knew it was my dream. You have the best pal and business partner, right here, never forget that, Ed."

Ed moved into the guesthouse with Sheena and they began saving their money to make a down payment of twenty percent on my property, as their bank required them. I began looking for businesses who may utilize my plans and assist Ed with my dream, which was now Ed's and Sheena's.

Chapter 19

Now that I was semi-retired at a young age, and I could still get around quickly, I did some of the things I always wanted to do before I got too old, but hadn't the time. I planned them all, while my kids were still in school. But, I felt badly that I didn't get to see them much; they were growing up much too fast with lots of activities.

Sheena was always driving them both somewhere; here, there, and everywhere. Usually the trip was for some sort of school function that I felt as though I wasn't really equipped to handle, or they just wanted Sheena, not me. It was my fault for letting it come to that.

I don't think for a moment that Tom or Jillian did not love me, it's just not "cool" to have your parents always around, especially like at proms and such. Younger Sheena was always cool, knew their friends on a daily basis and sometimes sort of hung out with them to secretly supervise their activities. It was Sheena who was always cool and I wasn't ever, I guess.

I looked for other things to do. Soon as the sun shown strong and the rains came, I searched for morel mushrooms along the creek and found enough for two meals and that night's supper, in just one morning.

In the creek bed, I found a yellow belly catfish hole that I played at for a week, until the creek flooded. Then I still fished out in my lake for the largemouth bass that grew big, because no one fished for them. I caught an eight-pounder, too, which about yanked my rod right out of my hand, but threw it back in, because I knew she was full of eggs.

I had time to think, just walking around that lake while fishing. I could get there at sunrise and fish until sunset without even stopping for a bite to eat or sometimes not getting one single bite. Sheena mentioned that, but I told her I was dieting and wanted to lose weight.

I flew out to Texas one spring day for a "guaranteed", three-day hunting trip for Russian Boar.

"No kill, no pay, no kill, no pay…I'll give ya every penny back, guaranteed… if you don't get your pig, I mean boar, how's that?" the outfitter promised.

That sounded good to me over the phone, but what did I know? I told him I would pay cash upon delivery, which made him drool, I'm certain.

My eyes got opened wide. I was a bit selfish, too, and told the owner, who said to call him Old Dusty, that I wanted his whole place to myself. I actually didn't want someone to shoot me. That suited him just fine.

Old Dusty told me he had the best "hawg-huntin' " dogs in Texas. He said I'd better come prepared to climb a tree, if a huge black boar caught my scent. They would instinctively charge me and try to eat me alive, as their huge tusks ripped and tore my flesh apart.

It was intriguing listening to his stories of past customers who hadn't heeded his advice. It was his build up for a sale, but I liked it.

"A big hog will kill ya; he'll eat ya alive!" he vividly told me.

Old Dusty had personally saved fifty persons who were in near-death situations, fighting three-hundred pound, blood-thirsty, wild-eyed boars.

"They woulda sure been kilt, iffin me and my fellas with their Kerr dogs hadn'ta moved in when we did to save 'em," he went on to further excite me.

"Yes, I've had to save many a dude from disaster, soin's you better be prepared for the adventure of your lifetime…Let's see, ten to fifteen hogs, that will come to about thirty-seven hundred…cash at the door, or I do take plastic," he told me, right after building up my excitement of that hunt.

Well, I hadn't much training with guns, but I knew how to aim and pull the trigger. Before I left on the hunt, I drove into the old Army Surplus Store and bought an old British 303 with a scope on it. It was easy to shoot at long distances, but hard to aim at a close moving target, so I returned and bought an old, used, single-barreled shotgun. Now that ten gauge I bought packed a punch. It wasn't too heavy, but it kicked like hell. My shoulder was sore after the first shot, but it tore up the chunk of firewood I used as target practice. I was ready.

Dusty met me at the Austin airport with a big smile and a bigger drawl and hat that looked kind of cool. He grabbed up my luggage and gun cases and put them in the rear of his exceptionally, filthy-muddy F-250 Ford pickup, and took off for somewhere. He wanted to be paid then, but I took out my big roll and flashed it at him and he ran off the road and about nearly killed us hitting a road marker.

I told him no problem, but he'd get his, only after I killed my first big hog. I reminded him of his deal of guaranteed kill. He reluctantly okayed that, but he kept looking at the big bulge in my jeans…I hoped he wasn't another Ferd!

He drove and drove, until he finally stopped, and then turned that old pickup down a long dirt road that led to a big, thick timber of oaks and an old deserted ranch house, where his GPS directed him. I thought it odd that he didn't know where he was going. But his buddy who owned the ranch did.

As it all turned out, it was a big scam for dreamers like me. Dusty had actually taken me to the back of his friend's big pig farm, where some of his accomplices then released hogs from the guy's pen.

Old Dusty told me to fire my gun to see if it was working well and to aim at an old mesquite tree branch. I didn't realize immediately, but that shot was their signal to release some hogs and they'd begin herding some hogs toward me to shoot them. That shot sheared off the tree branch.

I quickly wised up when I saw several men I thought were holding switches tapping those same hogs on the rump to get them to move. They were old sows that had been used in breeding and spray-painted up black. From a distance, they could pass for a big boar to a dummy like me.

"What's wrong, feller?" Old Dusty said, as I raised my shotgun to shoot and didn't pull the trigger.

"I'd like my rifle, please…it's in the other case in your truck."

"But this shotgun is good, you're sure to hit one with that."

"Nope, it kicks too hard for all the shooting I intend to do. I just might stay for another three days."

That did it. Feeling he had one of those "dudes", he hopped right over to his truck and brought my rifle back. Then he took my shotgun back, while I loaded up. Like a rookie, I had brought along ten boxes of high powered bullets.

"There's a biggin'!" Old Dusty pointed out.

I could see three men herding pigs and using cattle prods. The pig out front was huge, coming fast, with a cattle prod shocker zapping the poor thing to get it to run my way.

"Who are those people out there and what are they doing?" I asked.

"Oh, those men, there…let me see," he said, as he raised up a pair of opera glasses for a look-see…"Ahhh, hey, they must be my specially-trained employees, those are my hog trackers acomin' up behind. Didn't I mention them? Well, you see the hog is a naturally born hider…he waits for his prey to walk by and he goes out and attacks. These fellers know how to get them out…it's a bit safer than you going walking out into the bush, not being a hog hunter before…ya see? But tomorrow night, I'll take ya nighttime hog huntin' and we can sit in a tree and use lights. Then you can still be safe and shoot your pick of the litter, too."

What a fool I was, and with every doodling word he spoke, I felt he knew it, also. I then spotted that hog running faster, as if its butt hams were on fire from the zapping of that cattle prod.

I raised my rifle quickly to fire, but the huge bullet missed the hog considerably and instead struck a tree a half-mile away with exploding bark, about a foot above the head of that guy; just where I had aimed.

When I discovered its accuracy, I kept jacking in bullets, as fast as that old five shot, bolt action would allow, taking aim at other hogs that came running on the scene, or at the people who herded them.

In minutes those "pushers" were high-stepping it back to where they came and though I must have fired twenty or thirty times, not one hog did I hit.

"Darn, those hogs are tough to hit, ain't they?" I played him.

Old Dusty got wise to me and just kind of simmered there, until he said, "All right, I know what you did. You did that on purpose. But, you still got your hunt and you still shot your gun, pay up!"

"Dusty, here's two hundred for my fun and experience. I'm renting your truck to go back to the airport. I'll leave it there, but 'No kill, means no pay'. Take it or leave it. I should call the Texas Rangers out to get you."

He looked at my artillery then said, "I'll take ya back if ya don't tell a soul, promise?"

"Okay, let's go," I told him, as I raised my 303 and fired one last very long shot that hit the "o" in an old metal sign that read "No Trespassing", just to empty my rifle.

I stayed in Austin two days, until my scheduled return flight and that night I stayed in the Hyatt. The next day I saw the University of Texas, a beautiful place, then went to see Willie Nelson's show on "Austin City Limits" that night.

I decided hunting that way was just senseless, so I went to a pawn shop and swapped the guns for a big scary boar's head and had him send it COD to my address. That was all the proof I needed to tell of my big hunt.

I landed in Springfield on Friday night, just in time to get home and watch the last two innings of Tom's very first, grade school baseball game under the lights.

"Hi, Sheena, hi, Ed, I thought I'd try to see this home game, if I could. How's our player doing? I see it's six to three and we're ahead."

"You'll just have to be on time from now on and not off on some big safari someplace when your kid's the star of the show," Sheena said, trying to humiliate me.

I knew Sheena had great interest in Tom's abilities and probably thought she was solely responsible for everything good about him, including his athletic abilities.

I looked at Ed for some support, but noticed quickly Ed's attention wasn't on the game, however. His eyes were locked upon a group of young studs who had surrounded one smart-looking, well-dressed little lady with the look of a Hollywood model. Her hair was up with curls, dangling like tight-knit corn rows that I also had seen lots of young girls at my old office wearing with a pigtail braid.

She looked pretty neat and cool on a hot summer's evening. But this girl wore lipstick that was so red, I could read her lips saying, "No, thank you," and I kind of thought she looked like someone I knew. So, I kept thinking of who that might be, until she looked up and waved at me.

I thought she waved because I was staring too hard at her and she wanted to break my stare. But then she got up amongst all those boys and used one's shoulder to get down off the stands. I saw him litterly hold his hand against where she touched him with that love-sick, dumb, gaze in his eyes. She sure had his heart and the guys around him wanted to sniff her fragrance when she left. They watched her every move headed away.

Her eyes were painted in shadow, just enough not to detract from her pretty smile.

"Oh, my God! That's Jillian!" I shouted out after the ump called strike three on a batter. I could not believe my girl was that girl. Suddenly it was not all right and I stood up and was fuming.

Sheena reached up and yanked me down and told me I was blocking everyone's view from behind.

"Don't you dare make a scene here for Jillian's sake or I'll feed you dog food for a month. She's growing up now, so you just better get used to it. Now be her loving father cause here she comes...Hello Jill!" Sheena greeted my daughter, who came and sat close to me right after she gave me a short preppy hug and a peck on the cheek.

I almost died when I smelled that Coffee perfume she wore. I quickly decided I was too deep in over my head. I kept one eye on Tom's play and one eye on Jill.

"Hi, daughter. My, my, have you got the admirers," I told her, looking back at the boys with the best unyielding grim look of a concerned dad that I could muster, without showing mad teeth, too.

"Now, Father, you know you'll always be my only boyfriend. I know how much you care for me and you'd come to all of my performances, if you really could. Sheena came to all my teacher-parent conferences, but that was okay, because all they wanted to tell you was that I had always worked my butt off and made straight A's...and you'd loved to have been there when I played the part of Juliet in our sophomore play...I knew all that.

"But now I've figured out how you could really make up for missing all of my plays, award banquets, and parent-teacher meetings to mention some. My sixteenth birthday is next month and I thought you could spend some time shopping with me for a new convertible. I want a Beemer."

Holy shit, it was Jill, my sister talking through my daughter to my father, exactly. I was stunned.

"Sixteen! What happen to ten through sixteen?" I shouted. "Car! What happened to that bike I bought...that I never...got time to put together."

I slowly saw my ineptness as a parent and pleaded the fifth. If I opened my mouth again, I would be cutting my own throat. "Can we talk about it at home?" I questioned.

"Now, Father, I did lots of thinking and considering. Look at it this way…example…I need to go to the grocery store for Sheena…there's my new car."

"I'll go…next!"

"Ah…I need to go mail a package and I have to ask you and you're busy and so is Sheena."

"I'll stop and take you," I said again, to fend off saying good idea.

"There's an emergency at home, and someone of us has to go to the hospital?"

"Easy…dial 911! Next!"

She thought and thought, then said, "I'm at a Friday night basketball game, it's over, it's late and one of those guys over there asks to take me home, instead of calling you?"

"What color are you considering?" I said, in defeat. "But, you must never, ever, get in anyone else's car as a passenger. If you see that someone has been drinking, don't let them in your car and don't ever let some boy drive your car, ever…you promise?"

"I promise, until I go off to Illinois. Then I'm on my own."

When I got up to go to the restroom, I looked in the mirror as I washed my hands and saw my first gray hairs. My worries began. Then I heard the crack of his bat and hustled to see that was Tom trotting around second. He had hit another walk-off home run. Well, not really, because he got carried off the field by the other players and received a standing ovation from everyone in the grand stands, including me.

"What'd ya think, Pop? He gonna be a pro?" asked the man seated behind me. I had to look hard, but it was Grub, with a Cubs hat and dark sunglasses, a little bit grayer and had a pooched belly, holding a can of Miller's. "Joy would really have been proud," he added.

I turned around and thanked him, but one whiff of his breath made me turn back. Thankfully, Tom came to me from the field. I shook his hand, congratulated him, and gave him a fatherly hug.

"Nice work, son!"

"Gosh, I looked up and saw you were in the stands and it made me so proud that I hit that last one for you. Did you have a good hunt?"

"Actually..." I began, but noticed the sweetest looking little girls all standing behind Tom, smiling, giggling, and I guess waiting for Tom. "I think your fans want you. Where are you headed?"

"That's what I was going to ask you...ah, Dad...you think it would be all right to have some friends over this Friday night for a campfire and weenie roast by the lake?"

I took a deep breath to assess what this 'a few friends' meant?

"Well, how many people are you talking about?"

"Just my closest friends, that's it. Maybe we could swim or sing songs. Jill will be there, too, right, Jill?"

"Yes! But give me your ten bucks before he says no," she said, an image of Jill, my sister.

"Wait a minute, wait a minute...ah, Jill, by any chance, have you ever thought that you might ever want to become a Marine?"

"What? No way! I wanna be a fighter pilot," she said, pulling my strings.

I sat down, getting the business that every parent who has teens must go through. It's God's way of telling you not to have any more kids when you get my age.

"Okay, Tom, you've always been very responsible and I'm certain you invited Sheena, so okay, but...no liquor and no sex...got it?"

The little girls 'eked' and ran away giggling. I turned to see Sheena's brown eyes showing their whites.

"Tell me I didn't hear you say that! My God, are you ever a pill of a dad."

"Sure, Tom, just your closest friends. Here's twenty for you tonight. Go have some fun and here's a twenty for you, Jill. What are you thinking of doing with it, if I may ask?"

"I'm headed to the clubhouse and a shower. If you wait, I'll hitch a ride, Dad, if you don't mind. Can you haul my bike in the back?" Tom asked.

"Certainly...ah, hum...and you?" looking at Jillian.

"Well, if you really must know, Daddy. I wanted to ask if I could go with Judy Phelps and Ptomaine to the late movie at the Ritz in Pawnee?"

"How are you going to get there and how will you get home?"

"Her mom."

"Who's mom?"

"Ptomaine's mom!" she said, getting huffy with me.

"Ptomaine? Such as Ptomaine poisoning?"

"No, silly, her real name is Germaine, but we nicked her Ptomaine, because she's poison as a domestic in Family Care, a cooking class at school."

"Cooking at school? Hummm…that's educational. Okay, I said I trusted Tom. What will you do with the money?"

"Party on dude! What'd you think?"

"Well, I know that was for the entertainment of your friends, but party your ass home by curfew at eleven, or I'm never trusting you again. No car, no nothing. Got it?"

"Well, curfew is twelve and I'll try. It's up to Ptomaine's mom, right?'"

"No, it's your responsibility, right, Sheena?"

Sheena had left us with Tom and was hand in hand with Ed. I hugged my little girl and gave her a big swat on her keister. "That's a reminder… curfew, no later."

I went to follow Tom.

"Well, you handled that much better than I thought you could. Where is Jill going and what time is she supposed to be home?"

"Late show, Ritz in Pawnee…home by curfew," I proudly told her to show her my parenting skills.

"Ha!"

"What?"

"The Ritz closed two years ago. You figure it out."

I quickly turned to Jill, but she had vanished. My worries got worse, then Tom came out and said the water heater had broken in the city park club house. He'd shower at home. Without saying anything, he put his bike in the back of my pickup and jumped into the passenger's side. He immediately put on his seatbelt and waited for me.

I saw Jill getting into someone's car and she was seated on top of this guy's lap. I started after her, but the car sped away, which direction I wasn't certain because of the dust it churned up. Then it was gone. I felt ill.

"Sheena, you get a retro-active raise starting from five years ago, and it starts tomorrow," and I meant it.

Tom was bushed, but kept looking at me, then asked. "Dad, did you ever play baseball?"

"I thought you'd never ask. They called me 'Gregor the Terrible'. I was a pitcher, I threw really fast, but I had this little problem."

"What was that?"

"I didn't know where in the heck it was going after I threw it," I laughed to his amazement.

"Sheena said her roommate named Lila dated you. Was that before Mom?"

"I didn't actually have a date with Lila, we just both went to the same place."

"Did you kiss her?"

"I don't remember."

"Did you date any other girls before Mom?"

"Why all these questions?"

"Because Sheena said she once loved you. Is it all right to love a black person?"

"Well, if you really love someone, then the color of their skin doesn't matter. But, when you consider all the interracial problems that arise, mostly by relatives and bigots, sometimes you have to let your heart decide if it can take the punishment. Let's talk baseball."

Tom's questions revealed more than he knew. Maybe I had made a grave mistake with Sheena. I still loved Joy, but her memory was all that was left. I always thought that was enough. Sheena was the best mother to my kids and she wasn't even my wife, or their mother.

Tom was a very good son and I could see being as young as he was when his mother died left a lot of questions unanswered. I thought one day I would try to tell him how much I loved his mother and she me. Until then, I wanted to become a better father and spend that father-son time together my dad had substituted with money.

I showered, as Tom did, then I sat down to wait for Jillian to come home. When it was eleven, Tom left me to go to bed, because he couldn't keep his eyes open.

"Good night, son. Love ya, sweet dreams," I said, as Tom left me half asleep.

"In the morning, Pop…love you, too!"

I kept looking at the clock and the minutes kept ticking away. It was ten minutes before the midnight curfew and no Jillian. I got up and walked out onto the veranda overlooking the lake. I saw the light on in the guesthouse and the silhouettes were slow dancing and kissing. I sighed and felt lonely.

I didn't know what to do, when the curfew expired and still no Jillian. I became very upset and started thinking what I was going to say to her after I whipped her little butt.

At one o'clock, I couldn't stand it any longer and was going to call the police. Oh why had I trusted her? Hadn't I learned from my sister's behavior? I reached for the phone, but I had to get the number from the directory because all I knew was 911.

As I found the Sangamon County Sheriff's Department number, the phone rang. I froze, thinking something terrible had happened to Jillian. I wasn't completely wrong, but it was Sheena.

"It's about Jillian, she's at the hospital."

"Is she dead, hurt, in a wreck? Oh, God, I knew I shouldn't have let her go. I'll..."

"Listen up...hear me? Jillian collapsed at a party. She was taken to a hospital in Bloomington. They need your okay to proceed. Call 217-999-1234. That's admitting and call them now, then call me back afterwards. No, Ed and I are coming over."

Sheena hung up.

"Admissions, who are you calling?"

"Hello, my name is Gregory Wetmore and I was told to call this number because my daughter was brought in to your hospital. They said you needed my permission to continue."

"I don't. I'm transferring you to the emergency room, hold on," the tired sounding receptionist told me.

"Emergency Room, Nurse Howard."

"Yes, my daughter was brought into your emergency, her name is Jillian Wetmore, I'm Greg Wetmore. They said to call because the doctors needed..."

"Hold on...hey, here's her father. What should I tell him...ok...sir, you live in Springfield? "

"Yes, it will take forty-five minutes to get there."

"Okay, what's your social and birth date...and middle initial for the release by phone? All right...I'll give the doctors the okay, if it's necessary, and you go to admissions when you get here and...sorry, have to go...click."

That sudden 'click' scared the hell out of me, until I saw Sheena and Ed walking into my kitchen door.

"I had hurriedly given a nurse all the information, however, she didn't explain a damn thing about what was wrong with Jillian," I told Sheena.

"The doctors told me they thought it might be a roofie, the date rape drug, but they don't know, as yet. They have her stable now, but she's confused."

"And how did you know that?"

"Jill told them I was her mother, before she passed out. When they called and found out I wasn't her mother they had me call you for them."

"How in the hell did she get way up to Bloomington?"

"I think she went up to the college with some college friends."

"College friends, too! Oh, God where have I been all this time?"

"I think we can forgive a man who lost his wife. I think you're recovering now, you better, because Jill really needs you…let's go."

"What about Tom?"

"Ed, sleep on the couch, the sheets are in the hallway…you better go up and tell him you're leaving, Greg. Hurry."

Sheena had it together.

It took the forty-five minutes to get to that hospital admissions and about that long to see Jillian. She was sitting up with a drink in her hand seemingly fine. I pulled up a chair, but Sheena sat on the edge of Jillian's bed and began straightening Jillian's hair from her eyes.

"Hello, sweetheart," I said to Jillian, trying to look around Sheena.

I think Sheena wanted to keep me from making an ass out of myself.

"You've got lots of explaining to do, honey, when you get out. You better start saving for a car…that Beemer's history."

Jillian was quiet and there was no backtalk, so I was concerned.

"Are you Gregory Wetmore?" came the question from the doctor entering the room.

"Yes, sir!"

"Would you please stay with her, miss, while I speak with her dad?"

"Certainly," Sheena answered.

"Would you please sit with me in the hallway, Mr. Wetmore?"

We sat down together and the doctor began.

"Your daughter came in unconscious with a possible subdural hematoma, so with a bump on her head we rushed a blood screen and an MRI. Her blood came back zero, meaning there's not drugs or alcohol or anything like that. Is there anyone in your family that has MS?"

I revisited the words of Doctor Metz telling me that Joy felt Jillian had begun with symptoms of MS, but I couldn't speak.

"Mr. Wetmore, did you hear me?"

"Sorry, yes, my wife had MS."

"Then it's a probability the diagnosis was correct. Your daughter is in the advance stage of MS as revealed by our radiologist. I'm sorry, because you know what that means. The contusion on your daughter's forehead is superficial. We can release her yet tonight. Again, I always hate to see this in anyone. Please take this release to admissions before you leave."

I returned to Jillian's bed and apologized to her. I told her she was released and we would get that Beemer for her birthday. She smiled as best she could, but she knew. Joy had told her long before that this night might be coming and warned her when she was very young. Jillian was very quiet; a very different person looked at me through her sad eyes. I searched for something to say other than I loved her. My hug was unreturned.

The ride home was quiet and my mind told me I would not act as selfish as I had with Joy. I could be strong as need be and I hoped I had Sheena there always. When Jillian fell asleep in the backseat, I felt Sheena's hand gently grasp my arm. We rode the distance up to our home and then I carried Jillian to her bed. Martha was upstairs and looked worried.

When I came downstairs, Ed and Sheena had gone home. I needed a strong drink…lots of them. I laid down on the couch getting blitzed, while watching ESPN replays, but couldn't sleep nor concentrate on any of them.

It was the dawning of morning and I had finished off a bottle of Southern Comfort, once made known to me by Kurt… "Kurt, I wonder how you are. I hope you have my wife near you, because I need to thank you, honey, for telling Jillian about her illness. That helped her and me. Miss you…" I remember, saying before I fell asleep. Then Tom touched my arm.

"Dad! Dad! What happened to Jill?"

"Tom, sit. Jill is okay, but she has her mother's illness."

"No, there was a commotion that woke me up…she's not in her bed."

"Jillian! Jillian! Tom…go check upstairs. I'll see if she went over to Sheena's."

"Hello," his voice was garbled.

"Ed, sorry to call…is Jillian over there?"

"Sheena here, what's up?"

"We can't find Jillian. Is she over at your house?"

"I don't think so…she has a key…let me check and I'll call you back, but you call us if you find her."

She hung up.

I ran around like a chicken with my head chopped off. I checked every closet, under the bed, then walked out on the veranda upstairs. That scream told me everything, as Ed held Sheena back, as she stared down to the water frantically with her hands about her face screaming. Jillian had drowned.

I was still drunk and stumbled down the staircase and fell flat on my face. Tom came running to assist me, he hadn't heard the screaming.

"Tom, dial 911, Jillian has drowned, God help us!" I screamed to myself.

Tom's mouth fell open, but he still had the composure to tell the emergency station his sister had drowned and we needed help. I jumped up and went to Ed as Sheena ran back into the house to also dial 911.

She lay there floating lifeless below the surface. Jillian's long hair had spread out in the water, as she was face down, still in her nightgown that she had worn to bed. However, she had evidently put on her robe. That was three hours before.

From the light of Sheena's nightlight, I knew it was useless to even attempt to go out to get her, so I sat down on the bank and started crying. Crying because she might have lived if I had said the right words to give her hope. I heard the distant wail of the emergency vehicle sirens and wondered how many times were they to come down our lane. This place was jinxed…I was jinxed.

The EMT came to me, first, then I pointed to my daughter down in the water. She had sunk deeper and was hardly visible. But a man in a diving respirator, wearing bright orange swim flippers, entered the water and slowly pulled Jillian up to the surface, but left her in the water.

"It's too late!" he told us, removing his diver mask. "I have to leave her in the water until the coroner arrives…you better not stay."

"Can I touch her?" I asked the EMT.

"How much have you had to drink?" was his response.

"Not enough, not enough," I repeated.

"There's nothing you can do now. Who found her?"

"We did, sir."

"Sir? Sheena, this is Dick Holcombe you're talking to," he spoke up as he removed his yellow EMT hat.

"Oh, hi...Dick...we found her down there at about dawn...about five-thirty or so, after Greg called she was missing. I think I know what happened, if you want a statement."

"Well, Sheena...why don't you tell me so I know, too...damn it!" I cried out.

"Greg, Jillian had MS coming on for a long time. If you had been with her as much as Martha and I had, you'd know...by the way...where's Martha? She was sleeping the night upstairs with Jillian."

"Something's going on at the other side," the EMT said, then listened to his radio message.

"We've got another one...a white, elderly female."

Now it was Martha, too.

"Oh, God, what have I done to deserve this?" I screamed up into the morning sky.

I felt a hand on my shoulder and thought it was Sheena's. It was Tom's.

"Dad, come, let's go back up to the house."

I was shocked by his adult behavior and did get up. Ed came and helped me, too, because the alcohol's effect was excessive. No one had ever seen me in this condition before, not even me, but it was not going to end that day.

That afternoon, after I had regained sobriety, I learned from Ed and Sheena that apparently, according to the footprints left from Martha and Jillian that Martha had tried to catch up to Jillian thinking Jillian had jumped in.

Apparently, because it was dark, lighted only by Sheena's outdoor pole light from across the lake, Martha fell in by accident. Because she, too, had on her night robe, it swamped her efforts to swim. Unfortunately, she had fallen into the deepest part of the lake near the dock and couldn't get out. Martha's tracks led from our house to near where Martha fell into the lake.

Jillian's tracks led from the house...she was running, as if she might have been headed to Sheena's place. Nevertheless, her tracks reversed and went back to near where Martha succumbed.

The investigators thought, Jillian couldn't drown herself then, but went back to save Martha. Martha pulled her down. She shook loose and swam towards Sheena's pole light, but herself succumbed. It was a strange circumstance that was later ruled inconclusive, but accidental.

We buried Jillian and Martha next to Kurt and Joy. I was too ashamed to speak anything and turned away. I felt that everyone had to think I failed my own daughter and my promise to Kurt was tainted.

It was an empty house with just the two of us; Tom and me, and only Sheena during the day. After the double funeral, most everyone sent their condolences to Tom, because someone said I was too drunk to save either. They were right, but my life resumed with Tom's help.

Tom became my mainstay thereafter and at seventeen, his senior year in springtime high school baseball, Tom was already getting pro baseball scout's attention. His shortstop position was switched back and forth to second, since the scouts told his coach they wanted to see how versatile Tom was. His arm was very strong, he was fast, he was agile, and he could hit the cover off that baseball, they all agreed. Tom was getting lots of local newspaper print in the sport columns.

When someone said the team became "all about Tom" and their team started losing, Tom called a team meeting and asked if they had given up, because of his star status. He said he would stop playing and never play again, if his friends, which he had grown up with, ever thought he was thinking only of himself; he had no takers. The team returned to form by dedication to tough practices as their coach's trick worked, without anyone the wiser.

That seemed to spark the team and they won a few more games to keep them in contention, in the lower brackets. Tom, was their cleanup hitter, batting .489 for the season, with sixteen homers. Good for any kid.

When playoffs came, Tom decided to step up to the pitching rubber to help out there when his best friend's arm was being overworked and developed a twinge in his pitching elbow. He had never pitched one game, ever, but he knew how and showed his future's ability.

I had been in the stands for every game after Jillian's and Martha's demise, and this was the first game that gave me the jitters. When Tom threw his first warm-up pitch off the mound, it sailed ten feet over his catcher's head and caused the other team to begin hollering "rubber arm". That only pissed Tom off, though he never showed much emotion when he was about to destroy you.

After walking the first batter on a questionable call, he moved from the uncomfortable windup stance to the stretch; a pitcher's stance with runner's on base, or the stance most good relief pitchers use from the get go. That was Tom's salvation. He struck out ten batters, others just hit grounders and his team backed him to a win over the first ranked team, 6-0. They were put in the winner's bracket and that set the pace.

At home between games, I iced his arm after he threw and rubbed it down with Atomic Balm Aid, a vapor-rub type analgesic. It helped loosen Tom's muscles when I applied it with massage to his pitching arm a half-hour before he pitched, just as I had when I threw off the mound. Tom liked it.

Choices, choices, choices, that's what Tom had after he pitched two more games into the championship game, winning one 5-4 and losing the championship1-0, going all nine innings and losing when the opposing coach put in a left-hand batter, who caught Tom off guard and bunted with two strikes. The ball trickled on the third base line and spun to a halt, still fair, allowing the man on third to score. It was a big disappointment for Tom. Nevertheless, immediately after his last playoff game, college choices arrived in the mail daily.

Tom seriously looked at Arkansas Razorbacks, Texas Longhorns and the Miami Hurricanes. He finally chose the Canes, who were perennial participants in the ACC conference playoffs.

I couldn't go to Miami to see Tom's first performances, but I bought a satellite dish that could. I taped his games. Then, Sheena, Ed, and I watched them over and over. Their pitching coach had tweaked Tom's delivery movement to the plate from his windup stance to allow for better movement through his shoulder delivery. Then Tom really was "Terrific".

Then one evening, Ed told me he had a substantial down payment for purchase of my entire place and we arrived at a mutual deal. I sold the home place of twenty-two years to Ed and Sheena before the end of that month.

In an effort to appease my burning desire to deep sea fish once again, I decided to drive out to Vegas for old time's sake and then on to Southern California, to fish for dorado, off Baja. This time I contemplated I might try for that world record class fish, if I got there at the exact time for the migrating run along Mexico's shore.

With Tom at baseball's off-season down in Miami, I took off in my brand new truck and had two thousand miles on it in four days. I needed three thousand to break it in, read the owner's manual, before I did any serious fast driving.

The closer I got to Vegas, the more intensely I remembered my time there with my wife; it became painful, as I thought we both might have died there and never had known our love could have been so strong.

Therefore, I made a drive through the city, mostly, and looked for a man whose name I imagined might be highlighted on any marquee. I could not find that name of Hajji. I should have been looking for a guy named Carvey. I didn't know it then, but someone told me he was Doctor Hajji.

Anyway, the guy was very talented and made Joy and me laugh. I hoped he and his wife enjoyed a good life and he had a better view of things in life as a comedian, not as a proctologist.

I finally got to the Pacific Coast but was held up ten days by a weather situation that was caused by turbulence of a dwindling hurricane named Eddie. Eddie had crossed the Yucatan Peninsula and my charter owner from Tijuana called to ask me to delay, because he could not go out at all.

Therefore, I laid around on the beaches and saw San Diego and our Marine Corps training grounds of Camp Pendleton. There was a list of Marine casualties on a sacred wall there. I found Captain Will Char and Staff Sergeant Jillian Char, both casualties in Afghanistan. I was a bit saddened, but very proud as other visitors stood beside me rubbing their lost loved one's names.

I did not know much about Will, but it really caused me to understand about people moving their own different ways in life, such as Jill had. No one could have predicted her behavior of being "Little Miss Rich Bitch" would turn into a Congressional Medal Winner…no one.

Then the second-most important detour of my life occurred, while I was lying on the beach in San Diego catching serious rays. An attractive woman who apparently was on a mission to save the whales, was walking the beach, obtaining everyone's signature that she could, in support of PETA. I saw her working her way towards me and she wasn't moving very quickly. I think she was forcefully obtaining those signatures.

I tried to avoid her, by pretending to be sleeping. Nevertheless, when the sand was kicked up upon me from under her feet and hadn't disturbed me yet, the drippings from her ice tea glass did. She dripped ice water onto my back, which caused me to squirm in distress of its cold, so I rolled over really peeved at her.

I know now it was her intention to spill a little ice water on any sunbathers who tried to roll over and ignored her. She was merciless.

"Whoa, Nellie! Watch it, lady, that was cruel!" I shouted, to this gal in a bikini, wearing very dark sunglasses and standing over me with her clipboard and that tall ice cold glass of Lipton.

"Kind, sir, I'm from PETA and we're concerned with the Japanese over-killing of our water's blue whales. Would you be so kind as to support our cause by signing this petition and include your residence and state address?"

"If I do, will you stop torturing us people by dripping that ice cold water on us?"

"It does grab your attention, doesn't it?" she giggled. "Well, then, will you please?" she requested, extending down to hand me the petition.

Her bosom just hung down right in my face. Maybe that was my reward.

I quickly signed my name and address and handed it back, and then rolled back over to get my tan.

"Greg! Greg Wetmore! It is you…hi, don't you remember me?" she squealed.

I was looking directly into the sun, she had a big brimmed Hawaiian hat on and her sunglasses were very dark, I told her. She plopped down beside me, spilling more of the ice tea upon me. I again let out a pretty ghastly tirade, but stopped short of anything in God's name, when I realized I knew her. It was Carla Dionne.

"Carla Dionne, I'd know you anywhere. How have you been?"

"Well, Greg, I want you to know I'm about to finally marry. A girl can't wait forever," she laughed. "Would you believe I hit forty last year and a virgin? Yes, yes, so how have you been, dearie?"

"Wonderful, now that I see someone I know. What are you doing for PETA?"

"Really, it's piece work. I get a quarter for every valid signature. I work hard and get by," she told me easing up to me to block the sun out of my eyes.

"You live around here?" I asked.

"Oh, no, I'm out here for this project only to help get sixty-thousand signatures. I still live in Chi-town. That's where I'm getting married, can you come?" she almost immediately begged after not having seen me for all those years. I was surprised, but it might be something to consider for laughable entertainment.

"When is it exactly? I'm headed down to Tijuana to fish in ten days. Thought I might hang out there, until I get tired. I also have a son, he's down in Miami, Florida and goes to college there. I'm planning on getting a condo near him soon to be closer."

"Well, for goodness sake, he's one of those Florida Gators, huh? Good school, I've heard about…Gatorade, and all."

"No, not hardly, Miami is home of the Canes, the Miami Hurricanes."

"Oh, sure, I know them now. Where's your wife?"

"She passed about fifteen years ago. Without her love I've almost been celibate and single, ever since," I said, to deter her thoughts of getting back together, but it didn't register.

"Oh, I'm very sorry to hear that. Almost? You really mean you actually haven't been with a woman for fifteen years?"

"That's right!"

"God, I bet your hard as a rock…oops, exxxxcussse me!" she said, thinking out loud on purpose.

"You're excused. Remember, we dated once and we might have been together, if you hadn't flunked out," I chuckled.

"Well, poo, poo, on you…I graduated from college; only took seven."

"It took you seven years to graduate from UIC?"

"No, baby, it took me seven men to graduate from Parkland College. I couldn't make up my little mind."

She had that right.

"Seven years, in a two-year school is too much, Carla. What was so hard that you were studying all that time?"

"As I said, I was studying, hard men, ha!"

"Ha! Carla! You don't want me to believe that, now do you? You just told me that you turned forty and you were still a virgin."

"Let's change the subject, and let's talk about you…what do, you, think about me?" she giggled, and allowed me to see her still-firm, tanned body.

"Carla, you're a real peach. You still look great in your bikini and your fiancé will be a lucky guy."

"Think so? I still have a month before I tie the knot. Wanna mess around for old times sake?"

"Shucks, Carla, if I were going to mess around and enjoy the company of a completely outrageous, sexy woman, you'd be the first I'd try on for size, but I'm going to be celibate from here on out."

"From here on out, could be a long, long time. She must have really been something, your wife?"

"Thanks, she was."

"Well?" she asked.

"Well what?"

"Well, will you come to my wedding, or what? As a matter of fact, would you actually be in my wedding? I have a best friend who's perfect for you. She won't walk down the aisle with just anyone and my fiancé can't seem to find the right guy for her, she's very picky, picky, picky…always has been.

"But you remember Amanda Morgan, back at UIC, don't you? I think we were double-dating then and you found some of her books in the library…she was so relieved…remember, I saw you there in her little apartment and later she said she wished she was dating you that night instead?"

I sat up and asked her to repeat that, that haunting, stirring name.

"I'm getting married and I'd like you to be in my wedding."

"No, what's that part about Amanda Morgan?"

"Amanda is single, like you…but she's a spinster…you know, she's never been married. She told me she didn't have time and never met a man of her equal…intelligence or financial status."

I stopped hearing Carla gabbing and remembered Amanda for the first time in years.

"Yes!" I told her.

"Yes, you remember Amanda, or, yes, you'll come, or, yes, you'll come and be in my wedding?" she asked.

"I'll be in your wedding. Do I need to get fitted for a tux or something?"

"Sure, you think my future man is a bum? There's a fitting in Arlington Heights, where he lives, and I will live there, too. Here, when you get there, look up Dennis Melton, call him, he's my guy," she told me, writing down his name and address and giving it to me. "You sure you wouldn't like to mess around, just a little?"

"Sorry, but I'm not ready. See you in about four weeks. Maybe, we can work something out on your honeymoon, if your new hubby likes threesomes!"

"Oh, you shit head, you, that was crude…good-bye," she said, acting rather insulted, getting up and walking away, but laughing, then turned around smiling and said, "Maybe!"

I must have been crazy to say I'd do it, I later thought. But thinking back to Amanda, I had visions of her thirty years ago. People change a lot in thirty years, I had. And, Amanda was never married…humm, maybe I bit off more than I could chew.

Ten days later, I was fishing off the Baja Peninsula upon a charter fishing boat, reeling in rooster fish, yellowtail, and grouper, off the deep rocky shore, because the dorado left with the bad weather. I still had fun.

After almost two weeks fishing, till my heart's content, and getting a deep, dark tan, my intentions were to drive back to Springfield, then down to Glenarm to visit my family's graves. After that I'd be off to Chicago, just in time to get that tux fitting for Carla's wedding.

When I left California my new vehicle was purring like a kitten, seemingly broken in with four thousand miles, so I floored her to see what she could do out in the desert, nearing sunset. One hundred was fast enough, because there were no cars in sight in the cooling, nighttime, desert air.

I had driven only a few miles at that speed when I slowed down, thinking to myself, what if? What would I do if I broke down out here, and I also saw that my gas gauge had quickly dropped almost a quarter tank. I wondered how far it was to the next gas station, too, so I eased up on that gas pedal.

I drove until dawning and finally found a station, with less than a quarter showing on the gas gauge left in the tank. I was dead tired. I could have stayed at the truck stop, but I wanted to keep going.

Hours later, when I was getting even more sleepy, up popped the bright, warm sun, beaming through the windshield from the east into my face. That recharged my biological batteries. I just let my foot get too heavy again and was seeing those cacti fly by like a green picket fence.

Later in the heat of the day, while I was driving very fast east on I-80, west of Elko, Nevada, I stopped to help a woman who was apparently stranded. She just popped up out of nowhere from lying down upon the hot sandy shoulder with her thumb stuck out hitchhiking and holding onto a back pack.

She was dressed somewhat scantily. Her long legs first drew my attention to her white, low-cut, tight fitting jeans. It appeared she was braless under a camouflaged, long-sleeved shirt, tied-up, which slid up high above her thin waistline as she frantically waved me down. Also noticeable was her army boonie hat that shaded her face and the well worn cowgirl boots she wore. She was quite a sight, like a cactus flower out there alone in the desert. I think she had camped overnight there along the interstate.

She held up her olive drab army knapsack, and then took off running towards me frantically, waving her arms to flag me down long before I even got close to her. Her slender body looked very tanned out there in the hot wilderness sun.

I could have zoomed right past her for she hardly stood out, even under the clear blue desert-like sky, except for those gorgeous long legs. Nonetheless, there she was, way out in no-man's-land. She probably had been dumped out there by a trucker. I suspected she might need my help desperately, because I did not notice if she had any water bottles or a canteen. I always carried extras, just in case. She had to be thirsty, it was almost one hundred five degrees.

I shut my truck down from doing ninety-five and the engine moaned from my hard braking. I stopped short of her, so I could see her better. She might have something in her backpack…like a gun. My mind said she was not a criminal, so I rolled forward slowly.

Then I cautiously drove up to where she was still frantically waving at me. I became anxious when she removed her dark sunglasses. With just one good look at her face, I was stunned how she remarkably resembled my long lost love's appearance. My first thought was it could actually be Amanda, and after all these years.

I eased off the hot asphalt onto the sandy berm slowly, so as not to raise dust. One's radial tires could actually melt down and get out of round being stopped too long on the hot black asphalt. I was also cautious to save my tires from any broken glass or sharp debris. It was easier to be overly cautious than to try to change a tire in this hot weather.

I was still watchful and alert driving up to her, aware some thug might jump out packing a gun or a knife from behind one of the many cacti, which speckled the area surrounding her; but she was alone.

The astonishing woman smiled excitedly showing her bright white teeth, and came running and hollering something to me when I stopped short. She rushed to my truck and did not hesitate to get inside.

I guess she didn't care if I were a rapist or murderer, she'd have died soon outside there anyway without any assistance. She did not even ask where I was headed when I took off eastbound again, nor did she worry of my character. All this woman needed was the cold air conditioning inside my truck. She took several deep breaths right out of the vents and pushed her sunglasses onto the top of her head.

Then she grabbed my air conditioning vents and directed them from me onto her beautiful face; and let out a big sigh of relief. I watched as she began untying her shirt and then leaned forward. She waved the air under her shirt and I quickly noticed she really wasn't wearing a bra. I almost ran off the road. She just looked over and smiled, then sat back up.

I soon learned she was different than she looked. She became one strange and lonely woman, who could be spontaneous trouble and living in a world of her own. Still, she was so attractive, it bothered me.

Her speech was a bit slurred, her lips touched by the sun, and she strongly smelled a horrible mixture of cheap perfume and sweat. But she looked so helpless, I decided that I could not begin to leave her there for humanitarian reasons. And even if I wanted to, she reminded me so much of Amanda, I became anxious to know her name without sounding too pushy. I kept thinking…what if it is her?

The sun had burned fine wrinkles into the back of her neck and forehead. Still, I was stunned by her resemblance to Amanda, just hoping to hear her say, "You look familiar," and we would embrace and my world would brighten beyond imagination.

Unfortunately, that would certainly be too much to ask, since I hadn't seen Amanda in many, many years, and I thought she was from the east, not out here in the west.

When she moved closer immediately and put her arm around the back of my neck, as if we were dating, I suspected this woman was a hooker. But there was that mystique about her that turned me on. Under her magical charms, I could do nothing, but surrender to her, if she were so inclined. My heart was beating faster.

"Weren't you afraid of those diamond backs and sidewinders back there?" I questioned her to start a conversation when she neglected to thank me for stopping to help her.

"Hell, no, ate two of them raw this morning! They were little," she casually related extending her hands apart about a foot's distance. "Couldn't find any matches or sticks to rub together, that's why I ate them that way. I saw Yucca Indians do it many times. They, of course, had mother's little helper lend a hand tolerating them, you know, peyote. Why people come to the desert is beyond me. Give me the good life," she seemed to reminisce.

"Good life, eh…what's that?"

"A delicious meal in a fancy New York hotel, a handsome guy with a big dick and a bottle of good wine."

"Sorry, you're out of luck here. This isn't a New York restaurant and I don't have any wine," I laughed.

"Ahhh, ha, ha, ha," she chuckled weakly, but started to stare at me. She had lovely blue eyes.

"See any alligators? No. See any elephants? No," she suddenly jumbled and mumbled out in delirium. "Can I have some of that water?" she begged.

"Sure, take one of the blue labeled ones, they're regular H20. Or, the red ones have a teaspoon of salt in them to help from losing electrolytes in case I get stranded."

"You shittin' me?" she said, sitting up. Then she turned around backwards in my front seat revealing her nice rear end, as she reached for the water in the back. I could see her fine breasts again under her shirt with no bra. I think she meant for me to see her that way.

This woman seemed to possess every wild emotion, though probably caused by a mushroom, or an opiate. She sometimes spoke with an educated tongue when she tried, which when added to her extraordinarily, beautiful physical quality, lit a fire burning inside of me, again.

I was helplessly drawn to her like a moth to a flame. I guess she was an old pro, but I was lonely for a woman like her. I could make love to her and never see her face again. But found myself asking "what will I do if I couldn't see her again?" Now that really bothered me. I knew the other.

Awed by her sleek looks and close resemblance to Amanda, who I assumed was still in New York, or Chicago, I succumbed to her physical appearance and allowed her to run her fingers through my hair and then nuzzle my ear. This perfect stranger reminded me of Amanda so much, even a bit more than I remembered; maybe it was in my best dreams.

Nevertheless, while slowly accessing her overall appearance, she seemed older with wrinkled skin; almost old enough to be my mother. She was certainly wild and crazy enough to be exhilarating, and surely could fulfill any man's desires at any time she wanted to grant his wish. I was beginning to wish harder, not wanting to be the first to ask if she wanted to become intimate, for fear she might scream rape.

The dark circles under her eyes told me she might be hooked on drugs or something. When I also mentioned the needle tracks on her arms, she withdrew them behind her back to hide them, but then exposed her voluptuous bosom. She was working me.

She sadly told me it was heroin that she needed so badly; a fix for the moment. She was hurting, would do anything to get it right then, as most users explain succumbing to their addictions.

She told me she had only begun using drugs to ease her suicidal anxieties, because life was rough. When she asked if I would help her, I was in over my head, and I knew it. I knew absolutely nothing about hard drugs, or did she mean suicide? She really worried me that inside her gorgeous body a real suicidal nutcase resided; that's just the way she wanted it.

She needed to kick her habit, she said, or get relief in a few more minutes. Somehow my thoughts quickly ran all the way back to my first love, Amanda, and I wondered if she had gone astray something like this. Then I looked over and she was sleeping. Now that was strange. Someone in a dire need of a fix couldn't sleep. I became more suspicious.

An hour or so later, I stopped for gas and checked my radiator overflow. I saw the woman awaken and stretch, then get out of my truck doing the same. She looked back at me and somehow now seemed to be straight. Maybe her problem had lessened, I thought. She came to me at the pump and asked where we were.

"I thought you'd surely have been this way before," insinuating her hooker dates must have dropped her off here before. "I'd say about one mile due east of Wendover…needed to fill up before crossing the Great Salt Desert."

"Why the scorn, junior? Are we still headed east?"

"I was meaning to discuss that with you. Where are you actually headed?"

"No where in particular now, just east out of this damn desert."

"Well, I'm headed to Illinois…ever been there?"

"Sure, once lived there for a while, but once was enough."

"Hey, be nice, that's my home state," I said, just as the gas pump clicked off and I finished topping off my tank.

She seemed much better and began to walk around very daintily, you might say like a lady, and that was even in her boots. When she stopped, she raised her hands up to really stretch out some more. I could see the shape of a model standing before me again. She really had a great body.

Why this whore-ish woman had chosen her Nomadic lifestyle I would never understand. She could have been a model on the front cover of any fashion magazine, maybe even still, with makeup. She wore none, but I liked that in all women.

"You want some breakfast? I'm buying," I said, returning the gas nozzle to the pump.

She looked at me, but just yawned with a silly little girlish shriek. It seemed so appropriate for maybe a teenage girl, but not her.

She didn't say a word, but followed me into the little roadside diner. I told the waitress we wanted two breakfast specials, but she said breakfast was over, so it was now the dinner-delight going on.

"Okay, and could we have some coffee?"

"No, would you make mine ice water, please!" the hitch-hiker told her.

The waitress looked at me as if to say, "What you doin' with her?"

Then she hollered out our order to the cook and he sang out, "Yo!"

"Say, I don't want to be nosey..."

"So don't be," she said, before I could ask her her name.

I guess it was her lack of sleep that caused her to talk so wildly. Being out in the desert heat can do that to a person, too. She was fidgety, tapping her long fingernails on the table, and staring hard at the cigarette machine.

"I'll buy you some cigarettes if you tell me your name."

"Ollie...now go get some Winstons," she quipped instantly.

I spotted cigarette cartons up on the top of a cabinet, so I thought I'd give her a thrill and paid forty-two dollars for some illegally, untaxed cigarettes.

"Here!" I said, pitching the carton across the table to her, as I also bought some gum.

"Where's the matches...need some fire on the end," she barked at me.

I picked up several books of free matches and took them to her, threw them down for her unappreciative attitude, then sat down.

She had that carton torn open almost immediately. Then hurriedly she removed the cigarette wrapper with her long fingernails and wrapped them around a cigarette and lit it up fast. She really seemed desperate for a smoke.

"That's why I don't smoke," I just mumbled watching her extreme anxiety.

"I don't either, the cigarette does…I inhale the smoke and I like it…like it a lot," she said, probably thinking I was going to criticize her for doing so.

But I really wasn't, because I would have said how beautiful she could have been, if she hadn't had that cigarette dangling off the corner of her mouth like a croupier in a card game. Instead, I said something totally off the wall.

"You don't do that while having sex, do you?"

She crushed the cigarette out in the ashtray, then lit another, looking me directly into the eyes all the time, staring hard even, trying to figure my angle.

"What do you want? You never touched me all night coming across the desert, why now?" she asked, looking very provocative.

"Nothing, I just look at you and think how beautiful you are. Sometime in your life, you must have been a gorgeous model, I'm thinking, a very high class girl. Did you perform on the stage or in the movies?"

"Where'd you say you're from, kid?"

"Really, you think I'm a kid? I'm not much younger than you, kid. I was born and raised in the suburbs of north Chicago…how about you, kid?"

Her immediate defense was her silence, but her look made it seem I had touched her secret accord. Then she puffed her smoke, blew it in my face and asked me my real name.

"I'm Gregory Jonathan Wetmore," I told her proudly.

"Yeah, you're shorter, but you could be his kid…I'm Olivia Morgan. I knew both your father and mother…I used to live on the North Shore, near Evanston…they still around?"

"No…my parents have both passed on…but then is your daughter named Amanda?" I asked to her complete surprise.

"Oh, Jesus, you know her? How is she? I left her as a child, you know. It was a big mistake and I can never set it right with her. I haven't seen or talked to Amanda Jean since she was six…almost thirty-five years ago, or so…she probably thinks I'm dead or wishes I was. Her daddy forced me to sign papers relinquishing my rights to her. I did it because...", she said, quickly on the defensive with me.

"I know all about that. It was scandalous back then and the Tribune had you in their society columns, when I really was a kid...but, but you were so much younger than your husband and my parents, too...I can't believe I'm talking to you...it's incredible!"

"Small world, nothing's incredible these days."

"Oh, yes, it is! Have I got something to tell you, but here comes our lunch...eat up, first, you're really going to be amazed."

I didn't want to discuss this openly before strangers, so I held off until we were driving down the road again and I was very tired.

"Do you have a driver's license?" I asked.

"Heaven's no...I always used a bike to get around and to keep myself in shape, but now I have a good right thumb, see?" she said, smiling for the first time, and extending her thumb like a hitch-hiker. "My cross-country trek ended with my last spare tire. I dumped my bike behind a big rock next to a very peculiar-looking cactus...it looked like someone's hand was shooting the bird. I think I can find it again someday. It was a really expensive old Chanel bike...limited edition."

"Never heard of it...then we'll just have to put up for awhile in a hotel, because I'm exhausted and I want to tell you everything. Okay?"

"I've had men use all kinds of behavior to seduce me; never had one ask me if it was okay," she laughed loudly.

"Don't think it isn't on my mind," I told her.

I pulled off the roadway, and checked us into a little hotel. It was the first one I found.

I grabbed my luggage and we went to the room. It was a double queen but Ollie was dead set for the shower.

"Tell me all about everything that you seem so excited to tell me about when I'm done. I stink like a pig," she said, closing the door of the bath.

I pulled out my clean clothes, then peeked into Ollie's bag, while she was in the shower. Her clothes were few, all dirty, stinky, wrinkled-up clothes. There were no real drugs or syringes, just some marijuana-looking grass seeds, so I pitched the whole caboodle into the outside trash, just so she couldn't retrieve them. I had decided to give her some of mine, including a pair of boxers and a widow maker to sleep in.

I would be more than happy to help her, Amanda's own mother, and in the morning, I would buy her all new clothes for my new mind-generated plans.

A lonely man can get some awfully wild feelings, especially with a lovely, half-naked woman in his hotel room. My heart was on fire, listening to her shower, imagining her wet, soapy body, thinking I could get romantic with her, since she seemed to be so receptive to me.

Ollie came out with her head wrapped in a towel and one around her body.

"Where's my bag? I need my clothes," she said, looking at me.

"Here, sleep in these, I ditched your stinky clothes, backpack, too… tomorrow I'll go out and buy you some new ones…my treat. Now, I know why you were so silly when I found you. You had hit on some of your stashed weed, hadn't you?"

"So?"

"So, I like you much better now. You're a real knockout, Ollie, especially in that loose, wet towel. I really can't believe how my luck has changed in two weeks."

"Oh, yes? And who told you that you were going to get lucky?"

"You did!"

"I certainly did not…was I trippin' then?" she seemed ashamed.

"You'll see after I get out of the shower. I think I can make us the happiest people in the whole wide world."

"You're not expecting much, are you?" she said, a bit sarcastically.

Then I thought Ollie just might put on my clothes and run out that door, before I could explain to her I was planning to try to reunite her with Amanda. So I grabbed up all my stuff and put them in the bathroom. She wouldn't dare go out naked.

I quickly figured that if I brought her mother to her, Amanda would also have to appreciate me. My giddiness was almost uncontrollable as I shaved, then took my shower. I heard the TV on and the weather report was severe thunderstorms; unusual for the desert. It wasn't the desert weather; Olivia was watching WGN Chicago on satellite.

After I showered, I returned to find Ollie in one queen bed, so invitingly propped up on pillows, then patting her hand down beside her on the bed, as if that is where she wanted me.

"Come right here, let's get it over with," she said, sounding disgusted.

I thought she meant for me to tell her my good news, but she was opening up her legs to receive me. I lost my train of thought and it was really confusing. I did lay down beside her, but outside the cover.

"Ready?" I asked, to a now bewildered looking Ollie.

"I'm waiting, get it on, already."

I quickly gave her a peck on the cheek, which caused her to laugh. But when I began to tell her of my first meeting with Amanda, she suddenly realized my real intentions, drew her legs together, then pulled the cover up, as if she were now overexposed. I didn't see Ollie Morgan lying there, I saw Amanda's mother, and that made all the difference to me, and apparently to her. She didn't want to reunite.

"I can't do that and I won't. She doesn't even know I exist, after her father told her bad things."

"That's just it, he's dead now and she's become a lonely spinster."

"I don't believe you. Her father wasn't ugly, and I'm not …"

"No, you're not, you're the most exceptionally beautiful, sexy, vibrant, challenging, intelligent woman, just like Amanda. The last time I saw Amanda, she looked just like you, gorgeous. In fact, I thought you were her when I picked you up. I'm going to see your daughter next week at a wedding… you're going with me, no ifs, no ands, no buts," I demanded. "Best thing is, Amanda doesn't know I'm going to be in the wedding party either and I'm her escort…neat, huh?"

"I can't do it. She'll see me and make a scene."

"Again, she won't know you from Adam…well, Eve, then, and you can sit in the crowd and at least see her."

"I haven't got that kind of money to dress as I should," she mentioned, as I knew she was now considering the options.

"But I have, and it's all on me. We'll go to any store and outfit you with a complete wardrobe."

"Why? Why, are you doing all this?"

"Don't you realize…I want my future mother-in-law, very close, and very happy."

"Well, now, I've got to see this play out," but she stopped, and looked hard into my longing eyes; she knew my thinking was hers.

Somehow after that moment we lost our goal, because not either of us was then really attached to anyone. Convenience, that's what led us together. With all of my exuberance, all my good intentions, stoked by our closeness, our unfed needs in consensual freedom, Olivia managed to give me that look I had craved for, as being Amanda's. We suddenly began to create a wildfire.

Olivia, not Ollie, slowly reached out to touch me; I met her touch with mine. We kissed slowly at first, but we drew closer and closer together, until we were embraced in an uncontrollable frenzied passion.

I felt I was safe with her and thought perhaps I may never have completed the conquest of Amanda, anyway, so it was "Love the One You're With" type situation.

I moved in to satisfy my burning desires. Her kisses were igniting and my thrusts caused her to want me more and more. Boy, was she a good kisser. She felt so good in my arms, we seemed to meld into a human fireball of sweat and energy. She was the most incredible love-partner I had ever experienced. Then, after a while, we lay back and rested; both feeling very satisfied.

"My daughter may never know what she has missed all these years. Hell, if she throws you down, come back to me, anytime," she told me laughing, much like I remembered Amanda's smile.

Our fires rekindled, however, this time we were more satisfied, under control of our emotions, much closer than before. We reset our goals. But as I looked at her nakedness and realized she was such a prize, I considered Olivia's words, and might have actually stayed with her forever then and there, but my cell doused the flame.

"Dad! Where are you? Did you see our team on TV?"

"Tom, son, I'm sorry, but something suddenly came up and I was held up by Hurricane Eddie, did you get hit by it?"

"Nope, it passed below the Keys and hit Mexico."

"Well, I was put on hold for fishing, or I'd been down there to see you pitch…I was about to board a fishing charter when Eddie came up. The captain called me and said I had to wait ten days. I did, later caught some great fish, but forget that, how are you doing, son?"

All the while I was talking to my son Tom about his accomplishments at his school, Olivia was touching me there and would not stop, as if she were now obsessed. Any other time I would have been thrilled talking to my son, but again, this time for selfish reasons, I left Tom hanging like a bad curve ball and halted our talk to another day.

"Tom, something just came up and I must get off. I'll call you tomorrow and the week after next I'm getting a condo in Coral Gables and you can move in with me if you want. How's that?"

"Good, Dad, but..."

I had to hang up abruptly, because Olivia was seriously distracting me. We made love again, and then again before dawn, and I was just as tired walking out as when we entered that room. A good woman can do that to a man. In a moment of meaningless sexual heat, Olivia told me she loved me and I almost returned her words because she was so wonderful; but those other fires, both Joy, and the thought of Amanda, overpowered me from saying I loved her, too.

Nevertheless, I knew it was indeed possible to love her when it was over and after we showered, we wanted the other again. But I dressed and we both left to go out to buy her new clothes.

A size eight, tall, is hard to find, but going through Salt Lake City, I saw several Mormon folks on the street and asked where the sinners bought their clothes. They walked away rudely, but we were directly in front of a wonderful store.

Dressed in my jeans and looking a bit like a ragamuffin, Olivia had found just the place. It was a bridal shop that also sold fashionable dresses. I dropped seven grand, before Olivia came out ready with her last dress to meet her obligations of looking good enough for the wedding and seeing Amanda. It was a bit pricey, but she was worth every penny.

Non-stop, we drove on into St. Louis. I noticed my planned bridge was non-functional. There were no signs of workers as we passed over. Springfield was farther that Glenarm, so I explained to Olivia that I had to pass by my family's graves. Olivia understood, when two hours later, I parked outside the church and walked to the rear cemetery.

"Hi, honey, it's me. I just came by to say 'hey' and tell you I miss you all. My life isn't much, except Tom has broken the starting rotation at Miami. He's doing really well in his academics, also. I'm sorry for letting everyone down...well, until next time."

I stood there waiting to feel that sensation that I had always felt, but nothing developed, so I left. I figured everyone had gone elsewhere or they lost their faith in me. I headed for Chicago with a different feeling.

We checked into a hotel in Arlington Heights, then I called Dennis

Melton, Carla's fiancé. Dennis was a graduate from Illinois State. He was a security camera installer-engineer with the job of overseeing business surveillances. Dennis was happy that someone had stepped up to be Amanda's date. So was I. I quickly drove over to his chosen men's clothing store and instead of renting, I bought the entire tuxedo ensemble.

It didn't seem enough to show up in just a pickup, so I stopped by Mack Cadillac and traded off my almost-new truck on a new Cadillac, suitable for impressing Amanda. I was ready.

In the meantime, Olivia had taken a taxi into the suburb of Evanston to see old friends and to get a makeover. I thought Olivia had chickened out on me and fled. However, when she returned to our room very late, Olivia appeared twenty years younger, she was really beautiful then, looking just like a magazine model should. I swooned over her appearance and needed to possess her.

We couldn't help being together and alone, so to keep her coiffure intact, she stayed up and I was down. Our spontaneous lovemaking was becoming habit forming and each time Olivia made love to me, I amazingly forgot all the others.

"You look very lovely, Madame!" I told Olivia when she strutted her stuff to my car exactly as a model should, then gave me a kiss.

"You look very handsome, Greg!" Olivia spoke to me, also with a kiss.

We both had dressed for the wedding rehearsal and Olivia wore one of her designer dresses just for meeting her daughter. I had a casual sport coat, but my new shoes needed stretching.

I opened the door for Madame Morgan and assisted her into her seat. The new car smell impressed Olivia and she said she had not smelled new-car leather since 1967. I drove her to the church on time and met with the future bride and groom and also with all of the groomsmen. Amanda was delayed one day, Carla said, but since she was the last maid of honor, her presence was not that important. I finagled Olivia into Amanda's stead and the proceedings continued smoothly.

"She looks almost like Amanda," Carla told everyone.

That made Olivia cry, however no one knew why. They ignored her sniveling, because they had no idea who she really was. I went to her when she went to the rear and sat in a pew. But there was no time to weep, it was a happy time for Carla as everyone headed out to the rehearsal supper, including Olivia and me.

"Keep a stiff upper lip, only one more day," I told her.

I think her emotions had built up on the premise Amanda would be there then. When Amanda was not there, that was her distress.

On our way following the caravan, I asked Olivia a question no man asks a woman; her age.

"I'm old enough," she said, without reservation of showing her dissatisfaction.

"You look my age and you feel like you're my age in my arms, and I'm dead serious."

"Why would you even try comparing our ages?" she asked.

"I don't think I've ever been so happy in a long time. Maybe..."

"Don't ask...I just might say yes," she said, looking toward me, holding my hand then quickly placing her fingers softly upon my lips to hush me. "If I knew I had stolen my own daughter's man, after all I did and didn't do for Amanda, I think I'd rather be dead."

"Oh, but Amanda is only my dream girl. I never even kissed her, never a date. But when I saw her, I wanted her more than anything in my life."

"What? How can you even consider her? You're difficult to understand. You seem so intelligent, yet so mesmerized on an apparition of thirty years ago."

"I shouldn't really, should I? It's just I met her that once and that was enough to inflame my heart, my mind. I lost my heart to her. She had left college before I could find her."

"I hope for your sake, Greg, your dreams aren't shattered tomorrow by a single word...no. I'm sure if she knew you intimately, as I have these past few days, she wouldn't say no."

We dined and drank fine wine at the Arlington Country Club. I wondered why Carla hadn't spoken much to me. Obviously, to her I remained irrelevant without Amanda here with me. That is how I could best describe my life without her. Nevertheless, even Amanda would not really know me when she arrived, I thought.

It was eight o'clock when our wedding groups' time in the Eagle Room had expired and we all had to leave. The arrangements were simple, and I had been to enough weddings to play it by ear.

Suddenly I remembered, "I haven't even gotten a present for them!" I told Olivia.

"It's late, but I have an idea. I have an old friend back in Evanston, who is an artist and a painting would be a great present."

I didn't even ask where we were headed, because Olivia punched that address into my GPS, which automatically lead us to his drive. It was her friend she was leading me to meet. What amazed me more was her knowledge of a Cadillac's GPS after telling me she was a biker.

When I saw the home, of course, I knew him. Yes, it was a small world and suddenly I felt as if I was revisiting my entire life, one friend at a time.

"Hello, Mr. Stuart. Do you remember me?" I said, to Olivia's surprise.

"Hello, yourself. No, I'm sorry, I don't remember you, but hi, Ollie, please come in."

Olivia kissed Stuart and remained in his arms. They both looked to me as one and I felt very uncomfortable.

"Donald, this is my dearest friend, Greg Wetmore…he's Jonathon and Genevieve's son."

"Oh, my goodness, Greg, of course, you've changed after all these years. I've thought of you many times. How have you been and what have you become?" he asked, putting his arms about me, then pushing me back, holding me out, as if to get a really good look at me.

"I'm a retired civil engineer, enjoying the fruits of my crimes and I've found Olivia here to ride shotgun, so to speak. I've read a lot about your astounding accomplishments, as an artist, a painter…world renown. I thought you moved out to California…to Sacramento."

"Well, thank you…I did, moved back here where I belonged and realized I was too old to do all that traveling. So, I just piddle around mostly, taking pictures of things I dreamed to paint one day. But, I am a pretty good photographer now."

"Donald, we need a favor. A friend of my daughter is getting married. Amanda, who lives in New York, is coming and Greg hopes to capture her heart. He needs a gift, not too pricey, but substantial. What do you have here?"

He took us to his vault, led by his man servant, who unsealed it and turned on the lighting. There were hundreds, but Stuart quickly picked one he liked best.

"Does this one suit your tastes? I dubbed it 'old friend'. I did it in '72 and could never give it up, because it's of your mother, Greg."

"Oh, my! I would want to buy that, never to be given to anyone. It looks just like mom. Have you a price?"

"I hoped you would react that way. I never imagined I would ever see you again. I read of Jon's and Gen's deaths. She was Genevieve Vandameer then who posed a moment for a picture. I took it by the lake front on Sheridan Road that year. The wind blew through her hair and I captured that by photo. I used that to incorporate the lake and park behind her."

"You're a genius," I told him.

"It's yours, my friend," he said. "You deserve this more than you'll ever know," he said, placing it upon a table, then wrapping it up like a butcher in an oiled cloth. "Wasn't that simple…follow me."

Olivia was still holding Stuart's hand as he led me to a panoramic picture of an Italian bridge in Venice he called, Vespucci's Column Bridge. It was very attractive, a still, he painted only five years prior, he explained.

"See that yellow building? The one with a wrought iron veranda balcony I painted? That man's wife used to sit there for hours and watch the gondolas push by. She waved at many of the gondoliers every day. Occasionally, gondolas would tie up to the home's lower front veranda and enter there.

"Her husband wandered by me one day, while she was sitting there and I was painting that building. He somehow imagined I was her lover. He kicked my easel over, but it didn't hurt this painting. However I had not finished it and dare not return for fear of my life. He showed me the sharp blade of a stiletto he carried, it was a switchblade knife. Therefore, this part was done by memory. I have no idea, now, how close I made it, but it's a twenty-five hundred painting."

"That's perfect. We'll take it," I said, looking at Olivia.

I reached into my vest wallet and withdrew the money and handed it to him.

"You do that so easily, my friend. This amount represents the first twenty years of my work. I should have been an engineer!" he laughed.

Stuart again began wrapping the painting, but one extra painting I recognized caught my eye. It was of a beautiful nude woman. I moved to it to point out I had peeked at that very oil in this house, when he was in Italy.

"I used to peek at this one, sir. I saw it once, while tending to your humidifiers. Is it for sale?" I asked.

"I'm sorry…it usually is not on display. I only took it out to admire her and check for dust. No, that one is from my personal collection, it's priceless," he explained, with a gleam in his eye, as he moved to cover it back up with much care.

"Wait, please! That woman…had you known her well for her to disrobe? Or, did she need the money, if I'm not too bold? This painting of her is exquisite; is she still alive and as beautiful as I remember? Too bad, I'd have bought this one certainly," I said, moving in to see a close up of her face.

"I often wondered who she was. I would have loved to have known her then, too. Can you tell me, what was her name? She must have been…some… kind…of a lady…" then, I realized it was Olivia. I turned to her and she was red-faced.

"Olivia? Olivia? Olivia!" I couldn't stop saying her name, knowing I had discovered that beautiful lady myself and she had been with me in my bed.

"Sir, it's been my entire pleasure seeing you again. I really thank you for the painting of Mother…I will cherish it always. You have the gift. Ready, Olivia?"

"Greg, I'll meet you there tomorrow. I want to stay here with my friend," Olivia told me.

I looked hard at her, but she moved next to him; I felt empty inside. Olivia wanted this man's love more than mine now, and I wanted hers more than my dream girl's, then. I was heart-sick and confused, but it was her choice, always her own decision. Though I did not like it, I would not attempt to force her in front of him. I took the paintings as gracefully as I could, left my ego behind, and sucked it up, as Joy had always told me to do. I went to bed alone that night, except I couldn't sleep.

Chapter 20

When the phone rang in my hotel room at ten, I picked it up quickly thinking it was Olivia.

"Gregory Wetmore, hello, this is Amanda Morgan. I just wanted to touch bases with you and tell you I was surprised to learn you were my partner. Carla has always been my best confidant, but sometimes she doesn't realize how hard it is to accommodate all her wishes. Are you ready?"

"Well, no…the wedding is at three, until midnight."

"You'd better check the time…the wedding ceremony…it's at one. The reception is three until midnight. She'll really tie one on with that much time. Will you help me control her drinking? She has a real problem, after just one.

"I vaguely remember you, Gregory. Whatever happened to you? I thought way back then that you showed some interest…or was it my perfume I remember had you up on your toes? I guess I was a foolish little girl then," she rambled, but had answered the question of my lifetime.

Maybe that's what it was all this time, that Coffee. I quickly wondered if that was why the words "the air of romance" began, maybe long ago in someone else's romantic adventure, but I caught myself thinking.

"Oh, boy! Sorry, where are you now?"

"You were supposed to be here, now, to pick me up at the Hyatt, on route twelve; actually a half hour ago for us to go to the church for pictures. But I'm in a taxi headed there now. I guess my best friend was too busy to tell you. Look, I'll meet you there, okay?" She hung up, a bit rudely.

I dashed into high gear to get ready. I was out of the hotel's parking lot by ten-thirty…I could make it. Taking of those precious wedding pictures always seems to take too much time anyway…everyone just sort of hangs around watching the bride try to look beautiful, before and after. I wasn't the star of the show anyway nor was Amanda.

Somehow, Amanda seemed like any ordinary girl after I talked to her over the phone. Amanda sounded a bit arrogant and pushy, too, so she had big money, who cared? I had lots of money, too. She had a career, I had mine, and was already retired. She was not going to intimidate me this time. This well-traveled man would treat her with a controlled heart…pulling in my heart strings this time.

I zipped into the church parking lot just as a green and white taxi drove in also, behind the groom and his best man. His white limo was rented, I'm certain, as two men with twisted bow ties and wearing wrinkled tuxedos got out with a pint of bourbon. The groom chugga-lugged the last of its contents with a long gulp and pitched the bottle into a nearby bush. He pulled himself together, waved to me as I got out of my car, then commenced to run into the church for a bathroom.

"Boy, is he nervous, or what?" came the voice from behind me. I turned around.

It was Amanda, the dream girl of my life, still looking as impetuously vibrant, just as I last remembered her. She was just as lovely, too. I could not help myself from openly comparing her to her mother…they looked like twin sisters to me.

"You look just like her!" I exclaimed.

"Like who?" Amanda asked with a wry smile.

I couldn't tell her Olivia, her mother, was here, so I said, "Just as I remember that little college girl on campus."

"Thanks, I guess that's your best compliment…is that your car, or did you rent it?"

"Bought it for the wedding," I proudly told her.

"Kind of tacky, leaving the window price tag up, don't you think? Sixty-grand, not bad," she informed me, while looking at the sticker price.

"You look absolutely beautiful, but where's your bridesmaid's dress?"

"I flew in for the fitting a month ago, Carla was out in California doing her PETA thing. It had to be altered, I couldn't wait, so Carla has it. I was supposed to try it on…what do you do?" she suddenly asked.

I had felt that she had checked out my appearance completely, from head to toe, and now she was digging deeper. Was there some interest on her part? I had to hold back the reins to my heart for this woman. She was bleeding back into my soul very quickly, still that girl on the pedestal where I had placed her.

"Well, I was a civil engineer, I took a position down in Springfield's district with the state, right after I left UIC. Through the years, I became the state's geotechnical service supervisor, but resigned into private life, when I retired. I guess you can say I'm now a freelance vacationer…how about you?"

She did not answer, though Carla had told me her father left her several of his fortune 500 industrial businesses, although I actually didn't remember what they were. Amanda avoided my question and asked another. She was really digging.

"Well, Gregory, you must get a healthy pension then, huh? Where do you live?" she continued to grill me, as we walked to the groomsmen gathering in front of the wedding photographer, out in front of the church.

"I'm about to move down to Coral Gables to watch my son Tom play baseball. He is part of the Canes baseball team."

"Oh, you're married?" she asked, just as the photographer took my arm and aligned me with his expertness to stand tall in the groomsmen's line-up picture.

When I turned to speak with Amanda, she had vanished. I guessed she went to get her dress on. I wouldn't see her again, until the ceremony. I noticed more vehicles flooding the parking lot, men, ladies, children; all who were dressed in their Sunday best, much like the church times in Glenarm, I thought.

And there was my Olivia, looking stunning, but on the arm of Stuart. They appeared friendly walking together. After talking with Amanda, I was stymied, in neutral with my feelings, which was a relief. Either, or, was a prize in my mind, but I wasn't through with Amanda, quite yet. I was putting too much pressure on my decision-making, because the only thing I knew was confusing, nothing stable.

It was time for the big event as the flower girls threw petals at everyone on the aisle, instead of onto the carpet as they were instructed to do. I followed the men's line and was last. It suddenly dawned on me if Amanda was Carla's best friend, shouldn't Amanda have been the bride's maid of honor? Instead, came this different woman, who I learned later was Carla's sister. The bridesmaids all looked very nice. Then I saw her.

Amanda entered last, but she was unbelievably gorgeous. I could not take my eyes off her and when she barely noticed me, I affectionately winked at her solely out of nervous happenstance. I looked to the audience and Olivia was also staring at her Amanda. It was then I realized I had lots of maneuvering to do to make things happen the way I had dreamed.

When the winded preacher kept dwelling upon the life's journey the two stars of the show were entering upon, it wasn't so unusual what transpired. I'd seen it once before, but not twice. First one of the groomsmen had become fidgety and locked his knees. I was surprised though, a bridesmaid fell back onto the front pew, but was caught by the seated people and fanned.

That didn't stop the ceremony, only complicated it, as everyone's eyes found hers. Then, "thump". That lock-kneed groomsman wobbled, and then collapsed onto his knees as if to pray, but I broke his fall. With help, he too became seated. He was embarrassed, tried to return to us, but sat back down. That evened out the wedding party anyway. Both fainters remained in their unplanned place, until the last "I do!"

Following behind the procession, Amanda took my arm, as we all exited down the aisle together to greet the newlywed's forthcoming exit. However, Amanda balked as we passed by Olivia and looked back hard twice, but saying nothing.

I think she either knew instinctively, or saw someone as beautiful as she was, but it was moving, as Olivia stood there applauding with the others; their eyes remained upon the other. Amanda became weak, but that was good, because she held on to me much tighter, until she asked, "Is your wife here?"

"No, I'm widowed, fifteen years."

"Amanda was confused, between looking up at me, then back to find Olivia in the crowd. She, too, fainted immediately after we all got onto the merry wedding bus headed to the country club reception. I allowed her not to make a scene as she regained her spirit in my arms very quickly.

"Sorry, I should have eaten something. Did you see that lovely woman in there?" she asked, and I knew who she meant.

"Yes, she's seated next to me, the prettiest of all," I complimented.

That confused look upon her face, as she peered up at me, was my assurance that she, too, was bonding into our friendship's renewal. She smiled and held onto my arm more tightly then, as the big bus swayed when the driver maneuvered the turns and sped up.

"Did I tell you how beautiful you look today?"

She gave me another one of her crooked smiles, then said, "Three times, but who's counting...keep it up. You look absolutely dapper yourself...thank you for the lovely compliment."

I didn't want to seem pushy as Amanda seemed to relax her businesswoman's demeanor and began to let her hair down. We entered the country club's huge reception hall in front of the newlyweds and showered their entrance into the room with a fanfare of applause.

The planned event was going strong during the roast beef supper. The best man got up to deliver his commitment to the memory of several funny incidents concerning the bride and groom. His salvo of joking was greeted by our raised glasses of wine to salute them. The wine was superb, Amanda said, of her first taste. I saw the label and went to the open bar to see if they had more. Yes, I was in luck.

"Keep several chilled!" I told the bar man, and tipped him accordingly to get him to do it, since they were one hundred ninety dollars a bottle each and the beer crowd was moving in around him to get served draft. I returned to Amanda and she was staring at Olivia.

"What is she doing here?" came out weakly from Amanda.

Of course, a daughter would recognize her own mother, especially one so beautiful as she, and her mirrored image...she pouted.

"Wish I hadn't come. I thought she was out in California. I despise her."

"Who?" I coyly asked.

"My mother...she's over there and with some man. How did she get invited?"

"I invited her."

Amanda was absolutely astonished.

"You! How do you know her?"

"Actually, she's my best friend."

Amanda rose up quickly to vacate my presence, nevertheless, I pulled her down roughly.

"You're making an awful mistake," I said, holding her tightly. "After this dance, we have to talk."

The bride and groom were dancing as the wedding party joined them. Then the music picked up and everyone was grooving to the seventies music, that Carla loved so much. Surprisingly, Amanda held me tightly and did everything I asked of her. Then, we strolled out near the fountain and sat upon a concrete bench to talk.

"Before you say anything, I want to tell you how lonely I have been for you my entire life, just searching for your memory."

"What?"

"Be still…I have to say this, now, before I lose my nerve. The moment I saw you standing in that blizzard in front of the UIC library, I loved you."

She leaned away from me as if I were a nut.

"Bear with me, please. I had so much going on in the classroom I didn't have time to return to you and I wanted then to ask you for a date. You left before I could find you," I tried hard to explain.

"My father had died on a business trip. I flew to London to bring him back."

"Oh, I didn't know, I'm sorry," I spoke.

"How could you have known?" Amanda then spoke. "Continue, if you will."

"Then, I took the position with the state, got married to a wonderful woman but she died. Nevertheless, before she left, we had two children, a boy and a girl."

"Where are they?" she asked, and seemed interested.

"As I mentioned, my son Tom attends the University of Miami. My daughter died trying to save my wife's foster mother from drowning, they both succumbed."

"Oh my, that is terrible…how could you survive a child being taken away like that? How old was she?"

"Just turning sixteen. Joy, her mother, had developed MS. My daughter inherited that from her mother and she became despondent one night and…" I could not finish.

It was quiet, but Amanda needed more.

"So tell me, how do you know my mother?"

"It's a God thing. It was a miracle, pure chance, that I met her out in Nevada. We…we accidentally sat down next to each other in a little restaurant and when I dropped my utensil, we just picked up on a conversation, until we discovered we had so much in common."

"That sounds a bit confusing to me. How could one just sit and discuss your lives so openly in a restaurant with someone you never knew before and tell everything about your lives?"

She had me. My white lies were biting me in the butt, because she wasn't very gullible. But I continued.

"Well, I don't want to cause your head to swell, it's perfect now. But when I saw her face, I saw yours. That beautiful face that has kept burning in my heart."

"You carried a torch for me? Ha!"

"And your mother is such a kind person, she let me intrude. I told her I had graduated from UIC and knew you there, but I really didn't, not very well anyway. I took advantage of her kindness and hounded her to discover through many questions that she was your mother. You're so very lucky, don't you miss her? Her life was miserable after her husband did what he did to her…it was a crime."

"Hold it…that's my father you're talking about. He was a fine man."

"I'm sure, to you, and everyone else. Your mother was a fabulous model, young and upcoming in the world. He smothered her when he married her."

"Stop! It's all lies!" Amanda shouted and started to get up.

I yanked her down again and held her tightly.

"Look, I don't know what your father told you, but these are the facts… he had Olivia committed for her drug problems, she admitted her addiction to me…your father probably induced her use when she found out about his affairs. He had the power and lawyers to put her in an Indiana facility she couldn't get away from, unless she signed his waivers on never seeing you again.

"She went west and stayed there, until I met her. You're making the biggest mistake of your life if you don't seek her out and discover the truth yourself. She cried telling me everything and glowed when telling me how much she loved you before leaving you at age six, never returning, afraid she'd be chastised by your father.

"I told Olivia he had died and she wanted to see you immediately. Don't you see, she loved you all that time, and wanted to keep you out of the ruckus."

Amanda listened well. Her look was confused but she asked me to go back inside with her and we danced. While we danced, she saw her mother looking at her. Olivia had that "wanting" look upon her face. Amanda finally got it together and took my hand and headed for Olivia.

Without so many words, "Mother!" followed by "Amanda!" they embraced a long awaited reunion before me. Stuart was smiling and patted me upon my shoulder as the women hugged long, with tears falling upon their lovely cheeks.

"By God, you did it…the wrong has been righted," Stuart told me as we stood beside the women, who regressed to the table holding hands and talking frantically.

When the DJ played a slow song, I asked not Amanda, but her mother for the dance. She looked to Amanda, then Donald; guardedly, she rose to my extended hand.

"Yes?" Olivia asked.

"I wanted to thank you for making my dreams come true. I still think I'm a better man than Donald, although I admire his skill and tastes. What I wanted to tell you is that I think, with God's help, Amanda and I can have a very special bonding. It seems your daughter thought of me fondly back in college as I did her. Nevertheless, your husband's death divided us, unlike it allowed you to return. Thank you for showing your love to me. You, too, are amazing. I'm going to see that you get your share of Mr. Morgan's vast estate's inheritance, if Amanda and I connect. I'm going to try my best, believe me, but I'll have a hard time forgetting us," I whispered then held her more closely.

"You two will make a wonderful couple. Amanda told me just about the same as you did concerning your distant romance. Except she wants me living back in New York with her.

"I think I'm staying here with Donald. He asked me to live with him. He was a dashing young man when we were young. He has no hair now, however he was a real ladies' man back then. We were what they called Hippies. It was 'love the one you're with' back then. There's more of Donald's pictures and spray painted murals that got covered-over by paint themselves, left on the walls in Washington, D.C. when we were there. We shared our first doobie, cooling in the shade of the Washington Monument one afternoon at a rally."

"That's another thing I wanted to quickly cover. Have you kicked your habit? I will send you to a rehab to help you."

"Ha! You mean how I led you to believe I was a dizzy, pot-headed, druggie out in the desert? That was my gift. Should have played the part in a movie. I do it, or I did it, many times to avoid men from attacking me. I planted those seeds in my pack to throw anyone off. Cops don't arrest you for just having seeds. You should see the faces when I told some overly aggressive truck driver to make love to me, but I had herpes and AIDS. Ha!"

"Why would a gorgeous woman, such as you, become so nomadic?"

"It was burned into me as a youth after I left Stanley; a Hippie, remember? I made it wherever I went and always stayed clean. You were the first man, since my ex-husband to touch me. I wanted to get out of California, so I just did. I found an old bike at a pawn shop that had a little bag in the back, enough for my things. I loved that bike and it turned out the pawn broker knew little about a Chanel bike's value.

"I started out biking across America from the west coast to the east coast just to prove it to myself that I still could. I got to Nevada, had a flat on my bike's last spare tire, so I hid the bike at mile post 122…remind me of that one day…put it behind a rock near a cactus that looked like someone was giving me the finger…how apropos, huh? Then, I made a mistake and hitched a ride with this trucker. The first guy to come along was so fresh I told him I was willing, but I had AIDS, if he didn't mind. It worked. He let me out right where you found me."

The music had stopped and we found ourselves being applauded by the gathering and looked-at suspiciously, by Donald and Amanda.

"Someday, you and I should talk about all this, but for right now, I'm going to try hard to become your son-in-law."

Amanda was curious as to what her mother and I had taken so long to discuss, so I jumped the gun while we danced.

"Remember how we parted and it took thirty years for this night? Well, I've promised my son I'd move to Coral Gables to be near him to watch his games. . .I want to, have to. . .I taught him almost all he knows and he's really good. I must head out tomorrow. Would you be willing to become my bride when we get down there?"

"You mean live in with you?" she questioned.

"Until you decided to marry me, or leave. I wouldn't hold you back. I love you, always have. . .will you marry me?"

"It's too sudden, but I'm, I'm. . .wait. Let me talk to Mother."

Amanda left me to go to Olivia's side and it looked as if I'd started a quarrel between them, until Olivia took Donald's hand and pointed Amanda my way.

Amanda hesitated, then shuffled over barefooted in her long dress. Then she just stood there before me looking up for what she was going to tell me, still undecided, but quiet.

"Amanda Morgan, I love you. . .will you become my bride?" I then repeated but this time I got down on my knees in front of everyone and took her hand in mine, which drew much added attention.

Amanda still cringed in indecisiveness. So, I arose as if I was giving up and looking pretty sadly, when I walked over to the table and got our drinks. Olivia winked at me, but I couldn't smile walking back onto the floor to Amanda who still just stood there, like a child wondering what to do next.

When I gave her the drink, she quaffed it. Amanda then quickly said, "Let's try living together in New York."

"Flip a coin?" I bargained.

Carla bumped into us just then and created a stir, teasing us when she saw the half-dollar.

"What's this, a cheap proposition?" Carla hollered out, causing everyone to listen and causing much embarrassment to Amanda.

"I just asked Amanda to marry me, Carla, but she needs your help. She's wavering, hesitant, can't make up her mind and wants a coin flip!" I shouted out, so everyone could hear, hoping for encouragement, while holding the coin up for everyone's eyes.

"I'll do it to make it fair!" she said, taking the coin, again holding up the coin for everyone to see. It was obvious she was feeling the champagne.

Then she threw it, "Call it" she shouted out, as it went out of sight.

"Heads!" Amanda hollered.

When it hit the floor, it wobbled and rolled over to Donald and Olivia's table.

Donald picked it up, then yelled out, "What'd you call?"

Amanda shouted out, "Tails I go to Coral Gables, heads, I go back to New York!"

"It's tails, honey, pack your bikini!"

The verdict was swift. We kissed, and Amanda said, yes, she was mine. We danced and smooched a lot that night at Carla's wedding. I was finally holding that dream girl of my life in my arms, she was mine, and this time I was never letting her go.

I had three bottles of that wonderful wine still at the bar chilling, so before we departed to my hotel, I retrieved them at her request. Amanda and I found ourselves in my hotel room, exchanging thirty years of waiting for a wonderful day, another blissful night and then finally breakfast. Like the Good Book read, "And on the Third Day, They Arose From There, Dead-Tired" or something like that. That set the pace.

Amanda and I found ourselves on the direct flight to Miami International Airport. It was just a three hour flight, but we had so much to discuss. Soon it became evident we were going to be together forever.

We forgot the hoopla and decided to marry in Coral Gables. The first we told was Tom. When Amanda met Tom, he was very surprised, very cordial. On the other hand, Tom was not as much surprised as I was, because Tom himself had designs on a lovely girl from the campus who wore his engagement ring. It seems lovely Carra was from New York, and that made it very comfortable with Amanda.

We married five days later in a Coral Gables' cathedral with Tom as my best man. Olivia was maid of honor.

The honeymoon we had planned to Jamaica was ended by the threats of a hurricane, so we shopped realtors instead for that perfect place to live. We bought a very luxurious home on the Gulf of Mexico, at Naples, overlooking the water through palm trees. That beautiful place became our honeymoon Shangri-La and has remained as such.

My lovely wife quickly sold her interests in all of her businesses for too many millions to worry about. Daughter Amanda and Mother Olivia shared their rightful halves, and we all became regular fans of the Miami Hurricanes for almost two years.

However, Olivia moved back to Chicago with Donald, right after the first category five hurricane barely missed Naples. We had all left together at the first of the NOAA precautions of a possible land fall near the middle gulf coast.

Our highly structured stone home, which had been specially designed to withstand a hurricane approaching that force, had never endured one before; nevertheless it withstood its force. All of our beautiful palms were flattened or bent over, however, and had to be replaced or replanted immediately. We replaced only some of those palms, so as to allow for more eloquent views of the gulf sunsets.

Our Tom signed with the St. Louis Cardinals farm club several years later. He was called up from the Memphis Cards, just as Amanda and I were leaving out of Vancouver, British Columbia, Canada. We had just finished a two-week vacation and fishing for silver salmon off a chartered yacht.

We were driving south on the west coast near Seattle when Tom called. He wanted to say he was to pitch his first major league game, in any one of four next scheduled games, against the Colorado Rockies. Nevertheless, they didn't tell him which game, just to keep him from over-anxiety. We decided to try to make the games. I headed south on I-84, to hit I-80, near Salt Lake City and luckily needed gas.

I asked the attendant as I paid him, at which mile post were we? He told me mile post 132. I had to think hard before I remembered. I drove to the first possible turnaround place and headed back west. Then I drove up to mile post 120, where I illegally drove through the bumpy median and headed back east.

"What are you doing? Are you lost? Use the GPS for gosh sakes," Amanda scolded me, after the crossing was really rough and she'd gotten shaken up a bit while sleeping. Nevertheless, just as soon as I was smoothly headed back east, she again closed her eyes to sleep. I slowed down and ran onto the emergency lane shoulder, until I got near mile post 122.

When I stopped, I was confronted again by Amanda's quip, "Why are we stopping here?"

"I have to take a whiz, dear," I said. Then her eyes rolled up and around in disbelief and she began shaking her head in disgust; poor girl.

In my mind, I always wondered if Olivia had been that truthful with me from the beginning. I searched for that certain cactus, which Olivia had told me appeared as if it were flipping off the bird to everyone. I needed to know now she wasn't just a truck stop's whore when I met her. It really wouldn't have mattered, I loved her then anyway.

I was going to see if my mother-in-law's bike was really behind that rock near that peculiar fingering cactus, the place where she once had mentioned to me she had hidden it, when I first met her.

I looked around, then saw something leaning against this funny looking cactus. Sure enough, it was there, almost buried in the blowing sand. I suppose because of the dry weather, it was still in good shape, almost. The front tire was flat and the back tire was shredded, just as Olivia said. I limped it back to the car.

"What, in the holy name of God, is that?" Amanda complained.

"Honey, look what I found while taking a pee!" as I put the bike in the trunk and closed it.

"You mean you couldn't have gone back at the station? You had to come all the way out here to extricate your penis from your apparel to urinate upon the Earth's surface?" she asked curtly, but still very eloquently in her educated, angry tirade.

I had to think about that one..."Yep!"

"Oh, geeze!" she sighed.

"Now, dear, you know your gynecologist says you have to simmer down or else our baby will have your bad temperament."

"She did not! I'm going back to sleep. Just be more careful, and try not to hit anything!"

I forgave her crabbiness, because getting her into that "delicate condition" was oh so much fun, and worth all the trouble that followed. I loved her. But I had plans for that old Chanel bike, come Olivia's next surprise birthday party. It would be a great present she would take pleasure in, and a secret only she and I could share.

Then we made a beeline for "The Mile High City" Denver, Colorado. Tom pitched only five innings of the second game. He hadn't allowed any runs and the score was 3-0. He was taken out and relievers continued the shutout performance. It was his first win.

We didn't get to talk to Tom very much that day, because he had a meeting with the general manager and a contract was forthcoming. Eventually we did see many of his best games of his long career, alongside his lovely wife,

Carra, who he brought along from Miami; and later our first grandson, Mark, their handsome son, and a chip off the old block.

I recall, we drove more leisurely home the next two days, and not too soon. Our only child, little Olivia Genevieve Wetmore was born just one week later. She was my Amanda all over again.

I look back upon my life's episode and its many unforeseen occurrences, unexplainable passions and their many twists and turns, which have shaped my life for so many years.

I remember about all the good people in my life; how could one ever forget any of them? Especially, the ones I loved so dearly, but who left me so quickly that I could not even say good-bye. Somehow those losses remain strongest in my brain; they all still seem just a moment away. I can see their smiling faces clearly, never sad ones.

I could never forget my beautiful, wonderful, soul mate Joy. She will always share a big part of my heart. Joy was never complicated, yet she was concernedly honest, straightforward, generous, a forgiving, God-fearing woman. We only shared part of our lives together, first being friends, then lovers and husband and wife; it happened so swiftly. She wasn't the one who completely blew me away at first sight. She stole my heart and made me love her through her goodness. I made her a woman, she showed me how to be a man.

Nevertheless, what we shared was beautiful. Joy gave me two children, strength, direction, and made me believe; all before she was taken away from us, as swiftly as we had been joined together. I had no time to mourn her loss or say good-bye. It says in the Bible, "The Lord giveth; the Lord taketh away."

Nevertheless, I do believe in my heart that Joy planned it that way for me, her gift somehow; it was her way to ease everyone's pain, except her own. I always assumed our "I do's" meant forever, but only time could heal my empty aching heart.

I frequently wonder of my Jillian's last moments and what was going through her mind. Had she given up? Yes, my lovely daughter, Jillian, another of my unforgettable memories. Was she, too, at loss with her own helpless passion as her mother's; something over which she had no control? It is the good parts of her short life that we shared together that I'm so grateful for

Him allowing into my life. She left another void in my heart, as quickly as an arrow strikes its target, she was gone.

I learned the hardest way possible that you must take full advantage of your time on Earth, give and share your love, plan it well, be prepared for anything, because in an instant your life can drastically change and there's nothing you can do, except try to endure; you'll need His help.

I do know God left me a strong-willed Tom. He helped me in my deepest sadness, even as a boy. The Good Lord helped me find Amanda, though in the most complicated and roundabout of ways. Maybe He felt Olivia's passion also needed a result. Amanda filled both of our voids; enough good to continue on with our lives.

God blessed me. Why, I don't rightly know. Maybe it was the baptism, or maybe it was done for my Joyce, or maybe even all along He knew that eventually I would find Him, too. God used part of my own heart to mend it.

Yet, sometimes while we are making love, when Amanda and I are alone in our bedroom, and Olivia, our daughter, is sleeping, I find myself looking deeply into Amanda's eyes, and I remember her passion for me. Now and again, I perceive that same passion as being upon that other face, who once I found longingly looking back at me.

I begin thinking of those sultry moments in the desert, where I first met her. Both of our lives changed there, because of our long stays of mutual devotion to Amanda. I loved her then, also. I will never forget our passion crossing.

I've walked life's path, in happiness and sorrow
Searching for a dream, always arriving tomorrow
I've left behind regrets, and must repent
I could have done more, time better spent
Though time heals most wounds, and eases most pain
I can never walk that way again
I think of them all, in some form or fashion
I loved them all dearly, only one with passion.

composed by
PHILLIPE` / Philip W. Kunz

A VERY HAPPY ENDING!